HARD CHANGE

Dawn Reeves

sharedpress

First paperback edition published in Great Britain in 2013 by Shared Press

Published by Shared Press
www.sharedpress.co.uk

ISBN 978-0-9574981-0-5

Designed and typeset by Quarto Design
www.quartodesign.com
Edited by Lisa Hughes
Artwork by Ben Kelly

Shared Press' policy is to use papers that are natural, renewable and recyclable products from well managed forests in accordance with the rules of the Forest Stewardship Council.

*To everyone struggling to deliver and improve public services
in the narrowing gap between a rock and a hard place;
and to my uncle Tony Reeves.*

Saturday 13th November, 10pm

He carries the girl as if he's a fire-fighter; one arm under her knees, the other under her armpits. Her head is slumped against his chest; her neck and face are hidden by thick, straightened hair. The narrow Fold he emerges from is no more than an unlit alleyway. It's about thirty metres before he'll hit one of the roads that lead off the High Street, where there'll be lights and people milling around the edges of the ritual chaos of Saturday night.

There's a brief clatter as a mobile falls out of the girl's thin jacket pocket onto the road. A navy, sequinned ballet pump dangles from one foot, the other is bare. The skin on the front of her foot shines in the white of the streetlight. As he turns out of St Mary's Fold and into Silver Street, he sees three lads coming towards him. They are loudly drunk, but maybe they'll offer to help? He slows, catches one of them sniggering at him, but is unsurprised that they say nothing and wander off for a piss. Almost there now. He bends slowly, back and knees engaged to put her down on the ground. Her head rolls back onto the paving slab with a gentle thud.

He stands up, looks about, then takes a few steps back, as if he might leave her there, but this time he lifts her over his shoulder, like a dad giving a kid a sack-of-potatoes ride. There's a skinny arse and two translucent stick legs on show. Now he moves quickly away from the lamppost and towards a big, green tub bin. His free arm lifts the lid and it takes only a forward shrug of his shoulder and she falls in. She's on a bed of broken glass and cans. Blood and ketchup seep out from the polystyrene takeaway box that is her pillow. "Night, night," he says.

The smell of the bin, like a cheap burger frying on a misty, damp night, makes him feel hungry. In the distance he sees a refuse truck, but he isn't sure whether it's coming towards him or not. He walks off in the direction of the High Street and Mr Sizzle.

CHAPTER 1

JESSICA

Saturday 13ᵗʰ November, 10.30pm

Deputy Commander Jessica Reid breathes in through her nose and out through her mouth, pulling her stomach muscles tight, rolling her shoulders down her back, enjoying the calm. It's an hour since she finished her shift and she's grateful that the universe has given her time and space to deforest three weeks' worth of paper. The City Centre is quiet, but before making tracks for home she wants to eyeball a group of young men who've been hanging around the Chickenshack takeaway opposite the Library. This is not something she would normally bother with, but she thinks she's recognised one of the bored teens on the CCTV. It's not procedure, she'll be alone, but she's off-duty and it's only a ten-minute recce. From there she can cut back through the pedestrianised shops, take a left up to the High Street and circle back to pick up her car.

The youths have been flagged by the Anti-Social Behaviour Team three weekends running. Jess thinks they're moth boys, drawn to the zing of the neon light and the warm glass of the shop front. Or they could be vampire kids, only seen drifting through the city at night, looking for trouble with the potential to take blood. They aren't a known gang. There are no specific incidents to report, but it could be a sign of something significant emerging. Even if it's not, Jess has to take account of the public intimidation and the small businessman whose takeaway could be losing money.

Helpfully, she's not in uniform tonight. She tightens the belt of her thick, charcoal cardigan, wraps a black woollen scarf round her neck, and heads out, glad of the warmth of the soft fibres. It's clear to her that the gang is a diversion. She knows she's avoiding going home. Stewart is finally moving his stuff out this weekend. It ought to be a relief, but it's taken so long to get to this point that her skin flares irritably at the thought of the kitchen cupboards still full of his body-building protein tubs.

"Excuse me, please, lads."

She's been walking faster than she thought, past the gang's outliers, until she's blocked by two six-footers with their backs to her. There is no movement. She remains calm and has another go.

"Excuse me lads. Can I get through?"

"Miss wants chicken," one smirks. The two taller ones turn round.

"I'd like to get through, please."

"This is our side, man." Another points menacingly at the pavement.

They seem to be looking at a youth wearing a village-green, upside-down golf visor, twisted backwards on top of a black balaclava. She knows better than to laugh. This young man wants to be taken seriously, right down to his matching green laces. Jess sees how desperately he's trying to distinguish himself through the tiny details important only to him and his mates. She holds her ground and returns the look directly. These lads have managed to create a nasty vibe that this part of the City Centre could do without – and they're well aware of the tension they're cooking up.

Her colleagues don't see the subtleties. A collective mistake had been made with a group of goths who had moved into the Market Square a few months back. While she was on annual leave, her Chief and the Council Leader had imposed a Section 30 dispersal order. It was a press-driven reaction that had seriously antagonised a whole range of young people into occupying public places. Jess was angry that it had undermined her longer term strategy to build community trust and astonished that they didn't know goths are congenitally passive and just want to hang out with their darkly dressed friends. The goths were never going to be the problem, but maybe this gang is part of the backlash? She suspects not. Hiding your face with a balaclava isn't a new trend. There's more going on here.

"Run away." One youth leans in from behind her, almost spitting in her ear.

"Run and cry, old bitch lady." She feels the tip of a baseball hat on her neck. Stay calm, she tells herself. Stay calm. He won't touch you.

Strictly speaking this has escalated into an unsafe situation and she should call for back-up, but she knows what she's doing; procedure won't help her here. Intuition and experience tell her to concentrate on the leader. Where is he emotionally? What will he respond to?

"I'd like to get home."

She meets his eyes through the gap in his headgear. She adds weight to her shoulders, making them low and heavy, conveying the look of a proper mum, maybe a mum like his, who tries hard, who won't be pushed around, but who is tired to the bone.

The rest of the group watches for maybe another thirty seconds. Their silence causes a shift. Gaining their attention, maintaining discipline, seems to be what he's after.

"Old teacher lady can walk." He gives his permission, turning his visor round to the front. As Jess weaves quickly through the rest of the group, her bleeper goes. She releases her shoulders, breathing deeply. That was close, but she refuses to resort to getting her badge out. Her instant reflection on the incident is that someone was missing. On the CCTV there was one particular boy in a distinctive black hoodie with P.I.M.P. written on it in gold. These kids don't realise how much their fashion choices help the police. Maybe she knows him? There'd be time to get someone onto them on Monday, but, relieved for now, she picks up the call from her DI, Alan Jones.

"Ma'am? If you're still hanging around, looking for action, we may have a major incident. Possible homicide. A girl's body found by the bin men. It's the corner of Silver Street and an alley round the back, St Mary's Fold. Where are you?"

"Up by the Library..."

Jonesy is new on the murder squad and she can hear him controlling the excitement in his voice, but as far as she's concerned he's got it completely wrong. Jess isn't interested in that kind of action these days. Most of her colleagues, and her soon-to-be-ex-husband, can't understand why she likes going to meetings, but when she hears herself arguing about the importance of tackling underlying causes her voice has an authenticity and confidence that resonates in her core. Outside the dire plodding realm of enforcement, outside the confines of a command and control culture, Jess revels in the nuances of meaning and implications. She delights in debate and is jealous of the freedom other public servants have to sidestep the corporate line. Her school friend, Anne-Marie, who works for the City Council, relishes her ability to question and challenge decisions, but the wilfulness with which Anne-Marie often refuses to comply would mean the end of a police career.

It's true that the Council and the other public agencies could also drive Jess mad. Talking about getting to the heart of tackling crime is one thing, but solving it is another and resolving it for good – that's what they all seem to struggle with. The lack of black or white, the reality of complexity, keeps Jess motivated. Still, thinking about Stewart, she returns to her phone call.

"I'm probably ahead of you. I'll be there in five minutes," she tells Jonesy.

As she turns into Silver Street, she sees a refuse truck and two men standing with their backs to the bin, partially obscuring it.

"Evening lads, I'm Deputy Commander Jessica Reid." She flashes her badge. "Thanks for your help. How did you find her?"

"Standard practice to bang on the side of the bins," one of them grunts, "but I thought summat didn't sound right – odd like. Summat big in there."

"You've got good ears, then. Must've been a shock?"

"Never seen a dead body," he says shakily, "I could do with a drink."

The squad car and ambulance draw up behind her. It's been a long time since she's pulled on a pair of sterilised gloves. She opens the bin lid. Poor kid. The girl looks more grey and green than a freshly dead body should. Maybe it's just the light? Jess moves around to view her from another angle. There's no colour in her face, but the effect of the white light and the bin lid doesn't help. Feeling an emotional rush, she focuses on the other contents of the bin. There's something domestic about the scene. A two-litre milk carton, empty cans of pop, sweet wrappers and rotting food. It's not unlike her bin at home.

Jess scans the girl's body. The sole of her bare foot is black and grazed. It's not been the night the girl must have imagined when she neatly painted her toes a metallic pink. Her vest-style T-shirt dress has ridden up on the left. A thick black belt with a fake gold buckle is no longer around her hips, but up under her breast.

"We're securing the scene, ma'am." One of the sergeants makes her jump.

Finally, Jess gets to the girl's eyes. She's always relieved when they are shut, but the panda-sized smudges of mascara suggest she's been crying.

"Good. Thanks." Jess pulls out a hanky from her bag and blows her nose hard.

That's weird. From behind the white tissue, out of the corner of her eye, she thinks she sees a slight movement. It may have been nothing more than a tear on her own eyelash that she's hastily flicked away. She bends down. Could it have been a shadow? Maybe a rat running under the bin? Or a rat in the bin with her? No. She looks at the girl's arm. It definitely twitched.

"Wait," she shouts. "Get the medics over here now. She's alive."

CHAPTER 2

ANNE-MARIE

Saturday 13th November, 10.45pm

"What's your poison?" The barman winks at her. Anne-Marie marvels at the under-lit glass shelf full of coloured spirit bottles hovering magically in front of her. She's seduced again by the glittering array of poisons on offer, wondering whether it's just her who's forgotten what is and isn't poisonous these days. The young man is just playing with an old phrase. There's no hidden wisdom or warning of imminent death, it's just marketing – and that goes for the wink, too. She arches him an eyebrow to stop right there.

"I'll have a Dirty Black Russian."

With the soft crack of the ice in the sweet coffee liquid and the anticipation of a vodka and Coke kick, she licks her lips and returns to Bob. They've set up camp in a boutique hotel, enjoyed medium rare steaks with the perfect combination of blood red and charcoal, and polished off two bottles of velvety Shiraz. The Lovell Bar is in late-night mode; muted lighting and space to slink into one of the low leather sofas.

"You look fantastic," Bob says. He's tall and solid. His stubble is just the right side of coarse sandpaper.

"Why don't we get a room?" It's their fourth anniversary and she wants the excitement of the first few months back.

"Are you going to switch your phone off, then?" he taunts.

They both know that she can't do that. She's a senior manager and this weekend the emergency phone is in her bag.

"Why would that matter?" She tries to keep her voice light, but the reminder of the phone grates. She's at the beck and call of the Council Leader.

"We wouldn't want to get interrupted," Bob says, feeling her thigh through her thin knit black dress.

"Exactly," she says, getting a shot of desire. A room would avoid any chance of an interruption from her teenage son Adam. She knocks back her drink and wrinkles her nose at him, thinking about the king-size bed and stiff sheets.

"Steady love," he cautions.

"Come on, why don't we let our hair down?"

It's a joke. Bob shaves what hair he has left and hers is cut short and tucked behind her ears.

"OK, but we're not teenagers and with the prices of these rooms I want to be able to make the most of it."

"Don't you think we deserve this?" She skates fast across the deep ravine of their pay differential. "It's the one decent place left. Use it or lose it."

His smile is wry. "Job done, then, is it? That's the night-time economy sorted?"

She opts for a distraction rather than a fight. "Can you imagine any of our new councillors in a wine bar?"

While it's easy to picture Council Leader Davina Clarke in a classy place like this, Bob doubts that any of the newly elected members who are keeping her in power, or most of her own party for that matter, would drag themselves into the City Centre for an evening out, despite the secure parking and extensive CCTV. Anyway, as he's told Anne-Marie many times before, he's convinced the Coalition won't last long enough in a place like this to do any real damage. Local politics isn't everyone's idea of an aphrodisiac, but it works for them.

As the emergency phone rings, Anne-Marie's legs automatically spiral upwards until her knees lock and she's on a firm footing. It's a dog and bone alright. Delving in her bag and mouthing an apology to Bob, she misses the call. Davina's tone is measured.

"I do apologise for calling you so late. I've heard from the police that a girl's body has been found in one of our commercial waste bins. It's dreadful, of course, but nothing we can do now. We'll need a statement, though, and we don't want any negative impact on our plans for the City Centre. We must avoid anything sensational. I'll leave it with you, talk to your comms team, make sure the story is right and brief me on Monday morning."

Anne-Marie's body straightens, her brain refocuses. Celebration and sex are cancelled; her night out is over.

"The City Centre clean-up team have found a girl's body in a 660 tub."

"Come again?" Bob doesn't comprehend.

"Big, metal, commercial waste bin, green lid."

"Is she dead?"

Anne-Marie lowers her voice. "Sounds like it. Davina had her respectful voice on."

"Lucky it was the weekend or she'd have been in the compactor, through the transfer station and straight to landfill, or," he says shaking his head, "in a waste container on her way to India."

"Christ on a bloody bike," is all Anne-Marie can manage.

They are shocked into a cold pragmatism.

"How the hell did she end up in one of our bins in the first place?"

"How the hell should I know?" she flashes back.

Her Regeneration and Planning Department had taken flack for putting those bins just out of sight in dark corners, where the street drinkers and junkies hang out, but that was only after they'd taken flack for putting the bins on the High Street, making the City Centre look like a dump. The lurid headlines are all too predictable: 'Feral Youth Out Of Control... Underage Drinking... Alcopop Town... Moral Outrage'. The Council didn't tip the alcohol down that girl's throat, but the article will end with a lazy refrain, that the Council ought to do something. It's just sport for the *Post*.

"There's a poor, daft kid in a bin. A kid who hasn't got a clue; who's got the whole world telling her that getting pissed is cool and will get you a shag. It's not like when we were young," Bob grunts.

"I was drinking when I was 14," she says. "Weren't you?"

Anne-Marie's internal organs contract as she visualises her teenage self, swaggering around uncontrollably. The red monkey boots she used to love hadn't stopped her tripping over a curb, twisting her ankle and head-butting a shop door. She remembers being too drunk to move.

"No, actually, I wasn't. These kids need to be told when to stop and we need to do more."

"Not now Bob…"

As the shock subsides, apprehension invades her brain space. Davina's message was odd. She was flagging the potential impact on a plan Anne-Marie has heard nothing about and talking as if they could control the way this story unfolds – and how did she know about the girl's body being found so quickly?

Bob reacts angrily. "I'm trying to stop landlords fuelling the underage hordes. The police waste half their resources trying to contain the chaos and A&E are patching them up and sending them out ready for another go next week. It's got to stop."

They are on different tracks.

"I hope there's no video footage." Anne-Marie is thinking of an incident with a cat in a bin that went viral.

"Hold on love, we've both just made a massive leap there. We don't know the story. We've assumed she was out drinking. It's not that easy to get into one of those tubs."

Anne-Marie looks down uneasily at the chocolate rug, trying to think creatively. Maybe they could say something like,

'Council Clean-up Teams Help Tackle Anti-social Drinking' or 'Bin Man Saves Trashed Teen From Masher'? Not the best lines she's ever come up with, but they're a starting point.

She knows from the way Bob has slapped his hand on his knee, elbow jutting out towards her, that he's about to start arguing, arguing for more enforcement, more regulation. Being his boss means constantly negotiating boundaries, but with a Council Leader clearly wanting light touch policy and a local economy in free fall, she sees sketchy fault lines begin to darken. Bob has a point, but he needs to evolve as much as public services do.

"There's a dead girl in a bin. We don't even know how old she is… was."

Anne-Marie nods, sobered but in need of a final drink alone to focus her thoughts.

"I'm sorry, love. Let's leave it for tonight, shall we? I'll get a cab home. I need to work tomorrow."

They kiss briefly and Bob heads off. Staring into the warm glass she plays with the swirling liquid, seeing the colours of a dying fire, but realising there's a risk those embers could catch and she will find herself fighting on a new front. Her approach has always been, 'Don't spin the story, start it.' This story is off and running, but she'll do what she can to tell it her way, for her reasons. As she empties her glass a phone rings somewhere in the bar. She rises quickly and heads for home.

CHAPTER 3

BARRINGTON

Monday 15th November, 7.05am

It's a 'clean' day if, on the final four-mile cycle around the ring road, it's possible to reach 18mph, maintain good cadence and time it to perfection, to ensure that you can sail through five sets of traffic lights, turn up the final hill and coast into the city without putting your feet down. Of the last 90 days, 76 have been clean. His aim is a clean ride followed by a clear run at the day, which means avoiding any interaction with his colleagues at least until 10am. If he could make it through the entire day without distractions that would be a rare treat. Focus is everything.

To keep his interest he's made the ring road stretch into a series of time trials. On Mondays the traffic is always heavier. Today there is light drizzle, the tarmac is wet so he must adapt his speed for safety, and there are Council workers cutting the verges – minor obstructions, but seconds count. There is a grounds maintenance vehicle picking up the cuttings from the verges. The car in front sees it late and pulls out sharply, causing Barrington to swerve into the fast lane. The car behind him is too busy hitting the horn and doesn't break hard enough. It catches the back wheel of his racing bike. Lightning reaction and upper body strength allow him to jump the front wheel up onto the central reservation, but he's no BMX specialist so he's over in a second. Thigh and shoulder hit the grass. He hauls the rest of the bike out of the way of the cars streaming past as his head bounces down. A woman in a passing car is staring. He looks away.

Shaking slightly, he checks the bike and gets straight back on before the anger kicks in. Bright blood is seeping through his Lycra shorts and he feels the heat of his shoulder swelling. He hits the next three sets of lights. The bike is performing well as he presses on up the hill. The heart rate monitor on his handle bars is still functioning and he's glad to see it climbing. He feels the familiar pinch in his quad muscle, eases out of his seat and undertakes two cars before he hits the brow.

He's in the office at 7.28am, though. That's good. There's a basement shower room, which he hates, particularly when other people are using it. Today he's alone and enjoys soaping up, running his hands over his thighs, reaching down to his lower calf muscles. Blasting the blood away now with cold water, he decides the cut is more of a graze and that a cold pack on his shoulder will sort it out. Standing tall, running the fresh lime-smelling soap over his chest, taut stomach, the lower back and buttocks, he washes away the sweat, the ride, the accident and half a sniff of the smell of last night. The drain blocks and his feet are swimming in dirty water. He's argued that it's a public health building and requires a deep clean, but there's no money, so the hygiene standards remain poor.

In his locker he has a suit bag with two identical suits and three shirts, delivered straight from the dry cleaners. His wife, Corinne, loves to see him dressed for work in these sharp midnight blue suits with a fine pin stripe. He puts on the light blue cotton shirt, navy tie and black loafers. No need to check himself in the mirror, but he manages a smile at the sharpness of his collar. Corinne says that as the only black man in the building people will notice what he's wearing. Maybe she's right, but he also likes wearing a suit. It's certainly better than the white coat he continued to wear long after every other doctor had stopped. That white coat had established an appropriate distance between him and his needy patients, but when expectations changed his colleagues were clear it signalled that he lacked the skills to talk to people in a way that made them feel better. Yes, he thinks, a suit is the perfect uniform for his public health role.

On his desk is the action plan for tackling alcohol misuse in the city. He grips a red pen in his hands like a scalpel, taking the knife to the 65 pages with relish. Alcohol is the single most serious issue facing the city and this plan is drivel. He cuts through to the appendices for the numbers. How many drinkers are there in A&E, in GPs' surgeries, in police cells, in the bail hostel, in rehab, in divorce proceedings, in car crashes, on the streets, round the back of the bike sheds? The city is host to 42,000 harmful and hazardous drinkers and 6,200 dependent drinkers aged 15 to 64. The numbers illustrate why this is the issue Barrington has to focus on. The numbers are his allies. They are entirely themselves, straightforward, their meaning fixed. It's a minority view, but to Barrington a trajectory is a work of art.

His five-year-old son, Nelson, is learning fast. Only yesterday he'd pleaded, "Dad, Dad, can we count the money in the box again?" It's not Barrington's favourite pastime as his hands smell unpleasant afterwards, but he'd relented. Numbers connect them. Numbers make patterns and the patterns reveal a story truer than any of the frankly questionable and unsubstantiated opinion he's currently reading.

No, today isn't going to be good. This is a critical issue; complex, dense and professionally challenging. It's the only thing that matters. What is Anil thinking? Barrington has briefed his policy officer, Anil, on the priority level for this piece of work, so he knows what is expected. Barrington puts down the pen and turns to his screen. He's learned that his emails don't always have the desired effect, but not having to speak to his colleagues is time-efficient.

Anil

The report is unacceptable. I will take it forward myself.

I refer you to the article in today's paper: Trashed Teen Fights For Life – body of young woman etc. She had almost 0.40% alcohol in her bloodstream. She should be dead.

Barrington

CHAPTER 4

ANNE-MARIE

Monday 15th November, 4.30pm

Andrea, the mouth of the Highlands Estate, and Carol, the elbow grease, have bullied the young barman to open up early.

"Let's start as we mean to go on," says Andrea.

"Whether we win this award or not, let's drink to a great night out, to the community and our hard graft," Carol joins in.

The Highlands, though, is Anne-Marie's estate. From a grubby-kneed kid who knew the occupants of every house, to a power suit, managing the services that matter, she's the artery. Getting nominated for this award is the first time in years that the estate has been in the news for the right reasons.

It was a simple economic equation and a silver tongue that convinced the judges to hold the Regeneration Awards here. The Football Club were happy to show off their new Drummond Stand and Hospitality Suite for a reduced rate and it had proved to be more of a draw than she'd expected. Bob thinks that it's sealed the club's fate: build a new stand and you're doomed to relegation. The evening has to go well, especially after the incident on Saturday. The Council Leader, Davina Clarke, will be here later and wants to talk budgets.

While the community reps get her a drink, she checks the article in today's *Post* to assess the damage. The Council has a bright, competent comms manager who has used Anne-Marie's 'Bin Man Saves Trashed Teen' line to good effect. The girl in the bin is alive, it's gruesome, but maybe she was over-reacting. Is it really such a big story? The final paragraph reads:

The Chief Executive of Alcohol Concern, Ed Forby, said today, "The harm caused by alcohol has already reached epidemic proportions. We're asking everyone, especially policy-makers and those with responsibility for our health and well-being, to take action." The City Council, who have a duty to ensure our well-being and are the Licensing Authority, were unavailable for cement.

Literacy is no barrier to success in the world of local news. They were available, she thinks, but it suited the *Post* not to call and get a proper quote. Her PA phones and she steps away from the bar.

"I've had to swap tomorrow's meetings around. Jess Reid wants to see you urgently about the incident." Anne-Marie rolls her eyes.

"Your management team is starting at 8.30am." She expects to pre-load on the coffee, if the pesky machine is still working, that is.

"You've got the meeting with the solicitors about the disciplinary hearing at 11am." That gives her about three minutes to cadge a quick fag from her mate Ken in the Keepers' Office.

"Then 12.30pm is the Shared Services Project board." Which means lunch will be a few biscuits left over from the previous meeting, if she's lucky.

"At 2pm you have the Homes and Communities Agency, transition funding arrangements." She'll have to strangle their two key officers if the last session is anything to go by.

"You're chairing the Skills Strategy at 3.30pm." Then she'll have to strangle herself.

"And you can fit Jess Reid in between 5pm and Planning Committee at 7pm." Jesus.

"Can you tell Jess I'll actually be dead by then. I'll speak to her on Wednesday."

Andrea shouts across to let her know they are waiting.

"Not thirsty then?"

The Regeneration Awards gang have been waiting to conclude their toast. Andrea raises her glass. "To us, to you, boss, and to Sandra…"

She's glad they've mentioned Sandra. She's the best manager Anne-Marie's got. It would be rude not to join the toast, but it's early even by her standards.

"…who has given us so much. Like that attractive high-vis jacket…" Vital for the night-time patrols she has going on the estate.

"…and those classy, green, triple-thick rubber gloves." No-one can pick up used johnnies and junky needles on the estate without them.

"And without Sandra, our back passages would still be a dirty hellhole."

"Speak for yourself." Anne-Marie is drawn back in. Simple alley-gating schemes, they work every time.

The group are naively enjoying themselves, but surely they must've listened to the news recently? There's no money left. The days are gone when they could make the Highlands liveable with a targeted project or two; when there was government money to employ intelligent operators like Sandra.

Andrea ploughs on. "And if you hadn't bullied me into volunteering, I'd have had nothing to say at that job interview. I wouldn't even have a job and we wouldn't be here."

They raise their glasses again, but Anne-Marie has slipped back into her own world. The Highlands team and all the local services will be lucky to exist unless she can get them mainstreamed into Council budgets. Hosting this event has cost a few hundred quid, but that's small beer if she can shift the neighbourhood work onto the priorities list and park it safely – well, for now, at least – in black and white in a departmental budget line.

"You got us those skips." Carol's gaze seems to drift off to a past memory. "Those skips were rubbish… in the end." It ought to have got a laugh, but Carol's voice tails off to nothing and no-one replies. Seconds pass, holding them still. Anne-Marie sees the silence become a shadow at the bar. She looks at Andrea's face. They all seem to know what Carol's talking about. "To our absent friends."

"What is it about bloody men and bins in this city?" Andrea scowls at Colin, one of their community wardens.

"We'll enjoy it for her, won't we?" Carol says.

She sees pain on their faces. Not knowing what it is raises her anxiety levels, but if it's another girl in a bin this is back to being a major problem again. The reason she doesn't know what they're talking about had been spelt out pretty clearly by Andrea a few weeks back when Anne-Marie had been trying to talk to the women about boosting the local economy. "Do you actually know what the local economy is like?" Andrea had interjected. "A couple of betting shops, two knock-off pubs, a so-called supermarket that sells orange food and tins of foreign lager, and a loan shark who's got the place sewn up. You're well out of touch." Anne-Marie had had to accept that it was true. Although living on the estate makes her sound edgy to her leafy suburb-dwelling colleagues, in reality her house is a grand, old terraced house perched on the hill above the Highlands. Anywhere else it would cost a fortune.

Colin breaks the mood of the group. "Don't forget the free swimming tickets and the Friday kids' disco. I'll drink to that. Before I got this job, before all this," he raises his pint gently, "the house next door to me was empty for five years. The housing manager told me there's a waiting list now for the Highlands." Middle-class officers in the Council refused to believe that a kids' disco and a trip to the seaside could be enough to make a family move house, but it was true.

"Yeah, and I'm still waiting to be re-housed somewhere else," Andrea jeers.

Anne-Marie focuses on the reference to the woman and the skip. There had been stabbings, but no murders on the estate. Never, in fact. Whatever it is, she doesn't need anything spoiling the reputation of this work, especially now. That could be why they are keeping so quiet. She reminds herself that these women aren't stupid. They out-smarted her at school and would do so again given half the chance. Anne-Marie decides to talk to Colin about it later.

Seeing Colin, she remembers back to a tired Friday night mixing Rioja and Night Nurse. She'd sat with misery at the kitchen table, looking through a pile of returned CRB checks for the Community Wardens' Service. The service had been politically kicked in all directions since the beginning. One minute the councillors loved the wardens, then they were a liability and they wanted shot of them. Then it was Police Community Support Officers who found favour, or rather that's what the Home Office had given them money for. She'd had a skirmish with the Police Chief, who'd argued that the extra external resources could have been better spent elsewhere. He'd meant paying their overtime bill and he'd held sway, saying, "Give me one constable who can make an actual arrest rather than three PCSOs and a load of wardens and I'll be happy. They create so much bureaucracy that our constables never leave their desks."

Anne-Marie had quickly mobilised local support, leaned slightly on Jess to persuade the Chief to rethink and they'd managed to employ a small number of Community Wardens. They turned out to be the best investment the public purse could have made in keeping people safe. Now, though, it wasn't clear where it would go next.

Looking at the returned CRB checks, she'd read story after story about the lives of local people, tarred with the black end of a bureaucratic brush for minor offences, tagged in key worker reports for teenage misdemeanours, scarred for life by petty crimes. Colin was a classic case. He was now a happily married man with a young family and youth work qualifications. He was an enthusiastic volunteer in the community, who'd been involved in starting a gardening project and, as a former West Midlands hammer-throwing champion, he was perfect. Except for the criminal record he'd dragged around his neck since the age of 14. In a fight at school he'd belted a teacher with a bag. The zip had cut the teacher's face. That's not great, she'd thought, but she'd looked at the risk assessment forms and the box marked 'Suitable for employment?' and she'd ticked 'Yes'. For ten years Anne-Marie has constantly feared she might drown in the waves of initiatives. It's been invigorating, but the waters are still now, on the surface that is – there's just a powerful current swirling below, threatening to pull them all under.

CHAPTER 5

BARRINGTON

Monday 15th November, 4.45pm

Barrington stares out at the city. From the fifth floor he can see the seventies red brick of the Council House building. Counting the number of dirty windows, he recalls a report that highlighted the stress levels of the workers, although the figures had been unsurprising given the annual build-up of grime in the city and the low glimmer of daylight that gets through the glass.

He sees the eighties shopping centre, a prematurely dated edifice in black and red that's been up for sale for twenty months. The spire of St Mark's needs a sandblast. The Market Square looks as small as a village green and there's the roof of the football stadium, a container for levels of testosterone significantly above the national average and fuelled by the 48,000 pints of beer that are sold there every week.

To the north, the market sells sustenance-free food, which causes him to reflect on a presentation he'd given recently on the current incidence of rickets, which his colleagues had seemed greatly affected by. There are half-empty luxury housing developments without internal windows. There's the ailing Highlands Estate, derelict land and too many pubs for him to remember. There's the hapless hospital and, in the distance, the ring road, its arms gently kettling it all in.

This is a small city about to keel over. In fact, it ought to be downgraded to a town – anytown. His wife Corinne doesn't agree. She accepts it as where they live and likes how people are here. She cares about it in a way that he has never understood. There is work to be done in this place, thinks Barrington, and I will make the difference.

It's been a day of too many meetings; the endless talking, posturing, action points noted and never taken. To him a meeting is a prison, a cell full of the last people on earth you would want to be locked up with. The prospect of an early release is appealing, but then he loses two hours to interminable emails. He's not sure how and that's worrying for someone who monitors his own cadence, who knows how many revolutions of the wheel his legs can push per second. As he is finally about to leave for home, he sees a message about a budget cuts meeting. He ignores it, but opens a reply from Anil.

Dear Barrington,

Naturally I've already picked up on the Girl in the Bin, but the level of alcohol in her blood is only part of the picture. We need to know her story. We need to find out about her as a person, the pubs she went to, who she was with, why she drank. We need to explore the patterns.

With respect, I've been working on this project for months, building a picture of alcohol abuse in the city, getting a feel for drinkers' impulses and motivations, making connections with the agencies already working in this field. It's an immensely complicated issue and I am astounded that you simply dismiss my report as 'unacceptable'.

I'm sure it would be helpful if we could meet informally to talk about the alcohol work face to face, over a coffee. I am free tomorrow. Please let me know what time suits you.

Yours, Anil

The email agitates Barrington. He needs to remind Anil of their priorities and he also needs to remind Anil that he is his line manager.

Anil,

*I am not interested in individual 'stories'. They add unneces-
sary complexity and lack the credibility of statistics. Contact me
only if you identify any quantifiable trends that can be utilised
as the basis for action.*

I do not drink caffeinated drinks.

Barrington

It's 7.30pm when he arrives home. Corinne is reading the even-
ing paper at the kitchen table with a glass of white wine in hand.
There are plates on the worktop. She's obviously fed Nelson but
Barrington prefers the surfaces to be clear.

"How was your day?" she asks, not looking up.

"I had an accident on the bike this morning. That was a shock."

Corinne's glass makes Barrington think about the physical
manifestation of that much alcohol in the body of the young
woman in the bin, but he's distracted by Nelson, who is playing
with a box of Lego. The Lego is dirty.

"Shall we clean that up?" he says, patting the boy's head. He
has his hands in a bowl of soapy water on the kitchen floor.
Nelson is not allowed to splash and so wanders off to get a biscuit. Barrington patiently cleans the bright block.

"Are you OK? No broken bones?"

He shakes his head.

"Monday is an alcohol-free day for you," he states.

"Hmmm..." she says, turning the page.

"I've got a bit more work to do, but I'll put the boy to bed."

"Thanks, but it's OK."

His head twitches as he puts the Lego onto one tea towel,
picks up another to begin to dry it and begins building a brick
version of his to-do list. The bottom brick, the red one that holds
it all together, has to be health inequalities. From there he adds
a chunky yellow block for obesity, a blue one for mental health,

grey for dementia, a smaller one in violet for sexual health, a single orange piece for the six cases of rickets. He's made a neat tower, but then fixes a long black brick on top for alcohol, on the basis that, if the alcohol issue isn't addressed, life expectancy will never improve. Corinne leaves the wine glass on the table and takes Nelson upstairs.

Anil's report can't go into the public domain in its current state. The kind of personal and public change in attitudes he knows is required will be difficult enough to achieve without substandard evidence. It took public health professionals sixty years to get a ban on smoking in public places, but people are still wedded to their right to drink, drive and kill themselves, and others. He has to take action now and with budget cuts on the way he needs to accelerate the pace, but he's short on allies. Every recent discussion about alcohol has been about making it more available. The Council's promotion of the night-time economy is madness; relaxing licensing is a recipe for irresponsible drinking. With that thought he prods at the black Lego block with his index finger. It tips over easily, flat out on the carpet.

CHAPTER 6

ANNE-MARIE

Monday 15th November, 7pm

The house lights dim in the Stadium hospitality suite, a spot picks up the minor celebrity at the podium, a regional newsreader. Glossy hair and expensive teeth, the golden envelopes are held up as a signal to the audience. It's that time. The expected hush takes a while to reach their table, long enough even for Anne-Marie to catch a temporary dose of the child-like excitement. Andrea and Carol are seeing each other afresh in their frocks. The Highlands' women have scrubbed up well and hide their nerves beneath a torrent of alcohol. Anne-Marie sees how much they all want to win. Carol rubs away goose bumps on her bare arms, not caring who sees her fading scars. Andrea taps the table impatiently, reminding Anne-Marie of the time she'd thumped her desk, threatening to hit someone if nothing was done on the estate. Sandra rolls her eyes. Colin continues drinking quietly. Councillor Davina Clarke, the Council Leader, sits back, relaxed, focusing on the stage.

It's almost time for their award category. Anne-Marie practises an alternative acceptance speech in her head. "For the arses I've kicked, the budgets I've fixed, the stories I've told, for being bold, for seeing it through, I thank you. No, I pat myself on the back, because I doubt you lot will."

The hushed atmosphere is already wearying.

"And the winner is… The Street Speaks, an innovative youth engagement project." The celeb makes it sounds as though the team from the neighbouring borough have won the lottery. Christ. The programme states that The Street Speaks is in development, which means it hasn't even started yet. A project that's delivered nothing, an idea that's barely more than listening to random kids in a video booth, has won an award.

"What a shame," says Councillor Clarke, 50 per cent genuine.

Anne-Marie had really needed that award to keep the Highlands work on the Council budget sheet and she'd really wanted the girls to see their photo in the *Post* as winners.

"Let's have a toast." She bangs the table loudly. Others look round at them, but she wants to lift the team before they fall. "To the Highlands, to us, to our communities and to proper programmes of work that deliver real change."

They raise their glasses. Andrea adds a finger in defiance.

"I'm gutted," says Sandra.

"Yes," Anne-Marie nods. "We deserved that."

"Has Councillor Clarke said anything to you about next year's budget?" Sandra whispers.

"Sod that for now. You worked bloody hard for this. You're a finalist for a prestigious award and we'll get some good publicity out of it. Come on, let's enjoy ourselves."

"Cheers, boss."

Anne-Marie moves her chair back, stretches out her arm and leans over to the neighbours' table, picking up a nearly full open bottle of red wine. "Thank god I still smoke," she says, taking her glass and the bottle out of the fire exit door onto a terrace. The steadying effect of the nicotine and the mental shift that she makes moving from a superficial white to a serious red are disturbed as she realises Davina has followed her outside. Davina's wearing an emerald silk dress with chunky ethnic jewellery and clever natural make-up.

"Obviously we're all disappointed in the result this evening, Anne-Marie, but while we've got a quiet moment I wanted to talk to you about pressing ahead with our agenda. We've decided on the savings programme, we want you to lead it and we've got an exciting new City Centre development scheme we want you to head up. We see you as an agent of change and there's potential for you to go far if you deliver for us."

Anne-Marie takes a slow sip from the wine glass. Clever that. Of course she likes the depiction of herself as an avenging agent of change, but it irritates her that Davina has made it sound as if she is bestowing an honour. Of course it's impossible to give the Leader a direct 'no', not unless you want a short battle and a speedy end to your career, but if Davina's City Centre plan is a development scheme, why hasn't she heard about it already? As Regeneration Director that's her turf. She doesn't look Davina in the eye yet, but nods. She's wishfully thinking that Davina may not get the savings package through the Coalition cabinet, but at the same time she knows the reality is that councillors will keep on cutting and still expect officers to provide the same level of services.

"Let me put it like this," Davina continues. "Our only priority is to get the City Centre sorted and we need to make sure there are no, shall we say, blockages for the businesses involved. And make sure the Girl in the Bin story dies."

Charmingly put.

"I know we're here to celebrate the progress made on some of our more difficult estates, but I need you to review the Highlands work." Davina means that Anne-Marie will have to take an axe to her own empire. "Some of my group have never been happy with Neighbourhood Services. They don't know what they achieve."

Anne-Marie mentally grinds her teeth. That's because most of Davina's party have never even been to the Highlands Estate. If the local councillors had seen the difference this kind of intensive problem-solving at local level makes, they'd want it in every neighbourhood, but that's the kind of challenge Anne-Marie loves. To start with a blank page, to fundamentally do things differently. Still, that's a fantasy.

"I know you're close to this neighbourhood work, but it's not a priority in relation to the real challenges."

Anne-Marie looks at the ground, surprised it's not moving. She feels Davina's hand briefly on her shoulder and senses that the Leader is enjoying this conversation. What would she do in Davina's shoes? She notices her own shoes could do with a clean.

"Councillor, we are well used to making what we've got stretch further." Anne-Marie aims for a tone which isn't negative, but which holds off from full commitment until absolutely necessary.

"And we've always been committed to getting value for money. Some of our group want to be more radical."

Anne-Marie groans internally.

"The important thing is that our economy thrives and people prosper. In the current climate, it has to be business that provides the lightening rod for change."

It's half a relief to hear Davina say that. There's a practical logic to it. The public sector is almost on its knees, bound up in government knots, unable to drive a mini-bus let alone turn around the leaking tanker of the economy.

"Look, shall we go inside and talk more?" Davina looks disapprovingly at the bottle of wine. Anne-Marie looks pointedly at her watch.

"We've had a good night, but to be honest I've got to prepare for tomorrow and could do with getting an early night."

There's a short cut round the back of the stadium that will get her to the New Mechanics in five minutes. It's a public footpath, with impressive brickwork walls in parts, but it's unused and feels risky. In the thin light of the cold November evening Anne-Marie sees where Davina's going, but not how they'll get there. Not without a decent vehicle to clear the path. Not without filling a few potholes. Her eye is caught by a flash of metal in the headlight of a car. It's a commercial waste bin. Davina won't get what she wants without dealing with the rubbish. There's always something in the way and it usually takes some heavy lifting. Something Anne-Marie will do when she has to, when her battery is charged and the juice is flowing. That's not now.

Heaving open the door of the Mechanics is an effort. The lights welcome her. She's safe for now, relieved that Frank is at the bar and that Bob's gone home. Before joining Frank she sits on the toilet, her fierce miracle pants around her ankles. Christ, these buggers are coming off. Why is she here? It was an automatic reaction to head for the bar. One she's now regretting. It might've been a better idea to see if Adam was home. If she's not careful she'll go another week and might not see him, although it's possible he's avoiding her. This mother and her 17-year-old need their space.

Her sweaty thighs are sticking to the seat. She lets her head drop into her hands, elbows digging a red hole in her knees. The whole evening has been depressingly ugly. No award. OK, so that shouldn't have been a big deal, but Davina's words have pinned her to the floor. It's been clear for a while that the Council is in this position again. The organisation is quietly self-harming. A thousand tiny cuts have already gone un-noticed, but from now on there will be broken bones, bleeding arteries, amputations and unidentified mass viruses to deal with. And she's down to be Sweeny bloody Todd, although she's not seeking sympathy. That's what they pay her for.

She hears them calling time and heads to the bar. Frank has already bought her a VAT.

"Nearly sent a search party in there for you. Are you alright, girl?" Strange she still lets him call her that, as if she's his daughter not his ex-wife. Frank is happy at the bar on his own; it's like his front room. So much so that he's holding a mug of tea. He's known for his tea and his 'I'm no mug' mug. He's happy to buy anyone else a drink, if they are foolish enough to want one, but it's best not to ask him why he won't take one himself or you'll get a lecture about surplus value and why he's not giving his hard-earned cash to those that rob the working man of their livelihoods. He used to be an opposition councillor, part of the political furniture, and, as a college tutor, he can lecture for the city. Anne-Marie necks the drink as if it's cold pop on a hot day.

"We didn't win," she moans.

"We never win." Frank loves to be enigmatic. "But we always fight."

"Not at this time of night. I'm only just in the business of living to fight another day."

Frank has a rare twinkle in his eye. "There's a meeting about the cuts in the week. Bob's lot are having a go already, so fight again we will."

She manages half a smile. "Davina's been briefing me on her priorities for the City Centre and the savings programme."

"Let's call it cuts, love. That's what it is."

Her smile fades. "She wants to see the city and the community prosper."

Frank appears to read the swirls in his tea. "Careful, girl. She'll have you choosing between the devil and a big black hole. Or maybe that should be the Highlands and Bob?"

"But…" She hates the way Frank can strip an argument to the bone before it's even begun. She's too tired for this.

"Remember you don't make the choices. You aren't forced to do anything."

"I know. We're all trying to do our best in difficult circumstances."

"Don't be so sure. Never underestimate the dark side. You think you know their ways…"

Anne-Marie picks up her bag. "Look, I'm done in and I've

missed Adam again. We'll catch up on Saturday. I need to get my head together for the morning."

He's right, though. She needs to know more about the chalice she's about to drink from. What's in Davina's cocktail? She makes her way to the taxi rank. The drivers on that rank all know where she lives. The last thought she fixes on as her brain shuts down is that this has happened before: a different girl in a different bin. She climbs into the taxi, rests her head on the window and stares blankly out.

CHAPTER 7

JESSICA

Tuesday 16th November, 5pm

It's the first opportunity Jess has had to talk to her Chief Super, Richard Haynes, since the weekend. All is quiet in the station below. The Chief's office is on the top floor. He sits with his back to the expansive window. That's always struck her as a bad idea. It means his head is a black, egg-shaped silhouette against a vast ellipse of grey that includes the railway station, sidings, multistorey car parks and the low-rise flats that mark the start of the Highlands. It's hard to make out the shape of his mouth and difficult to focus on what he's saying unless you get up close. Is he being clever? Not that clever. He calls himself Dick rather than Rich and his Victorian tone alienates most of the station.

"Jessica, I am at your service," he pronounces.

"Sir, we need a radical rethink of our approach to alcohol. Since we discussed it last, we've had the Girl in the Bin, and GBH, ABH and domestic violence are all up. We can't have another report of weekend carnage from the custody suite and do nothing about it. We have a duty of care to our staff that we aren't meeting."

"The demon drink," he says, ignoring her point.

"Absolutely. Alcohol is on the agenda for the next partnership meeting and we need to have our own position clear."

"How is our Trashed Teen faring?" he asks.

The *Post* headline rankles. It isn't helping her push the alcohol work up the priority list, a list that has grown to the point where the word has become meaningless.

"Laura Awsworth. Her name is Laura, Sir. She's still in ICU. Hasn't regained consciousness. Likely brain injury. We're due another report from the hospital later. I'd like to take time to do some digging. Investigate what's really going on across..."

"Youthful inebriates?" he butts in. "Your role is rather more strategic, don't you think? Let me give you some advice."

Being her boss is just one of the reasons she doesn't pick him up on his patronising attitude. There's also history, incidents going back twenty years, the death of her father, whom the Chief knew well, and tactics.

"Yes, I'll take the overview, but I'm talking about something more fundamental. This is about the sort of society we want – one where we take alcohol-related violence seriously. At the moment we do nothing unless there's a serious crime. We should be focusing on the causes of crime. Sir, you've said yourself we're wasting precious resources."

"When I first joined the force..."

She can't bear to hear his 'good old days, good old ways' speech again. The world has moved on, but the Force hasn't. Yes, catch criminals, but what about prevention, not just saying the word loudly and often enough in an attempt to convince people things are changing when they're not? The resistance baffles her. Every officer knows that it's the same few families at the same addresses, front doors open, poverty, mental illness and alcohol spilling out into the street, mostly with a load of verbal if you're in a uniform of any sort. The Police, the Council and others do some good work on the front line, but it's too slow and Jess can see a meteorite hurtling towards them.

While the chief is breathing in his memories, she gets her ask in. "I want two DIs and one of the analysts to do some serious work on a new approach. We can't keep saying the Council needs to pull its finger out and not put some insight and muscle into it ourselves. We all need to work together on this, get health involved, business, the community, everyone. Launch a special task force."

He pulls out his Blackberry. Normally she would stop speaking and wait to get his attention, but she's on a roll. "If the girl dies, we'll be in a very different scenario. We'll need a major investigation and we'll need to demonstrate leadership." This line would normally work with the Chief, although as he nears retirement she's not clear what he wants to leave behind. Not this it seems.

"Alcohol is everyone's problem," she says.

"And not our responsibility," he replies sternly. "And unless the girl dies we'll manage this as is. After all, as I said, this is a nasty incident, which we'll investigate as normal; but I remain unconvinced at this stage that a wider response is required. If we make a big show of this it will become political and we'll have to get the Police Authority involved in the damn thing..."

Jess notes that it's already become a 'damned thing' in his mind.

"You suggest the task force idea to your Council friends. If they lead it, you could participate."

It sounds like another good idea that will be suffocated by his quiet life-ism.

"As it happens, I'm meeting one of the brewery managers later. I'll get his take on the City Centre and what some of the less reputable publicans are up to."

"I'd like to sit in on that meeting, Sir, if you don't mind."

"No," he says firmly. "It's not that kind of meeting. It's more of an informal parley."

She knows they'll be meeting on the golf course, but there's no point in antagonising him further and losing focus. "That's fine, Sir, but we need to do something. I'm passionate about this work. It might not be murder this week, but what next? We've got to get a grip."

He plays with his phone. "I'll ask Stewart to work with you and link up with DI Jones on the girl. That's as far as I'll go for now."

He's done that deliberately to end the conversation, or worse, to ensure that as little as possible gets done, or to wind her up. Professionally speaking Jess now finds Stewart slack and self-serving, a description that goes for him as a husband, too. His interests won't be furthered by this investigation. He'll be a slow-moving vehicle and will happily sit on his soap box, talking about the scum who don't deserve his consideration.

Jess stands to leave. "Am I OK to put the alcohol work on our next management agenda, before we go public?"

He shakes his head. "Let me come back to you on that."

"Sir, you're wrong on this." She's unusually blunt.

He becomes a silhouette again. This is basic. Alcohol is at the top of almost every chief super's list. She sees the girl, Laura, as a call to action. Ignoring her is high risk. Something else is definitely going on, but frustration blocks her intuition and she gets no further.

She changes tack, jogging down a floor to Alan Jones' desk. "Any more on Laura Awsworth?"

"There's an initial medical report."

She pounces on a few points for Jonesy to check. The probable cause of the injury to the back of her head is reported as a concrete post or flag stone. A pencil note in the margin suggests the brain injury could also have been related to a hairline fracture to one of the neck bones, which could've cut the blood supply to the brain. Possibly a martial arts manoeuvre? That's interesting.

"Is there a toxicology report?"

"Not yet."

"Have you had a chance to look through the Saturday night CCTV I marked up?"

"Not yet."

"Can you check through and let me know if we've got anything in any of the City Centre pubs. What about…"

Jones is young, keen and normally an easy target for a favour.

"Excuse me, ma'am, Deputy Commander, ma'am, but is that you pulling rank? You'll get the intel up the chain, won't you?"

The young man has a local accent that softens the challenge. Yes, but, Jess needs leverage to get the task force idea moving.

"This isn't pressure. Senior officers are paid to keep tabs. I'm talking to the Chief and our partners about an alcohol task force. This incident is one reason we need to do more. Are you interested in taking part?"

"Can I let you know when we've made progress on this?"

Smooth answer, but she needs to strike while there's some momentum, get hold of something concrete before she tackles the Chief again.

"What did you make of that boy band gang?" Jonesy asks.

"Nothing the beat officers can't deal with, but you've reminded me to check something. Thanks."

The fresh air will do her good. She'll walk and think.

"Sharon! Sharon, stop! Shaz, how're you doing?"

It was one of those edge of consciousness things, a dog of a thought, an *ought to* action that had dropped off her list, maybe more than a year ago. The fact that it hadn't been done meant that she hadn't dismissed it completely and she'd half expected to see Sharon, here, at the wrong end of the city, among the pound shops and vertical drinking bars.

"Hey, Shaz. It's great to see you. It's been too long. God, don't tell me it's, what, 18 months already?" Jess grabs her friend's hand then lets it drop. The fingers are icy.

"I'm fine. You look great. No, really, you look, well, classy."

Jess is wearing her own navy coat. Underneath are boot-cut, black slacks and a thick purple jumper over her white short sleeved shirt. Not obviously uniform, but smart.

"What are you up to? I've got time for a quick drink. Have you?"

In contrast Jess realises her friend doesn't look well. Her skin is grey. She's put on weight and her gaze wanders too quickly down to the pavement.

"I need one," Shaz says, without an invitation to enquire further. That doesn't bode well, but Jess welcomes the chance for a quiet word.

"Where shall we go?"

"What about the Anvil? It'll be empty this time of day."

They turn around and walk towards the station, although the Anvil isn't a great choice for Jess. Without the smell of smoke it just smells of beer and sweaty men, the lights are too bright and the drinks too cheap.

"How's Ben?" asks Jess, sensing a connection emerging. "What's he doing now? Finished college? Hoping to go to uni?"

"Yeah."

"Yeah to which bit?"

"Sorry," says Shaz. "He's still at college."

"What's next? Has he got a girlfriend?"

Jess doesn't want to start interrogating her friend, but finds her irritatingly vague, almost disinterested, or maybe it's that she's guarded.

"I'm the last to know what's happening these days."

"That sounds like teenagers in general." Jess' non-judgemental response is a learned one, based on her colleagues who have kids rather than the teenagers that end up in the custody suite, who seem to talk all the time and give little or no information.

She's known Ben since he was born and loved looking after the toddler when his dad left. Carlton was Shaz's on/off child-hood boyfriend. They'd all lived on the Highlands Estate until they were ten and Jess' dad had bought his own house out of the way of any obviously criminal neighbours. Jess decides to ask about Ben again later.

"And what about you? Can I take a couple of those bags for

you? Looks like you've been on a bit of a spree."

"I've not been at my best," she replies. "Nothing a bit of retail therapy can't shift, though." Shaz sounds defensive.

Jess takes a bag from her friend. One contains a set of kitchen scales; the other a couple of thick, dark hoodies. Hardly a binge. They arrive at the pub and Jess offers to go to the bar.

"What do you fancy?"

"I'll have a Whiskey Mac. I've got this cold and can't shake it off," Shaz says.

"You sure you're OK?"

"You aren't on duty are you? I've just had a bad year or so."

"What's up? Or is it something you don't feel like talking about now?"

"Yeah, best not to go there now." Her eyes are darting around the room.

"Course, no worries, but you could've rung me. And I could've rung you," Jess admits.

At the bar Jess wonders at what point she'd gone from best friend to big sister to distant cousin. Joining the Force and marrying Stewart hadn't helped. Maybe she's just being nostalgic for a friendship that hadn't been there in any honest sense for over a decade. The pub is empty, but Jess observes three men at the bar who are locked in an intense discussion. Bar staff and boss. Not studying form or football stats. It could be a rota, but customer service is clearly not on their agenda. The boss, in a sharp-collared, navy shirt is writing in a Moleskine notebook. It's the type she would buy for her sister in London, if she had time to think about shopping.

"Excuse me?"

One of the other men is wearing a dangling cross in his ear. Now she looks closer, he could be a cellman, bouncer or general heavy. He stares coldly through her and returns to his conversation. Was that just rudeness or had he guessed she was Police? Still, there was a time when she'd known most of the landlords in the City Centre. Turning back to the table, she sees Shaz suddenly look at her, eyes bulging, stand up abruptly and scrabble to pick up her bags. Jess hurries back to the table without the drinks.

"Are you alright?"

Shaz begins to pull on her coat, won't meet her eye. Jess only just manages to keep up as Shaz speeds to the door. Once outside she links arms and takes the weight of her friend's crumbling knees. No words come out.

"Right, breathe deeply, keep your head up, lean on me. That's fine. You're not even that heavy." She maintains a light, practical tone.

"We'll go straight back and pick up my car. I bet you could do with a cup of tea. Lucky I've been on a first aid course. Yes, we went on one just to be told to make a cup of tea. Will Ben be home?" It's probably not ideal for him to see his mum so distressed, but Jess has so little to go on.

"I'm sorry, I just lost it. I get a bit panicky these days. Ben won't be home, or he might be later, not sure, but I'll be OK. I'm fine at home." This doesn't ring true, but Jess doesn't push it. Inside the car, her friend's breathing returns to normal.

"Stop apologising would you."

"Yes, sorry. I mean, I'm OK. I know I don't look it. I could really do with a good job. Any job really."

On the journey through peak-time traffic, Jess hears about Shaz giving up college, then volunteering for a project that closed down, succumbing to daytime TV and not hearing from her mum. Who wouldn't be depressed by that picture? As they draw up to her house, they see the lights of a massive and presumably very expensive screen through the window.

"Great, Ben is home. Can I come in and say hello?"

While they are walking up the path, Jess' phone rings. She sees Stewart's name flash up and switches it off. Ben comes to the door. He has a shaved head, but his features are kind and unthreatening.

"Wow, look at him. I didn't recognise him. He's a man now."

"Yeah."

"Shaz, can I ask, are you talking to anyone? You don't have to tell me what's going on, but you need someone to talk to. Look, I will definitely pop in on Friday for a cup of tea, if that's OK?"

"OK. OK, thanks."

Jess gently hugs her friend. She knows it won't make anything better in the short term, but the physical contact feels like a contract, a commitment to stick with whatever this is.

CHAPTER 8

ANNE-MARIE

Tuesday 16th November, 6.15pm

Anne-Marie's normal survival toolkit for a Planning Committee meeting is a pack of cigs, a can of pop, a packet of Ibuprofen and a trip to the first-floor east wing. Partially obscured by filing cabinets, one of the committee clerks trades misshapen Cadbury's seconds from a plastic basket. Next to it is a tin labelled '20p', a voluntary contribution which no-one dares disobey for fear the basket might one day be empty. If only management was so easy. Get people to do what you want by letting them think they're getting a bargain and implicitly threatening to take it away. The chocolate will keep her going until the meeting is finished. Although the strip light in her office is bright, the corridors are dark after 6pm and the temperature drops. It used to be about reducing CO_2 emissions, now it's about cost-saving.

The planning meeting requires all her mental strength, both to look like she's paying attention while covertly answering emails and to give credible answers to stupid questions. The situation is exacerbated by fifty minutes of discussion on what ought to be a straightforward approval for a garden shed in a posh outer suburb. An incoherent letter of objection, laced with bile, has meant the application has to be dealt with by committee rather than simply processed by her officers. "As you'll see from the report, your officers have recommended approval. The application is in line with your policy, councillors." She thought it would go through without comment. Then there is a councillor's chance remark about the proposed shed being bigger than her sister's new house. Anne-Marie rolls her eyes, knowing this means the end of all hope. The councillors are off enjoying themselves, speculating wildly on the nature of the housing market, reminiscing about the Parker Morris space standards. The level of debate has sunk to barely above the gossip line. These are the councillors who'll have to deliver a sensible decision on Davina's City Centre plan, god help her. She smiles and calls their bluff. "Chair, could I propose we set up a sub-group to review the policy on sheds and could I ask for volunteers?" No-one puts their hand up. "So for now, the policy stands and the application," which they've now wasted an hour on, "is passed." It's no wonder they are a laughing stock.

As the meeting winds up and she trudges along with the crowd, trying not to start a stampede, she overhears two of the older male councillors talking.

"I heard that girl in the bin was raped. She's a vegetable. Might never wake up."

"It's not safe to walk the streets and our clever-clever officers think we should switch the street lights off to save money. They're on another planet."

Anne-Marie doesn't make eye contact. What she wants to say is that if they weren't protecting their pet services and projects, in this case the city's bowling greens, she wouldn't be forced into making those kinds of cuts. The madness has begun.

She escapes the Council House buildings, but hovers at the night boundary, where the light of the building bleeds into the shadows. Empty buildings increase the density of the gloom. She struggles to light a cigarette in the cold wind, but doesn't want to stand in the designated smokers' area. Too close for comfort and today she's had more than enough of that place. Sod it, she thinks, and finds herself almost jogging to the Mechanics. Her mood lifts slightly, confident in the knowledge that a stiff drink will help. Andrea is at the bar.

"Have you recovered from the awards night?" Anne-Marie asks.

"We know how to celebrate losing alright. Where did you skulk off to? Not like you to leave while there's still booze on the table."

"Yeah, sorry, it's been a hell of a couple of days."

"So, you've heard last night's estate news?"

"Er no, tell me." Again Anne-Marie feels out of touch.

"Some incompetents nearly burned down St Peter's Primary."

"That's not like the Highlands lads. We expect a more professional approach to arson. I blame the parents." Anne-Marie manages a hollow laugh, but it isn't funny. She loved that school.

Andrea shakes her head. "It started on the tennis courts. They had a brazier going. Colin spotted it on his way home and called the Police. They got there just as the building was going up. Colin filmed a bit of it on his phone. Have a look before you start lecturing anyone on parenting."

"What?" Anne-Marie dreads the implication as Andrea gets her phone out.

"Listen, I'm only saying this one mother to another like, but I hope you're going to give your lad a good hiding."

Seeing her son in the middle of the gang, Anne-Marie tries to hide her fury. The idiot is wearing that P.I.M.P. hoodie again. Without that she might get away with arguing that it's someone else.

"My old man gave our Kerry a mouthful, but she's just a sheep. She wasn't the one with the matches. Community will do what we can, but, like you say, it comes down to the parents."

"Jesus, I'll kill the little bugger. I'd better get home."

Anne-Marie grabs at her drink, but fills her mouth too quickly and snorts as bubbles go up her nose. Smacking open the toilet door she throws down her bag. More madness. He's supposed to be doing well at college, taking exams, not setting fire to schools. How dare he? How absolutely dare he jeopardise his future like this? As she splashes her face with unexpectedly hot water she knows that he's jeopardising her future as well. The hand towel is stuck and Anne-Marie is forced to dry her face with toilet paper. The toilets are clean, but smell old. They've got a chain pull like the one at her gran's house. Of all the pubs in the city surely the Mechanics is making enough money to upgrade the loos?

She chews on the inside of her cheek trying to compose herself. OK, it might be possible to avoid a complete disaster as long as Davina doesn't get to hear that her son is an arsonist. Angrily she works up a scenario that will drag something positive from the ashes of this fire. It's not strictly Sandra's job, and it's not strictly appropriate, but if she can get Sandra and maybe Andrea to stoke up some community reaction, suggest there's asbestos in there, get a petition going, it will help keep the Highlands in the news. Councillors need to physically see what the issues are and who's sorting out their problems, so now seems like a good time to show them the damage to the school and how Colin's prompt action saved them resources. 'Simplify and exaggerate,' is always Davina's message.

Then there are the land issues. Davina wants to sell sites like the St Peter's Primary one for housing, but she's kidding herself if she thinks there will be developers queuing up to build on the Highlands. It'll be empty for years, but while it is Anne-Marie can work on getting a principle established. If she can get agreement that the proceeds of the sale of any school site will be ring-fenced for community use, it will give her something to work with. It's hardly a quick fix and she'll end up in a dogfight with the Director of Education and the Finance Director, who will both want to appropriate the proceeds of any asset realisation, but now's the time for open minds. She brightens a smidge. 'Managing the political interface' – it's crass management speak, but it accounts for the bulk of her job and she's good at it. Just a shame it's not so easy to manage her son. What she needs is a couple of months to get through this round of cuts and kick off Davina's development. Then she'll have time to sort out Adam.

Out again in the cold night air she is suddenly ravenous, having eaten only a crooked chocolate bar in the last nine hours. Cooking a meal when she gets home isn't an option, especially if Adam is there. Maybe Andrea's right about giving him a good clout? He's as tall as she is, but she could give him a scare. She loved that school. Jesus, she thinks, a brazier. Frank can answer for that. He'd have taught him that on some picket line, no doubt.

Exhausted, she makes her way to the taxi rank, but is distracted by the fatty smell from a burger van parked off the High Street towards the Concert Hall. It's a quick victory. The burger she can take or leave, but not the fried onions, the way the burnt ends contrast with the soft translucent strands.

"Fancy a big one?" Mr Sizzle's downbeat delivery means he gets a quarter of a smile rather than a sharp tongue.

"Regular with lots of onions, please."

The big man nods. "I like a woman who knows her onions."

Anne-Marie fishes in her bag for her purse, leaves it on the counter, pulls out her phone and get's Adam's voicemail. "Adam, I'll be home in twenty minutes. Stay put if you're at home. If you're out, call me."

Next she tries Frank, turning her back slightly on Mr Sizzle. "Is Adam at yours?"

Mr Sizzle fills the burger and wraps it elegantly, turning down the corner of the serviette.

"And I suppose he wasn't there last night either?" As she repeats the story, Frank's predictable response is to try to ease the edge off her anger. She takes the burger and chews on a mouthful, tuning out from Frank's apologist chunter. "I'll call you as soon as I hear anything." She puts her phone on the counter next to her purse.

"I should have divorced my kids not my wife. Watch your stuff love," says Mr Sizzle.

She's not in the mood to chat. This time she puts the whole bag on the counter, takes another bite of burger, then searches for a cigarette, pulling out a hair brush and a packet of tissues, as well as a folded train ticket. Don't lose that, she reminds herself. Useful notes scribbled on that.

"Got a light by any chance?"

Mr Sizzle pulls out a gun-shaped gas lighter at speed. "At your service," he says, blowing out the gun, cowboy-style.

She puts the burger down amongst the mess of her things. "Sorry. Nightmare week."

"And the nightmare continues... that'll be £3.50."

A text arrives.

Staying at bens. Will call dad.

She finds four coins in her purse, then sweeps everything from the counter back into the bag, hooks it over her shoulder and takes a long draw on her cigarette. She decides Adam can go and live with Frank. Frank can sort this mess out. Davina will hear about the Highlands everywhere she goes and the rest of them, the Planning Committee in particular, she will just have to shoot.

"Right, I'm off." She stubs out the cigarette into the barely eaten burger and heads off to the taxi rank.

"Charming," Mr Sizzle says into the wind.

CHAPTER 9

JESSICA

Wednesday 17th November, 1.30pm

The Chief increasingly palms this sort of event off onto Jess. To her, though, the launch of a Healthy Living Centre on the Highlands Estate is good news. She's happy to have the time away from the station and the prospect of a lobbying opportunity with Anne-Marie is icing on the presumably low-fat carrot cake. In between the free baby massage, taster self-defence class and condom distribution there are the standard speeches, and Jess hovers at the back. The room is packed with staff, patients and members of the community Jess recognises from their police liaison meetings; those people who will turn up to the opening of a crisp packet and prefer a live soap to a televised one. Anne-Marie gets the proceedings underway.

"Welcome everyone. I'm Anne-Marie Morton, from the City Council. It's fantastic to see you all on this very exciting afternoon. The formal opening ceremony will be starting shortly. I've had a message to say that the Council Leader, Davina Clarke, is stuck, not sure in what, presumably traffic, but in the meantime we have Dr Barrington Edwards, who helped secure the funding for this building, and he's agreed to say a few words on the local health challenges."

There is vague applause. Jess can tell Anne-Marie's smile is forced, but isn't sure whether Dr Edwards is the cause. All she's ever heard about him, which isn't much, is that he's a bit of a liability. She watches him pull at his tie and stare at the tracks of hairdressers' spotlights hung on wire across the ceiling. The level of chatter in the room drops as if someone has switched off a radio.

"I have three things to say about public health challenges in relation to this building. The first is that you, the community, need to use it. Average life expectancy in this neighbourhood is 68 years. That means that simply because of your postcode you are likely to die 12 years before someone living on the west side of the City.

"Secondly, your biggest problem is alcohol. You drink too much. Alcohol-related deaths have doubled in the last ten years. This neighbourhood is estimated to have 3,800 harmful and hazardous drinkers and 620 whom we consider to be alcohol-dependent. And there was the incident of the Girl in the Bin at the weekend. She was found with the equivalent of 132 units of alcohol in her body."

The crowd mumbles. Anne-Marie rolls her eyes. Barrington doesn't seem to care.

"You might not see it, but alcohol-related domestic violence is increasing. The Supermarket on Simpson Street sells a can of strong lager for 39 pence, cheaper than carbonated water. The Three Lions is famed for its lock-ins and we are working to shut down the Booze2U dial-a-drink taxi service."

Anne-Marie cuts in. "I'd like to re-assure Dr Edwards that we won't be giving out the number!" The crowd laughs nervously. "We take alcohol harm very seriously," she continues. "I know some of you may have spotted the wine glasses laid out at the back of the room, and we'll be offering a small toast to celebrate the opening of this fantastic new centre, but it's for special celebratory purposes only."

Barrington shrugs his shoulders. "My final point is that the GPs and nurses here will do their jobs, but you've got to start taking responsibility for looking after yourselves and your neighbours. You need to eat less and exercise more. Obesity rates in both adults and children are the worst in the City. This is the unhealthiest estate in the Midlands and it's in the bottom 5 per cent nationally."

Jess watches Anne-Marie almost pull his arm from his socket, dragging him to his seat. "That sounds like a good point to pause for a minute as I've just spotted Councillor Clarke arriving. Thanks again Dr Edwards for standing in."

The volume in the room beings to rise. Jess hears the word 'pillock' slung in Dr Edwards' direction and is relieved that his address has been cut short before he's been seriously heckled or Anne-Marie has hit him. He's blunt, more than she would ever be, but he was exactly right about the health of the community and she wonders if he could be an unexpected ally. Jess can see Dr Edwards' comments making dangerously good copy for the press and from the way Anne-Marie is laying coats over community puddles it's clear she's on the case. The Council Leader, though, seems unfazed, sweeping her way royally around the room. That kind of straight talking might chime well politically. Interesting, Jess thinks.

"That's one word for it." A thick-haired young Asian man standing slightly to her left makes her realise she's spoken aloud.

"You know Dr Edwards?"

"He's my boss. I'm Anil Desai. I've been doing the leg work on the City Alcohol Plan, liaising with your intelligence analysts."

She hasn't heard of Anil, but sees it as an opportunity to find out more about Edwards.

"I'm Deputy Commander Jessica Reid. Is this something Dr Edwards is personally getting behind?"

"It's his number one priority."

Jess intuits there's a 'but' coming, so gives the young man a sincere nod, inviting him to say more.

"He's hot on the data and knows his stuff, so we're focusing on developing an evidence base for the problem."

That's good news for Jess, she waits to hear the downside.

"I'd like us to be doing more qualitative work. Take the Girl in the Bin, for example. We need to be thinking about her behaviour, her choices. There are other girls with similar drinking patterns that link to other violent incidents. I mean, the City Alcohol Plan, at the moment, it's nowhere near what's really happening, is it?"

She zooms in now, nodding, seeing a further potent ally. She agrees that data isn't everything. They could spend all their time digging into the stats, going deeper and deeper under the surface, hoping to find a golden nugget that explains everything, but the further down they go, the murkier it gets. It's as if they believe there's something they've been missing all along that will give them the answer, but everyone knows there's not one rational answer, no straight line between cause and effect, in the same way that there's never just one easy solution. It's not that the intelligence-led approach is wrong. She definitely doesn't want the pendulum to swing back to over-simplistic gut reactions and the personal prejudice that inevitably entails. What seems to be more important for Jess are the basic connections, the choices, the incentives and consequences for everyday life. That's what needs sorting out and Anil has just talked about a trend.

Jonesy has left her a message saying that Laura Awsworth, the Girl in the Bin, was living in a residential care home in Derby. What's her connection here, a boyfriend or parts of another family? What choices did she have? Could she just choose to work hard at school, get a good education and rise above the predictably depressing results for kids in care? Or did she make another choice – to get drunk and pick up an older man who might give her a route out? A man who might have cash or a flat, who might make her feel that she's wanted and attractive, however temporarily? Did she knowingly put herself in a high-risk situation and take the consequences? Or maybe, like many teenagers, she wasn't thinking at all. Although Dr Edwards might take a bit of managing, they could make a useful alliance. She needs his statistics to make the case for a proper investigation and Anil could be an extra resource.

"We'd be interested in the qualitative work. Would you be able to do some research at A&E on girls with similar profiles? Intelligence on that could be critical to us. I'll have a word with Dr Edwards. If we can support you in any way, let us know." Anil looks relieved. Jess sees Dr Edwards loitering at the back of the room, checking to see if he can get out unnoticed.

"Thanks, but please don't say it was my idea." Anil holds up his clean palms, embarrassed. Things must be bad for him to be so open in front of her.

"It wasn't your idea," she responds.

"Sorry. It's just that Barrington likes a more direct focus. Like the prostitution work."

"I need to hear more, but you'll have to excuse me for a moment." She's seen a *Post* journalist heading for Dr Edwards. It's a sarky boy who works the courts and is known to the Police. He's been cautioned for being drunk and disorderly before, but double standards mean nothing when there are column inches to fill. It won't be helpful to have Dr Edwards discredited, especially for telling the truth in a way that she envies. If the reporter gets an interview and asks Edwards to explain himself further it's likely that he will. She shouts across – a verbal body-check. "You're from the *Post*, aren't you? Great to have a good news story, isn't it? I'm Deputy Commander Reid. Would you like me to give you a quote? I think this centre is a fantastic resource for the community and they are out in force today to support it. You can expect to see our Police Community Support Officers out here, working in the neighbourhood..."

The hack interrupts. "Could you comment on the negative portrayal of the community from the NHS guy. He didn't have a good word to say about the place."

"I heard him say there were challenges and he's right. You know that as well as I do."

Dr Edwards is leaving the room. As he does, a small boy throws a samosa at him, but he seems not to notice. The second attempt catches his elbow as heads out onto the street. Jess holds the journalist up a moment more, wanting to make sure the doctor is in the clear. Then she turns her attention to Anne-Marie, who's escorting the Council Leader out of the room. That's annoying. Jess already has the feeling Anne-Marie is ignoring her. Usually Jess could rely on her primary school pal to share her aims, although her performance so far on the alcohol issue doesn't bode well. Their differing ways of getting what they want have sometimes been a source of conflict, sometimes admiration, but they've managed to stay pretty close. The potential new allies Jess has just encountered have shown her a different door and behind that door there's a corridor to another part of the public sector – and some intelligence to help her wedge it open.

CHAPTER 10

BARRINGTON

Thursday 18th November, 10am

Barrington had been up working until 2am, until his eyes, gravelly and raw, had begun closing of their own accord, but it was a waste of time. The report is vague, directionless, lacks any statistical analysis and, worse, has already been sent out without his corrections. At these partnership meetings, with the Council Leader sitting in a high-backed chair like a judge, it's unacceptable to table an update and the prospect of presenting a shoddy report with no tangible recommendations makes it daunting, even for someone with his experience. He had slept badly.

The meeting started at 9.30am, but in order to limit his suffering Barrington has made an art of arriving just in time for his agenda item. Meetings in the formal Committee Rooms at the Council House are particularly painful. The fixed, lacquered tables are set out in a rectangle so long he has to strain to see who is sitting at the other end. The wood panelling increases his feeling of claustrophobia. He feels on trial, the thick air seeming to eat his words. "Good timing," notes Councillor Clarke. "We're about to turn to item four, the City Alcohol Plan. Dr Edwards, could you kick us off with your report?"

"I apologise Madam Chair, but I'm obliged to make a verbal presentation due to an administrative error an earlier version was sent out. I'm seeking partners' approval to make this our top priority and set up an emergency task force on alcohol." He'd discussed this with Deputy Commander Jessica Reid and it had been surprisingly fruitful. The task force was her idea and she'd cleared it with her boss, the Chief, who is now sitting opposite him. He'd also instructed Anil to brief the Council's Regeneration Director, Anne-Marie Morton, but from the dismissive shrug she gives the Leader it seems it's the first time she's heard about it.

"That isn't in the report is it?" Councillor Clarke looks at him blankly.

"No. I'm proposing it now."

"Is that appropriate?" She looks around for someone to give her an answer.

Owen Cork, the Chief Executive, leans across to her and shakes his head. It looks as if this simple negative movement is the only way his head ever moves. Police Chief Haynes looks doubtful and walks off to take a call.

"We have the worst alcohol abuse figures in the Midlands. It's our job to discuss what needs to be done."

He stops abruptly to look at Councillor Clarke. Her voice is terse. "I understand your concern, but I don't see how we can make decisions on what needs to be done when there's been no consideration of the issues."

Aware he's out on a limb, he appeals to the room, more politely than he feels.

"We've all got resources committed to this and people have been working on alcohol harm for years. I'd be grateful if we could address my proposal."

Anne-Marie Morton speaks first. "I'm happy to have the debate, if that's the general consensus…"

It's hardly what he would call enthusiasm. Anne-Marie waits for the Leader to nod agreement and continues. "I have to say, though, that I don't agree this is our top priority and certainly not based on this." She throws the paper on the table.

"Is the later version any better? The evidence isn't exactly robust and the conclusions… Frankly I just don't believe them. People drink too much because they don't know the dangers? No, people drink too much because they can and because they want to."

Barrington has been expecting something along these lines and he can't say she's wrong, based on what's written here, but he has to get them onto the issues.

"People in this city, people everywhere, drink because we let them or because they are addicted to the effects."

"We've had task groups before and they've made no difference," interjects Anne-Marie dismissively. "You say individuals don't make the right choices where alcohol is concerned, but do we? We're supposed to know better."

Barrington tries to keep it simple, but the lack of a strong case means he has to ad-lib. He notices he's starting to perspire. "We need to make progress on three things. Firstly, alcohol-related crime. I remind you that we have the worst stats in the region on domestic violence. Secondly, the idea of a safe and sensible culture of drinking within the context of a deregulated, 24-hour economy is nonsensical. We need to tackle the alcohol industry through licensing and regulation, because we have more vertical drinking establishments per square metre than any other city in the country. And finally, we have to improve access to alcohol through..."

The Leader speaks over him. "Dr Edwards, I take it you mean access to alcohol services?"

Councillor Clarke's interruption agitates Barrington further. He's embarrassed by the obvious slip of the tongue. He goes back to the numbers, talking over the low-level laughter. "Half of all teenagers as young as 16 admit to binge drinking and around 25 per cent of children aged 11 to 15 drink an average of ten units of alcohol a week."

"Hang on." Anne-Marie comes back straight at him. "Half of all teenagers? That just doesn't ring true. I have a teenage son and there's no way half his class are problem drinkers? They can't afford it. I recognise there are families with chaotic relationships to alcohol…"

Barrington is sure she's playing this for laughs and deliberately trying to undermine him, but his thinking is clouded by his own family experience.

He'd have been about seven years old when the first serious incident happened.

"Please don't go out. Mummy's too ill."

His father was wearing clean, black shoes, a stiff jacket and was definitely going out. The tall man had looked at him and told him not to start unless he wanted a lick. "Boy," he used to say, "my ears are too tired of you."

After the front door had slammed shut, it was so quiet he could hear her breathing. That breathing scared him. She breathed in and seemed to stop, and then breathed out for so long he started counting each second until some air went back in. He sat on the floor by the sofa where she was lying. She was sweating, but cold and wanted a blanket. She used to like a smelly old hot water bottle, but he hadn't known where it was. It had seemed like ages before she spoke, saying something like, "It's the pressure, son. Stay there, Barrington. Don't you go anywhere".

Her legs felt damp and she kind of laughed like she was drunk, but not drunk like his dad could be. Why had his dad gone out? He couldn't stand it anymore and had decided to phone the Police. His father didn't like the Police and he would get in trouble for using the phone. He rang 999 or, more accurately, 9999999. He remembered the feel of the telephone button on his fingers, he'd pressed so hard. When the ambulance came they'd taken her straight to hospital. The ambulance men had asked him grown-up questions about his mum and her condition. They'd commented on how well he'd answered and he was proud that he'd acted responsibly in spite of the lack of regard shown by his father.

The next time she was ill he'd written everything down in a yellow notebook, drawing a body shape and marking where it hurt with a cross. He'd practised using the phone when no-one was looking. He'd even hidden his father's 'going out' clothes for a while. Not that it had made a difference. He had carried on drinking, going out when he felt like it, leaving Barrington in a constant state of anxiety. Looking back, it was so obvious. His mother had been suffering from angina and was over-weight due to a high cholesterol diet. Black women had twice the rate of heart disease of white women and in many ways his mother's death had been inevitable. The tragedy for Barrington was that it was all so avoidable. The causes had been ignorance, apathy and a lack of action.

He hears Anne-Marie talking again. "Shouldn't we be more concerned about the small number of young girls who are drinking, getting themselves into risky situations, ending up on teenage pregnancy lists? If the Girl in the Bin incident shows us anything, isn't it that we need to be more targeted?"

Barrington finds himself on his feet. "We already have a teenage pregnancy strategy. This is about acting to reverse the practices that encourage people to drink dangerously." The temperature in the room can't be rising, but Barrington feels hot. Momentarily distracted, he counts five, large, old radiators, the type they had at his senior school. He wonders if that's the only reference that will be made to the Girl in the Bin? Five of them haven't even spoken.

Anne-Marie challenges again. "I'm interested in the demographics. Where's our population group and geographic breakdown on alcohol? I've heard you say the Highlands is the worst estate in the Midlands. I've heard middle-class wine drinkers are a problem. Which is it? I'm sorry Dr Edwards, when I have a drink I often like a smoke as well, but at least I'm not obese yet."

He twists his cufflinks, blowing out a long, loud breath. Anne-Marie gives him a wink and he spots a meeting of eyes between her and Councillor Clarke. "What? What's going on?" he blurts. "Is that why no-one will take the problem seriously? I'm not interested in middle-class drinkers' inability to control their own intake. This is about a large proportion of the population who are literally drinking themselves to death and being encouraged to do so. You won't take it seriously, because you think you can't afford to." His feet want to take him out of the room right this second. Councillor Clarke motions him to sit down.

"Colleagues, I can assure you we are all very aware about alcohol harm, but we need to keep this in perspective. We're talking about something that's part of most of our lives. It's a legal product. It's an industry that generates significant revenue and jobs for our economy. Dr Edwards, we've consistently said that the economy is our top priority and there doesn't seem to be the backing for a task force. Are there any other views around the table?"

"I don't agree, Chair. I know the Police support the task force." Barrington looks directly at Commander Haynes. He's missed some of the debate, but now sets out his stall.

"Thank you, Chair. Please accept my apologies. It was most rude of me to leave the room. We are here to fight crime. We have, indeed, had a preliminary discussion about the idea of a task force. My colleague, Deputy Commander Jessica Reid, has been working tirelessly with our partner agencies on this, but unfortunately our focus from the Home Office is on tackling gang-related crime. I'm sorry to say that I don't understand young people's idea of a good night out these days. It's an education issue."

That's not what Barrington agreed with Jessica. Even to Barrington Haynes' words sound ill-considered. "We need to get moving. We need to do something practical," he responds. "We can at least look at the areas where we can have an impact, like licensing. I'll be asking the Council formally to review their licensing policy, task force or not."

Anne-Marie picks up the paper in front of her. "Doesn't this report say supermarkets are the problem, not the landlords? We've recently reviewed our licensing policy and your health colleagues were fully involved. However, I'd like to be positive. Could I make a suggestion that might help everyone move forward? The Highlands is in my remit. I'd be happy to look at alcohol as part of a more joined-up approach. We could link this in with the excellent community work that's going on locally."

Councillor Clarke sighs, relieved, and smoothly moves on. "Sounds like a good way forward. Dr Edwards, I'm going to ask you to set up a meeting with Anne-Marie to progress that."

Barrington sits down sharply. He stuffs the papers back into his rucksack, focusing on pulling the two side zips to the top of the bag together. "That's ridiculous. Completely inadequate." He isn't aware that he's mumbling out loud until he looks up to see everyone staring at him. Councillor Clarke fixes her lips in a straight line. "I, er, with your permission, Madam Chair, I have another meeting to go to," he says. He needs to escape. His shirt is stuck to his back. He has to have a shower to cool down, to wash away his humiliation

CHAPTER 11

ANNE-MARIE

Thursday 18ᵗʰ November, 8pm

Anne-Marie is relieved that Frank hasn't pushed for Adam to come out for a pizza. She detests family meetings. Too much like work and equally ineffective. Another late night at work has left her hungry and with a thirst on. The restaurant is small, local and empty. It normally annoys her that there are no mainstream pizza chains in the City Centre, but tonight it's a blessing, because she won't bump into anyone she knows. She gives Frank a generous hug, aware that he might not automatically go for her plan for Adam to move into his place full-time. The way to get around Frank is leave things open and let him step in to fill the gap. If they finish in an hour, she'll have time to do some work before the morning.

"Adam told me what you'd said on the phone. You didn't think of holding something back until we know a bit more about what's going on?"

"Yes, well, he wound me up. It's always someone else's fault with that boy." The comforting hot dough smell of the restaurant and the sense of a useful sortie amidst a longer term, soon-to-get-bloody battle, keep her mood from hardening too quickly. "I suppose I could have been a bit more..." Frank opens his hand as a prompt. "More...?" More what? She's not having this turn into a lecture on what a good mother would do under these circumstances. "Frank, I was in shock. Weren't you? He's a good lad. He doesn't set fire to schools. My old school."

"What did he tell you? Or did he not manage to get a word in?"

"He did tell me it wasn't his idea, but he's no sheep. He always does what he wants."

"Like mother, like...?"

She ignores that. Frank has been home to change and is wearing a blue-checked shirt she'd bought him years ago. She smiles at the waiter and they order quickly.

"This couldn't have come at a worse time. I've got so much on my plate at the moment. I need some space from Adam, to be honest."

Frank's starting to look like her dad these days, but he's no fool and his bright, piercing blue eyes drill into her. "How much space do you need? I get the impression that between your job and these new mates of his that you barely see each other."

"It's different if I know he's meant to be with you."

"You mean you feel better. What about Adam? What about the two of you, your relationship?" Frank is direct, but that's fine. It's a function of both their former intimacy and a common enemy – the lack of time.

"It's not unusual for teenage boys..." he starts again.

"It's not exactly normal."

"OK, setting a school on fire isn't normal, but all parents worry about who their kids hang around with. We don't know yet what's going on, but you can't just palm this off to me. There won't be a quick solution."

She saws off the pizza crust, preferring to wrestle the chewy edge than play with the sloppy middle. Irritatingly, she has to admit he's probably right.

He continues, "I'm relieved we got to hear about this, whatever it is, now. We have to sort this out together. He needs both his parents."

"Did I need both my parents? Once mum left, dad and I were pretty much alright on our own."

"That's not how it sounded to me," he says.

There had been good times. Restaurants and birthdays went together. She'd loved the feeling of being in a grown-up restaurant and the attention she got. On her ninth birthday they had gone to a Berni Inn. It was unheard of then. She'd had chicken in a basket – in a basket! – and tackled her first knickerbocker glory. Her mum had looked like an angel in a white, sort of flowing, sleeved top and long skirt. The celebration for her tenth birthday was in a new Italian restaurant, not dissimilar to the one she and Frank are in tonight. She'd laughed along with her mum when her dad spilled spaghetti Bolognese down his shirt. Her mum had laughed too loud, though, and people had turned to look at them. She remembered concentrating hard on snapping off the melted wax from a candle stuck in a Chianti bottle, until her mum had shouted at her to stop. On her 11th birthday they'd driven out to a pub in the countryside and her dad had gone on about it being the best ploughman's in miles. She'd just eaten the crisps and her mum hadn't really spoken at all.

Shortly before her 12th birthday her mum left. The next-door neighbour had brought round a pineapple upside-down cake and then it was her dad's turn to stop speaking.

By the time her 13th birthday came round, she'd had a few domestic science lessons. They'd fried some sausages in a Teflon-coated pan and her dad said they were truly in the space age now, but he'd looked old, not modern. On her 14th birthday she'd sat behind the garages drinking cider with some lads. She remembers she'd started a scrap when her dad called her in for a packet curry.

On the basis that those were the good bits, Frank is right, it wasn't great, but at least there was a time when she'd tried to please her mum. Has Adam ever done that? Maybe she'd given

Adam too much freedom, but they couldn't have predicted this, nor stopped him.

Frank changes tack. "Do the Police know Adam was involved?"

"God, I'm not informing the Police on him. And you better not either."

"I don't want to, but it's arson. He's got to go of his own accord, which I've already told him, but he's not having any of it and he won't tell me who else was involved."

Anne-Marie reasons that if Colin took the video, he'd have sent it to the Police already. It's a long shot, but Adam isn't known to the Police, so maybe they won't get his name? That bloody hoodie is going in the bin.

"He's spending a lot more time with Ben," continues Frank. "Ben used to be a great student and is now a complete nightmare. There's some kind of involvement with a gang, possibly drugs, but we don't really know, so I've asked our Student Support to investigate."

"But you aren't going to call the Police?"

"As I said, I want Adam to go of his own accord, but if he won't, I'll have no choice…"

Anne-Marie tries a different tack. This could have a long-term impact for Adam. Would anyone be willing to give him the same chance she'd given Colin?

"Wait, let's find another solution. Adam is being influenced by Ben. He's the problem, but we need to support them both, not criminalise them." That appears to chime.

Franks says, "I could have a word with Jess, just to get her advice, hypothetically speaking, or you could. You're her friend."

Now isn't a good time to be asking favours of Jess. If this can be made to go away quickly Anne-Marie might eat some humble pie, depending what it's made of, but it's much better if Frank can sort it. She shifts Frank onto more helpful ground.

"What's bothering is why he'd get wrapped up in all that?

He's on track with his A levels, seemed set on uni, but maybe he's got other ideas?" Frank is a senior manager at the College and while he wouldn't normally get involved in individual cases, it's his territory. "You can help him think it through. He's got to know what he's doing to his own future prospects. He listens to you. Always has." She backs off, leaves a space, looks up at the wall-sized photo of the Coliseum in Rome. The golden lighting makes her wish she was there. After another moment Frank steps into the void. "Maybe he does need more time with me." She's tactically silent until he nods. "OK, he can stay at mine until further notice." Relief spices up her pizza. Frank can keep tabs on Adam and keep him away from the gang. This is bad timing for her and terrible timing for there to be an active gang on the Highlands. She needs the estate to be fixable and the community to appear deserving.

"Thanks, Frank. I mean it. I'm sorry I was so knackered on Monday I didn't get to ask about the College?"

He knows exactly what she's asking. "We don't know what level of cuts we'll be looking at. The funding mechanisms aren't clear yet. It's a mess."

"Davina's put me in charge of the cuts."

"What about Owen? He's the CEX. Shouldn't he be leading that?"

"This time last year he was talking about retiring."

Frank and Owen have history. As a backbench councillor Frank was frustrated by the dense bureaucratic fog the Council's chief created around himself and the organisation. He continues, "Our principal is controlling everything that moves, right down to part-time art tutor contracts."

"I've got to talk to Owen about it, you're right." Operating in fog is not Anne-Marie's style, but she sees Owen's deliberate tactic for what it is and feels it could provide some useful cover. "Either I've got the power to do the job or I haven't."

"Slow down, girl. You haven't got the power. Not in your shoes or his."

He sounds like he's gearing up for another lecture. "I know, I know. It's going to be dirty, but unless I'm right in there it will be carnage."

He's eyeing her every blink. "Stop thinking about the CEX job. Make the leader do the job she's elected to do."

"I don't trust her."

"It's not about trust, it's about giving politicians options. Your job is to make their decisions happen and to treat people as fairly as possible."

"I can limit the damage more if I'm in control."

He begins to roll up his shirt cuff as if it's a sleeve. "Trying to control things is a waste of time, is it not?" He means Adam.

"Don't patronise me, Frank. I'm not talking about one teenager now. This is the time the City needs me most. Sorry, the City needs us all to be doing the best we can."

"I know what you meant and I'm not saying don't try and do that, but have you got super-powers I'm not aware of? Davina's not like the councillors you're used to. She may look soft round the edges, but she's got the heart of a Russian oligarch and the killer instinct of Putin."

"Frank, she wants to boost the economy of the City. That's to be expected and it's right, isn't it? She's got to make cuts, but she's also promoting a major development for the City Centre. It's more than Les and the opposition have come up with."

"Hang on a minute. You're more interested in getting a promotion, aren't you? You're sitting here telling me you're going to deliver her cuts and it sounds like you believe you can make it alright. Like you can influence her, when in reality you're some sort of nodding dog." That dig goes straight under Anne-Marie's rib cage. He might as well have said poodle. "You're forgetting what's important here. Stay critical. Do what you can. Do what you're asked to do, but stop trying to impress Davina. She'll be off as soon as a parliamentary seat comes up. In any case, you might be useful to her for a while, but she won't think twice about leaving you on your tod, just like your mo..."

Anne-Marie clenches her fist. She'd punch his lights out if he hadn't just agreed that Adam could move in with him. Frank pulls back. "Look, I didn't mean to go over the top. Now's not the time to be thinking about a CEX job. Bob and the union branch have got the placards on order. The opposition is meeting to discuss our response. What I'm saying is it's high risk."

"I know that..."

"...and don't think we've finished talking about Adam and protecting our family. Work isn't going away, but right now we've got a crisis of our own to deal with."

She doesn't reply. The waiter asks if they've finished. If Franks intends to go around that loop again, they definitely have. He'd normally offer her a lift home, but it's not like her taxi habit is going to break the bank. It's only a fiver and she can get the driver to stop at the off-licence on the way.

"You get home, Frank. I'll get the bill and then I'll get a taxi. I've got a lot to think about."

"You have." He's not smiling. "I'll see if I can bring Adam round tomorrow. You two can spend some time together over the weekend."

She nods, hoping that Adam will still want to go out and she'll still be able to fit in some work, but now's not the time to mention that.

CHAPTER 12

JESSICA

Friday 19th November, 4pm

Ten minutes in and she's already regretted turning up. It's winter and her sweaty backside is stuck to a green plastic stacking chair. The Hospital Trust Improvement Manager who's been chairing the meeting has sucked the remaining air out of the room and the participants. These are powerless people behaving powerlessly, without the energy or sense to admit it and move on. There's no time for this. Jess is too senior to be here, but she has to unlock new intelligence and then get to see Shaz.

Days are slipping by and there's a shadow at her heel. The task force idea has been shot, in the foot probably. Trusting Barrington Edwards to sell it was a risk that hadn't paid off. There's CCTV of a group of three young men close to the location of the bin at roughly the right time, but so far they haven't been able to trace them. Stewart has told everyone that a doctor has said Laura Awsworth could make a full recovery, but that hasn't been confirmed. She can't think why he would make it up, but it has her worried. Jess' leverage on this issue could discharge itself from hospital and disappear as randomly as it had arrived. Without the direct power to command these people to get on with it, she relies on influence, guilt and over-egged urgency. She takes up as much space as possible, letting her arms slide out across the table, showing the room her palms, as if she is gifting them a solution.

"From a policing perspective, if we don't get this intelligence now we can't do our job. I'm surprised I need to say this, but I passed by ICU on the way up here. If the Girl in the Bin dies we are into a major investigation and none of us will have any choice about this. We'll all be under scrutiny. I want this data so that we can prevent this happening again."

A woman in a lime cardigan nods agreement. The chair tries to shut the meeting down.

"Thank you everyone. We'll be putting this on the agenda for our management meeting and I'll make sure the notes are circulated."

Barrington's colleague, Anil, who she'd met at the community centre, jumps in. "I'm sorry, but do we have an agreement or not?" Anil looks at his notes. "You said it shouldn't be a problem. You clearly implied agreement to provide this data. What's changed? We are serious about this and I can't leave without an agreement."

Jess has watched Anil's frustration grow broadly in line with her own, although he hasn't managed it well. The sweat patch on his pale blue shirt has raced out from under his arm. She hopes hers are more slow-moving. Why didn't they open the window sooner?

The manager loosens his tie and puts his faded conference bag on the table. "Nothing has changed, but you know how it is. I'll need approval from the management and I know people need to get off for the weekend."

"I'm sorry, but you've wasted our time. We believe there is a trend. We need it confirmed." Anil is incensed and he's right, Jess thinks.

"If you can't say yes, who can?"

"Sorry," the manager shrugs. "Data protection." He's not rude, yet is refusing to budge. That's the third time he's put up the data protection shield and it doesn't wash. This manager doesn't want to do the right thing, not because it's going to be more work for him – long term it isn't, even short-term it isn't – and it isn't about the chain of command. He's resistant to change because he doesn't accept that the way it's always been done, his way, is too slow. It just isn't good enough.

Jess takes control. "Here's what's going to happen. I'll personally speak to the Trust Director on Monday. You let him know we've had this meeting and I'll make it clear we want to start immediately with the interviews we discussed earlier. The data from A&E – maybe your colleagues can chase that up?" She looks across at the woman in lime, who nods immediately. Just when you think you are going mad with a system that seems unable to cope with the smallest request, you find a poorly paid administrator who's prepared to go way beyond her role to help.

"Anil, could you set out a draft interview schedule and mail it to everyone." Anil mouths a silent 'thank you'.

The brisk flight from the sauna means she's taken a wrong turning down an almost abandoned corridor. As a kid she'd never been able to resist running down any corridor, but she slows up. The silent grief of this place contains her energy, compounds her frustration. Her mother's hospital despair hadn't been the pain of multiple miscarriages, it was the lack of a son that hurt. There had been no need for her father to voice his disappointment with the birth of two girls. Taking her mum's arm, guiding her slowly in and out of the hospital while her dad was at work, the referred failure had become ingrained. This place is suffocating.

Finally hitting the car park the cold air revives her. She sees Anil getting into a car near to hers and waves. It's a mistake. Anil comes over. "Thanks for your help in there. I looked too desperate, didn't I? I'm struggling with Barrington and this alcohol work is so personal for me." Anil looks down at a pothole in the tarmac. It's getting late and Jess has to get to see Shaz, but she nods him on. "Not that I drink." He shakes his head. He's hesitant now. "Remember when we were in that meeting talking about the Booze2U service? I was wondering if there's a connection between that and Laura Awsworth, the Girl in the

Bin. To have that much alcohol in her body she must've been pre-loading, because there isn't any CCTV on her, and that means she could have been using Booze2U." Anil takes a deep breath. "My family runs Booze2U. It's an extension of their corner shop." He's the lead officer on the City Alcohol Plan. The grim irony tastes intriguing.

"If I can be open with you," he continues, "the alcohol off-shoot is causing a rift between the older generation and my brothers, and the shop's been vandalised, which is worrying, because it seems connected, but they won't report it. I normally keep my professional life and my personal life separate, but I have a dilemma" – and here he takes another deep breath – "I know they haven't got their license sorted. You, me, our colleagues, we have been trying to tackle the alcohol problem for years, but my family has spent years trying to build a business. If I shop my family they would never forgive me. I am weighing up what's in the public interest against my family interest and my own interest. I can't sort out what's right."

"What are you asking exactly?" says Jess. Anil is still looking down. She can feel his cheeks burning and the shadow at her heel has grown. She kicks her boot, trying to shake it off, then presses the automatic key lock to open the car door.

"Look, sorry to be blunt, but I've run out of time. Talk to Bob Jackson, the Licensing Manager at the Council. He's a good bloke. Morally, I can't help you. Talk to your boss." Slamming the car door, she sets off for the Highlands.

As she pulls up in front of her friend's house, she notes that the grass has missed a cut or two before the winter and empty cardboard boxes are stacking up in the garden. Before she gets to the door, Jess can hear the TV. Her friend looks calmer and reasonably pleased to see her.

"Kettle on by any chance?"

"It's a mess in here. Let's go through to the kitchen."

There are piles of ironing on the dining room table, envelopes and papers spread onto a chair, large-footed trainers litter the floor. The kitchen is better. There are chocolate chip cookies and a gate-leg table half folded down with two stools for them to perch on.

"How are you doing?"

There's a pause before a nervous reply.

"I'm so sorry, Jess. I was, er, it was rubbish. I lost it, didn't I? Thanks for driving me home."

"You're welcome. Glad I was there."

"Maybe you could escort me every time I go out? I shouldn't be allowed out really, should I?"

There was a time when it had been the other way around, when Shaz was the one who played nurse to all the younger kids.

"I'd be delighted, but I'm not sure my boss would be too happy!"

"No. I was… I was, I mean, I wasn't joking about not going out."

"Agoraphobic?" It slips straight out.

"No, no. Not that bad. And this estate, there's nothing to go out for is there? Seen this?"

The *Post* headline in front of them reads, 'You're Drunks And You're Too Fat! Highlands Officially 5th Unhealthiest Estate In UK'. There's a picture of Barrington Edwards.

"Bugger." Jess is annoyed that she hasn't managed to save Barrington, and the estate, from the negative press.

"Well, he's probably right, isn't he?" Shaz sighs.

"He is, but most people won't believe him and this doesn't exactly help does it?"

"I don't know. He can't help himself, can he?"

This is new. Is there some sort of a connection between Shaz and Barrington Edwards?

"Come on, Jess, don't you remember him? He went to our school, although I suppose he might have been a few years younger than us. Carlton lived two doors down from his aunt and he lived with her. He was always coming out with weird stuff."

"No, maybe I was away then?"

"You've forgotten all that trouble? Or you just haven't made the link, but why should you, it must be nearly twenty years ago, and he's a doctor now, if you can believe that?"

"Yes, but not a GP."

"Whatever. He's Darren Wilson's cousin."

Jess stares at the photo of Dr Edwards as if she's never met him before. It's a bad photo. His head is at an awkward angle to his body, his mouth open. It can't be.

"God, I had no idea."

"Looks better in person, I guess. He's done well for himself, hasn't he?"

Swallowing hard and digging her nails into her leg, Jess manages a nod and draws on all her training to keep herself in check. Dr Barrington Edwards? She feels another shadow.

"So, how about you, are you really OK?"

"I'm alright, but don't ask me to say any more. Honestly, it'll set me off."

Jess happily takes this as a sign to stop probing, to finish her tea. "Sorry, Shaz," she says looking obviously at the kitchen clock. "I need to nip back to the station. I'll call in again next week? Maybe I'll get to see Ben properly then?" As Shaz closes the front door, Jess catches a look of relief in her friend's eyes and hides her own.

CHAPTER 13

ANNE-MARIE

Friday 19th November, 10pm

Bob Marley, in his London lover-man phase, is singing. They are lounging on Anne-Marie's sofa, a deep red three-seater with a poof to match. She's aiming to switch from the working week into recovery mode, but can't help herself trying to wring out a last drop of information from Bob. She massages his palm with her thumb. "Come on, tell me what the branch is planning on the cuts."

"What's left of regional office are leaving it up to us, so hold your nose for the stink. We had the best turnout for our AGM in years. I've asked Les for a joint union and party campaign, but they don't want to play in case it stops them winning the Council back. He's scared we'll come across too radical, like we're the problem."

This is typical Bob, stuck in the eighties, when working for a council was a common expression of your politics. He's forgotten he's a manager now. He's too excited by the thought of the fight and not thinking big enough.

"He's in a difficult position, though, isn't he?"

Anne-Marie has time for Les. He's a wily old shepherd, patiently rounding up his party members, coralling them in roughly the same direction.

"No, he needs to come out hard and fast against Davina, simple as."

"Isn't he just playing for time so Davina has to make the worst of the cuts and he can come in on a more positive ticket?"

She leans in and nuzzles at Bob's neck, not wanting to tip into an argument. "We've got to fight together for public services. Public service cuts hurt and hurt the poorest most..." It's a poor impression of Les, the careful Welsh opposition leader. He sneers, but doesn't move away, so she catches his ear lobe in her teeth. "...and it needs managers, staff and service users to stand together, to get closer together, to get really close..." She puts his hand inside her jumper... "...to get in bed together and sweat." She lingers on the 't'. "Sweat, long and hard, and harder still...." Her lust draws Bob's hot hand onto her stomach. She has a brief moment of doubt. Should she have taken her time or gone upstairs? Did Frank say Adam was due round? Her hearing is still as tuned as a teenager's to a key in the lock. She won't hear the footsteps on the path, yet will know the second before the door goes that it's him. Adam's never caught them in an embarrassing position and right now neither of them needs that. If there is conflict between Adam and Bob it's another man management job for her.

She pulls away from Bob before the key goes in the lock and wanders into the kitchen for a couple of beers and a bottle of white wine. Adam doesn't take his jacket off.

"OK love?"

"No and I'm only here because Dad told me to come over."

"Don't worry, I won't say a word, but if you want to talk, you know you can." She stops herself taking a step towards him.

"Mum, don't start."

"Showing concern is my job."

"Yeah, but I don't want to talk so don't start trying to wheedle anything out of me."

"I'm not even thinking about it..."

"Liar."

She knows Frank has 'had a word' about dobbing himself in so backs off, feeling that they're not a team anymore, not a group that sticks together. The glue isn't holding. It used to be super glue and now it's more rubbery, easily picked off into a dirty snot ball and flicked away.

"Thanks for the beer, Mum," she says sarcastically, as he takes the bottle and goes straight upstairs. She's losing that ability to prize a word or two from him that's helped keep the bond going through his teenage years. Noticing he's left his mobile on the side, she stops herself from shouting up to tell him. It could be useful.

"Don't worry, love." Bob is consoling. "I know it's hard but that's what lads are like. Be glad you haven't got a girl. One that ends up like our Girl in the Bin…"

Is that supposed to make her feel better? She can't hear another word about the Bin Girl. It's become a song stuck in her head, on a grating loop, with a chorus of Davina bellowing, 'Kill the story'. The thought takes her temperature temporarily down.

"I've got so much on my plate at the moment. Davina wants me to lead the cuts programme. Owen has his head in the bloody sand again. The management team are simmering."

The weight of hundreds of redundancy notices, due to be sent out two weeks before Christmas with her name at the bottom, is already pressing on her spine. Anne-Marie's had two 'at risk' letters of her own in the past. The formality had been unnerving. However much a manager might want to tell you you're safe, processes can't be predicted. These days it's the only time she sees letter-headed stationery. How did they get here again?

Bob confidently undoes her shirt buttons.

"I'm sorry. I said I wouldn't talk about work. If you want to go it's OK, you know." She knocks back the white wine in one.

"Nah," he says. "I'm here and it's my problem as much as it's yours, but if we talk about it now is there any chance we can avoid talking about it in bed as well?"

She turns the music up a notch and barricades the poof against the door, just in case Adam comes down. Pleased that Bob thinks they are in it together, she decides to dig down a level. "You know

Davina wants a lighter touch on all regulation." She feels his hand creep up towards her breast.

"I know. Why are you telling me this now? Does that mean she's going to cut our budget?" He massages her breast. She doesn't move. He goes on, "Tell me something I don't know. Davina'd like our service to disappear completely, but it's statutory. That's what annoys her. They can't totally privatise it and we'll carry on protecting the public."

"Our hero," Anne-Marie replies. This probably isn't the time to say that Davina has already asked her to look at other ways of providing the service. "Can't we just have a website?" Davina had said casually. Anne-Marie suspects she's already been checking this out legally. Protecting the service for the residents is what's important, not who provides the service. It's a principle Anne-Marie believes, but it's complicated. A website is not a service for an old lady fleeced by a rogue trader.

He licks her ear and whispers, "I meant to say, it'll be you that cuts our budget." She kisses him hard on the mouth to avoid a response. He's not stupid. The sharp edge is what makes him sexy.

The problem is that Bob thinks regulation is the answer to everything. They'd had a recent bust-up about his relentless pursuit of an infirm pensioner whose nephew dumped his soiled mattress on the pavement. Bob thinks the nephew in question is acting wilfully; he could've picked up the phone and the Council would've picked up the offensive item. Anne-Marie thinks that's wishful thinking and culturally naïve. It just gives the Council a bad name and solving it is more than that, it's about the people. It isn't an art gallery. If it's a tip, people will carry on decorating the street with dirty laundry, stuffing nappies down the drains, and no amount of tax payers' money spent on enforcement education will work. If the people are OK, if they have a job, a decent house, they'll want to live in a nice area. They'll want to keep the place tidy.

Bob doesn't buy that. The general public probably don't buy it either. They think they're alright jack, but leave the Highlands to sink and the inequality, the crime that it generates, spills over into the city and into their leafy part of it. Or even worse, like Davina, they see the connections only too well, but think they can build walls high enough to keep it all out. She's better letting her tongue focus on his mouth, but Bob pulls back.

"If you gave us some time we could find a solution, find another way, maybe share services, team up with our neighbours, keep some expertise in house."

Bob surprises her. It's a good idea and for other areas sharing services and reducing costs might work, but with Bob's lot the culture of suspicion, the petty leadership battles and endless altercations over terms and conditions... Well, it's a very long shot at best.

"If you're doing Davina's dirty work you can make sure we have time."

As he lifts himself on top of her, she lets out the longest breath she has.

"Come on Anne-Marie, you want a solution as much as I do. You can fix it."

She doubts she can this time, but undoes his belt buckle.

She pulls up her trousers and sneaks to the kitchen. She feels blissed and ready for more, but Bob's nodding off. There's not enough left in the wine bottle to bother taking it back into the lounge, so she knocks it back. Adam's mobile stares up at her from the worktop. Her information-gathering habit doesn't normally extend to Adam, but she can't resist a look. How else is she supposed to know what's going on? And he's burnt down her school. There are new rules. She rifles through his texts. They are mostly rubbish, but then she looks at the Ben strand and her heart thumps.

At anvil
Will come
Not your prob bruv. I gotta do it
Will come
Holler me. They don't trust you. Worse for me

CHAPTER 14

BARRINGTON

Saturday 20th November, 9pm

A long ride on a Saturday night is unusual, but not unheard of. It will help defrag his brain and stretch out the tight muscles that have shortened at the rate of 0.4 millimetres per minute as a result of today's concentrated session going over the spreadsheets. In the face of budget cuts he's been forced to rethink every aspect of his work on alcohol, layering spreadsheet upon spreadsheet, exhausting all possibilities to find resources.

Corinne and Nelson are at her sister's and staying the night. She said she'd left three messages on his mobile. He'd checked. That was correct. There's an old couple she seems unusually obsessed with, but he hasn't seen enough of her to hear the detail. Cycling along the A56 spine road he is flanked by warehouse sheds looming over corrugated steel fencing. The white street lights bounce off his Team Castrol lime green Lycra shirt. Zipped up, head tucked, elbows pinned to his torso, knees fixed forward, quads pumping, his sense of control increases with every mile. The dual carriageway has a string of roundabouts that he barely notices, cogs with spokes leading nowhere. Eyes flick right to check the road is clear and he ploughs on. There's no break in the urban sprawl; there's no traffic; it's safe. He breathes deep and even.

Thirty minutes on, though, and he suddenly notices that the lights are dimmer. There's a familiar sign heralding the Spine Road Project, funded by the European Union and a host of organisational logos it's too dark to read. With the cash they've spent on this road he could have pegged back the rate of alcohol-related deaths by 8 to 10 per cent, he estimates angrily. That's 320 completely avoidable deaths and, with the budget deficit as it is, he can do precisely nothing. Don't these people understand basic maths? Two plus two equals four. Two minus two will never equal five. He grits his teeth.

The shadows of the huge boxes alongside him grow darker and he suddenly hits a T-junction. He must have taken a wrong turn. He spins around, thinking he'll retrace his route. He climbs out of the saddle and sprints, then finds himself at the end of a wide cul-de-sac and a gated entrance to an anonymous site on an industrial estate, indistinguishable from many others dotted around the outskirts of the City. Wait, this is wrong too. As he turns away a 200-tonne truck eases off its brake and slides out behind him. The dark cab appears driverless and the hiss of the brakes makes him shiver.

Now cold, with his body temperature dropping, his energy levels dip. Distracted by the spreadsheets and with Corinne visiting the old couple again he hadn't bothered to eat anything substantial. On the wrong side of town, Barrington decides to cut through the city instead of taking the ring road. He hits the centre exhausted, realising he's hit a wall of glycogen depletion. He needs fuel and feels faint. It's now 10.40pm and people are noisily emerging around him. The lights of Mr Sizzle's burger van draw him in. He dismounts, staggers across the pavement and slowly sits down on cold flags five metres from the van, almost vomiting at the smell of cheap fat and blocked drains.

"Drunk in charge of an expensive looking bicycle, is it?" Barrington hears, but doesn't follow.

"What?"

"Oi mate! You there! Bradley Wiggins! Except you're not, are you?"

"What?"

"From Yorkshire are you?"

Barrington's attention is drawn to the way the bulbous burger man with Shrek hands delicately flips a row of burgers.

"Bradley Wiggins was born in Belgium and lives in Lancashire. I was born here," he groans, wanting to get back on his bike, but his legs feel like concrete.

"Alright, alright, Bradley mate. Hungry are we?"

"I am. What have you got?" Barrington surprises himself. He's so hungry he's almost prepared to eat something from Mr Sizzle, he thinks, while simultaneously wondering how environmental health have let this character continue to operate.

"What have I got? What does it look like? There's the list. Doesn't matter what you choose, it all tastes the same. With onions, ketchup or in a scud? It's not 11 yet, so you're lucky, it's freshly cooked..."

"There must be something else I can eat? Something edible?"

"You can't offend me, mate, with your demands for edibility. It's sugar for you then. Full-fat can of Coke?"

"Yes, please." Despite his usual discipline Barrington can feel an involuntary craving in his body for sugar and caffeine.

"And what about another of our local delicacies? Bar of Cadbury's Dairy Milk?" Mr Sizzle appears to have made himself laugh. "That's what all the girls have when they're queuing for a cab home. Sobers you up fast and guaranteed you won't chuck it straight back up – £3.50 to you mate.

There's a small compartment under his saddle that contains a key and a two-pound coin. He holds it out like a small child in a sweet shop.

"You owe me £1.50." Mr Sizzle slips him the chocolate bar and moves on.

"What can I get you Miss World?" His thick, soft Black Country drone generates an easy laugh.

"Two chilli dogs, Mr S."

As a queue quickly forms Barrington backs away with the cold can, pulling his bike into the shadow of the van. Recovering slowly, he finds himself transfixed by the translucent blue-white skin of a young woman's legs. He watches the muscles in her back working hard to stabilise her body as she teeters on odd-shaped shoes. Her friend is barefoot, carrying similarly dangerous-looking footwear. She briefly makes eye contact with Barrington.

"What you got lurking back there, Mr Sizzle? Tasty piece of meat?" She cackles.

Barrington has no idea the young woman is talking about him. He is trying to work out just how drunk they are. Ten units each? Next in the queue a couple, the woman in her early twenties dragging an incoherent male. Her: eight units. Him: three units times ten pints? Two men about his age swearing loudly: possibly 20 units each? Suddenly in danger of becoming aroused at the naked shoulders and arms of a woman wearing what looks like a silk nightie, he focuses again on his impromptu research. He hears the sounds of a good time being had, but that does not compute. To Barrington, these people are clinical conditions on legs. The barefoot girl lurches to the edge of the pavement and vomits at great speed, stands upright, holding a clump of hair matted with fresh sick and shrieks, "Urrrgh, gross!"

"You still here, sunshine?" Mr Sizzle is pouring two old mugs full of hot fat down a drain at the back of the van. "Enjoying the freak show? Well you're part of it tonight, mate."

"What? No, I'm in Health." Barrington jerks into action, picking up his bike.

"Alright, don't panic, you're safe for another twenty minutes or so, then it turns nasty."

"What do you mean?"

"Our Friday night puke, piss and punch-up session, and that's just the fairer sex. You ought to see what the lads get up to. It's a sight to be behold and let's just say there are certain landlords round here who fuel the fire. It's all business to them and never mind where our girls end up."

"The Girl in the Bin? Is that what you're talking about? You know about that?"

"We all know about that and let's just say I'm not the only one around here who knows where the bodies are buried."

"Exactly what do you know?" Barrington finds he can't hold his voice steady.

"Who did you say you were? Not Police, dressed like that."

"No, Primary Care Trust. I'm a doctor."

"Whatever." The big man looks away. "Our city doesn't need that," he says.

"Oi, mate, you open?" Another drunk bangs a hungry fist on the counter and Mr Sizzle disappears.

The petrol station on the Newbridge Road closes at 2am. There are two private hire taxis refuelling ahead of him. A souped up Punto crammed full of twentyish lads cuts in front to the next free pump. He wouldn't hesitate to have a go normally, but doesn't want to attract attention. The cashier's head keeps flicking round to check they don't drive off. He slides two £20 notes under the tray to pre-pay, does a heavy end-of-shift sigh, nods and wanders back to fill his tank.

The men in the Punto don't seem to have understood. They hammer the horn to get the pump switched on. The driver gets out and charges over to the cashier box. The driver's mate, shouting in an unrecognisable language, walks round to the driver's seat and revs the engine. The car lurches forward and back.

He pulls off slowly to their left in the direction of the far exit, past the water and air pump, round the back of the shop. He wants the darkness and the absence of cameras. There's a padlocked toilet door and a tall metal bin. He stops, pulls on his gloves, opens the boot and reaches in.

The girl is lying on a checked car blanket. She's snoring. He shifts her body around so that he can get his arms under her shoulders. It's good lifting technique. He sits her up with her back against the toilet door, decides the blanket's had it anyway and tosses it into the bin. "You won't remember a thing," he says, putting his hand up her skirt and easily ripping the elastic string of her knickers, "but you'll know."

CHAPTER 15

ANNE-MARIE

Monday 22nd November, 8.30am

The Council House heating has been off all weekend and the recycled air is as close to fresh as it gets. The scent of musty settees is masked by the recently deposited odour of bulk-buy disinfectant. The regular service desk clients and their pre-school children haven't dragged themselves and their complaints in yet. The reception is an assault of laminated signs, leaflets wilting like dying daffodils and maze-like queue management. Anne-Marie blasts the temporary calm by shouting a loud "Morning everyone" in the direction of the Keepers' Office on the far side of the reception.

Sunday has been productive and she's confident that selling her plan to Davina will be straightforward, as long as she doesn't make the mistake of calling it a strategy or attaching any status to it. Owen, the Chief Exec, is manageable, a soft touch, Davina's duvet, and he might be useful to Anne-Marie if she needs someone to smother a few flames along the way. The Council's management team aren't stupid, but none of them can teach her organisational games. Anne-Marie has done a nifty jig in every round of cuts so far, changing pace and direction so that no-one around the table can predict her tactics or stick any lazy labels on her. Her careful self promotion casts her as a corporate street fighter, but how possible will it be to maintain that image? These days how can anyone do the dirty work, keep their allies on side and keep their career on track?

It might be slightly easier if there was any internal opposition to Davina in the Council, but the Coalition is in name only. Davina's group play-act like it's their organisation, but politics isn't win-win, it's win-lose and they've lost for so long their sense of ownership has gone, too. Even the ones arriving on the hot ticket of a shake-up breathe the dead air, smell the settees, ingest the failures of their predecessors and find themselves adrift. Davina's councillors have never been to a community centre, send their kids to private school and, if an elderly relative threatens to slip into dependency, they ship them off to a swanky care home. What's surprising is that none of them are that rich, it's just they don't want to think they're in the same boat as their estate cousins. The councillors ought to be holding the leadership to account on behalf of local people, but it never seems to work like that. Any idiot can make cuts and sod the consequences, but if Anne-Marie is going to protect services and tackle real need in the Highlands she needs to shift gear and move forward on all fronts – which makes it all the more important to get time alone with Davina to find out where the trip-wires lie.

Making her way energetically enough to Davina's third-floor office in the Elected Members Suite, Anne-Marie enjoys the echo of her clompy heels on the low maintenance, bare brick staircase. She's not as fit as she used to be, but isn't panting yet. At the top there's a worn Kidderminster carpet and smoked glass balustrade, leading up to a wall of faces known as the Chains. The old-timers, men like Chamberlain, Walker, Leverhulme, had real money to commission favourable likenesses and the power to put them up in galleries named after them, but Anne-Marie cringes at the portraits of more recent mayors, men with no power, money or vision. Their likenesses are now photos with marbled studio backgrounds that make them look cheap. The Chains get wheeled out for a year's worth of ceremonial functions while Davina as Council Leader holds the purse strings.

There's a security code to the suite, giving protection against marauding local residents with legitimate questions and staff with unwanted truths. The final door on the left is Davina's, shielded by an office for her PA, but this morning it's open and both rooms are transparently empty. She takes a quick look at Davina's diary, which says '8.30am, GFB, Owen Cork, Daniel Croft and Paul McGuire – DNB Holdings'. 'GFB' is the Gold Fish Bowl meeting room on the second floor, in the corner next to the CEX's office. That's good, she can drop in, start her story there and then. Owen won't have one yet. He goes on the G of the bang, when he's sure he hasn't been hit by the starter's gun.

The GFB has brown-tinted windows, floor to ceiling, and a great view over the back of St Mark's Church and the University. It always reminds her how small this city is. As she marches towards it, she sees the meeting in progress. One of the men is portly, wearing a pinstripe suit, definitely not local. The other, sitting back slightly from the table, has a tailored matt grey suit, with a box-fresh collar and thick, black-rimmed, sixties-style glasses. It's a studied look, one that says 'I know I look good and I know you're looking at me'. She is. There are no notebooks out, but Danish pastries on a table she doesn't recognise. Anne-Marie expects a nod or a wave from Davina to motion her in, but gets neither. She catches Owen's eye. He half-smiles and shakes his head vigorously, to say 'No, no, not now'. What did he think she was going to do anyway? Barge in? It wouldn't be the first time, but if they're talking about a development, why blank her? It's her department.

It's a small snub but she decides to blow off steam with a cigarette while considering her next move. Davina wants her to lead the cuts and this development, so is she in or out? She thuds her way down the stairs to the Keepers' Office to trade gossip and cadge a cig from Ken. He knows plenty about the new GFB furniture. "Her Majesty ordered it weeks ago. Scandinavian retro I think they call it. Matches the windows and the cheese plant. Price code A, for Arm and Leg. She wants to be careful that kind of thing doesn't end up in the *Post* when they starting announcing cuts."

"And what do you know about the guests?"

"What Croft serves is not what we call real ale, like."

She notes the guarded response. "And mixing with royalty?"

"Strange days indeed."

She thanks Ken and, turning to make her way to the outdoor ashtray, she sees the four meeting members already emerging from the lift. She decides to hold back, slowly nodding in their direction. A full-length view of Croft reveals smart brogues, probably hand-made, and a neat triangle shape to a black silk handkerchief in his jacket pocket. This is a face, not someone who hangs in meetings in the City Council. Davina waves, but walks on. Croft stops and looks directly across at Anne-Marie. That's good, he knows who she is.

When they've gone, back at her desk for five minutes, Anne-Marie looks up DNB Holdings. The first stab gives her a company data site. The company status says 'dissolved'. There's a P McGuire listed as a director of a land-holding property and mention of the Brewery. It's surprising she can find nothing on a local Daniel Croft, but a Mrs D Croft is the licensee of the Anvil. Maybe a wife or relative? None of that adds up to the man she's seen with Davina.

She remembers Adam's phone and the text messages from Ben. Frank says that Adam wants to earn some cash and has heard of work, vaguely described as distribution and collection linked to soft drinks. That prompts childhood memories of the Corona man in a gentle lemonade float, shaking slowly up the street every Saturday morning. Maybe it's a good sign? Her phone buzzes with a text.

Can you get to childrens centre now. Call me. 100% emergency.
Sandra

"Unusual to get a message like that from you. What's up?"

"Thanks. I know this isn't something you'd normally deal with, but it's Andrea. She's in a bad way. Her daughter, Kerry, I think you know her, seems like she's been raped. Could have been drugged. On the Highlands, I think. They won't go to the Police. She's with Carol and they're asking for you."

"Jesus, no. I do know her. She was in Adam's class. Lovely, funny, blond girl. Poor them. Poor bloody kid."

"It's happened before and they've had enough. Carol's sister was raped and dumped in a skip, too. She never recovered. I think she's been sectioned."

Anne-Marie twigs that must've been what they were talking about at the awards ceremony only last week. "I don't know what I can do but I'll come."

There's just about time for a quick fag break to compose herself before she enters the Children's Centre. The winter sun is low in the sky and lacks warmth. The side door to one of the rooms on the ground floor is open to a small, gated play area. There's a black girl, maybe four years old, with a blue plastic ruler measuring a painted tyre. There used to be tyres aplenty in playgrounds across the city, when the tyre factory was still open. Her mind jumps from tyres, to small dirty hands, to skin and eye infections, to carcinogenic health risk assessments, to angry parents, to malicious law suits against the Council, to skyrocketing Council insurance premiums, to the closure of play areas and the death of creative play. She carefully puts the butt of the fag into the ashtray and walks towards the door.

There are only two grown-up seats in the room. Carol has tilted hers against the window, tense and swearing under her breath. Andrea is slumped, her head barely lifted. Anne-Marie squeezes her shoulder and pulls up a red plastic child seat next to her. She sits down awkwardly, knees bunched up into her chest, unsure how she'll get up again. She's lower than Andrea, enough to make eye contact. She realises this woman doesn't need her asking how her daughter is and she's not sure she wants to hear the details either. Mirroring their anger, she starts. "The Police will get the bastard. Chop his bollocks off and lock him away. It's psychopathic behaviour, pre-meditated and inhuman. What's wrong with the men round here? Why aren't we all looking after our girls? Our estate is better than that." Andrea doesn't respond. "It's Kerry's choice, but if you can, if Kerry can, get the Police involved and make sure he doesn't get away with it. We'll do everything we can to support you..."

"You could shut that pub down now," Carol says rocking, on her chair.

"Sorry, what pub?"

"The Three Lions. She was drinking with a friend. Next thing she knows she wakes up next morning beaten and dumped by a bin in a petrol station miles away. She was drugged, defo, and she's not the first. Don't you people realise it's another girl in another friggin bin. You've got to do something."

"That's the old Red Lion. Are you sure? Have you told the Police?'

"Of course we're bloody sure. You can buy any bloody drug you like over the bar. Everyone knows that. It's got a great big sign over the door saying 'Lowlife Scum Welcome'. And what've the Police done? What've you lot done? Nothing."

"I told you my old man'd given Kerry a slap for hanging around with that gang. I warned her about going in there, but it wasn't enough. I want it closed down. Either you shut the bastard place or we will." Andrea's anger has set hard.

"What gang?"

"Don't give me that, lady. It's the gang your lad knocks about with. They hang out in the pool room at the back of the pub. They're underage and the landlord knows it. We'll start a picket."

Carol is defiant. "And we're coming to demonstrate at the

Licensing Committee. How d'ya like that for community action?"

Anne-Marie stays calm. "Let me talk to my Bob, he's in Licensing. It was closed for ages that pub. Is it new management?"

"Management? I don't think so, love. It's Croft you're talking about."

Anne-Marie blinks, but concentrates hard on fixing her facial muscles.

"Let me sort this. Will you talk to Kerry about going to the Police. We'll need evidence. We can give him a condition on his license."

"Is that you trying to sound hard?" Carol sneers.

"No, it's me trying to help. This centre is safe. Would Kerry chat to one of the women police officers down here?"

That gets a nod. These women love this place. Sandra does too, but she can't help herself and gives Anne-Marie a look that says, 'Is this centre really safe?'

Andrea spots it. "What's that look for?" she demands.

"Nothing," Sandra blurts guiltily. "Sorry, I'm just horrified by it all."

"Don't treat us like idiots. We've all seen the paper, we know cuts are coming, but if you lot are thinking of closing this place down, then you really will see trouble." Andrea is livid.

This woman is in shock and agony. Her baby has been hurt. Anne-Marie would love to be able to say this centre closes over my dead body, but that's naïve. Thinking carefully about her next words, because these women remember everything and she doesn't want to get caught in an outright lie, she says, "You saw the Council Leader last week. She hasn't said anything directly about the estate and the community is her main concern." Her tongue shapes itself. "I've promised I'll sort this and I will."

Anne-Marie normally thinks of power as a commodity to trade, sometimes to invest, sometimes to stockpile. She is active in the market. Today, though, any value her power might have had has plummeted. Neither buying or selling seem like a good bet. She can't align herself with the community and alienate Davina, but she won't hide in Davina's pocket or she'll never be able to hold her head up in the neighbourhood. She'd have to move house. She is torn. "Let me talk to my colleagues. Give me your mobile number and I'll call you later. Please, both of you, let's get whoever did this locked up and get Kerry the support she needs."

"And the rest of the bastards?" Objectively, Anne-Marie knows Carol is right to make the link with the pub and that she is wrong to be preparing to do as little as possible about it. Her integrity has developed its own convenient habit of absenteeism. "I can't tell you what to do," she says, remembering the scary of version of Andrea and Carol who owned their school playground. "I never could. I'll call you later, Andrea."

It's not officially lunchtime, but as she approaches the Council House entrance she turns on her heel and takes a left down to the Mechanics. The morning has felt like a ride on the waltzer when you've had a curry and three pints. Her neck hurts from the force of it. She's glad she has to knock on the pub door. It means the place is empty. It would be impossible to get through the next few hours on only a chocolate bar. "Vodka and slimline. Make it a double." The optics are directly in front of her; steady, stable, supported. There's no magic or glamour here. They promise respite, numbness, a stronger calming effect than nicotine. She stares into them, instead of the abyss. Handing the barmaid a fiver she's surprised to get a two-pound coin in change. "It's happy hour" is the young woman's deadpan reply.

Could Andrea and Carol achieve more than she can? In theory, as a resident, Andrea ought to have a better chance of influencing change than a council manager. Residents elect councillors who still hold the purse strings and they listen to real people. The problem with that is Andrea's the wrong kind of resident; a poor inner city one in a ward that will never be winnable for Davina, so unless it's something that hurts the whole city, forget it.

When she'd started out as a manager she'd put her shoulder behind the boulder, trying to change the way things are done, and in the process she'd soaked up responsibility everywhere she went. All that got her was a frozen shoulder and a chilling bout of disillusionment. She knows she would do a better job than Owen and if she was in charge she would have a better chance of influencing where the cuts are going to fall. Not that that would mean anything to Andrea, Carol or Kerry. She could hardly say, "The current bloke is a waste of space, but don't worry, Andrea, love. If I get promoted – and by the way that will mean a massive pay rise for me – it'll all be fine. And ladies, it would be good if you didn't demonstrate outside the Council and put any pressure on a Croft pub while the Council Leader is trying to do some kind of deal with him."

She plays with a beer mat, grabs a pen from her bag and scribbles. Andrea, Highlands, Croft, Davina. She can't write Kerry's name. She wonders if should she tell Jess what's happened? What about Bob? She says his name aloud. Adam's name comes out more quietly. Knocking the drink back, she nods to the barmaid and walks back to the Council House unseen.

CHAPTER 16

JESSICA

Tuesday 23th November, 3pm

Jess has agreed to meet in Anne-Marie's second office – the art gallery café. The huge roof lights let in a natural light that beams peace and goodness into the room. The kitchen clatter and lack of soft furnishings provide a convenient hum, so it's impossible to overhear anyone on the next table. Beginning to get annoyed at having to wait for Anne-Marie, she attacks a chunky slice of lemon drizzle cake, picking off the icing and wolfing down the sponge.

"I'm sorry, Jess, but this will need to be quick. My leader is barking." Anne-Marie is speaking before she's sat down.

"And mine is out to lunch. Permanently." That makes Anne-Marie smile.

"Are you developing a sense of humour?"

"No, that's only temporary."

There are some jokes only they can share. As survivors of the ravages of middle management, they have the stripes of five or six restructures, the scars of bullying, harassment or victimisation processes, the odd community backlash, any number of incorrect or defamatory stories, incoherent quotes and unflattering photos in the local rag. Now in senior management, they recognise they've had times when they've been sitting on the sofa with a partner or in a pub with mates and been there only in body, smiling vaguely but mentally still in the office. They can deal with the loneliness, even though work never leaves them alone, and mostly they can manage their emotions, holding their tongues and controlling any honest facial expressions, although that's something Jess thinks she's better at than Anne-Marie.

"You've been avoiding me," she says.

"I haven't, but you know what I'm going to say. We're not changing the licensing policy. Davina's message – our message – is any development is good development. We can't say we want a vibrant night-time economy and shut down as many pubs and clubs as we can. I'm protecting what we've got left of an economy. You know how bad things are. When we've got more unemployment, we get more crime."

"That depends on what sort of economy it is. If it's the black economy, you're right."

Jess isn't impressed by lazy causal links that happen to momentarily suit Anne-Marie. Still, she wants to keep things on an even keel at this stage. "Where is this pressure on the landlords coming from?"

"Laura Awsworth, Girl in the Bin. Have you forgotten already? And we're looking into the possibility of similar crimes."

"Is it a crime then?"

"This is not something you get to wind me up about. I was there. I was checking out a gang when the call came in. I saw that girl's face in that bin, her smudgy mascara…"

Jess spots a hint of a flinch. She continues, "There was evidence of intercourse and with that level of alcohol in her body it would have been impossible to give consent. She'd have barely been conscious, whether or not the sex was before her skull was cracked against the concrete."

Anne-Marie drops her head towards her shoulder. Jess folds her arms and talks at pace.

"I wanted to warn you that we're going to formally request a cumulative impact policy and recommend that we all get our act together on enforcement."

"Is Bob behind this?" Anne-Marie shows her irritation.

"No. I'm working with Barrington Edwards and the Hospital Trust management."

Anne-Marie sneers, but Jess retorts, "You've got a legal enforcement and a development role, but it sounds to me like you've got them out of balance. Don't you think the City is getting out of hand? You need to be protecting the public, not landlords."

"I'm not protecting anyone," Anne-Marie snaps, "and it sounds to me like you're on your own."

Jess logs the over-reaction and presses on. "I'll work with anyone who's up for change. Why do you think you can't have safety and a night-time economy? Isn't that what investors want?"

"What investors? We can't chase them off before they've arrived."

"A girl was dumped in a bin. There are young women in the City Centre who are vulnerable. It's violence against women, but it seems to me that you're not in the slightest bit interested and I'm questioning why?" That is less diplomatic than Jess intended, but what strikes her is that there's something new in this. She raises an eyebrow.

At sixth form college they'd disagreed about a group called Women Against Violence Against Women. Anne-Marie had got to know the older women through her dad's trade union mates. They were organising a reclaim the night march. It wasn't the cause that was the problem. Jess thought that the turnout would be dismal and they'd be a laughing stock, but Anne-Marie didn't care. Jess suspected that Anne-Marie was responsible for spray-painting a bra advertisement on a hoarding. The ad had said said 'Lock up your daughters'. The addition had said, 'and let your sons roam free???' It was clever, true and she'd admired her friend for doing it, but the good girl muscle in her stomach had always stopped Jess agreeing with Anne-Marie's methods. What's new is that Jess has just questioned Anne-Marie's motives.

Anne-Marie reasserts herself. "Let's start again shall we? I'm doing exactly as I've been told to do, by which I mean I'm implementing Council policy and, yes, we need things to change, but what kind of change? Your approach is taking us backwards. And why make it so formal? A cumulative impact study never changed anything and you'll never get the data you need from the Hospital. It'll take forever."

"Can't you see it the other way round? OK, it maybe a bureaucratic palaver, but it'll mean that you'll have a legitimate reason to turn down any licensing application you want. It gives you more control. Blame us, if it helps you manage Davina." That gets her a 'back off' look.

"We wouldn't be doing it if we didn't need to. The problem is what else are you doing? Nothing's happening. Barrington and I, we need..."

"You and Barrington? Dr Edwards? Now I feel like I'm missing something."

"Don't start. I don't know him that well and, personally speaking, he'd be the last person I'd want to be working with right now..." That might've been too honest but she needs allies. Anne-Marie looks like she might pounce. Jess speeds on. "I heard what a difference he made on prostitution. Three years later and it's still having an impact, especially on your estate. The neighbourhood teams couldn't get it sorted by themselves. He was literally on the street stopping mini-buses full of punters. That's impressive, isn't it?"

"He's a liability. He doesn't seem to recognise we work in a political environment. All that crusading intensity, it pisses me off."

Jess had watched a video clip of Barrington being interviewed. The way his jaw jutted out gave him the look of a vigilante in a suit. "We're clearly saying, to anyone who uses prostitutes, get out of this City and stay out. And if you don't, you'll lose your driving licence, you'll have your name in the *Post*, your reputation, your job, maybe your marriage will all be at risk and we'll do all we can to ensure you end up in court and with a criminal record." Jess would love to be able to actually say that, but never would. Barrington can say it because he isn't Police and because he's a man.

Anne-Marie shrugs.

"Come on, pimps were bringing mini-bus loads from the Potteries. We had no idea there was that kind of volume. He got to grips with it."

"Not born again is he?"

"Give the bloke a chance. That sort of thing doesn't happen often enough round here."

"It's always a one-man show with him. And don't get carried away, there are still a hundred-odd young girls, kids, working the streets. We've got him to thank for Davina getting such a high profile. She started coming out with the 'Saving children from slavery' soundbites and took the credit for the drop in street prostitution. Maybe if there was more of a team effort..."

Jess sees Anne-Marie eyeing up the icing on her plate and offers it up. "Look I can see why it might be a problem for you, but I'm just seeing someone who seems to do a good job, an odd bloke, but an alright bloke, who gets things done. We need more of that and, yes, we do need a team effort. That's why I'm here."

"Just make sure you aren't mopping up after him that's all and thanks for the warning about the impact stuff. You do what you have to."

"We need you. It won't work if you won't make it happen."

"I am but a humble servant of my political masters."

"Now who's being funny?"

"I have to shoot."

"Wait... there's nothing else? Nothing you need to tell me?"

Jess looks for a reaction, but gets nothing. Anne-Marie is on her feet and making her way down the stairs. Why didn't she just tell Anne-Marie she's had a personal phone call from Frank and she's going to see him later? Frustrating exchanges makes life harder and Anne-Marie doesn't normally hide behind the 'just doing my job' wall. Jess knows there's something there.

Everything in the reception area is new; the caramel-coloured, varnished desk, the clean, black, brick flooring, the leather chairs that haven't had time for bum imprints to stick, the pot plants that are just growing into their own. Walking through the college to Frank's office she feels invisible, but also freer. The young people don't notice her. She's only forty, but here she might as well be seventy. The energy of the place is infectious; the possibilities, the undetermined futures, the sweet smell of potential.

"Thanks for coming, Jess. Sorry if I was a bit cryptic on the phone." In contrast to the entrance, Frank's office is crammed with the messy reality of teaching; books, files, timetables and a half-eaten sandwich. Frank's eyes are weary, his body language unusually wary.

"That's fine. Good to see you outside of a meeting for a change."

"I take it Anne-Marie hasn't spoken to you then?"

"About?"

"About Adam. I'm sorry. I'm not exactly sure what to do about him."

"And you think I will?" Jess shakes her head, glad not to be a parent.

"Don't get me wrong, I'm not looking for any special favours. It's advice I'm after. Here, look at this. I'm not sure if you've seen it." Frank gets out his phone and presents a shaky, dark video of a group of young men setting a fire.

"No, I haven't, but that doesn't mean someone at the station hasn't. Do I take it one of the group is Adam?"

"That's him with the ridiculous P.I.M.P. top. Don't you recognise him?"

"No, I've not seen him for years." But she had seen him on CCTV the night Laura Awsworth was attacked.

Frank nods. "No point in him denying it. I've told him he's got to come forward himself. He's not a bad kid, but, obviously, things aren't right. I'm glad you said group not gang, though," he adds.

"What's a gang and what isn't these days? Trying to define what's going on and how serious a risk a group of young people is... Hang on, who's that standing behind him? I can't quite make him out."

"That's Ben Wright. I'm worried about Ben's influence on Adam."

"Ben? No way. I just saw him two days ago."

Jess has known Frank the best part of twenty years. She'd been invited to the evening do when he and Anne-Marie got married. They had always seemed mismatched to her, the age difference magnified by the fact that Jess' dad knew Frank when he was a councillor and on the Police Authority.

"How serious do you think it is?" He looks out of the window at the already black sky.

"How serious do you think it is?" she throws back.

"I know he's been involved in arson, but my guess is that Adam's probably just trying to act hard."

Jess reflects that hard has always been cool at some level, but it wasn't always criminal.

"How do you know Ben?" Frank asks.

"I know his mum, who's an old school friend, but I didn't know Ben and Adam were close."

"Too close. Ben's behaviour has crashed off the acceptable scale in some style. He's hardly been here and when he was he assaulted another student and spat at a tutor."

Jess sucks in her cheeks, finding it impossible to believe.

"We were surprised. He's an intelligent lad, could go to

university if he wants. We have a member of staff who's been working the system to keep him in college."

"What's caused it? What's changed with Ben?"

"We don't know the whole story yet, but it appears to be about him repaying some debt, financial I think. I also suspect him of some involvement in drugs in college."

"Have you informed us officially?"

"There's a separate process for that." He pours all the scorn he has into the P word. "It's with our Police Liaison. It might not be dealing and we aren't sure what drugs."

Jess tries to be positive. "Adam will have to talk to us. I can't say what will happen, but maybe just a caution, especially if he's willing to be open."

On top of a filing cabinet Frank has a small kettle and a tray of mugs. Sorting through them to find one that's clean, he manages to drop one on the floor. It doesn't smash but splashes a remnant of tea on to Jess' shoe. "God, I'm sorry." He hands her a piece of blue paper from a roll that's bloated at the bottom from other spillages.

"It's fine, Frank. I know you deal with this all the time, but it's different when it's your own kid in trouble. I appreciate you being honest. Do you recognise any of the other kids as students?"

"There's definitely one ex-student Adam has mentioned, Leeroy Wilson, but there may be others."

She makes a note of the name on her phone. "What about the drug connection? Do you have any evidence? Any CCTV? You're sure Ben's involved, but Adam isn't?"

"We believe so. Anne-Marie's seen some texts."

"What did the texts say?"

"Nothing we could make sense of particularly, sounded like a meeting in a pub. The texts were on Friday, but no times or anything. It sounded like something heavy that Ben was scared about and Adam wanted to support him with. He's staying at mine at the moment and I practically locked him in and he didn't leave the house until Saturday afternoon."

"Did it say which pub?"

"The Anvil. Do you know it?"

"I know of it. It's dodgy, but no more than many round here."

"What will happen next?"

"My colleagues will interview them both and the drugs issues on campus will go the normal route. It's out of my hands, Frank, but I could ask them to do the interviews here. I'll tell them that Adam's helping us with some background."

"I want you to put the fear of god into him. Obviously if there's a hope in hell he can come out of this without a record we need to make sure he knows what he's got to do to make that happen."

"There aren't enough kids in this city with a real chance and we're not in the business of criminalising the ones who've actually got a future... unless we have to."

Frank's face broadens. He almost smiles.

"I saw Anne-Marie this afternoon." Jess can't resist mentioning it.

"And she didn't say anything about this, did she? Let's just say I'm fairly sure us having this conversation will piss her off, but I'm trying to do the right thing for Adam."

"Thanks, Frank." She means it and gives him a brief hug as she leaves.

Anne-Marie complicates things by keeping them so close to her chest and if she hasn't told Jess about Adam and Ben, what else has she left out? And did Shaz freak out the other day because of Ben? This is important. Sitting in her car, she calls Jonesy to get an update. He's on voicemail, but she manages to get one of the sergeants who was chasing up the CCTV from the night the girl was found in the bin. "Those three lads on the CCTV who were in the area – did you identify any of them? Do we know where they'd been drinking?" The sergeant has spoken to one of them and they'd been in the Anvil. This time Jess leaves a message for Jonesy, trying not to sound too hopeful or excited. "Call me. Did you pick up the link between the Girl in the Bin and the Anvil? I want everyone working there interviewed. And the City Centre Chickenshack kids I was looking at. There's a connection to the same pub. This could be useful."

CHAPTER 17

CORINNE

Wednesday 24th November, 11.50pm

She fills the glass again, to the rim. No point in pretending she's not going to finish it and she doesn't care if it spills. It's almost midnight and the still, silent house magnifies the thoughts in Corinne's head as she sits, distracted. She is tactically avoiding another bad night's sleep by making sure she's too tired to think, too tired for that monkey to start jumping around inside her brain, too tired for another nightmare. Robbed of the relief of a few undemanding chores by a germ-free husband she's already irritated with, Corinne decides to join the Action Men in the bunk bed underneath her son Nelson – again. "You're 42 years old for god's sake. Get a grip. You did your best, so switch off and get to bed," she chides herself, except her legs are like solid concrete posts sunk deep into the floor and they won't carry her up the stairs.

She pictures Barbara and Stan. It's late, but they would still be up, listening to the radio. Barbara would have a small glass of whiskey in her hand, having pestered Stan all evening. "Stanley, pour me another would you love?" The Bells would be on the wooden table between their two favourite chairs. He'd pour it and get short shrift for a short measure. She'd be chuckling about the bags that needed to go to the charity shop, the untouched bags that had come from the charity shop or the merits of Aldi.

Corinne rubs her hands, feeling the piercing pain in Barbara's stiff, bony hand like a house alarm going off inside her head.

She'd been in on Monday on her rounds, a normal event ever since the old lady's stroke three months ago and a normal enough case for any occupational therapist, but the Barbara and Stan double act, a team in constant sickness and poor health, stood out. Barbara had had almost no movement in her left arm and her fingers had contracted into an ugly arrangement of chickens' feet, their sharp talons touching the paper-thin skin of her palm. Her right arm, crippled with arthritis, was not up to much. Her leg was heavily bandaged, her knees gone and her back stuck, pain and frustration hidden under a glamorous rainbow of BHS' finest knitwear.

"Looks like this ring is causing you problems." Barbara's finger was puffy and swollen tight around her wedding ring.

"It's telling me something this ring, Stanley. After forty years it doesn't fit. Maybe it's a sign for me to get a fancy man or take up with the milkman?"

"Can we have a go at taking that off?" Corinne had pressed lightly on the top of the ring and tried to twist it. It wouldn't budge and she realised the skin was broken underneath, red-raw and bleeding. She'd tried Vaseline. She'd tried dental floss. She'd pulled out some antibiotic cream and tried again. No joy. There was no option but to lift the arm up and let the blood drain out to reduce the swelling. Barbara's eyes filled and she backed off. This was medical, it wasn't really her job, and she had already stayed too long.

"Barbara, I know you aren't going to like this, but you really ought to pop into the surgery to get this sorted out. I could call the nurse or Dr Allan and we could arrange a taxi."

"Sorry ducky, but we can't be spending our pension on taxis."

"No, no, of course, but this looks nasty. Think about it and I'll call round tomorrow."

Tuesday's call to the old couple had found them sober and sombre. Stan, who'd been sitting in his chair, playing with a box of ciggies, had got up and shuffled a marked path to the kitchen to put the kettle on. "One lump or two, young lady?" The couple marvelled that you could still buy sugar in lumps, but that was useful when you couldn't see to pour a teaspoon of sugar or clean up the mess after. Until that point it hadn't been clear how bad Stan's sight was. "I can't see a bloody thing these days. Totally gone now," he'd said, resigned. "See no evil, do no evil. That's us."

"We'll have another go with that ring shall we?" Corinne had said and, after failing to arrange Barbara's hand in a cold bowl of water, she'd rested it gently on a cold pack. It had been obvious then that she'd underestimated the seriousness of the situation. There was an infection in the wound around the ring, dried black blood under the finger and white skin on her palm, where her finger nail was growing determinedly inwards. The ring wouldn't move and neither would the finger.

"Cheap gold," Barbara had snorted, "but we just didn't have the cash in those days."

"He could buy you a lovely new one," Corinne had said, regretting the words immediately.

"I don't think so, young lady. It could be a brass curtain ring, but they won't be cutting it off, not unless I'm in my box and won't know anything about it." Corinne had let it drop, but with her options running out she'd pleaded with them to let her drive them to the surgery. "No," Barbara had said. "I don't want to be causing a fuss."

She'd done what she could to dress the wound and said she'd be back in the morning. It hadn't been right, but what else could she do? Her manager had clearly said, "If a patient refuses treatment, even a patient in her eighties who's under the influence, there's nothing you can do about it. It's not your job, but you can contact the GP and if you want to pop in again that's fine. Just make sure everything is recorded and you don't get behind with your other cases." She'd called the surgery straightaway and spoken to the practice manager, who'd sounded concerned, but only in a way that didn't commit anyone to doing anything.

"I can't understand why you're so upset?" Barrington had reproached her. "They are adults and they are making their own choices. They don't want help and you aren't seeing the bigger picture. Presumably they have family, they have neighbours, or there should be a local voluntary sector network they can access. Corinne, make sure you fulfil your duty of care by all means, but respect their wishes. It's not your responsibility." Better not ask for his view next time.

Except that she'd had to talk about it, because it was important to her. He might have been right, but whose job was it to take that extra care and what happened when there wasn't anyone else? She'd wanted to say more, but felt they were at the edge of a mountainous old argument. What she'd seen in Barbara's eyes was a thick concentrated pain as she'd hopelessly tried to lift her crippled finger, sensing the infection crawl through her hand and into her wrist, the jagged tip of the uncut nail growing through each layer of her skin. Corinne walks upstairs, kisses her sleeping boy and eventually falls into a fitful sleep on the bottom bunk.

At 5am a silent scream caught in her throat shocks her awake. In the nightmare she'd been walking to her car. It was night and she was being followed by a zombie-like creature, a swollen, decaying woman's head with no eyes and an old man's body with no hands. She recognises the blood-stained dressing gown as Stan's and the thin, grey-purple hair as Barbara's. There is no real chance of sleep after that. Strangely, though, as the new morning light hits her eyelids, she sees that Stan and Barbara have begun to morph together, not as a monstrous nightmare creature, but as a whole, weird, wonderful, life-sustaining entity. The opposite of her and Barrington.

She gets up, goes to work early, clears her normal visits swiftly and goes straight round to Barbara and Stan's. Stan's blank eyes seem to disappear back into his head, he is too quiet. He has put an old blue tea towel over Barbara's hand. "Can I have a quick look?" Barbara shakes her head. "Don't worry, young lady. It'll be fine. I've got my medicine here." She points to the half-empty bottle of Bells. Corinne gently ignores her and raises the tea towel enough to see that the nail is now embedded in the palm and there is a red-blue tinge to the rest of the hand. "I know you won't like this Barbara," she begins, "but the quickest and easiest way to sort this out is to nip down to Casualty. I'll ring the ambulance now." She begins to pull her phone from her bag.

Stan stands up more quickly than she's seen him move in weeks and guides himself straight to Barbara's chair. "No, no, there's no need. We've come through worse together. We'll sort ourselves out, thanks." His mouth is hard, his instruction final. Corinne digs her fingers into her own palm to hold it together. "I'll just tidy it up for you, shall I?" "No, honestly, thanks, love, you're a good girl, but it's a bit sore to be honest and I'd rather you didn't touch it." She gets Stan to put her personal mobile number into his phone. "Call me anytime."

Anxious, distracted, head fuzzy with guilt edging to anger, the day passes. One of her own Gran's sayings – "I wish I was a bird and the cat had me" – keeps coming into her head. On the way home she stops at the GP's. No, they aren't able to take any action, but will act immediately if instructed to do so by the patient. After a quiet dinner has come and gone, she explains to Barrington what has happened.

"So what about your training and supervision arrangements?" That is his reaction. Bloody Dr Barrington Management Edwards. "What about your arrangements with adult social care providers? Who bears the risk?" She falters, not knowing and already doubting herself. Could she have been predicted the ring would be a problem after the stroke? Why hadn't she seen the other nails on the hand growing? Has she got too emotional, wasted too much time chatting with the couple and not dealt with the problem? Why hasn't she been more assertive and simply brought one of her friendly nurses along anyway, taking the choice out their hands? She twists her own wedding ring. It catches the skin and pinches sharply.

CHAPTER 18

ANNE-MARIE

Friday 26th November, 9pm

"Switch that music down, will you mate," Bob instructs the young Pakistani mini-cab driver. A throbbing techno beat blares as they get in. From the review mirror she notices the driver's eye movements flick up and down in time with the lights in the car's display panel. She's mesmerised, too. It might not be safe, but Anne-Marie knows that if she was on a Friday night cab shift she'd want something to distract her from the rest of the madness. That and a six-pack of Red Bull. The driver makes no comment, but does as he's told.

"Come on, Bob, this is the nearest we're going to get to clubbing tonight. Enjoy it and be grateful you haven't even got to dance."

"How do you know we won't end up clubbing? It's Grab-A-Granny at the Irish." "That's sexist, Bob." She digs into the seat to pinch his bum. "It might not be long before I'm a granny. Maybe I'll check it out."

"Don't tell me Adam's gone and..."

"No, Bob. Get me a VAT and I'll follow you in."

They like the King's Head, the grandest original pub building in the City Centre. It's the first point on any pub crawl and a good people-watching spot. She's trying to pace herself, because after this week she knows she's likely to burn bright and crash early. It might have been a better bet to stick to the sofa, but what swung it was the need to see that life outside work still existed. And to get a look at the Croft pub, which is technically work, but she's determined to enjoy it. There's been no breath to catch in the last three days, or weeks or months. She could even say years and wouldn't be lying. Nodding to the other smokers, a couple of young lads about Adam's age, she calls, "Managed to drag yourself away from *Call of Duty 5* then?" The boys aren't sure they've heard that right. "Yeah, me too." She stubs out her fag. "So addictive isn't it?"

Inside the volume is on full and the air is thick with the voices of thirsty men. Bob's standing at the bar with two men she doesn't recognise. She looks around for a chair, even though she knows this kind of City Centre pub avoids providing seats. Vertical drinking. If you stand, you drink quicker. Until you fall over that is, which makes her think that, without a pick-me-up or two she'll be vertically sleeping fairly soon.

"You might remember Eddie? He did a stint as Markets Manager after me. He's in security now."

Eddie has very clean hands and there's no smell of rotting cabbage – always a bonus. Bob shows her off with an appreciative look at her arse that's just about acceptable, but Eddie's a tall creep and she catches him looking down her bright red T-shirt top. The silent bloke isn't introduced. For a few minutes she's happy to listen in to their Friday night bollocks. It consists of re-telling stories from so called legendary pub sessions: "Remember when that lawyer, Peter Potts, tried to sell me a gypo horse?" Or tales of England football supporter trips: "This beer might not be great, but it beats drinking cement in that miners' bar in Kazakhstan." The men don't ask her any questions and she isn't expected to express an opinion. Then she registers Bob's talking about away matches over the Christmas holidays. God, is Christmas only four weeks away? She'd better find someone to outsource that to. She hasn't broached the subject with Frank, Adam or Bob yet.

"My round. What are you having?" Eddie offers.

"No, not for us, thanks, we'll be moving on for the next one," Bob says. "We're aiming to do the whole circuit tonight."

"Is the Anvil next?" Anne-Marie asks, knowing it isn't, but interested in the reaction.

"The Anvil? You're kidding. That's a different circuit entirely," the silent bloke pipes up.

"Is it that bad?" she asks. "I mean, I haven't been in there in years, but I remember it as a student."

"They eat students for breakfast in there." He seems strangely animated.

Eddie grunts, "I wouldn't take a lady in there."

"What, I'm not safe with Bob? I can't believe that." Anne-Marie knows this is a challenge Bob won't be able to resist.

She stands outside the Anvil for her customary smoke while Bob goes to the bar. There are two puffer-jacket bouncers. The Frankenstein one nods her away from the door. She steps back a couple of paces. He nods again. She steps back further, giving him a 'whatever' shrug. The bouncer looks her up and down and speaks into an ear piece, staring upwards, possibly at a camera. Christ, the treatment nicotine addicts have to put up with, but Anne-Marie enjoys the minor discrimination. Smoking is a small act of defiance, a finger up and an entrance to an alternative club, an information-rich place where powerful bonds can be formed.

What looks like the boss of the bouncers comes out of the pub to survey the scene. He turns his nose up and sneers. She sneers back, his dark, wavy hair is slightly too long. He's too old for a gypsy earring and has the air of an ageing Maradonna. She decides to call him the Argentinian and is about to say something sarky when she sees Bob at the bar with the man she now recognises as Croft. She hasn't been expecting anything in particular from the trip to the Anvil, but this is a gift from the goddess of middle managers.

On closer inspection Croft is about fifty, this time wearing a fitted charcoal grey shirt, cut in at the waist, three buttons to the cuff and a neat ticket pocket. Normally he would have made it onto her good-looking list, but he looks as if he irons his own shirts and perfectionism is not attractive. As she joins them at the bar, Bob puts a proprietorial arm around her shoulder and does the introductions.

"Pleased to meet you," says Anne-Marie. "We saw each other briefly at the Council House, but didn't get a chance to introduce ourselves."

"Yeah, of course. You're welcome here anytime." Croft shakes her hand formally, which gets noted by the Argentinian who has followed her in and is standing close by.

"Those are on the house." Croft motions to the barman.

Bob barely nods in thanks. His arm slips from her shoulder to her back, guiding her in the direction of a table in the corner, as far as possible from the bar. She smiles compliantly for now. Danny has a full pint and doesn't look like he's going anywhere. Now she'll get a real chance to find out what Davina is planning.

"We'll just stay for this one and move on. It's dead in here." Bob rubs her hand, something that normally doesn't happen in public.

"Tell me if I'm missing something. First the scary build-up to what looks like a dull, ordinary pub. Then you aren't at all happy to see this bloke. Who is he?"

"I'd have Croft's licence off him in a second if he actually had his name over the door. I know him from way back. What was he doing in the Council House?"

"I didn't get to find out. Davina was meeting with him and another guy who I also didn't get introduced to. Is he a developer?"

"Wouldn't be surprised. One of my team said he's been buying up old pub property dirt cheap, running all sorts of cash business out of them."

"What's the connection between you and him?"

"We both went to Hilltop Comp. I'm not proud of it, but we were into moronic kid stuff, stealing bits of lead, copper. His uncle was in scrap. Lots of metal-bashers over that side. We both wised up. I straightened out. He took the other route."

"Unusual company for Davina to be keeping."

"You're telling me. Ask Frank as well. That family are seriously bad news."

She nods. "Fancies himself, doesn't he."

"He was a face, I suppose you'd say. Went up to the soul clubs, Stoke way, Wigan I think. He's smart. Like's nice things, quality."

"Where's the money come from?"

"Exactly, but let's leave it for now, eh?"

She takes his point. The pub is small, the tiled surfaces harsh. "How come you've never told me about your dark side?"

"There's not much to tell. I got an apprenticeship. Grew up quickly."

That's something they have in common. She sighs. "I can't see Adam just getting an apprenticeship and it suddenly being alright. If there are apprenticeships, they aren't like that anymore."

"He'd be bored in five minutes, but being with those blokes, great blokes by the way, taught me everything I needed to know about life, work, paying the bills, management, unions, organisation, right, wrong."

"And that's why you know nothing about women!" And very little about relationships, compromise, flexibility and tolerance for life's grey areas, she could add.

"Not true. Remember, I've been married twice and I've got you."

She rests her case with a peck on his cheek.

"Let's go." He necks the final third of his pint. "I'll have a quick slash first."

As she finishes her drink, Croft comes to sit at their table. "On to the next then?"

"Has to be done," she smiles.

"Make sure you have one in the Lions." Anne-Marie says nothing. After what she's heard about Kerry, she's in no hurry to check that one out.

"I'll look forward to working with you," Croft says. "I've got time for your boss. She means business. Better than the usual deadbeat councillors. She's got the vision to lift us out of this economic gloom. This place needs a real shake-up. Get the city on the map. Get people investing here."

Anne-Marie is surprised to hear he speaks the same language as she does, but however he's learned it, it's what Davina wants to hear.

"We'll need all the help we can get with that," she replies, genuine.

"And what we need is for you to cut the red-tape. Let business get on with what we're best at. We employ 150 people and we can make this city work. We're on your side. We're working hard to help deliver the vision."

That's news. All of a sudden he's a major employer, probably smarter than she'd thought, and probably richer, too. She sees Bob returning and stands, knowing that if Bob hears this it will be a red rag.

"How's the project going? Where are you up to now?" She doesn't have long and doesn't want to sound like she's out of the loop.

"It's exciting, but early days and we haven't got the full package sorted yet. Sites with mixed ownership always take time and the access onto the ring road is something your planners ought to have got sorted years ago."

Also interesting, he's put a land deal together before and she reckons it ought to be pretty easy to work out which site he means.

"What exactly are you into these days, then?" Bob can't help himself.

"Meeting people's needs," Croft continues calmly. "Helping them feel safe, providing jobs, finance and entertainment."

Bob rolls his eyes.

Croft is enjoying this. "You could call it a public service."

Bob almost spits his front teeth out.

"Don't forget, I know where you came from, Danny."

"We all had to start somewhere, matey. I don't see your problem. Never did. You were always scared of pushing the boundaries, but that's how we get on. I've learnt from Davina. Secure the bricks and mortar. Make a profit. Use what you've got. We're all on the same team now."

This is unexpected.

"No," Bob straightens up, "my job is to protect the community. I'll have a go when I need to, but within the rules. You haven't followed a regulation in your life."

"And whose fault is that? Enforcement – isn't that what you are now? Well, mate, you do your job and I'll do mine."

Luckily the Argentinian steps in, touching Croft's arm to beckon him away.

"Sorry we can't continue this discussion. You two enjoy your evening. We'll be seeing more of each other, no doubt."

Anne-Marie nods, Bob turns his back quickly. Outside, he seethes. "Smug bastard. Why didn't you just tell me that was what you were after tonight. Not that crap about a pub crawl?"

She screws her nose up at him and links his arm. "That's not fair. I had no idea he would be there. Yes, I wanted to see the pub, but you men don't multi-task the way we do."

"Just steer clear of any projects that involve him."

"Bob, love, do you think I've got a choice?"

Anne-Marie wonders about the point at which Bob's and Croft's paths split. What he actually said wasn't so bad. He's not that different to many of the developers she sees. If anything, he's better dressed and more articulate. Everything's so black and white with Bob. It's a scrap. Them and us. His eyes are sparkling, his chest out as he grips her hand. They walk a few hundred metres away from the main drag with a quieter pub at the edge of Station Road in mind. As they turn the corner he pulls her into an old empty doorway and kisses her hard. She puts her cold hands up inside his leather jacket and leans back onto the glass. "You can do that again," she says. They stay there like teenagers with nowhere else to go.

Minutes later the cold still of the Friday night is shattered by a screeching sound, a sharp crash of metal, a fizz of pressure, then an explosion, a deep, powerful blast. Jesus, is it a bomb? The glass behind her shakes violently. It's followed immediately by another bang so loud she raises her hands to her ears, her legs crumple and she clings to Bob's jacket. Screaming echoes up the street. A second later, there's the sound of ice cracking above them and a huge chunk of the top pane falls. It hits Bob's shoulder, his body buckling sideways under the weight, then smashes to the floor behind them just as another smaller piece of glass crashes down onto her shoulder and another guillotine-edge scrapes her neck. They lurch forward into the middle of the street and she gropes her way to the ground. Her hands are a fright of grit, cuts and gem-like shards. She wipes them on her jeans, then gently touches the back of her neck It stings like acid, her finger tips wet with blood. Glass is caught in the centre of her back, stuck in a bra hook. A blade jabs into her as she tries to shake it free. A screech spurts from her throat. More screams, alarms blare around them, people are running.

Bob crouches over her. "There's a fire. I can smell gas. Can you move? Come on, Anne-Marie. Let's move." There's a final bang, like an industrial Chinese rocket. Behind them, clouds of smoke gust down the street. They run, sort of. Anne-Marie gets another jab of sharp pain as the glass seems to fall further down the back of her shirt to the top of her jeans. She stops, breathless. They're back at the crossroads with the High Street. Maybe twenty or more people are there. She hears sirens. She looks in her bag for a tissue and blows her nose. More blood. She doesn't faint, but falls in slow motion back onto the stability of the road.

"Best to stay here. The ambulances will get to us quicker," Bob says, standing up straight, breathing heavily and looking around.

"Are you alright? Shouldn't we call someone? Silver Command?" She's desperately racking her brain for a procedure to follow.

"Never mind that, they'll be all over this. Let me look at you. Your jacket's ripped and you've got a nasty gash on your neck. What else?"

She looks him straight in the face. He seems unhurt. There's a sliver of glass shimmering by his ear. She point towards it and he brushes it off like a fly.

"My head's thumping. I have to get this jacket off." It's a thin, navy, Harrington-style zip-up that feels completely inappropriate. She'd known Bob would be wearing his leather jacket and hadn't wanted to look like twins.

"I'm not sure." He's worried. "Don't want to make it worse. They might want to cut it off. Keep your head back. Here let me." Bob holds the tissue firm on her neck.

Jesus, why didn't she stick with her first instinct? The sofa. A bottle of wine.

"Anne-Marie, are you alright? Talk to me. Are you OK?" It's Jess. She tries not to cry.

"I need a drink."

Casualty's a blur. The adrenaline wears off and the painkillers kick in. They stitch and dress her neck and back. She sits up on the bed in her cubicle. Her lovely red shirt is a shade card of blood, no longer wearable. Bob helps covers her with his leather jacket. Waiting for the doctor to discharge her, exhaustion creeps in and weakness pins her to the bed. She's confused. What just happened? That wasn't terrorists. This isn't London. She hears Bob on the phone talking to Frank and shields her eyes from the coarse strip lights above her.

About two hours later, she persuades Bob to take her home. Frank drives them. She hears them in the front, quietly discussing the explosion and the fire. The conversation sounds strangely low-key, a combination of facts and practicalities. It's a weird contrast to the violence of the experience. Frank says it was joyriders crashing into Bentley's yard. They hit part of the gas storage unit and an old warehouse went up. There don't seem to be any fatalities, but there's a significant blaze that's keeping the Fire Service busy. It's ripped through the adjoining derelict buildings.

"Is that it? I mean, how, how did joyriders do that?"

"Take it easy love, we'll find out soon enough."

"I mean why, why would a joyrider do that?"

She feels a draw of suspicion, but its pull isn't strong enough for her to focus. They say goodnight to Frank quickly.

"Drink this love." Bob pours her a brandy. She necks it, shivers and motions for another.

She spends Saturday on the sofa, dressed in yoga pants and a thick hoodie, wrapped in a pink comfort blanket, sleeping awkwardly on and off until lunchtime. The lump on her head feels as if it's grown. What's inside that lump? Fluid? Puss? Blood? How did her skin expand like that? There's a small but fresh smear of blood on the blanket. She lifts her head alarmed. There's a dot of blood expanding on the cushion and she realises it's on three of her fingers. Peering through a filter of co-codamol and brandy, she sees tiny shards of glass that must have fallen out of her hair while she was investigating the lump. A shower would be painful and she doesn't want to dislodge the dressing on her shoulder, so washing her hair isn't an option unless Bob does it, and he won't be back until around teatime.

Reaching for another painkiller, she thinks about work. Got to be back in the office on Monday, no question. The next meeting with Davina's too important. That's what they're paying her for; to get a grip on the situation, the cuts, the budget, sort out the process and come up with options that have a chance of being deliverable, never mind supportable. The fresh blood on her finger releases her of any guilt that she won't be working today. It's a write-off.

The sound of the key in the lock wakes her again at about 4pm. It's not Bob, but Adam.

"Hello, love." He looks so young, her boy.

"Trust you to get blasted last night."

She pulls an offended face.

"Not 'blasted' blasted." Although she was certainly drunk by the time she'd finally managed to sleep.

"You know what I mean. I heard you got stitches in your shoulder."

"Yes. Don't hug me. It smarts like hell."

Adam's carrying a blue plastic bag from the corner shop. He's picked up the local paper, a packet of fags and a bar of Fry's Chocolate Cream.

"What have I done to deserve this?"

She nods and smiles. She shouldn't be surprised. That's basic decent behaviour.

"Nothing."

The scary thing is that he's seriously considered the question and that's his honest answer.

"I'll put the kettle on."

While he disappears into the kitchen she looks at the paper. There are clichéd pictures of firefighters at the site taken from a mobile and a view of a burnt-out car. Four foot high gas cylinders are sprawled across the road. She tries to think through the geography of the area. What else is down there? Who owns the sites? They've commissioned a masterplan recently, but she hasn't seen a draft yet. There was damage to the area, not just the Bentley site, but he'd be insured.

Adam comes in with tea. "You haven't been through the City Centre today have you?" He shakes his head. "That's going to be a mess for a long time. It'll look even worse than it does now if you come in on the train. Land values will…"

"Give it a rest mum."

He sits on the floor facing the TV with his back against the sofa and passes her up the chocolate. Her eyes fill. She blinks hard so he won't see her cry.

"What are you trying to do? Make me fat?"

Adam flicks through the channels on the box, sticking at an old episode of *Columbo*. That'll do.

CHAPTER 19

BARRINGTON

On the twenty-minute journey to the terraced house on an estate on the far side of the city Barrington analyses the situation. The old couple are an interesting system test. The woman, a nurse all her working life, refuses to be a burden on her fellow professionals and is adamant about avoiding hospital at all cost. That's interesting. The husband could fall into a category of 'significant need', but isn't critical and, again, is determined to stay at home. As they arrive he is attempting to calculate the cost of Corinne's visits over the last week, except he can't remember her unit cost.

"Let me go in and check what the situation is. You stay in the car," Corinne says, but Nelson jumps out and follows her up the path. Barrington follows, too. To him the visit is unnecessary, especially on a Sunday evening, but he agreed to come after Nelson started crying when Corinne began to leave the house.

The curtains are closed. She bangs hard on the couple's old door. The rusty letter box and standard numbering tell him the house is still in Council ownership and the garden is a mess.

"Alright, alright, I'm blind not deaf." The old man eventually opens the door.

"Stan, it's Corinne. I came to see how Barbara is. I've got my husband and my son with me, but they can wait outside. She's OK is she?"

"Bring them in duck, it's bloody freezing out there."

They are bundled into a low-lit hall, stacked out with carrier bags clearly full of junk. Nelson pulls out a teapot wrapped in newspaper. Barrington gets his son to re-wrap it and sit on the stairs. They count the decorative plates on the wall, their size and the number of nails holding them up. There's a school photo of a fat mixed race boy. Interesting. He'd assumed the family were all white. Barrington watches his wife through the gap in the door.

"Come in," Stan says. "Barbara's asleep, but I warn you we've had a night of it."

There's a gas heater on full blast, but the woman in the chair is bone white.

"We did it. Don't ask me how we didn't wake the dead, but we got it off between us and the Brylcreem." Barbara's hand is resting on the arm of her chair with a tea towel covering her forearm. On the table next to her Barrington spots an empty half bottle of whiskey and the blood encrusted ring.

"Don't wake her," Corinne says. She leaves them a tube of antibiotic cream. "I'll call in tomorrow."

In the warm car Nelson begins to doze off.

"So, that's fine. You can move on."

"No, love, it's not fine. This time they managed, but what about next time and the time after that? It would've meant A&E probably admitting Barbara and Stan can't survive on his own. I've already been trying to sort out adult services to do an assessment, but people fall through the net every day. It's no-one's job to check or to spend the extra time. When the cuts come either I won't be here at all or I'll be doing three people's jobs. I'm doing what I can while I can."

"That's laudable, but ultimately pointless."

"Lord in heaven…"

"I agree you might've saved the public purse a sizable bill, but actually public services weren't needed. They sorted it out themselves in the end, despite the unnecessary intake…"

"You mean despite her drinking? If I'd told you she liked a drink, you'd have had a totally different attitude. You wouldn't have even got in the car."

"I didn't say that," he says, but acknowledges the veracity.

"Barbara's not a drunk, Barrington. She likes a drink and it helps her manage the pain. That's a normal couple. I see older people like this every day."

"Ideally, the family or the neighbours would take responsibility." He concentrates on the driving.

"What do you mean ideally? It's not ideal and it doesn't work. What about my family? They're two hundred miles away. And think about our neighbours. How good would they be at sorting out support services? They aren't medically trained. One side can barely speak English and the others are always at work. They wouldn't have a clue. We can't leave it to chance."

"And we can't design or afford a system for all eventualities. Individual needs are just that. Individual. Which means we're into rationing and…"

"Shut up." Corinne almost shouts.

"Shhh. You'll wake the boy."

The problem is that Corinne, like his colleagues, has made her mind up based on the beliefs she holds, but the NHS is no longer a universal service, free at the point of delivery. People already pay for parts of the service now. Why not make alcohol-related treatment chargeable, relative to the units in their bloodstream? Drink drivers pay their own costs and the costs of those they injure.

"You just don't get it, do you? We need a humane system, for human beings. What if it was Nelson who needed help?"

"That's not relevant. He's an innocent. You're emotional."

"So who's deserving and who isn't? Am I? I like a glass of wine now and again? I am emotional, you're right. I'm relieved. I'm happy that funny, inspiring old lady is alive to tell the tale and I don't want to talk to you anymore."

Corinne has a point, but with the mathematical certainty of the cuts, he isn't prepared to let himself see it.

Back home Corinne carries Nelson up to bed and Barrington heads for the shed to get his bike. He wipes it clean from left to right, finishing with the saddle, and sets off. He's not exactly sure why the ride doesn't go well. His breathing seems off. His legs are heavy. Maybe he could do with getting the bike serviced. He cycles past his aunt's house, then down past the park. Unusually he swings left and does a circuit of the roads around the park. This park. That bench. He stops, staring through the park's Victorian railings at the same bench he'd been sitting on that November day 25 years ago.

The driving snow and sleet had made his face sore. He was wearing a cheap baseball jacket that seemed to absorb the wet icy flakes. He watched the demonstrators amass, his aunt and uncle, their neighbours, the pastor and some friends of his mum he recognised from the church, huddling around their neatly painted sheet. There were around five hundred shabbily dressed students with Socialist Worker party placards, a trade union flag and a colourfully quilted banner he couldn't read. He wasn't sure why they were there, but he'd overheard the family talking about it and they were glad others in the city felt angry about his cousin's death.

Barrington had always hated crowds, but was desperate to do his duty and be there with them. He'd agreed with Aunt Hermin that he'd follow from a distance. She understood and, although she worried that there might be other teenagers hanging around the edges of the march looking for trouble, she knew he'd always fled from any sense of physical danger.

Impatient to get moving and desperate to keep warm, he set off to walk the mile circuit of the park, keeping an eye on the crowd as they stamped their feet and waited, increasingly impatient.

He wondered if it was deliberate, keeping them there as long as possible – freeze some of them into opting out. There had been talk of the Police steering clear, prioritising the football fans and the overtime they would earn from covering the match. As he walked around the park he clocked the Police and their positions, mainly at the gates to the park, but on the outside. He jumped as he heard his aunt's voice through a tinny loud hailer, her accent muted, intent clear, anger and pain in every syllable.

"Thank you everybody for coming today. Thank you. The organisers have asked me to say a few words and to remind you all that we want a peaceful march today. I appeal to you all to respect the memory of my son, Darren. We want peace and we want justice. Be sure that I will fight until my last breath and beyond – yes, and beyond – to get justice for my boy. They had no right, no right to take him away from us. Who murdered my son?" He hears a single voice in the crowd shout, "The Police are the murderers." There's a small cheer. Aunt Hermin continues. "My son was allegedly arrested for fraud. We refuse to believe this. He was arrested and now he's dead. We want answers. We are starting a campaign today for a full public enquiry. My son was murdered. We have a right to know."

He heard her voice break up as it had done so many times in the last few weeks. She handed the mike to a young black man beside her. Barrington couldn't hear him. He ran towards the crowd, wanting to hold his aunt's hand, wanting to listen to her voice, wanting her to keep talking, wanting to take his place in the line behind the family banner – 'Justice for Darren'. The crowd was thin. He could easily weave his way through, but right at that moment they started to move off and he lost his nerve. He stayed at the back with the stragglers, with their brollies blown inside out in the blinding sleet and snow.

They walked the short distance up the hill and into the city. As they entered Corporation Street, the crowd condensed and found its voice. The narrow street with tall Victorian buildings amplified the sound. The chant rang out.

"Who killed Darren?"

"The Police killed Darren"

"Who are the murderers?"

"The Police are the murderers."

With his attention more than a hundred metres in front of him, and the growing noise around him, Barrington noticed a group of around twenty young men, faces covered with balaclavas, coming up behind him and thrusting their way into the compact crowd. His instinct was to leave, but he found himself rooted to the spot. His aunt and uncle, the pastor, they didn't want this. No-one wanted this. Needing to see their faces, he took to the pavement, skirting the crowd and pushing past the shoppers.

"Fascist Police. Racist Police," the crowd yelled, over and over. A constant shrill of whistles pierced his ears. Frantic, he was still nowhere near the front. He barged through a young woman marshal who stumbled awkwardly and hit the floor. A policeman stepped in. "Oi, you!" he screamed at Barrington. "You little bastard."

As he turned, someone in the crowd spat at the policeman. Barrington saw the slimey gob hit the arm of his high-vis jacket and disappear in the melting snowflakes. Disgusting. From the corner of his eye he saw a bottle fly. He threw himself down onto the road, half on top of the marshall. He saw her grazed cheek, mucus running from her nose. His heart pumping wildly, he scrambled backwards on his knees. The policeman's attention was drawn to the direction of the phlegm. Jumping up, he ran full pelt back down the street away from the march.

Without stopping he took the next left and circled back behind the shopping centre. An old lady stared at him, shaking her head. What? What had he done? He felt sick, but kept running, through the alley and up the pedestrianised stretch towards the alley behind the shop where Darren had died. He hadn't been into the city since his cousin's death. At the other end of the street, maybe two hundred metres away, he saw the beginnings of the march turning in his direction. The thoroughfare had been cleared and was eerily empty for a Saturday afternoon. He slowed to a jog, then walked towards the banner, sticking to the shops on the opposite side.

He could see his aunt and uncle now, gripping their battered sheet, silent and focused on every step towards the spot where their son had died. Apart from the police patrolman on a bike leading the way, there was no sign of violence. Maybe they'd all gone back down Corporation Street? Maybe that was it. Could she see him? If Aunt Hermin could see him, just once, he'd have done his duty. She would know he'd been there and then he could escape the suffocating chaos of the crowd. Jumping up and down on the spot, counting the jumps as he went, he waited until Aunt Hermin finally nodded towards him. That was it. He had done what he promised. He could go.

CHAPTER 20

JESSICA

Monday 29th November, 8pm

Sitting on the low, wooden school bench, watching the children train, Jess enjoys the sense of order, of certainty. It's a small, scruffy church hall, the floor is a neat jigsaw-like floor of mats, the Dojang. There's a line of mainly boys, interspersed with two or three small girls, their hair tied back not quite tightly enough. They bow as they step on. Certainty is as valuable as gold these days – and found in unlikely places. They are bowing to Stewart, their assistant instructor, not their Master. She can see him enjoying it.

"Light as you can on your feet, guys. You can pivot easier."

She watches as he takes them through the basic stances, blocks and kicks. The boys try hard to keep control, but the excitement gets to them as they start an initial punching sequence. A lad of about ten is trying to do a spin kick and falls over. Stewart steps in and demonstrates slowly.

"Keep at it. Don't worry about feeling stupid. Try again."

The boy, who looks like he's trying to impress Stewart, falls again.

"Doesn't matter. You'll get it eventually. Look…"

Stewart motions to a tall, thickset man with the body of a bouncer and curly, shoulder-length hair. They are slick sparring partners, both third dan black belts, enjoying showing off their power and skill to primary school children, for god's sake.

"Did you hear that?" Stewart says. "That sweet sound when

your spin hook hits the target? That's the spirit in you that won't be crushed – when you know you've won." The Master signals that he should move the group onto the next exercise. Maybe she's not the only one who notices that the gleam in Stew's eye is a tad too much.

It's an uncomfortable reminder of a link she'd seen between Stewart and her dad. Her father's preferred policing style had included a traditional and painful hook to the ear, a well placed kick in the back of the knee or an unseen punch, but only in the moment, when it mattered, when the toerag was in no doubt that his actions and the injection of pain were directly related. Her dad wasn't violent at home. He never needed to be. He had approved of Stewart on the basis that he'd been accepted into the Force. It was enough to secure the engagement. Stewart had been certain of the need to get married, he'd wanted her, and Jess just wanted to be wanted. She hoped young women were smarter these days, but being in the Force hadn't given her much comfort on that front.

Stewart's reaction to the Girl in the Bin was typical of his policing style. "There's no crime there – forget it," had been his opener.

"You're the support to Jonesy. What've you been doing?"

She used to be reluctant to pull rank, but since they'd agreed to split, there was no reason to hold back. He'd always resented her promotions and his failure to make progress. She felt he'd never respected her, but she had been loyal. He owed her. He resented that as well.

"There's nothing to do."

"This isn't the only incident. There's a trend here."

"Yeah, I heard you say that before. You let me know when there's a new case you need me to sort for you."

Even though no information had come through from the hospital, which made a pattern of incidents harder to stack up, she wouldn't let him wind her up. "Come on Stew, the City Centre is a nightmare. The whole booze-and-brawl thing has got out of hand."

"We're keeping a lid on things. If we crack down too hard, the nutters will just go down the road and the Force can't afford the overtime bill to contain every minor piss hole."

"We can't just contain it. It's our job to improve the situation."

"That's politics not policing. You stick to what you're good at."

It's funny to be here for the first time. Jess has never been invited to the gym. She's never been interested, but needs must. Frank had mentioned Croft and the gang, the CCTV witness mentioned the Girl in the Bin and a Croft pub, the same pub that Ben had been in. Although a mixed race kid in a white pub feels unlikely, if no-one else is paying attention, she will.

"What're you doing here?" Stew says, joining her on the bench.

"Missed you at the station. I've been busy with the Bentley's explosion. The insurance team from HQ are in. Anyway, just a quick one, can you give me a bit of background on Daniel Croft? Jonesy said you were on a case a while back that he was involved in."

"Why do you want to know?"

Just give me the answer, she thinks, but then decides to tell him it's personal.

"How is it personal?"

"You know my friend Sharon? She and Ben are in a difficult situation."

"Not surprised to hear that she's a mess."

If ever there was a question that their marriage was over, he just had to open his mouth to confirm she'd made the right decision. Best to keep her focus on the action on the mats in front of her.

"Croft, Stew. Did we make any drug connection?"

"Has the soft lad been dealing then?"

Jess checks herself.

He continues, "Croft isn't the problem. I can't see any link between him and the likes of Shaz. It's a fair-sized development business. Not sure they're even landlords anymore. He's the sort of person that sits in meetings with you and your lot."

Jess bites half her tongue off. That's exactly the problem with Stew: this lot good, that lot bad; Croft is worth something, Shaz isn't. That's the way he thinks they should do policing and that's why the Force keeps finding itself in the papers, exposed by lazy prejudice and corner-cutting. He's got the imagination of a pigeon. Dealing with complexity, adapting, making connections? No, Stew and 'his lot', including the Chief, they can't see it or they think there's no time for it. Whatever is deemed to be too difficult gets chucked into a box and nailed shut.

Stewart looks over to his sparring partner, who's stretching out a hamstring on a separate mat at the back of the hall. "I know what's important. My mate works for DNB, Croft's company. They're moving into security. They could be working with us soon."

It's a scary picture. In the background, their budget cuts strategy is like pin the tail on the donkey. They're being forced to play musical chairs, with big brother in the Home Office telling them who they can and can't play with. In the foreground they're chasing traces of Croft like a game of tag. Worse still, it's like sleeping lions. Open your eyes and he's moved in close; him and his men are all around you.

"Introduce me, will you? It'd be good to make a contact. I know nothing about DNB. I need to find out who I need to talk to."

"We're due back on any second. Save you hanging around, I'll have a word with Jonesy and I'll be in the station in the morning when you need my help."

She pragmatically swallows it. If they're such good mates, she doesn't want to send him a warning that this is anything other than personal, so she resists the temptation to ask for the name. That'll be easy to get.

Stewart stands, half pointing to the door. "Glad to hear the Chief has shut down the Tart in the Bin investigation. It was going nowhere. Wouldn't have done your career any good."

Bloody hell. Here we go again. He can't leave it. She stands up too quickly. It's almost a jump. "No. That's not the case. You're out of touch."

She could tell him there's new information. The girl has had another brain scan. There is a map of the fractures, splitting off, getting thinner and fading to less than the wisp of a pencil line. Sitting here watching a martial arts session, Jess knows it wasn't an accident. There's also a picture of the damage to her liver cells, highlighted in electric green, like a live fungus feeding and growing on her vital organ. If the girl was regularly drinking that kind of quantities, Stew will say the incident was just one likely ending for an average Saturday binge. She certainly isn't going to tell him that they have discovered that there were three failed foster placements and no trace of the mum in Derby. Things happen all the time to that group of kids. To Stew, they put themselves at risk. He's made his mind up. It's a free world. A free world where you get what you deserve.

The problem is, on the investigation, she knows Stewart's right. The Chief left her a message, although she stopped listening after the first pompous sentence pronounced itself at an end. He thinks it's not worth investigating further, thinks the girl is not worth additional resources. Bloody men.

CHAPTER 21

ANNE-MARIE

Tuesday 30th November, 5.15pm

Making her way to Owen Cork's office, Anne-Marie's feet drag like she's crossing the Arctic. Although she's after compliance, she'll settle for acceptance that the cuts process is real and starts now. The most likely result is that she'll just about survive, thanks to a recent top-up of elephant-sized painkillers. On the positive side, her slightly blurry delivery and lack of paper might avoid the appearance of a done deal.

Owen's approach is death by bullet point. She speed-reads his presentation, while he rehearses his opening remarks. On TV important people walk briskly up and down the corridors of power. The corridors are short and the actors' lines are sharp, but this corridor is not long enough for discourse and Owen is not an actor. He is dependable, considered, thoughtful and a thoroughly nice accountant, but his mind has no room for big issues, for tackling poverty or regeneration. He knows it's a legal duty, but doesn't think it's his job.

Davina is expecting them to pull off a macabre slash-burn-and-make-the-bodies-disappear trick. This is harder for Owen, because, after 15 years at the top, the organisation is partly made in his image. It's like him, his grey-suited predecessors and the pallid locally elected councillors in their sixties and seventies. That's why Davina wants her to lead these cuts. The Council doesn't like being told what to do. It moves at its own pace; takes as few risks as possible. Organisations are full of people and plenty of people don't like change. Push the system to change and it will push back. Hard. She scans a bullet point at the bottom of the list. It says, '40 per cent overall reduction in the number of managers in the organisation'. Davina hasn't mentioned that. Normally Anne-Marie would be able to tread lightly over shifting sands, but in her current condition keeping her balance is tricky.

Owen slows up as he gets towards the meeting room. His frown lines deepen, he rolls his tongue around his mouth, stops, looks at his watch, the papers in his hand. He doesn't want to do this, but his ego demands that he goes through the door into the affray first. He begins. "Can I ask that we start with open minds and a can-do attitude." The more jargon he uses, the more old-fashioned he sounds. "This won't be easy, but remember we're not turkeys voting for Christmas, we're setting the menu." It's not what she would call humour. She's noticed a tendency for men like Owen, actually nice men, to use meat trade analogies. Talking tough, putting on the butcher's apron, as if that shows leadership. He means shape it or be on it and probably both, thinks Anne-Marie, ever the realist.

"Let me talk you through it." Owen hands out the sheets. Everyone has read it before he's made it to bullet point three, which gives them too much time to think. She thinks about what the 40 per cent means. There are five of them around the table, so that's five down to three, or does it include Owen himself? None of the team make eye contact. They are thinking shall we pack up now? How will we survive this bloodbath and keep some semblance of services in place? Where's the justification? How dare they undervalue us so fundamentally?

Anne-Marie knows, because she's been there before. She can skip the fear, outrage and injustice, leaping straight to the implications. What will that mean for her people, for the Highlands? The team are all pros. None of them voice their judgements on Davina's direction, not here. They are soaking it up, holding fire, until Owen takes a deep breath and says, "I've asked Anne-Marie to do some thinking on how we are going to make all this happen." And then they start.

"Sorry, but why have you chosen Anne-Marie to do this?"

"Shouldn't we have discussed who should lead and how we'll do it?"

"How many meetings have you already had to discuss this?"

"Unless it's robust, transparent and fair, my managers won't contribute."

"Look, we've been through this before and certain departments never take their share."

"Our service is 100 per cent statutory. Any further cuts to us and we will be facing legal challenge."

"We need a staged approach which protects the front line. There's no political heat around the back office. They go first."

"If we sack our most expensive staff, we won't be able to afford the redundancy bill."

"If we're going for another round of voluntary redundancies, my name will be on the list."

It probably will be, one way or other, she thinks.

"There will be strikes."

"We'll have a Baby P on our hands."

"The city will grind to a halt."

The vitriolic burst of steam starts to die away. Anne-Marie massages her knuckles. The chairs in the room are wooden, with cracked blue leather upholstery, nailed down with brass studs. They have been there for years, lumpy, uncomfortable. The team squirm, resilience thin. It's not unreasonable to fear losing your job, but the fear that they'll swing straight from high office to losing their homes and begging on the streets is ridiculous. It reminds her that they've probably always had money. They don't know what it's like to be on benefits. They don't understand how the people on the Highlands survive.

They say they do the job because they want to serve the public, but for Anne-Marie public service isn't just a line trotted out at job interviews. If you mean it, you act on it. It's a political issue and you fight for it. In that moment she decides this. This effort, all this, has to be worth it. If she's going to do this, she wants as much power as possible. She wants Owen's job. That or she'll walk, go and work in a garden centre.

Slowly, rubbing her shoulder, tired, but mentally ready for this, Anne-Marie stands. "We will make this work. We all know it's bollocks. We're about to spend time and energy on an entirely negative endeavour, which everyone else will hate us for. I'm interested in doing the best job we can under the circumstances. If you've got any ideas where we can find even the tiniest space for manoeuvre, I'm listening. Otherwise, see you on the other side – or not."

She marches out of the building and lights up. The nicotine helps, but a shot or two would be good. It's a politically shrewd move by Davina. No-one will grieve for managers at the Town Hall, but it isn't that simple. It means she will also have to cut her own management team by 40 per cent. Steve, the Housing Manager, is from Dundee, coaches a kid's football team. His partner is called Julia. She's a social worker and her job might be at risk as well. It could be a double blow for them. Chris P, her Planning Manager, has twin boys not quite two years old. A sound bloke. Chris S, Transport, has a dad with dementia in a Council Care Home. He's a smart arse and very funny with it, but it will be no joke if the care home closes, too. Audrey, Emergency Planning, her dad also has dementia and she's got a tough cookie act that Anne-Marie admires. Once Audrey actually told one of the councillors to stop talking, said he was wasting taxpayers' money in time and energy, and got away with it. That was legend. Kevin, Economic Development, fantastic, sarcastic, has just bought a wreck of a house in Brum. With no income he won't be building anything and a lot of building won't happen. And there's Sandra, Communities and Neighbourhoods Manager, her mate, who makes the Highlands liveable and never stops. What services don't they need? What expertise can they afford to lose? When people lost their jobs at the tyre factory, the city mourned for them, but what's different? Everyone has mortgages to pay, kids to feed, relationships to hold together. And then there's Bob.

CHAPTER 22

ANNE-MARIE

Despite her bullish performance at the cuts meeting, breakfast is guilt on toast. What should be marmite tastes like a bloody steak. They've agreed to meet for a coffee before work. Bob will understand that he'll be in the pool of managers at risk. He knows the way the political winds are swirling and, like her, he's a professional. Sometimes they administer the medicine, sometimes they swallow it. Because their relationship is public, Anne-Marie knows she'll have to declare a conflict of interest and it might mean she won't actually be able to make the decisions about his job. She'd rather have it in her own hands, though, as it's her best chance of protecting him. She won't be able to protect his team, though, and that will hurt Bob more. She can imagine him making a stand, preferring to lose his own job rather than see his team made redundant. It's the sort of cut off your nose thing he'd do.

They are in a warm coffee shop in the precinct. She's picked a table partially obscured by a pillar in case any Council staff see them, and a double espresso followed by hot milk with marshmallows. Her tactic is to get this over with quickly. She kisses him on the cheek, savouring the boy-like, just-shaved skin.

"So, I more or less told you it all on the phone last night. It's more for less."

Bob doesn't smile. "It's a bit early for Davina's bullshit. I spent most of last night on the phone. We're gearing up for strike action."

She winces. "Hold on, love. Is that the right tactic for now?"

"It's apathy or action. I know you'll have to jump as high as Davina tells you to. Leave the fight to us."

The slight makes her flinch. He's angry already, wanting the fight that's right in front of his face. He never thinks about the strategy, the broader landscape, the long game. She tries again. "I mean there are other ways. Work from within, get a seat at the table, negotiate. That's your strength."

"A seat at the table just gets you harder choices and a sore arse."

Starting the day with an argument isn't a good idea, but at least she'd been right to leave it until the morning. The problem is, she does love him, but she doesn't agree with him.

"Where has striking ever got anyone? Strikes are outdated. They're counterproductive and they'll give the press more ammunition. They pit Council workers against poorly paid private sector workers and we never win."

"Not striking is what's got us here. You don't believe austerity will work. It's more injustice, pension-raiding, unemployment and who benefits?"

"It's not about benefit, but work with me and we can minimise the damage, create solutions." She looks at Bob's neck, noticing there's now a dark Rioja-coloured rash creeping up towards his ear.

"Are you going to give us time to come up with an alternative solution then? A shared service could work, a wider approach with our neighbours..." Reading her body language, he knows that won't happen. She doesn't agree with him on this either. They don't trust their neighbours. It might work in other places, but not here.

"Bloody hell, you didn't even mention it did you?" He slurps his coffee loudly. "You aren't doing your job properly. You're supposed to look at the options for providing services and decide on the basis of what's best for the community, not what's best for your career."

She rocks in the chair, unable to hold herself still. "Piss off, Bob. I'm not having that. You're wrong about the strike. That's about your ego, not about what's best for your members. And you're wrong about your service. You're living in the past."

They both stand up. He looks like he's going to say something, but shakes his head and disappears out the door. She walks to the counter and orders a chocolate muffin. Back at the table, she fishes her phone out of her bag and dials to leave a message. "Morning, Davina. I know we're due to meet tomorrow, but I wanted to warn you. The union reps are planning an early strike. Talk to Owen. Get the legal team to take pre-emptive action. I'll brief you later."

Exasperation has fuelled her day, indignation has got her through the evening. She crawls into bed, exhausted, but convinced that her decision to put all her eggs in Davina's hamper is the right one. It will benefit those that survive the cuts and those who will benefit from a stronger economy. Those who live on the Highlands as well as those who live and work in the city, they will benefit. What other realistic choice is there in the circumstances?

She's not naïve. Davina's benefitted from this situation already. It's not pleasant and they aren't natural allies, but she judges that the devil you know is manageable. The devil she doesn't know is Croft and she doesn't know what the relationship is between Croft and Davina. In Anne-Marie's mind, the link to the Kerry incident casts a dense shadow over their plans. She has to confront Croft about that. And what about the impact of the explosion, the land ownership and the money for the City Centre development? Why does Davina need Croft's money and how much money can a bloke like him actually have? It's clear that Croft benefits if Bob's service is cut. It'll be free trade for all. Davina's reaction to the union action was hotter than she had expected. It might have been rash going straight to Davina, but she would've found out anyway. It might have been pride that made her pick up the phone, but Bob was genuinely wrong.

Almost tumbling in her tiredness, she gives up trying to sleep and decides to go and watch TV for a while. There's an old black and white film on, which turns out to be *The Bridge on the River Kwai*. Anne-Marie starts to engage with it, remembering too late how it finishes. She grabs another painkiller as she watches the Major's body fall and detonate the bomb.

CHAPTER 23

BARRINGTON

Wednesday 1ˢᵗ December, 10.45pm

Once a problem is resolved, Barrington sees no point in dwelling on it. Barely a word has passed between him and Corinne since they visited the old couple, but the nightly bedroom routine gives him no reason to suspect that she is any more unhappy than usual, although the measurements of happiness most commonly used are inadequate and their scientific basis is contested, meaning that any confusion is not down to him alone.

He'd announced that he was going up at 10.45pm as usual. He'd thought a quick shower would be enough, but he found his body tense and the power of the hot water encouraged him to stay longer. Focusing in his mind on his plan of action, he can let the water go to work on the solid knot of muscle lodged beneath his right shoulder blade.

The plan is about tackling the alcohol problem. The others have told him that the budget mess ought to be their priority, but Barrington's not prepared to engage with it until he knows the baseline position, the size and nature of the problem. He knows it'll mean a conversation about St John's Hospital. Budget issues always do. It frustrates him that people continue to flock unchecked to the bloated dysfunctional building in the expectation of a cure, as if an operation or pill can cure everything, particularly a drink problem. Ridiculous! He shakes the water roughly off his head.

The estimated cost of a liver transplant is £66K, yet they know the valuable, fresh organ will be re-poisoned by alcohol. They have re-set 205 broken bones related to domestic violence so far this year; bones that will be easier for a drunken husband to snap a second time. The incidence of fetal alcohol syndrome in newborn babies is increasing and, even to him, it's shocking, but the evidence suggests mothers do not automatically stop drinking once they get home again.

Stop the problems in the first place. Shift the resources to where they would make a real, long-term difference. Who can argue with that? Except that isn't his experience. All around are professionals who agree with him in principle, but in reality aren't prepared to change.

The weight of excuses dressed up as legitimate considerations drags him down. Their reasons aren't logical, they are emotional. They list the challenges as if they were facts, not conditions of the system that can be considered and resolved. They believe change can't happen. They believe it's too difficult. Whatever they say or believe, that shift never happens and public health suffers. The frustration makes him scratch his nails deep into the back of his skull.

He soaps his armpits generously with a sharp, lime-smelling gel. Today he'd been aware of his own ripe sweat. That was completely unacceptable and he ascribed it to the overheated council office in which he'd been imprisoned for most of the afternoon. Without the resources for public health work there will be no prevention activity, no intervention with problem drinkers, no-one qualified to deliver effectively.

Still thinking about his conversation with Mr Sizzle, he considers the landlords as an intriguing option. Sizzle said that he knows about what happened to that girl and there was a clear inference that some of the pub owners were involved. If he can personally force some change, get some purchase on the ones that deliberately sell alcohol irresponsibly, that could make an impact. The thought of action stirs him.

The Burger man said he knew where the bodies were buried. OK, that's a common phrase, Barrington reminds himself, but then he remembers what Anil had said about a trend – bodies plural. He's taken on the pimps in the city before, directly stopped the minibuses. He'd felt good about it. He had been proactive. It had been risky, but it had worked. Why not take a similar approach? The alternative is to go with Jessica Reid. Present a case to the Council and hope they change the licensing arrangements. But that's an unsatisfying slog and his recent experience was a humiliating disaster, not to be repeated. Yes, take on the landlords. Take action. He notices his arousal at the idea. He roughly towels his body. What's my next move? His lips are moving, but no sound emerges.

He is focused, feeling assertive, as he walks around the bedroom. He lays out his bike gear, a dry towel and clean underwear for the morning. Corinne is in bed waiting for him.

"We need to talk Barrington," she says.

He lays his head on her shoulder and she sighs heavily. Lifting his head, he begins kissing her neck, thinking that if he can get the landlords to start actively banning young women who are already drunk from the premises that will help, and he needs to get the bouncers involved, make sure they don't let them in if they have been pre-loading. He traces his wife's shoulder with his lips. Hmmm, and we need to get the policing rotas changed on Fridays and Saturdays, and we need more evidence of the danger those women are in.

"Barrington, stop that. I'm serious."

"What?"

"Barrington, we need to talk. I'm not in the mood."

"I am," he smiles, pulling her hand under the white cotton duvet to feel his erection.

"I know you are, but I'm not. That's an absolute, 100 per cent no, Barrington. Do you hear?" It's the sort of thing she says to

Nelson. "I know you're under pressure with the job and everything, but we aren't talking and this is serious."

He peers closely at her face in the light of the purple bedside lamp and notices the frown line on her forehead deepen. She looks tired. "Serious? We haven't had an argument recently? How exactly have things changed? I know I am working more hours. Is that it? " He holds her hand.

"No, that's not it and you don't seem to have noticed how much I've been working either. I need some space. I think you should go and stay at Hermin's for a while. We can talk tomorrow evening. I'll ask Hermin to babysit."

He's already shaking his head. "I'm going out."

"You don't go out on Wednesdays. What's so important?"

"It's important work." It's the best time to talk to the burger van man again and Barrington has overheard colleagues talking about the football match this week. Burgers and football. He recognises the positive correlation.

Corinne starts to interrupt, then stops again. He sees there are no tears in her eyes. She looks calm. "With you it's always going to be work, but I'm serious. Our relationship is in serious trouble."

"This is news. Whatever the problem is, just tell me and I'll fix it," he says, stimulated by the Sizzle idea and how he can build it into a useful bike ride. Nothing too exhausting, though. He wants to focus on what information he can get.

"It's not a practical problem I'm talking about, it's my feelings. How I feel."

"Let's talk about it on Thursday. Is that OK?" Barrington's mind is bright, his body alert.

"Don't treat me like a member of your staff. I can tell you're still thinking about work. Barrington, this is about emotions..."

He ignores her.

"Don't pretend you don't know what I'm talking about. This is desire, but it's not just sex. It's you feeling something, wanting something. You put your head on my shoulder, you want comfort. Why can't you see that?"

"It's…" Barrington stops, realising this is problematic.

"You say statistics and logic are everything, but you're kidding yourself, because it's convenient, because you can't be bothered to put the effort in. Or is it me who's the fool? I look after you, but my needs don't come into it."

He says nothing.

"You pack some clothes. I'll call Hermin and explain you'll be round first thing." Corinne gets out of bed and goes down the hall to Nelson's room.

He can't imagine what life would be like without her, because speculating about scenarios isn't his strong point. Their relationship has been a constant feature of the last 16 years. He feels no fear. It's just unimaginable. His desire subsides.

CHAPTER 24

BARRINGTON

Thursday 2nd December, 7am

Aunt Hermin's house seems smaller to him now than when he was a boy and he went to live there after his mother died. The logical explanation that he is now twice the height he was when he first arrived doesn't quite cover it. Once when he'd accidently dropped a carton of orange on the floor, he'd had to clean it up on his hands and knees, scrubbing it with a rough rectangle of green-backed sponge. In his memory it took him hours. Now he's pacing back and forth across the kitchen in two steps.

"Sit down, son. Let me make you some hot chocolate."

His aunt almost fills the kitchen herself these days.

"Do you mind if I open the back door?" he asks. This allows him to step up and down on the door jar and to avoid the oppressive heat. Hermin has always wanted her house to be as hot as the Caribbean.

"I need to make sense of it. I don't understand. Why do I have to leave?"

"What did she tell you?" Hermin passes him a mug with Coventry Cathedral on it that he must have used a thousand times before. He notes the handle is chipped. It must be full of germs. Barrington slams the cup down on the kitchen worktop. The handle snaps.

"She thinks the marriage is over, but she can't decide that on her own, can she? She says we're too different. Everyone is different. And she says that it isn't the best environment to bring

Nelson up in, but she knows I just can't agree with that. All boys need their fathers."

"Yes, but some don't have the luxury and they turn out fine. Look at you." Hermin smiles proudly.

"I work at being the best father and the best husband I can. I ask her to tell me exactly how she wants me to do that, so there are no misunderstandings. I have a stable career, work hard, earn a good salary. That was enough for her when we got married."

"Well…" he can't tell if she's laughing at him, "…that's not all of it, is it? You've got to give her time."

He sits on the step looking out into the garden. "It can't just be this thing with the old couple. We've had disagreements about work before. Things haven't always been easy, I know she thinks I'm hard to deal with, but we make it work." There's some analysis required. He has to work it through, what factors influence the success of their relationship. They've managed to hold it together for 16 years. Not now, though. He needs more information and realises that there isn't much. Has the alcohol work made the difference?

"You stay there if you want to." Hermin pats him on the shoulder.

He can't stay still, but the early morning mist is restful on his dry eyes.

"Corinne called me to ask if she can bring Nelson round here tomorrow."

His head jerks round to face her. "Where's she going? What time?"

"She's going to call into a family celebration of some colleagues. She told me she'll only be out for an hour, about 8pm. Me and Nelson can watch TV and you two can go out and talk."

"Aunty," he says slowly, playing with the 'tee' sound, like he used to say it as a child, "do you think I've changed?"

"No son, I don't think so, but maybe that's the problem."

CHAPTER 25

CROFT

Thursday 2nd December, 2pm

The view from the fairway allows him to see connections, provides him with quality intelligence that supports his business. He spots others, who, like him, are not there for pleasure. Like him, he imagines they can play most sports competently, but what they genuinely enjoy is perfecting the technique and they are selectively competitive. Bringing down his par, tracking his scores is easy. He does numbers; reconciles accounts, calculates compound interest, the odd exchange rate.

He'd gut the Club House, strip it all out and start again. It's a 1950s country house. It smells of wet dog and the large hall clock ticks too loudly. They've re-created their living rooms, when they should be thinking about an open plan area, glass extension maybe, like the place he went to in Portugal.

It's not that he doesn't like some of them as individuals. Some are self-made men, although they tend to be too brash for his liking, too soft, no killer instinct. Some are old money and, although he would never have been on their radar before, now he's got more resources than they could dream about. That the whole place is a cliché isn't a problem. Since his nomination at the Golf Club was accepted, the questions have stopped. To Croft, it's validation.

He lets the Leader of the Council tee off first. He has no problem playing with a woman. She doesn't slow them down. He lets the Police Chief go next, keeping his distance, preferring not to have his back to the old man. Some habits die hard.

CHAPTER 26

JESSICA

Thursday 2nd December, 2.30pm

The Chief's diary was ambiguous. Probably on the Golf Course. Jess is determined to drive out there if needs be. It would wind him up, but tough. Following procedures, waiting for the Chief to consider the situation, has lead to a loss of momentum around Laura Awsworth. Disinterest and inactivity at the station add insult, but Jess has found a way to sell it to him without it looking like he's going back on a decision. The Chief says his priority is gangs and now there's a link between a gang and the Girl in the Bin. That his priorities conflict, ebb and flow, is understood; it's become a way of life. The important thing is to get to the heart of what needs to change in the city.

The Chief doesn't answer his phone, so she tries the Wharncliffe Golf Club direct, thinking he might still be lunching. He's not, but she uses her most formal Deputy Commander voice to find out who he's playing with. Councillor Clarke and Mr Croft. She wonders if this was what Stewart meant, that Croft is part of this club, although how he knows isn't clear. Croft is no longer a rogue landlord, he's joined the Golf Club. It's a cliché and the cliché is the problem.

The city seems to contract in her mind. They know each other well enough to spend comfortable hours wandering the rolling greens. Well enough for the Leader to suggest that the Chief might be minded to change down a gear on the Girl in the Bin investigation and the work on alcohol? Well enough for Davina to direct Anne-Marie to muffle any complaints about landlords? Croft would certainly argue against a tougher approach to licensing, but she doubts there are even any arguments. She'll need to think this through and talk to Anne-Marie again, because their motivation isn't clear to her.

There will be a political angle, no doubt. Jess can leap out of bed if it's a question of social justice, especially justice for women and girls, especially when they end up in bins, but when it's about voting and winners and losers she loses interest quickly. She wonders how anyone in the Police could come to a different conclusion. That's what she sees year after year – women and girls, poor women and some poor men. They are the victims and if they aren't direct victims, they still suffer as a result of the crime. Mothers of stabbed boys, daughters of alcoholic fathers, school friends of abducted girls. Jess' office is too small today. Hemmed in with procedure, files, looked down on by badges and certificates, she knows she needs to get out more. Tomorrow will be a better day to make the case to the Chief, to argue for looking at the gang and testing his reaction to the licensing question. She's better informed this time and more aware how the odds are stacked.

Pleased to have a diversion, she sees Frank's number appear on her phone.

"It's kicked off at the College this afternoon. There was a fight involving the lad I mentioned, the ex-student in the fire video, Leeroy Wilson. Small beer for you, but I wanted to let you know."

"Thanks Frank. Were Adam and Ben involved?" She has to ask. They'd just been given a caution for the school fire and it's not good news if they're now involved in a fight.

Frank can't help sounding defensive. "Adam says he was trying to get Ben out of there. I'm worried Adam seems totally in awe of Leeroy and pretty scared at the same time."

"What was the fight about?"

"I was told it was a 'supply chain issue', if you can believe that. Seems a fair few of them work for this DNB. Adam says it's not a gang. They all work together, so they hang out together."

"Doing what?"

"He wouldn't go into detail about that. Something to do with a factory outlet, making collections and returns, cleaning up local sites. There was an argument over a rival operation doing the deliveries."

"And that's a code for...?"

"Your guess is as good as mine. Anyway, we'll do a College investigation. I'll let you know if anything else comes up and..."

There's more? Now a fog horn blasts in Jess' ear. Frank says it's small beer, but something's definitely going on and she'll make sure she gets Jonesy involved. She doesn't want to be accused of turning a blind eye because of Adam or Ben's involvement and she won't give anyone an opportunity to say she's played it anything other than straight. "If there's more, Frank, it's better that I hear it now."

"No, not that. It's not work at all. Did you get that email I sent about the party for my sixtieth? Don't think I got a reply. It's this Friday, but of course I'll understand if you've already got something on."

"God, sorry, Frank. The last few weeks have been so busy I'd forgotten all about it."

"Call in for a drink. It's at the Denham Suite. My colleagues have organised it. You'll know at least half the people there."

"Will they want to see me?" Jess is thinking of Adam and Anne-Marie in particular, but is sensitive to the fact that having a police officer at a party can change the dynamic. "I don't want to spoil the night for you."

"Not at all, love. We'll be pleased to see you and you'll be very welcome. You've been great."

Alright, she thinks, maybe it's not the right time to be going to a party, but it'll be good to loosen her limbs, do her bobbing from one foot to the other impression of a dance. And good to see Anne-Marie on neutral territory, get back on an even keel. It'll make a change from another Friday night at home alone and it'll make a change to feel welcome.

CHAPTER 27

ANNE-MARIE

Thursday 2nd December, 6.30pm

The self-dissolving stitch in Anne-Marie's shoulder seems solidly stuck. It was itchy and now feels hot and swollen. She suspects it's infected, but can't quite reach it to put on some antiseptic. Bob hasn't been around to do it for her. She's looked at his text twenty times.

It's over. Don't ring. I can't speak to you.

That can't be the last word. They could always talk. That was the attraction. What was important was that she could always cut through the domestic, test ideas and notions, dig around at given truths, get to the heart of things. This is what you feel like when you get dumped at the age of forty. Suddenly seeing all his good bits and none of the bad, panicked that you'll never have sex again, let alone meet anyone else, and resentful that this story will be about her lack of principles and not his inability to see the other side of the coin.

She looks at her reflection in the lift's mirror and is taken aback to see that she appears normal. Her hair is already way past the point of needing a cut. She licks a finger, smoothing it over her eyebrows and under her eyelashes to remove a smudge of mascara. Davina's immaculate appearance has meant that Anne-Marie has had to pay attention, upgrade her wardrobe. It all adds to the escalating cost of management.

There are no evening meetings tonight and the third floor is dead. The door to Davina's office is shut, but she can hear Davina's laughter, although there's a sarcastic edge to it. On another day Anne-Marie might chose to walk home in the fog of work, let it lie and see what emerges tomorrow. What's stopping her is that she's got to the point where she can't proceed without hearing Davina's plan. She needs answers to her questions to get her story straight and have a better chance of sleeping tonight.

"Let me sort out some tea," Owen offers.

She takes a fortifying cup of builders' tea, which makes her think of Frank. Davina is animated, walking quickly around her office. "Let's get a breath of fresh air in here," she announces dramatically, as if she's on a ramble in Shropshire. "We want to talk you through our exciting development."

Our development? Davina's and Owen's? How much progress have they made without her? She does the deals here. It's her legitimate role to talk to developers and it's their role to stay well out of it. For their own sake as much as hers, they need to be clean and to be seen as clean. For an old man who she'd thought was on the brink of retirement, Owen's like a puppy, lapping up the attention of an indulgent owner, seemingly unaware that Davina would just as easily have him put down.

"We will be the ones to finally get the Meadows development moving." Davina beams, meaning that they will do what the previous administration failed to do in good times. Timing is everything in small city economies like theirs, thinks Anne-Marie. They are always the first to sink when there's a recession, because they haven't modernised, they still have too many metal bashers. Investors don't rush here because the returns are low. It's iron filings not gold dust. Anne-Marie fidgets. Get on with it and make it good. She needs to be persuaded that whatever it is will significantly benefit the city, especially if it means they are cutting public services deeper to deliver it. They'll need her to deliver it and she'll need it to be deliverable, so that she can justify it – to herself, to the Highlands, and to Frank.

Davina does a mini-circuit of her office. She's all loose wrists and splayed fingers. "The development will help us deliver the economy that's appropriate for us. We are taking a pragmatic view of what is likely to be most successful here. We know it's radical, but we need to be bold."

Appropriate normally means limited and lacking ambition, and she doesn't associate Davina and Owen with bold, unless it's bold as in unacceptable.

"We're being pragmatic. We recognise we'll never attract any of the top 100 companies to the area and we're unlikely to pull in the top 250 either. We need to work to our strengths. We can't rely on shopping-led regeneration or upmarket retail when nearly 40 per cent of our population are on benefits. Any private investment will need a return and we need to work with those locally who want to invest."

The build-up is unnecessary and even more irritating, partly because this is true and because she's been saying it for years.

"Our development ideas will provide over a thousand jobs for our core labour market..."

That number gets Anne-Marie's attention. She could go with that.

Davina continues, "I've been accused in the past of not prioritising local people, but I won't have that with this scheme, because we'll invest in an on-site training centre."

Just get on with it. What we are going to build?

Owen can't help himself jumping in. "A quality, statement development for the city, this will be an entertainment-led centre – family restaurants and wine bars, a hotel, a destination nightclub, an upmarket gentlemen's club, a regional casino. We are talking to a major local landowner and investor. There'll be a bit of brewery land in there, too."

Anne-Marie focuses hard on the teacup. The handle is thin. She might break it. That's it – a bloody super-casino.

Davina adds, "We know it won't be popular with everyone and there will be wider planning implications that may well take the decision out of the realm of our committee, which wouldn't necessarily be a bad thing. They do this sort of thing in the US. It will put us on the map. The policy framework was established by the previous government and we'll use that to ensure our opposition councillors can't object too much."

Is that really it? She can already see a blizzard of objections, hailstones the size of footballs.

"I'm not prepared for this city to stagnate. It's not just jobs, it's spending power. I want people to have money in their pockets to support local shops. There are supply chain opportunities and existing businesses will benefit."

Anne-Marie holds her tongue, in truth because she doesn't know where to start.

"Owen has done a basic business case. We want you to go through it in detail. It's the only realistic option for this city. You might find it personally challenging to deliver, in some ways I feel the same, but we can't afford to confuse our individual moral positions with our collective responsibility."

She knows she ought to say something, but a sentence can't form without words and they've gone into hiding. Davina holds her hand out to Anne-Marie like an opera singer finishing an aria.

"We see this as providing the jobs we need for residents in our most deprived communities. We can't keep funding your neighbourhood work unless it delivers jobs. Here's the vehicle to make that happen. What do you think?"

There's an awkward silence as the mists clear.

"Er, yes, I can see the jobs bit. That's great." Davina has just set out a deal. If Anne-Marie delivers this, the neighbourhood work stays, but she commits the whole city to an economy in the likeness of Croft.

"This is it." Owen pulls out a site plan. It's a red line around the Meadows and a few neighbouring sites, slap bang between the City Centre and the Highlands. It looks bigger than she'd expected.

"Forty hectares. We'll put in our land for a peppercorn and we'll provide support, but private money will be the driver. We'll get some flashy looking architects' drawings done. It's irresistible."

She manages a nod.

"This scheme is happening. Your role," Davina says, looking at Anne-Marie not Owen, "is to drive out the benefits for the city. Sell it to the community. Make it work for us."

Anne-Marie judges her best bet is to beat a speedy retreat. "A park in the City Centre will be fantastic. A thousand jobs and a training centre is great," she says, trying to remember the positives. "I'll leave you with your plans and pick up the detail tomorrow. I've got some work to do for first thing tomorrow." That generates a harsh laugh, as if Anne-Marie was joking.

"Marvellous," Davina concludes. "We'll leave the numbers for another time."

Anne-Marie is dismissed.

CHAPTER 28

DAVINA

Thursday 2nd December, 7pm

This used to be a nice place. Her finger traces the red outline on the plan. She can't remember this site particularly, but wiping clean the dereliction is a must. The idea of an architectural competition appeals and she'd like a traditional market. The sort of thing they do in the villages, homemade cheese, cottage industries. She feels sorry for those without the drive and energy to use what they've got. They seem unable to bake a cake, let alone organise their lives. What they need is employment. Working provides structure, teaches them skills and team work, allows them to earn enough to feed and clothe a family. Employers are the backbone of Britain.

People in this city need direction. It's their own fault if they can't see what's good for them. Gigantic screens are one of her bug bears. A man from the Highlands Estate once said to her, "If the Government are stupid enough to pay me the benefits, who am I to refuse?" He'd just bought a new TV. "I'm just doing my duty and consuming, aren't I?" She'd blown her proverbial fuse.

It wasn't as if her family hadn't been through ups and downs of their own. Her grandfather was a bank manager who'd financed many of the businesses in the city. He managed assets and risks, made tidy profits. For her father, however, the risk was the fun bit. He'd found nothing worth investing in locally. With his list of business interests (the American car dealership, the vineyard in the desert, importing antiquities from the Middle East) speculate rarely meant accumulate. Luckily it didn't have to. There was always her grandfather, always connections, always capital to smooth things out and just about enough money for school fees, although cheaper schools had had to be found. She'd learned to be resourceful, quick to get stuck in, to make her mark, never to flap. These things sort themselves out in the end. It had done her no harm.

It would be the same with Pleisureland. Like her grandfather, the Council has assets to cover it. That's one of the reasons she likes Daniel. He has assets. Another is that, like her father, he's an entrepreneur. Not afraid of a risky enterprise and able to magic money from nowhere. She can leave it to him and if it doesn't come off she can simply move on.

CHAPTER 29

ANNE-MARIE

Thursday 2nd December, 7.30pm

In the lift on the way back down Anne-Marie sees her eyes are glassy. She feels as if cold wet sand is being shovelled on top of her from different directions. It's packing her in, fast approaching her neck. The Las Vegas of the Midlands will create jobs and training, but for whom? Lap dancers, croupiers, part-time bar staff? This is all Davina thinks the people of this city are capable of. Anne-Marie agrees upmarket might be unrealistic, but downmarket? Gambling drags violence and prostitution in its wake. They have obviously never been to Blackpool on a Tuesday morning in November. Grim.

She's argued with Frank before that any job is a good job. People hate nuclear waste plants, but they create jobs and communities just want jobs. Bob took that line, too, but Frank had disagreed and now she's forced into considering it in her city, for her estate, for the future jobs that Adam and Ben will want.

Pleisureland. Croft has land and money. Davina has Council land, no money, but licenses to trade and build. It's a match made in free-market heaven, but Davina doesn't know the half of what Croft brings with him. Anne-Marie gets out of the lift on the first floor, grabs her coat and heads out of the building, towards the taxi rank. There's not a taxi in sight. She walks down to the off-licence at the bottom of Cardinal Row and buys a litre of vodka. Spending the rest of Thursday night alone is a good option. She can't face the Mechanics. It would be good to see Adam, but not now. Getting herself injured in an explosion is the only way she's managed to spend any time with her son lately and she's not in a hurry to repeat that.

Back home she leaves the vodka and sticks to red wine. Midweek vodka feels too desperate and the dulling effect of red wine is what's needed. She leans back on the sofa. Never mind the dubious development with dubious developers, there's also the unwelcome prospect of having to dish out redundancy letters just before Christmas and the breakdown of her relationship with Bob weighs heavily. Trying to be grown-up, when you're a grown-up, is hard. The feeling of being buried is back. Sand is in her mouth, it presses on her eyelids. She can barely blink, but it's also somehow safe. The constraint takes away the choice. She can tell herself, at least for tonight, that, like everyone else, she's just doing her job, just earning a crust.

CHAPTER 30

ANNE-MARIE

Friday 3rd December, 7am

She wakes up feeling better, but is immediately hit by a giant spade, thumping down the last bit of sand over her head. It's a text from Andrea.

Going ahead with demo at Three Lions. You coming?

If it had been her daughter who'd been raped she wouldn't have let it lie either, although she likes to think that no daughter of hers would put herself in such a vulnerable position. She'd wondered how Kerry was doing and tried not to think about the Girl in the Bin. Placards outside the Council and a rally at the Licensing Committee meeting should get the *Post* interested. It's not exactly UK Uncut, but the *Post* needs to fill space. There's no escaping the fact that she'll have to talk to Croft. Chewing it over with a sympathetic ear would help, but who'll offer that. Not Bob or Adam or Sandra. That pretty much leaves Frank and it's his sixtieth party tonight. Raucous exposure is the opposite of what she needs. Still, she's pleased not to have opened the litre of vodka on the side. It's a small result, but they count.

On the way in she smokes a frosty fag out of the car window and then picks up a double espresso. Arriving in the office, she leaves a voicemail message for Danny Croft asking for an urgent meeting. She doesn't need to like him, she tells herself. It's hardly likely given the circumstances, but what's important is that he's someone she can work with and if he's willing to be reasonable maybe she can offer him a solution.

In reception she smells the weekend. It is strongest in the corridors nearest the IT Department where the bins are full of paper napkins that have mopped up drips of runny egg and wiped bacon fat from greasy fingertips. Near corporate finance there are more open doors than usual. The smells are of ripe shirts undone, sleeves rolled up to the elbow, as the temperature from a week's worth of over-heating overrides the need for ties. It shores up her mood. Wandering past Education she gets a mild mix of perfumes that could be part of a going-straight-out-after-work kit. The Council seems to speed up on Friday mornings. People walk faster as if in anticipation of the school bell. Before she can see Croft, though, there's a cuts meeting to endure.

The Deputy Leader of the Council, Councillor Bond, is another of Davina's duvets. Unusually he's an ex-bus driver, but his views are narrower than a cycle lane. Anne-Marie has worked with the Partnership Manager, Zoe, trawling through a list of the Government-funded activities that are first on the chopping block. Zoe looks ghostly; washed out skin, blond hair and a white shirt, without a jacket or jewellery. She is sitting in front of the window with the road, cars and buildings behind her. Anne-Marie sees that her face is a combination of shock and repressed anger, but can offer her no comfort. What Councillor Bond sees is an opportunity to talk about his life history.

He says to her, "Young lady, you won't remember the war. We learned the hard way what austerity is and how to make do. In the fifties, we left our damp terrace and we were driven in a mini-bus to this smashing new part of the city and told to choose a brand new house. We were given the keys that day. I worked on the buses, did alright, thank you very much, but we wanted better for our kids. My son's an accountant now."

Zoe nods, but avoids eye contact with the old man. Anne-Marie's heard it 123 times before. As he speaks, he is crossing out budget line after budget line.

Old people's luncheon clubs – £25,000
Vulnerable people central heating and boiler replacements –
£590,000
Health visitors, emergency food vouchers, domestic violence
support – £264,000
Improved cleanliness and green flag parks – £332,000
Homeless support worker – £28,000
Free bus pass removal bus company top-up – £817,000
Modern apprenticeships contribution – £156,000
Ready, Steady, Work scheme – £47,000
Adult literacy level 1 – £89,000
Targeted support for the recently redundant – £197,000
Local construction company support – £345,500.

"Look dear, it's all about the economy, getting this place back on its feet," he drones on. "It's not about fancy strategies or big words like 'regeneration'. No, it's about local businesses employing more of our people. I drink with some of these private sector chaps these days. Clever they are. I have every confidence they'll get this city working. Yes, young lady, in five years' time, you won't recognise the place."

"Councillor Bond," Zoe says, "I've been keeping a running total. These cuts amount to £2,890,500. That means 220 full-time equivalent posts are now at risk."

He blows his nose loudly. "Got to be done. On to the next, eh."

That's the livelihood of 220 people and their families, including Zoe's. Her face is now despondent. She's losing her composure. Bond is pretending it's not political, but it's his Government driving the cuts. He's got no problem with it, though, opportunistically seizing his moment to unpick what's gone before. Anne-Marie is incensed, but has nothing to trade in this situation. She's gambling on a bigger deal and can offer Zoe nothing but a quick exit out of the room.

"Thanks, Zoe. I'll pass by your office later."

As she herself is leaving, she picks up a message from Croft suggesting a drink at lunchtime. She prefers to meet in the Council offices, but doesn't want to bump into Davina or Bob. She pushes the meeting back until 6pm, when it'll be quiet.

Croft walks unhurriedly towards the Council House. An early evening frost creeps outwards, tracking the shadows of the buildings. Anne-Marie wonders how Croft's facial muscles can be so relaxed, dressed only in his Friday night shirt, but a shiver would show weakness. This encounter is a test to see how he responds. It ought to be a test for her to listen openly to what he has to say, but after the cuts meeting she relishes the opportunity for open hostility.

He's almost at the front entrance before he sees her. She doesn't bother to smile. "I need some fresh air. Do you mind a walk around the block?" He looks surprised, but says nothing. She leads off.

"Davina's briefed me on the development. It looks exciting."

"It's good you're on board."

"I am."

"It will turn this place around. We aren't borrowing to invest. This is my land, my money, and Davina has assured me it will progress without a problem."

It's not Anne-Marie's style to hold back. "We already have a problem, though. A specific one at the Three Lions. The police are investigating a date rape incident. The girl is underage and we've had a complaint from the community."

He stops to light up. She can't read anything into his face.

"I can see it's a problem for you, but it's got nothing to do with us. We leave our managers to run things for themselves. They're self-employed. That's our business model. We're not a brewery tying our landlords into beer volumes. It's up to them how they make their money. We own a range of buildings. That one doesn't have our name over the door. We just provide services and collect the rent."

It was a good idea to walk, because she doesn't have to look directly at him. His business model, for crying out loud. He's hiding his lack of responsibility in jargon. The wind whips around the back of the Council House, gnawing at her calves.

"When this kicks off, we all get bad publicity. What are you going to say?"

"Nothing. We are talking about a multi-million pound scheme, a thousand jobs. If there's a press problem, you sort that out, sit on it, whatever. We aren't interested."

Anne-Marie hugs her coat. The impact on Kerry, Andrea and the community isn't just a press problem. The arrogant assumption that she can just sit on a story like that, and that she would want to, stops her in her tracks. Practically speaking there's a demo about to take place in a pub he's connected to. Whether he likes it or not, there will be news.

"This development is an important investment and I don't expect you to bring this sort of crap to us," he reiterates.

Interesting. Might he be over-stretching himself? He clearly wouldn't talk to Davina like that.

"The value of your investment can go up or down," she says coldly.

His voice slows. "You mean to tell me some tart has too many, shags someone in the street and then cries rape, and that's going to affect this deal? No. I don't think so."

He's shown himself too soon. In five minutes he's gone from investment in the city to shagging in the street. She lights a cigarette after all. It gives her a moment to re-focus.

"Let's keep this professional," she says simply. "I'm warning you about a situation, but it's possible I can give you a solution. You and your managers have a business to run and licenses to think about. You need permission from councillors to run that business and the same goes for any development scheme. If this scheme is going to happen, we need to trust each other."

She's talking as if trust is her strong suit, but he's not playing. Maybe she's more like him than she wants to recognise. They are at the top of Corporation Street and she needs to be getting back to the Council House and away to Frank's party. "The Police will do their job, but to be absolutely clear, you need to clean your act up now." She says this not knowing if Kerry has come forward or not.

"We're not worried about an investigation. It won't have any comeback on us."

She wonders how he can be so sure.

He continues, "But as a favour to you we'll play along, for the sake of working together. You give our man a slap across the wrist..."

A favour to me? Jesus, she's going to have to deal with him for the next two years. Anne-Marie tries to sound final. "You accept an extra condition on your license, provide training and take the underage drinking policy seriously. One more strike and I guess the Council will have no choice but to walk away from the development as well."

"You need to talk to your boss again. Davina's going nowhere. This so called demonstration, you'll make sure that doesn't happen?"

"That's nothing to do with me. A generous donation to rape crisis might be a good idea, though."

He ignores that and she's had more than enough for now.

"Right. I need to go."

She smells the burger van of Mr Sizzle, it's just off to the right and will do to line her stomach before the party. Croft follows her.

"How's Bob then? Still in work?"

She suspected he'd be tougher than other developers and that is the case, but he's also more spiteful. He's hinting that either he's said something to Davina about Bob or is deliberately winding her up. Neither is good, but she doesn't take the bait. As she blows out, the smoke crystalises. In cold air she starts to see herself more clearly than Croft. She'd also said something to Davina about Bob and Davina wanted to sack him on the spot.

"He's fine," she mutters, "although we were caught in that explosion last Friday."

"Lucky that," he says flatly, making her wonder if he means the explosion was lucky for him. "You look alright," he adds. It's not a compliment. She stubs out her fag before approaching the counter.

"Burger, please."

Seeing the big burger man makes her smile for the first time in a few days. Maybe because he looks even more miserable than she does.

"Alright, boss?" Mr Sizzle asks.

Croft orders the same, then picks up a call. Her mind is drawn back to the explosion, the nod he'd got from his bouncer before it had happened. Anne-Marie offers Sizzle money for both burgers.

"You're quiet tonight. That's not like you," she says.

"It's not you, bab. Must be something to do with the company you're keeping." Sizzle looks at Croft, but doesn't make eye contact.

She bites into the burger, catching the big man scratching his arse and wrapping Croft's burger.

"No rest for the suits or the dirty money." Sizzle turns his back on them.

CHAPTER 31

JESSICA

Friday 3rd December, 8pm

The Denham Suite is already filling up with colleagues, friends and family. The function rooms above the old Co-op are the perfect choice for Frank's sixtieth. It's down at the quieter end of the High Street, just far enough from the hordes of young people gearing up for another Friday night on the stupid juice. That it's so different in here has to be something to do with the fact that everyone has been to a family party or wedding do there at some point in their lives. It's decent, cheap enough and copes well with a hundred people without being either a sweatbox or a corporate cavern.

Jess remembers that Anne-Marie and Frank had their wedding reception in the room next door. She waves at Frank and Frank Senior in his wheelchair in the corner, wearing his red tartan slippers. Random family members whose faces seem familiar swarm around them. She's struck by Adam's smile, sees he's trying to do the right thing and trying to hide his guilt about the worry he's caused his old dad in the last few weeks. She'll do the rounds later, she's a bit part tonight. Her priority is Anne-Marie. The wall she's been banging her head against remains unmoved. She's not dislodged a single brick in three weeks. Laura, the Girl in the Bin, still so vivid and clear in her own head, hasn't been the driver for change she'd hoped she'd be and what that says about the world view of her colleagues has been hanging gloomily over her ever since it happened. Everyone else in the city has forgotten about Laura, but patterns are beginning to emerge in Jess' own connecting wall.

Jonesy has mentioned there's been an accusation of date rape linked to a Croft pub. They are unsure if there'll be a formal statement, but the parents seem determined to make something of it. She doesn't believe it's a coincidence, but what has she got? There might be a link between the pub and the Chickenshack gang, who might or might not be working illegally for DNB, Croft's company. This morning she'd also had a message from Anil. He wanted to talk about his family and the Booze2U business. There had been another violent incident, on the same day she'd visited Frank at the College and there'd been the fight about 'the supply chain'. Another connection maybe, but still, hand on heart, no real evidence.

Anne-Marie is at the bar. Her clothes say 'I'm here to party', but Jess notices her face is pinched and her body tense. She gives her a quick hug and gets a stoic sigh in return.

"I'm freezing," Anne-Marie says. "Let me get you a drink? Fancy a double? I'm going to struggle through tonight without some assistance."

"Still suffering from the explosion? How's your shoulder?"

"Oh that? Yes, it's fine, I think... might be infected."

"Are you OK? Where's Bob?"

Anne-Marie stutters, "He's not coming. Long week I think."

Jess picks up on a shaky force field.

"Look, there's something I want to talk to you about. It's not the licensing stuff, but it's not for now."

Jess says quickly, "If it's Kerry and Andrea, I know."

"Good, but there's also... maybe I'll call you tomorrow?"

Jess nods.

"Let's try and enjoy ourselves tonight. Not enough dancing opportunities these days!" Anne-Marie manages a smile as Frank makes his way over to them.

"Happy birthday, love. Can I get you anything to drink?"

"I've drunk too many Cokes already. I'll be on the bog all night at this rate. I'm sure Adam will do his best to help his old man out." Frank is buoyant.

"Congratulations and less of the old," says Jess.

"If you're old that makes us middle-aged and I'm not having that," agrees Anne-Marie, meaning it.

Frank bends in close to her ear, but because of the music he speaks loud enough for Jess to hear. "Adam has promised to behave and we'll have a dance later, won't we."

A group of colleagues engulf Frank.

"Where do you want to sit?" Jess asks.

"Not with the family," she replies, looking at the various options available. "No-one linked to the Council either. Bad news travels fast."

They're both surprised to see Barrington push open the double-doors. A woman, presumably his wife, marches over and gives Frank a hug. Jess can see Barrington hovering, examining the ceiling, on his face is the kind of severe frown he usually takes to Council meetings.

"I thought you and him were best mates these days," remarks Anne-Marie.

"That's only work and I thought we'd agreed not to go there." Since Shaz had reminded her of Barrington's family connections, Jess has been unsure how to speak to him. She's also had a worrying email, clearly highly frustrated, telling her that 'he now favoured a more direct approach,' whatever that meant.

"That'll do." Anne-Marie has spotted a small, empty table next to the DJ box. "I'm aiming to be up dancing most of the night."

"In those shoes?"

"You mean these black suede Jimmy Choos with a unique T-bar and amber buckle?"

"Since when do you care about shoes?"

"My hairdresser told me to update my look and that these shoes are an investment – if I don't break my neck in them first, that is."

They are getting settled at the table when Adam comes over.

"You don't remember, Jess, do you?" Anne-Marie puts her arm round his shoulder. "She's a top police officer these days."

Adam flushes, brighter than the lights of the DJ booth. "Hello." He holds out a polite but awkward hand.

"Get me a lager will you, mum."

"The cheek of you. Get one off your dad."

"Not with your friend Ben tonight?" Jess is winding him up slightly. Adam physically steps back.

"Er, no. How do you know Ben?"

Anne-Marie laughs. "You think adults know nothing and don't talk to each other." She slaps his backside.

Jess holds her tongue. Talking to each other is not actually Anne-Marie's strong point.

"Go on, now. You don't need to entertain us."

Adam looks relieved. "Yeah, laters," he says and makes off in Frank's direction.

"Thanks, Jess." Anne-Marie looks protective, almost watery. "Adam's got a good future ahead of him. He's not a bad kid and he's already knuckling down."

"I didn't do anything."

"No, you did," says Anne-Marie, picking up Jess' hand, holding on tight.

The DJ knows his audience. The dance floor is soon packed with young kids running around, ten-year-old girls giggling and holding hands, a few mums are hovering. Anne-Marie drinks quickly and gives it twenty minutes before asking for some funk and kicking off her shoes. On the other side of the dance floor they both see Adam hide his head in his hands. At that age all parents are mortifying, although this is tame. Jess remembers their teenage selves and being scared by Anne-Marie letting rip in her bedroom to James Brown and Jimmy Hendrix. The sex and politics in the music had seemed too threatening for Jess at the time. Maybe it's the association of the music or the movement of her body, but Anne-Marie's mood seems to have shifted. Jess had decided to drive tonight, but wishes now she'd had a drink and could let herself go. Barrington still looks uncomfortable and isn't talking to his wife. Taking a rest from the dancing, she goes over to introduce herself.

"Hi. I'm Jess, a sort of colleague of Dr Edwards – Barrington. I just wanted to say hello. I didn't realise you'd be here."

"I'm Corinne." The woman holds out her hand. "I'm the one who was invited tonight."

"Deputy Commander Reid," cuts in Barrington. It's brusque even by his standards, but from the looks of things she suspects that it's nothing to do with her. His eyes are flicking around the room at speed. One hand is covering an ear, the other rubs the metal top of an empty conference chair. Corinne looks directly at Jess, to engage her on her own terms, not as Barrington's wife, or as if she'd rather he wasn't there.

"How do you know Frank?"

"I look after his dad – Intermediate Care OT support – and I've been working with Frank, supporting the college placements from our team."

"I want to talk to you about the landlords," Barrington interrupts.

Corinne rolls her eyes. "I'm going to dance. You can ignore him, you know. It's a party."

Barrington stands as if to follow her, then sits down again. "I'm going to talk to them." His insistence tells Jess that he's no different at home than he is in work.

"Sorry, shall we talk about this on Monday? Corinne's right, it's a party."

"I can find out what happened to the girl and who's involved."

"Hey, hey, slow down, please. I'm not sure what you know or who you think you might talk to and even less what you think you might say, but don't. I mean it. Don't! This is police territory. We need to work together, but let's do it properly. These aren't the sort of reasonable people we see in meetings."

Not unusually, Barrington doesn't seem to be listening and appears distracted by the music.

"It's great that you know how to get more information." Jess is positive, but doesn't want this to go anywhere tonight. "I know it's the weekend, but I'll call you first thing tomorrow, if that's OK?"

"I'd like to leave," he says and walks straight out onto the dance floor to where Corinne is dancing with friends. She seems to dismiss him like an annoying pre-teen. If Corinne wasn't there, she would spend some time calming him down, but she's not on duty and his marriage is definitely a problem she wants no part of.

As Jess returns to her table, she spots a cake being lifted to the edge of the dance floor. The room is hot and packed. Anne-Marie pats Frank on the back as he shuffles forward to make his speech. He wipes his upper lip and pulls his shirt down. The music fades out. Aunty Maureen waves a knife for a bit of hush. "I know Frank wants to say a few words." She points the knife at him. "And I've told him I mean a few words. We all know what he can be like." Adam wheels his grandad forward. Barrington stands by the door waiting for a quick exit. Jess catches Anne-Marie's eye. Her face has returned to its pinched position.

Frank shows the room his watch. "I'm taking my life into my hands keeping Maureen off the dance floor. All I wanted to say is a big thanks to everyone for coming. It means a lot to me. It's already been a great night and it's not even 10pm. I can't think of anywhere else in the world I'd rather be."

There are cheers, but then he starts again. "Since making it to sixty, I've been thinking a lot about my family, our community, this city... "

Maureen waves the knife at him, but most people are quiet. His views are respected.

Jess' phone rings and she's mortified, but she has to answer it. She puts a hand up in apology, moves quickly towards the door, then stops as she takes in what Jonesy is saying. The news rockets through her body. She starts again, not wanting to run, but stumbling into the double doors.

"This family, our community, I mean all of you ugly lot, related or otherwise, you're amazing. I know times are tough, but at times like this we surround ourselves with the people we love and people who love us,"

"I don't love you," Maureen heckles.

Jess jams the phone further into her ear, annoyed at the jeers, the laughter. Anne-Marie and Barrington follow Jess out.

"We stick together. United we stand, divided we fall and all that."

It's the last thing she hears as the doors swing shut.

"The Girl in the Bin has died," Jess says, her face hard. "I've got to go. I'm sorry. It's murder."

"Wait." Barrington demands. "Be specific. Do you mean someone's got into ICU, tampered with the equipment, or that she has died from her original injuries?"

Good question, they hadn't put a guard on her room, but not now. The whole city, everyone, has to know about this. Either way, the girl was murdered.

"Bloody hell," Anne-Marie stutters. "I thought, I mean, shit, I'd forgotten. Wasn't she recovering in St. Johnny's?"

Jess descends the stairs to a baritone round of cheers followed by a happy birthday chorus.

CHAPTER 32

JESSICA

Saturday 4th December, 10am

In the incident room, Jonesy addresses the team exactly as if he's leading his first murder enquiry. One or two of them give him a sympathetic look as he messes with the remote to show the relevant CCTV clips. Jess is sitting at the front watching the grainy, monochrome images, underlining the importance of the case.

"Progress is being made – the TV works." Stewart smirks.

"So why was she here at all? Who's her connection here? Where did she start the night? Our first sighting's at 7.45pm, walking down the high street. We've got her in the King's Head, looking for someone, then walking off in the direction of the Anvil, where we lose her until her body's found at 10.30pm. Stewart and Patrick, I want you on the pubs and clubs in that area, particularly the Anvil, the staff and regulars. There's also the Cave and Kenny's. Get the internal and the door tapes. Talk to the door teams."

Jess watches Stewart sitting there alert and attentive. She'd have preferred it if Jonesy had given that job to someone else. Changing his tune comes easy to Stew. He wants to be the one talking to his martial arts mates, not making life uncomfortable for them. Tactically Jess decides to mix keeping a close eye on Stew with a more conciliatory approach. He could be useful as a way into Croft.

"Karen," Jonesy continues, "I want you to go back to those witnesses in the Silver Street area around 10pm and see who else saw anything. She was dumped so close to the High Street someone must've seen her and whoever dumped her. Jill, I want you onto children's services. Chase the Looked After Team and the Derby connection." People move, but that doesn't necessarily mean action.

"I'll be going back to St Johnny's. I'm not saying it wasn't done properly, but we have to be 100 per cent sure on the security at the scene of death.

She nods encouragingly at Jonesy. The Force need more like him and it's not his fault it's taken more than three weeks for the case to be considered worth the resources. Aware that Stewart hasn't moved and is watching them, Jonesy wanders over to the crime board and pretends to look at the map. Jess follows.

"What do you think, Ma'am?"

Connections and cobwebs, she thinks. There's a web you can touch. Its tensile strength and elastic structure support a giant spider that catches flies. Look again and the web is barely there. Put your hand into it and the spider's gone, disappeared into nothing.

"OK, prioritise the Anvil," she says. The staff were interviewed, go over them again. I still don't think it's a one-off. See if we can get any more on the new date rape. I'm still waiting on some data from the hospital about other potential cases."

"Ma'am, there's the connection to Croft. You're not dropping that idea are you? There's definitely something there. I'm not sure what, but I want to keep digging."

Having your thoughts played back to you like that is a relief. "Yes, but keep that quiet, between ourselves. Nothing to Stew. Nothing that could get back to the Chief either."

Stewart's presence lurks closer behind them. Jonesy murmurs, "The Chief?"

"My agenda in this has always been the long-term strategy stuff, not just the crime itself, but I need time to work the Chief round to my way of thinking on alcohol." Now it's murder, her opportunity is back on and Jonesy doesn't need to know that the Chief and Croft played golf together last week.

"OK, good. Glad to hear you're not doing my job for me! Thought you might be getting a taste for investigating again."

"Yes and no. There's something personal I need to check out related to the Chickenshack lot."

"Alright, detective." He starts to smile, but sees she isn't joking. They shouldn't need her to be doing this.

The curtains are still shut at Shaz's house. The TV is blaring so Jess perseveres until eventually Ben answers the door.

"What do you want? I've been interviewed. This is harassment," he says, eyeing her coldly. This isn't the Ben she used to know.

"I'm here to see your mum."

He shouts up the stairs. "You got a visitor. I'm going to the shop for milk."

Shaz is quickly at the top of the stairs. "Thanks and get some Jaffa Cakes as well, eh?"

Ben grabs a jacket and heads out.

Jess call out, "Don't be long. You need to be looking out for your mum and concentrating on your studies." This isn't official, but she wants him to know she's on his case.

"Leave him alone will you. He gets a caution and I get two visits in a week. You must be after something."

Shaz isn't entirely joking and this might be tricky. "I am, including checking in on how you are. Have you, er, been out?"

They sit in the kitchen waiting for the milk to arrive.

"Jess, I'm not agoraphobic OK. I'm knackered that's all."

"Sorry. You had me worried and now I'm worried about Ben. There was a fight at the College. Did he tell you about that?"

Shaz clenches her fists. She doesn't bang them on the table. "What? The College have been talking to the Police about Ben and no-one's said a bloody word to me. They can't do that."

"I thought they'd have been in touch, but you haven't been answering your phone. I was trying to call you all week, and I came round and got no answer. You were avoiding me."

"I wasn't. Well, couldn't face anyone."

"Do you know what's going on with Ben?"

"He's got a part-time job. He's trying to hold it all together. He's a good boy."

"What's he doing?" Jess is trying to sound casual, but doesn't feel it.

"He's working in a factory unit and does deliveries, that kind of thing. It's manual."

"Sounds a bit vague. Who does he work for?"

"Stop interrogating me. He works for some bloke alright. Your lot interviewed him. Ben is studying hard. He's working hard. He needs a chance, that's all."

"Why don't you talk to Frank. Do you know him? He's Adam's dad, he works at the College. I'll give you his number. The College suspect Ben might be working for someone called Croft and that there might be drugs involved. I'm worried Ben's getting out of his depth."

"Why aren't you helping him then, instead of putting more pressure on him." Shaz pushes her chair back, stands and turns away.

"If he tells us what's going on maybe we could. Seems like Adam's getting back on track."

"Adam's out of it?" Shaz's face is a mess of emotions. She's biting her lip, screwing her hands up. She's angry, but there's also fear there.

"Why are you helping Adam and not Ben?" she demands.

Jess questions herself. She doesn't think she over-stepped the mark with Adam, but she does know Frank and Anne-Marie well. She is the Deputy Commander and even mentioning that to a plod issuing a caution might have been enough to... what?

Ben was interviewed again, Adam wasn't, and she'd just accepted Frank's view that Adam was helping Ben out of the fight.

"Shaz, what is it? I can help. I'm here. I want to help. Tell me what you want me to do?"

Shaz wipes her upper lip. She's sweating and almost spits, "I don't know. If I knew we wouldn't be in this mess. Ben would be fine. It's all my fault. It's not him. Leave him alone, can't you."

Shaz is on the brink of hot angry tears. Jess spots the kitchen roll and pulls off a few sheets.

"Start at the beginning. What's been going? I'm not asking you as a police officer, I'm asking you as a friend."

"Alright, I got in a mess. I'm on bloody benefits, I borrowed money. I got behind, I can't go to a bank. I can't go on the internet and get a loan. They come round here with wads of cash in their hands. I know I should manage better. It sounds lame, but I've tried, honestly. I'm on my own with Ben. He needs stuff. I mean, you don't know what it's like."

"I'm not a mum, but I work in a police station. I see people struggling, getting into messes, every day of the week."

Shaz gives her a withering look, one that says you haven't got the faintest idea, which is true, but what else can she say? In a professional sense Jess knows it's good to leave space, to let whatever needs to be said emerge, but she's in the middle of this conversation emotionally. It's all she can do not to fill the silence, but she lets her mind flood with silent questions until Shaz speaks.

"Ben's in a mess because of me, not the other way round. He was trying to pay off my DNB debt. That's how come he's working for Croft. How do you think that makes me feel? I'm supposed to look after him. I'm supposed to be the adult and I'm the problem."

The words feel old, like she's said them to herself a thousand times. Jess looks at the clock on the cooker. "Do you want a black coffee? Ben isn't coming back while I'm here, is he?" Shaz's face says it doesn't take a genius to work that out. "Tell me about Croft. He's on our radar."

"You won't get him. He's everywhere and nowhere."

"That I can imagine," Jess reflects. "I think there's a link to that girl who got dumped in the bin a few weeks back. She died last night."

Shaz goes to the kitchen door, wobbles, holds onto the work-top, tears now streaming down face.

"Hey, I'm sorry. Did you know her?"

Jess hugs her friend, taking her weight. From the smell of it, she's wearing Ben's hoodie and, like a teenager, she sobs as if her world is falling apart. Her voice is even quieter now.

"No," says Shaz, says, "it's just that it could have been me. I mean, it was me." She sinks to the floor, her back to a cupboard, head in her knees.

"What do you mean, Shaz? Tell me?" There is no reply. Jess sinks to the floor too.

"Except I managed to climb out of the stinking skip he dumped me in. That smell... a rat, a rat was chewing my hair." It's all whispers now as if she's talking to herself. "Perhaps if I'd told you, I know I should've told you really, maybe you could've got him and she'd still be alive."

"I'm so sorry, Shaz. Take your time. I'm here. I'm not going anywhere. Can you go back to the start? When we went for a drink after work? You were in shock because you saw the man that attacked you? Was it Croft?"

Slowly a story emerges. The attacker works for Croft, some-times behind the bar of the Anvil, could be higher up, sometimes in other places. She'd been to the pub to pay off what she could. The man had chatted to her, given her a free drink, offered her a lift home. The drink was spiked.

Getting to her feet, Jess moves slowly across the kitchen to make another cup of coffee. She moves into dealing with a victim mode, treading carefully, trying not to ask too many questions that she knows her friend will have to answer again.

"We'll get him," Jess says confidently.

In that moment, with the momentum building, it's possible to believe it. This could be the breakthrough she needs. Shaz can identify him.

Shaz rubs her eyes until she can see. "No, you can't tell anyone. I can't, I can't say anything."

"You don't need to say or do anything just yet, everything will be up to you, but we need to get you some support. Let me make a quick call. I won't mention any names."

"No. If I talk Ben could be in danger. I won't do it."

Jess sees Shaz's defiance. Protecting her son is what's important. The chance of progress starts to slip.

"We can protect Ben, we can…"

Shaz flares. "Don't patronise me. I want you to get that bastard, but I've made things bad enough for Ben already. I'm not risking my son's future on you lot protecting him. You've done nothing. When've you ever really helped young black kids like him?"

"I'm sorry you've had to go through all of this. Neither you nor Ben deserve any of it, but please don't make this a race thing. You know me. I care about you and Ben."

The skin around Shaz's eyes is a bruise full of reds, purples and black. "Yeah right, I don't see you for years and then you turn up like I'll make everything alright. But this isn't you and me, is it Jess? You're Police. You're them and we're us… I've acted like a bleeding idiot, but I'm not that stupid. I can't trust you and, much as you think you want to help, you can't. You couldn't help Darren all those years ago. Darren died in police custody. Is Ben going to be safe with you?"

"It's not the same Shaz. You've been attacked. Ben…"

"Thanks for reminding me." Shaz hauls herself up against the worktop. Energy spent.

Jess is lost too, arrested by the mention of Darren, thinking about Barrington.

"Just go, will you. Leave us both alone. All I want to do is sleep."

"OK," Jess decides, "but I'll come back."

Shaz shakes her head. "Don't bother. I'll find a way."

CHAPTER 33

BARRINGTON

Saturday 4th December, 4.15pm

How can it be that you can physically feel the atmosphere in the city? Some change in the mix of hydrogen, oxygen and carbon. The sky is already dark, no stars, thin cloud cover, a fine drizzle and in the middle of this December afternoon the lights of the stadium blaze, looking to Barrington as if a UFO has landed. He has no connection to the football, but notices an edge. It could be his own anxiety or the presence of thousands of men with a testosterone spike packed into a small space 200 metres away. Unusual. He identifies a string of unmarked police vans parked bumper to bumper along the Dales Road and cycles past, slowly estimating how many police are on duty and how much the football club contributes to the overtime bill.

He thinks he hears laughter coming from an open van window. From another there is the crackle of a radio mike. There is not a car in sight. Stacks of railings wait to be dropped into line to form a funnel. Pairs of police officers walk slowly down towards the underpass and back towards the road. It's a local derby, its half-way into the second half and the city is on lockdown.

Barrington has enjoyed a quick time trial around the city on his bike before finding Mr Sizzle. The burger van, parked between the University and the approach to the stadium, announces itself with the football commentary blaring from an orange plastic radio. As Barrington dismounts and clips his helmet to the cross bar there is a roar from the ground.

"Alright mate, what can I get you?" Mr Sizzle has a sixth sense for nearby custom. The distinctive clack of the shoes on the flags makes him look up and watch as Barrington leans his bike against the side of the van.

"Oh yes, it's you again. Big spender on bike. You owe me £1.50!"

Barrington screws his nose up at the smell of the smoky burnt onions left in the corner of the griddle. Sizzle scrapes them up and expertly launches them into an oversize bin in the corner of the van. "Back of the net," he chortles.

Barrington shrugs. "You said you knew about the Girl in the Bin. You know she died?"

"No, I didn't. Poor kid." Sizzle blows out heavily.

"You said you knew where the bodies were buried. I know that's a figure of speech, but there are bodies now. I need to know what you know. Who's responsible?"

"Hold your horses. I'm not Kojak. The mystery I'm interested in is whether we can hold on for a draw."

"You're not listening to me." Barrington glares at Sizzle's stomach wobbling as he laughs.

"I'm listening to the game." Sizzle settles his rotund frame against the edge of the cold drink fridge. "Look mate, everyone knows about this. Why not ask someone else?"

"I'm asking you. I don't know anyone else to ask." To Barrington it's a statement of fact.

Sizzle scoffs. "Don't you suited types get paid to know what's going on? Ask the Police, why don't you? Or the Council. They ought to do something about it."

"Believe me, they know considerably less than I do and it'll take too much time. Things need to change."

"Indeed they do." Mr Sizzle neatly refills the griddle in front of him. "I don't like the Council and they don't like me either. Are you eating then?"

Barrington shakes his head vigorously. "The problem is out of hand. Drinking is out of hand. You said the landlords fuel the fire. Piss. Puke. Violence."

"That's about right, but I've got a football match to listen to and burgers to flip, and there'll be plenty of punters dying for my culinary delights in about twenty minutes' time."

Barrington stares at him directly, tapping his fingers on the counter. "This is serious. It's not about football, it's about people's lives, young women's lives, lives we can save."

Sizzle shakes his head. "I'm guessing for someone as clever as a doctor or whatever you are, you don't know much, do you?"

Barrington knows the prevalence of every disease in the city. He knows the patterns of transmission, the risk factors, the treatments, the outcomes – everything from heart failure to a common cold. He knows how alcohol impacts on all of this to a level of detail that would make Sizzle's head explode. He wouldn't normally let challenges to his intelligence pass, but he takes a deep breath and determines to try again. "I need to know who the people are that let this happen. If it's publicans I can do something about it."

"You going to wave a health and safety certificate at them then?"

"I need to know."

"So you said, but you need to tone it down. I'm listening, but, how shall I put it, you're sounding a few cards short of the pack. You want to take on the dodgiest landlords, the breweries, the whole pissing drinks industry while you're at it?" There is a roar from the crowd and Sizzle looks at his watch. "Make yourself useful. I've got to fetch some supplies from the car. Watch the van for a few minutes and you can ask me anything you like until the final whistle goes."

Barrington is sceptical, but climbs the two steps into the warm van and watches Mr Sizzle waddle off down a side road. He turns the radio down and runs his finger around the small sink, finding it cleaner than he expects. There is something about the way that the uniformly circular burgers are lined up in two straight rows that Barrington finds acceptable enough. The way the sauces are arranged doesn't make sense to him, though. They should be on the right-hand side and they need a wipe. He starts cleaning then sorts through the tub of plastic forks, picking out those that are broken or dirty. If the smell was fried chicken he might even enjoy himself, but it's not and he quickly turns his back as a policeman ambles past, threatening to stop. I don't want to be associated with serving people this food, Barrington thinks, hoping Sizzle returns quickly. He makes himself busy rearranging the thumbnail milk cartons, sugar sachets and stacks of foam tea cups.

"Didn't scare any of my punters off did you?" Sizzle looks around. "Well, you've been busy. If you're ever out of a job like and need a bit of cash in hand you know where to come."

"So," Barrington cuts straight in, "who do I need to target first?"

"Something tells me you don't actually drink in town, do you? No? Thought not. They're not all bad. In fact, I could recommend one or two decent boozers I myself like to frequent. Thing is, times is hard. Some are just trying to earn their crusty cob, but, sad to say, all trades have their bad apples, mine included. People cut corners. Some are on the take, some are worse... Use your nod, lad. These aren't reasonable characters you can have a quiet talk with and everything will be hunky-dory like. I'm not telling you anything any of the traders, taxi drivers, bar staff or regulars don't know."

Sizzle lowers his voice. "The Anvil, the Three Lions, the Cave – take it from me, some of these landlords are, shall we say..." Sizzle begins flipping the burgers, maintaining the neat rows. "...evil bastards, like. Powerful people, with money and connections. You can buy anything and do anything on their property as long as you pay for it. They'll sell drugs, Ruffies, for the price of a pint. For the price of another you can watch and you can pay them to clean up after."

There's a roar as the final whistle goes. Men begin streaming past. Barrington looks at random faces in the crowd. They are loud, jeering, angry. Ruffies – Rohypnol? Who would do that? What about him? That one with a black football scarf tied round his head? Or him? That one with a sensible coat? Is he saying that other men would watch someone being drugged? Raped? "I don't understand."

Sizzle leans in. "No, neither do I, but it's a shame on all of us, that's what it is. Now, on your bike."

Barrington picks up his bike and begins pushing it through the crowd, but he's going in the opposite direction to everyone else. The density of the bodies around him increases. He hates crowds like this, crowds that could be capable of attacking and dumping a girl in a bin.

"Leave the bike with me, then," Sizzle calls, "and don't kill the moment. We should be celebrating. We only lost 1-0."

CHAPTER 34

ANNE-MARIE

Saturday 4th December, 6pm

Anne-Marie has laid low today, thinking mainly, recovering from a beating. She hasn't spoken to Frank and wonders how the party finished up for him. As she'd pushed open the exit doors, Jess was disappearing down the stairs and Bob was coming up. Bloody Barrington, his voice echoing down the stair well, loud enough to hear inside the room, telling the world that the Girl in the Bin had died. As the happy birthday chorus rang out, Anne-Marie had realised she was stuck in no man's land, alone with Bob.

"Christ, the poor kid," Bob had almost spat at her. "How are you going to spin this one?"

"Piss off, Bob," she'd managed to cough out.

"And what's that going to do to your precious bloody schemes? This'll be everyone's problem now. You'll have to do something."

Hearing his hatred wasn't a punch in the stomach, it'd been sharper, like he'd poked her in the eye and the corner of his nail had punctured her tear duct. Luckily the ladies toilet had provided an escape route. She'd thumped the door open, steadied herself on the sink, lit a fag, blew smoke into her eyes in an attempt to stem the tears, then, hearing someone coming, she'd locked herself in a cubicle and texted Frank and Adam that she'd been sick and had to leave.

Anne-Marie vaguely blots a red wine stain on the biscuit-coloured carpet with kitchen paper. She puts down the bottle for a moment and goes to the kitchen to get a tea towel and some chemicals to nuke the blotch. How did Bob get up on his high horse so quickly? The death of the Girl in the Bin does change things, of course she knows that, and after Croft's reaction to Kerry's rape she knows she's wobbling. The possibility that there is a serial rapist in the city is a dark alley she won't go down. Which is worse? That there might be one unhinged man who thinks he can get away with rape and now murder or that there are two, maybe three, random incidents and different men who are capable of this? She struggles to think about rape, let alone say the word out loud. Talking about Rohypnol, or putting the word 'date' in front of the word 'rape', somehow the words come out easier. She knows that's part of the problem. If we can't talk about it, how do we expect victims like Kerry to? How often has she used the word attacked or assaulted or even abused rather than just say the word 'rape'?

About eight years ago there was an incident. She'd sensed a bloke in a back street car park following her. She heard him laugh, sick and aroused, as she picked up speed and cursed her heels. Running past her car and straight into the street, she stopped a taxi, hoping to hell that the taxi-driver wasn't going to abduct her. Christ, it makes her rage. She knows it's a common fear, a kind of fear that most women recognise; a realisation, that sense of becoming a victim. What isn't fair is that women have to carry that fear around with them. It doesn't really go away. These men aren't looking at how attractive women are, they're looking for weakness. How different are they from the men in pubs like the Anvil? Drinking, leering, touching.

She tells herself to calm down. This isn't about Croft. It's the atmosphere, a permissive, anything-goes environment, where the modern day equivalent of asking for it is just being out in the City Centre. As a student she railed against that fear, those constraints. Kerry and her mates might feel the same. Isn't it their right to go out and have a good time? Anne-Marie thinks about Adam. He's careful what he says about girls in front of her and he's never brought anyone home. Is he scared to or not interested? Or there's just no story to tell. It's another subject that Adam has struck off the conversation list. How limited the stories have become; the range of stories that she gets to hear, gets to create, gets to live. It occurs to her that she might need to slow down or reverse, begin to write a new narrative. Come on, she tells herself. Create an alternative. Start another story. But while her thoughts are chasing around in a dense, contracting loop, nothing comes.

CHAPTER 35

BARRINGTON

Saturday 4ᵗʰ December, 6.30pm

An unmitigated disaster, Barrington concludes. "You're barred. Off the premises. Now!" the doorman at the Three Lions had said authoritatively, one arm stretched out, pointing the way towards the door, the other was grabbing the back of Barrington's elbow in a way that made it clear there was no other possible direction he could take. "Don't touch me." Barrington had barked. "I said, don't touch me. I'm going." Incensed, he'd stumbled into the street.

A vertical drinking bar was an accurate description. No chairs. Even the stools gave him vertigo. He'd sipped a warm Coke, watching the time tick past on his phone, not wanting to lose eye contact with the bar staff in case they forgot that he was waiting. The customers consisted of two groups of maudlin football fans and three young women drinkers whom Barrington was sure must be underage.

"Stop staring will you," one of bar staff had said bluntly.

"When will your boss be here? I'd like to ask him some questions. He knows I'm coming. I called in advance." It was the third time he'd addressed the selectively deaf teenager behind the bar.

If he had any choice in the matter he would not be here. That's fixed firmly in his mind, but he has to take action. Added to this, Corinne is out with friends and he desperately wants to see her. Hermin is looking after Nelson. After last night's disaster, Corinne's refused to speak to him all day.

"Who did you say you were?"

"I'm Dr Barrington Edwards, NHS Director of Public Health in the city. I have a right to question you as part of our duty of care under the Health and Wellbeing Act 2000."

"You're not Police, then?"

"No, I'm Health…"

"Whatever. You've got five minutes."

Barrington had become increasingly irritated at her responses.

"Don't know… You'll have to wait for the manager…. We only do what we're told…. No-one said anything to us about safety… Not my problem. We here to serve punters and that's what I need to do now." The young woman had wandered off without apology.

Barrington had counted up the hours wasted in the last three weeks. There'd been a Landlord Liaison meeting at the Council offices, where only the self-proclaimed 'decent' landlords had turned up and nothing but taxi marshalling had been discussed. There'd been a pointless and poorly chaired City Centre Scrutiny Review. The Keep It Safe campaign had lost its funding and had had to be re-thought, seemingly by reminding the public to act safely and look after each other, which had only increased the fear of crime. Writing to the landlords directly with requests for a one-to-one meeting had yielded nothing. He'd expected that, of course, although it had had to be done, but the 15 hours 45 minutes lost to his life had made him even more determined to spend however long it took to get to grips with the landlords, to make them see that they had to take responsibility for underage drinking and for the safety of their customers. The warnings he'd received from DCI Jessica Reid and Mr Sizzle had also hardened his resolve. He wasn't so naïve as to expect them to clean up their acts on his say so, but he wanted to hear it from the horse's mouth. The Girl in the Bin had died. There was a murder investigation underway, but, Deputy Commander Reid aside, who else was thinking about the bigger picture?

"Do you ask for identity before serving? Do you serve customers who are already drunk?" He'd begun questioning the young woman behind the bar again. "Do you know your company policy on drugs?" Barrington had thought she'd looked anxious. Maybe she knew something, but was afraid to say. There were no other customers at the bar, so he'd pressed on. "Did you know that there have been three suspected incidents involving Rohypnol in City Centre pubs? Date rape drugs? Spiking drinks? You're a young woman, do you have nothing to say about it?"

"George," she'd called over to the doorman, "this bloke's creeping me out. Can you get him to go away."

"That's it. The boss isn't here. You're leaving." The doorman had tried to grab his arm. They were three metres from the door. Barrington had jerked his body out of reach. A few customers had stared, but it had been over in a second. How dare they behave like that? Completely unacceptable.

Now out in the cold he wishes he'd put on a coat. A toothless smoker gawps at him. The smell of smoke in the doorway reminds him of his father. He might have come to a pub like this on a Sunday afternoon, although Barrington can see no other black men drinking here now. He does up the buttons on his suit jacket, ensures his tie is straight, then shakes his head. Riled up and without thinking, he launches himself towards the next pub. There's a slither of a second when he notices the corner of Corporation Street and the Bank, where he could turn left towards home, except he can't, because he isn't allowed back there. His heart is pumping, his body is ahead of him, physically moving him on until he's reached the edge of the bus station building site and Silver Street, where the Anvil is located. It's after seven and the timing isn't ideal, but he is in the moment. His saliva tastes bitter from a rush of humiliation-driven adrenaline. That's not good for decision-making, but there's no turning back. If he doesn't see this through, nothing will happen for weeks and there could be another incident.

As he walks towards the Anvil he notices two doormen. One is white, middle-aged and bulky, but judging from his tight trousers and fitted jacket it isn't down to excess body fat. He might be an ex-army type, but his hair is too long, probably unwashed. He stares in Barrington's direction and speaks into an ear-piece. The other one is black, slim and two metres tall. Barrington suspects they are either just talking about him or have been warned about his arrival. He turns his gaze back on the first bouncer. "My name is Dr Barrington Edwards. I'm here to see the licensee."

"Mr Croft is expecting you."

That's better. Barrington is relieved, steadies himself and makes his way to the bar. The barman effortlessly lifts a tray of pint glasses from the dishwasher, then picks up an unlabelled box of spirits. "Take a seat over there. I'll bring you over a drink. What are you having?" he shouts over his shoulder.

What arrives must be an unbranded cola; far too metallic and too much ice. Looking around, it strikes Barrington as unusual that a pub like this would need that level of security. There are original tiles on the walls, etched glass and dark wood panels that divide the tables. When he'd researched it on the internet, there had been no website, but it was listed in a directory of local businesses as a 'family pub'. He's on full alert after the Three Lions, although unsure what he might need to prepare himself for. The barmaid comes over with another drink and says the landlord will be down shortly. It isn't an apology.

The pub is filling up. There are a few groups of overweight middle-aged men, all drinking pints. They are scrubbed and ironed, a wave of aftershave hits him. He notes gold sovereign rings and less well cared for shoes. There's a couple laughing loudly and three young women speaking an Eastern European language. They look like children wearing too much make-up. He looks intently at his phone, feeling his body temperature increase, annoyed again that twenty minutes have gone by.

"I don't want another excuse and if I want a drink I'll buy my own," he snaps.

"No need for that attitude. He'll be out when he's ready." The barman stares directly at him and the group of men at the next table stop talking.

"I need to speak to Mr Croft," he says, unsure how loudly he's speaking, because of the music. "People in this city drink too much and pubs like this need to sell alcohol responsibly."

He hears the men at a table to his left laugh. "God squad twat."

Barrington drums his fingers on the bar, sick of the waiting. Nothing works. The Three Lions was a joke. This is a joke. I'm a joke if I don't do something. He begins diagnosing aloud. "I'm serious. Look at your customers, look at their skin, the early stages of rosacea, obese, statistically likely to have cirrhosis, possibly dementia..."

The laughter from the table stops. "What's it to you pal," one of them snarls.

"Definitely signs of brain cells being impaired." Barrington sees one of the men begin to get to his feet. He has silver hair and a faded Celtic tattoo on his neck. He's white, of course. They are all white. The only other black person around is outside on the street.

"One more word and you're out. We respect our customers in here." The barman speaks slowly, shaking his head at the silverback, who sits back down.

"How old are those girls you just served? Did you ask for ID?"

"What did I just tell you?"

"You and your boss need to listen to me. There's a problem and..."

"That's enough." The barman pulls up the bar flap and speaks directly into a radio mike. "I'm in charge while the boss is busy..."

"Wait, I'm here to..."Barrington steps back too quickly, finds he needs to steady himself on an empty chair and looks up into the smooth-skinned face of a slim, well-groomed man in his fifties. Croft's Black Country accent is patronising. "Looks like you've had one too many son. Can't take your drink?" Croft nods to the regulars.

"What? You're mistaken. I don't drink and I've been waiting for you. What's going on?"

The background noise of the pub drops. Barrington is unable to stop his mouth. "Your barman has put you in breach of your license and I could report you to the Police."

"You need to be careful what you're saying..." Croft pauses. "...Dr Edwards."

The tattooed Celt stands up. "That bastard's taking the piss. Come on, pal. If you've got something to say, say it." He pushes back the sleeves of his donkey jacket and shows his knuckles.

Barrington rears up to face him.

"Not in here you don't. I'll be speaking to the Police myself about you. Abusing customers. Aggressive behaviour towards my staff. We don't tolerate violence inside our pub."

People behind Barrington are laughing. "What? You've got it wrong. No way. You need to listen..." He tries again, but is cut off.

"I need to listen? To what? A lecture on alcohol from someone in your state. That's ironic. I was expecting a civil conversation. You need to leave now before you cause any more trouble." Croft turns his shoulder to walk away.

"Absolutely ridiculous," Barrington blurts. "I'm not the one causing trouble. I'm giving you the facts. It's your behaviour as a landlord that's in question. You're profiting from alcohol addiction."

"You know nothing about this business."

"There is evidence that you're selling illegal booze, serving underage drinkers, and we've had reports about drugs on the premises."

Croft motions quietly to the doorman, who has come up behind Barrington. "I'm leaving. Sort this."

"You're a disgrace to the city, you're poisoning young women and..."

There is a sharp pain in the back of Barrington's knee. He starts to buckle, but is picked up by a strong arm hooked under his shoulder and within seconds he's pushed towards the Gents. Barrington's brain feels like it's exploding. With his good leg he stamps on the squaddie bouncer's foot and gets no reaction. "Let me go," he yells. He panics, kicking out violently and is thrown through another doorway and onto the icy floor of the outside yard. Before he can lift his head, a boot makes contact with his ribs. Automatically he pulls his limbs into a tight ball. He needs to protect his head, but doesn't act quickly enough and a sharp heel lands above his eye, which fills immediately with blood. The third blow feels like a sledgehammer shattering his ribs. Finally raising a hand, he puts a thin barrier between a different dirty shoe and his ear. There is no air in his lungs to call for help. Pain signals flood his neural pathways and he can hear only white noise in his inner ear.

Alone now, his breathing partially recovers, but his brain is racing. I don't fight. I should've run. Get away now. Get the Police. I've been set up. I've been attacked. I did not start this. I need Corinne. The thought that he might be drunk rocks him. Sitting up is possible. He takes off his navy silk tie, wraps it around his hand, mops his face and stems the blood stream above his eye. Although his balance is poor, he manages to stagger away from the pub and into the back alley. It's barely lit. He makes for a lamppost, metres away from a large green bin.

"Are you alright?" A young woman stands in front of him.

"No, I'm not. Isn't it obvious I've been attacked?" He holds himself up against a concrete post, jabbing his foot into it angrily.

"You don't need to shout. Shall I call an ambulance? I know where the hospital is. I could get a taxi for you?"

The blood in his eye has stopped him focusing clearly on her face. Her hair looks healthy. She is wearing baseball boots, a short denim skirt and a rust-coloured bomber jacket.

"No, no. I can't turn up at the hospital like this."

"Whoa – keep the volume down." She steps back. "What's the matter? Someone bashed your ears? That cut looks nasty."

Being seen in A&E is impossible.

"Honestly, they'll stitch it up. Probably have to sit around for hours, though."

"No. No, thank you. I'm a doctor. I can look after myself. I just need some water and to get home."

"A doctor is it? I've been a nurse once or twice. I'm training." She laughs and fishes in her bag for a tissue. Barrington isn't sure what she means. He winces as she wipes his brow, dislodging some clotting blood.

"I work just around the corner. I'll get you a drink and you can wait for a taxi or someone to pick you up. I'm Holly, by the way. What's your name?"

"Barrington Edwards."

"Can you walk OK? You sure you don't want to go to Casualty?"

She puts her arm around his waist as he stumbles. He wants to pull away from the touch of a stranger, but she smells harmless.

"I just need water," he barks.

"Alright, alright, I'll sort you out. This is like one of them three-legged races at junior school. Wouldn't win, though, would we?"

She half drags him the 50 metres until they turn into another small fold and the doorway to a club with no name. Barrington looks up at the large CCTV camera above the door and into the bright, white security light. Unpleasant, but safe, he thinks.

"It's just down the stairs. Don't worry, we're not open yet. Can you manage?"

He throws his shoulders back and focuses on the stairwell below, wondering if he's made another mistake and is descending into hell. With every step down towards the basement bar the light grows darker and the music louder. He trips on the final step down, grabs onto the young woman's arms and finds himself looking up at the bar. He does a mental bodycheck. "I don't drink, but I could be drunk."

"Being pissed will make it hurt less." She puts him down in a quiet corner on a low, navy sofa and wanders behind the bar. There's only one other member of staff and the darkness of the club helps.

"Mum says you need brandy for shock. Water and a couple of tabs. You'll survive." She offers him a blister strip.

He looks at the painkillers. Co-drydramol. It will do for now. He's not bothered about the pain, but they will take down the inflammation in his muscles. Considering his options, a taxi is not a bad idea. Just get home fast. He looks at his watch. It's only 9.15pm. He didn't find Corinne. She could be nearby.

"What happened?"

"I..."

The girl seems to know already. "You were in the Anvil, right? You got drunk and you got beat up, like."

"No, they got me drunk. I don't drink. I'm..." He wonders exactly how much alcohol could have been added to the Cokes he's had? Not that much or he would have noticed. I've drunk too much caffeine, but that wouldn't have made me... what? Aggressive? He's alert, his heart is pumping fast.

"Nah." She looks directly into his good eye. "Looks like you're buzzing to me."

"What?"

"Probably speed. They do that in there. Spike your drink. Not been in before?" She shakes her head and answers her own question. "Nah, course you haven't."

If he goes to the Police they could do a blood test. He'd have proof, but doubts creep in. He'd argued with them. People find him confrontational. No hospital. No police station. The chaotic behaviour in the custody suite would be unbearable.

"I'll be alright. I'll walk home. It will clear my head. Thanks."

"Stay put for a bit. Drink that brandy. You're still in shock."

Barrington looks at her face. She looks too young to be in a night club. "I said I don't drink." He glares, but admits that she is right about the shock. "What are you? A barmaid?"

"At weekends, like."

"Are you 18?"

She laughs and puts a hand on his leg. "Calm down. I was only trying to help. Take your jacket off. I don't meet many doctors. What's it like then?"

"What's what like?" Barrington looks at her hand, up the thin arm to her shoulder, a UV light catches her bra strap under her pink T-shirt and he sees the shape of her breasts, the tip of a nipple.

"Being a doctor?"

"I'm not a GP. I work in primary care. I appreciate your concern. I, er... I have to go."

She looks at him, in a way curious, but also in a way sexual, like the one-night stands he used to have as a student. "You could examine me if you like. I've never been out with a doctor. You must earn a shedload." She fishes out her phone and holds it out to take a photo of the two of them.

"What? I'm married," Barrington says without conviction. Putting his head back onto the sofa, he looks up straight into the line of a strobe light. Christ.

"So, your wife isn't here now and you need someone to make you feel better."

"No. Stop it. You're too young."

"I'm not a tart, if that's what you think? Older men are cool." She leans her head on his shoulder. He looks up again at the ceiling. Her hand moves towards his crotch, but he doesn't stop her. I'm not interested in you as an individual, he thinks. As a problem to solve, as a member of an interesting socio-economic group, as a trend, a number – yes. Through his suit trousers she sees a bulge and smiles.

"You're not in that much of a hurry then?"

She puts the brandy to his lips. He swallows and shivers. She licks his ear. His brain won't focus. His eyes fix on her white skin.

"You had a girlfriend like me before?" She lifts his hand to her breast.

"Stop talking. I can't think."

"There's a room at the back. We could go there until my shift starts."

Head swimming, he grasps the proposition and thinks of the testosterone release. He heaves himself up and she guides him around the end of the bar and into what seems like a cleaning cupboard. She kisses him on the lips. Her mouth is small. He could eat it. A strong smell of bleach gets into his nostrils. The toxicity inflames his nasal passage. "Too many chemicals." He's babbling, still drugged. "I can't…" He holds the girl's upper arms, lifts her body away from his, then slumps back against a Dexion metal shelf unit. "Corinne. Where's Corinne? I need her."

"Like that, eh?" She shakes herself down. "Drugs'll do that as well. We can sit and have a chat upstairs, and then I'd better get ready for work."

He pushes past her, out and up the stairs.

Barrington makes it to his Aunt Hermin's place. He sits in one of the white plastic garden chairs in the back garden, desperately trying to focus on the washing line post. Historically it's always been safe out here. He remembers sitting out here while his mum and Hermin chatted in the kitchen, cursing the cold, tutting that he refused to come in. The inside of his head is spinning so much he's scared to shut his eyes. Images of tonight revolve in his mind. It's hard to believe that it's only 11pm.

The Three Lions, the Anvil. The actual experience of being there, is it always so extreme? Why hadn't he just walked away? That his behaviour was so painfully naïve had been confirmed by a well polished boot cracking at least two ribs. He'd made himself look ridiculous. They might have drugged him, but what did he think he was going to achieve in the first place? Was Croft right? Had he gone to pick a fight? Intellectually? Morally? There's the sour taste of bile in the back of his throat. He nearly... He could have had intercourse with a young woman less than half his age. He'd been aroused. He'd kissed, touched her.

Fortunately the light isn't on. He can't seem to find his keys, but remembers where the spare is hidden. As he bends to pick it up he vomits into a flower pot. A thin brownish liquid splays over the yellow leaves of the plant. He's a mess of sweat, blood and sick. With a downstairs bathroom and utility room leading off from the kitchen he can have a shower and wake no-one. The bathroom is unchanged from when he lived here as a boy: the cracked blue tiles on the walls, the smell of sandalwood, bottles of toxic hair products, a pallid green, plastic shower curtain and brightly coloured towels. He undresses quickly, looking with disgust at the pile of clothes, then scrubs his body hard under the hottest the water will go. He digs through the washing basket, finding a pair of slacks and a mustard fleece.

"Almighty god in heaven, Barrington. What has happened?"

In the dark he sees Hermin's shadow. No words are possible. He shakes his head. He doesn't know. Why won't his brain work? How could he break things so quickly – his marriage, his wife's trust? And Nelson, he wants to see Nelson. He tries to shut the back door quietly, as quickly as he can. Lights are still on in other houses in the road, cars pass him. He walks on alone. He is completely alone for the first time in his life.

CHAPTER 36

HOLLY

Sunday 5th December, 4am

Holly is glad she didn't get blasted at work tonight. Normally she'd rather get blasted, because you need a drink or ten to get through the night, like. They're allowed a Coke. It's rank, but they don't notice if she scabs a shot of rum or two. Vodka, no. It's evil and management get suspicious you're filling water bottles with it. As if... As if they care when there are pills everywhere.

Tonight she wasn't bothered by the local mongs chatting her up. It can pass the time, but they're losers and only want one thing. The lads at college are the same. They call Holly a slag if she has sex with them, same as if she doesn't. So she does, because all her mates do. Most of them just want her to watch porn with them while their mums are watching TV downstairs. She finds her body responds, so she can see that porn works, but, still, she doesn't get off on it. Not really. And she has to wipe it all up afterwards, which is so like what she'll be doing in her nursing NVQ. It's too gross.

She can't wait to tell her mates about Barrington, though. She could see straightaway he was decent, proper, a real actual doctor. Maybe she'd come close to blowing it, but it was alright, because he'd been beaten up. Yes, he was thinking about his wife, but that was alright, too. He's not a knobhead, so he would, wouldn't he? But he'll be back. She's got his Blackberry.

Yep, tonight was mad. Even though she so wants her bed, she says no to a lift from the boss. Too risky. Walking in the ring road when it's dead is alright. The lights make it safe.

CHAPTER 37

JESSICA

Sunday 5th December, 9.30am

Along the right-hand grass verge of the ring road she sees a tall black man walking at speed with his head down. Mental health, she wonders, then looks again. The mustard-coloured fleece isn't something she'd associate with Barrington so she slows right up to make sure. He looks away, not wanting to make eye contact, but it's definitely him. There's a lay-by about 200 metres ahead so she indicates to pull in.

Jess would've stopped anyway, but she has nowhere else to be. She's already been to Shaz's house, banging hard enough for the doorpaint to crack and fleck, but the curtains were closed and Shaz wasn't answering her phone. There's nothing she can really do at the station either. That's the hardest part of being management. Jonesy and the two murder detectives will be making up for lost time, although Stewart won't be contributing much, hovering in the background, playing down any connection to Croft. She will have to force herself to talk to him. Later will do.

Barrington crosses the dual carriageway at speed and walks in the other direction. He might have recognised her, but clearly wants to avoid contact, even though he seems to need help, a lift at least. It's weird even by his standards. Pulling out again she drives on to the next roundabout and turns back to see if she can find him. She sees him ahead of her, walking along the central reservation. She slows to a crawl, puts her hazards on and winds her window down.

"Can I give you a lift?"

"No. I'm fine." He jumps the barrier and walks back in his original direction.

She decides to stop and check what's going on. The last time she saw him was Friday at the party. He'd been awkward, distracted, there was a bit of a domestic and he'd been rambling about the landlords. She wants to tell him that his suspicions about the Girl in the Bin being murdered in ICU were unfounded. She parks back in the lay-by and moves towards him.

"Sorry, I said I'd call you," Jess starts, "but we've been busy since Friday."

"Yes. I've lost my phone and my keys." He looks at the sky as if deciding whether or not it might rain.

"That's OK. I'll give you a lift home."

"No. No, thanks. I can't go home."

"Barrington, what's happened? Let's get in the car at least. It's freezing out here."

"I'm exhausted."

Jess thinks he's in shock. He's clearly confused, blue-black blood crusted above his eye. His shoes are covered in mud and there's a leaf sticking out of one of the trouser pockets. He gets into her car, slumping down in the seat to avoid being seen.

"Have you been attacked? It's none of my business, but shouldn't you talk to Corinne? You can use my phone. Shall we call in at the hospital and have that cut looked at?"

"No. Absolutely not. I can't go there. I'm, I'm exhausted. I need rest."

He looks determined not to go to the hospital and she sees that professionally it would be a problem for him.

"I've been out walking all night, trying to get my head straight."

"All night?"

Lucky none of her colleagues picked him up.

"Corinne's told me to leave and I..."

Jess senses he needs someone to take control of the situation. She can't insist on normal procedure here. He's fragile and defensive. "OK, you need a change of clothes. Let's pass by the house. You can stay in the car, while I check with Corinne. I'll come and get you if she's happy for you to come into the house."

She'd do the same for anyone in a state like this, but he's not just anyone and she does have a personal connection with him. Under the circumstances Corinne is bound to assume the worst. So would she if a woman she'd met only once turned up on the doorstep with her husband. The fact that she's a police woman in uniform should help, but she wishes someone else had spotted him.

Even through the car window Corinne can see the state of Barrington.

"I think he's been in an accident or beaten up, but he won't tell me what happened."

Corinne shakes her head.

"I don't want Nelson to see his father like that. He's got a temperature as it is. I'll get some things, but he should be at Hermin's. That's his aunt. He's staying there for a few days. I'll call her now."

Jess tries not to panic. She knows who Hermin is and definitely doesn't want to go there.

"Look, he's not my problem anymore and he's certainly not yours, but thanks. Wait there a moment. I won't be a minute."

Corinne shuts the door. Jess is relieved, but wonders if she looks like she's helping too much, that Corinne might start asking why she's putting herself out for someone she barely knows? She wanders back to the car to tell Barrington what's happening.

"What is his temperature exactly? I want to go in." Barrington says, suddenly insistent.

"No, stay here. You can trust Corinne and think of Nelson. You look shocking. You don't want to frighten him."

He nods and they sit in silence until Corinne returns to the front door with a rucksack. Jess throws it on the backseat of the car.

"OK, where to?"

He is silent.

"Corinne said Hermin's. I could drop you there?"

"I can't go there."

She doesn't push him, she's relieved, but it still leaves her with the problem of what do with him. "A friend?"

He shakes his head. She realises she might have to take him back to her house. She is really reluctant to do that, but can't see another option.

"How about I drive you to my place? You can change and crash out there. The house is empty. I need to get some shopping and visit a friend."

"Empty. Good. Can I sleep there?" He blows out all the air in his lungs.

They drive off in silence. Jess' anxious thoughts drift back to the murder case. She's in the same place she was three weeks ago, knowing a crime has been committed and wanting it to be solved, not just for Laura Awsworth, but for Shaz and the others. She needs to get back to Shaz's. The man dozing in the seat next to her isn't the ally she'd hoped he'd be. She's ended up helping him more than he's helped her, and not just for the sake of human kindness. Guilt is in the driving seat.

CHAPTER 38

ANNE-MARIE

Sunday 5th December, 8.30pm

It doesn't start well. As Anne-Marie pushes the door open she can see Bob at the bar. The Mechanics isn't empty, which is good, and it's good to see people here, savouring the sanctity of a quiet Sunday night drink, spinning out the weekend, mourning the return to work. Bob's shaved his head and is wearing her favourite maroon and navy check shirt like a soldier. She wishes she could put both arms around his thick torso, kiss him firmly and send him off for a safe tour, but he sees her and turns away.

Frank is in his corner with a mug of hot chocolate. He could have stayed at home, but he prefers the company and it gives him the chance to review his big weekend. Anne-Marie has been in the ghost ship of the Council House since lunchtime. She'd woken on the sofa with a brain cell-killing hangover, but by 1pm she'd felt like doing some work and had been going over the Pleisureland outline. It isn't bad, although there are risks attached – planning issues, finance that might not appear, political implications if Davina can't persuade her group and the Coalition members – but she wants Frank's take on it. She doesn't need his approval, but he'll help her see where to bolster her arguments and what she needs to hold out for. If he has his sleeves rolled up he can pick any deal apart.

"So it's all off with Bob, is it?"

"For now," she says, more hopeful than she feels. "Enjoyed the birthday weekend?" She's more pleased to see him than she admits to herself. Close up, the familiarity of his straight back and soft, bobbly jumper are a comfort.

"I have. People get funny about birthdays with zeroes on the end, but not me. We heard about the Girl in the Bin. That's why you left, wasn't it?"

"Yeah, it was partly that. I'm sorry." She realises that to other people leaving a party because of a story in the newspaper, the death of someone you never met, would seem strange, but Frank knows her of old.

Moving the conversation on, she says, "I thought Adam was on good form. It was good to see him enjoying himself, chatting away."

Frank shakes his head. "But he's not on good form, is he? He seemed really down this morning, went out and I haven't seen him since. This thing with Croft, I've told him not to have anything to do with them, work or otherwise. He knows my views on that family, but he says he's watching Ben's back and he won't abandon a mate."

"Does Jess know all this?"

Frank nods.

She tries not to allow middle-class paranoia to take over. What's actually happened is that Adam was involved in a fire, he's been cautioned by the police and that's over now. He helped his friend get out of a fight and, as far as they know, he's getting back on track with his studies, so maybe now's not the time to get heavy. "Perhaps we just need to give him some space?"

"He needs his mum. He needs you to be around."

It's true that she chooses to spend her life in a pan full of hot water, but she's not in control of the dial and the temperature is increasing. She can see that Frank's mood is swinging from fatherly to critical ex-husband.

"I am around. It's just that Davina's new vision for the city has swamped me. She wants to…"

He cuts her off. "Don't start on that."

"I'm sorry if it seems like I've not been there for Adam, but that's only temporary. What I'm doing is working on a future for kids like Adam. Finally, we'll get the Meadows site sorted. We're creating a regional destination, a super-casino, leisure village, bars, restaurants, all privately financed. It could mean over a thousand jobs."

"Is that your pitch?" he scoffs.

"Look, we've done a few good things in the city so far, but basically we haven't really cracked it, have we Frank? We haven't created any real opportunities for our communities and families to get work and get themselves out of poverty, and that's because we've been tinkering when what we need to do is transform the economy."

Franks slowly rolls up his sleeves, looking like a street fighter. "You're sounding like Davina again. What kind of future career will this give Adam? Bar work? He needs qualifications, not a shiny new cage to get pissed up in. The town's full of empty pubs doing god knows what. Come on, this is depressing. Yet again you're giving us the next big idea ten years too late. You know all this, Anne-Marie. Do we need more violence, more alcoholism? Do we buggery. And why are you interested in helping property speculators get a short-term payoff? If they're lucky, that is. Empty luxury flats, market failure, land values lower than the conference league. It won't stack up for ten minutes."

So far he's been jabbing at her professionalism, but then he moves in close.

"What has Davina promised you? Owen's job? Tell me you aren't that naïve?"

"I'm not and it's not about me." Her defence is a basic denial, although if Davina makes her redundant after all this there will definitely be blood and entrails. "We get to keep all the neighbourhood work, rebrand it as 'localism', because that's what it is anyway, and we link people on the estate to the new jobs."

Anne-Marie clings to the ropes. Frank takes his time before putting together a flurry of punches.

"We talk about jobs for local people every bloody time there's a new development and it never happens. We can't tie employers down to local labour schemes, because they don't want local labour, they want mythical Eastern Europeans, and if we did get an agreement there's no political will to enforce it. Trickledown never works. It just makes a few developers richer and the community gets to scrape a few dog-ends from the gutter. Davina's 'vision' does nothing to shift the structure of the economy. It's just the shitty end of the service sector. A casino? All that will deliver is addiction, self-loathing and an increase in the suicide rate."

She wants a crash helmet. She doesn't want to hear any more. She could argue that other cities have been effective at getting benefits from developments like this, but before she can speak he's cuts in.

"So when you talk about keeping the neighbourhood work going, are you really talking about the work in the community or do you mean saving your department?"

"No, that's not it." She wants to raise an arm to stem the tirade.

"It had better not be, because that makes you just as bad as you think Bob is. Bob's defending jobs, but he's doing it upfront through proper union organisation. Your job is to make sure services get delivered by the people who can deliver them best and, as they say, that ain't necessarily you."

He takes a step back.

"What's happened to you? Do you think dealing with Davina will get you the result you want?"

She can see immediately where he's going with this.

"Davina didn't actually say she won't cut that neighbourhood budget did she? It must be around a million pounds or more. How can she promise that? She'll make you slash it and you'll have to come up with some line about the community doing it for themselves. Do me a bloody favour, tell me you haven't fallen for that as well. Who do you trust these days?"

Anne-Marie scratches around for a defence, feeling that any positives she's been shoring herself up with have been kicked from beneath her.

"Give me more credit than that, Frank. I'm as pissed off as you sound. I wanted to hear what you had to say, I always do, but don't patronise me. I'm using the tools I've got and don't you dare question my loyalty to the estate. I'm not the enemy here."

Concussed, she stumbles to the Ladies, holds on to the sink, splashes her face with cold water and pulls down hard on the towel reel. It gets stuck. It always gets stuck. Bloody thing. She manages to awkwardly wipe her face on the small loop of coarse blue cotton. Smoothing her hair down, she resolves to finish the fight. She goes to the bar, opting for a double. Her only relief is that Bob has gone. Back at the table, she hovers, half on the seat.

"I haven't changed. Three weeks ago I said I didn't trust them. I still don't, but what else are we going to do? What. Else. Frank? I'm not hearing alternative solutions?"

"Yes, Anne-Marie, that's exactly it. Where are your alternatives? I'm not expecting you to do it all on your own. It's political. If we're going to fight the likes of Davina – I don't just mean here, I mean nationally, the whole neo-con game of a global economy – we should be providing bigger-picture alternatives and starting to build bottom-up. The party needs to do that, to create the environment for it, but if you," he seethes, "if we, as a city, put all our energy and resources into this insult, this pissing farce of a scheme, we'll never build something solid for the future."

Still in the ring, she summons the strength to have a go back. "I agree, we need a national solution for places like ours, but this isn't an academic exercise. We've got a Government that isn't interested in growth. There are no solutions coming from on high. We can't wait around doing nothing in the meantime, hoping for the economy to improve. We need action now."

Frank takes a final shot. "Talk about action now if you want, but I'd rather do nothing than do more damage. This condemns kids like Adam to failure. Low-paid, unskilled work. It's exploitative, it's…"

Anne-Marie is on the deck. "Frank, give it a chance. We've got local investors on board, we're using our land…" She sees too late she's given Frank a gift.

"Who? Who has got money round here for something like that?"

She's deliberately avoided mentioning Croft's name, but he's spotted it. "Croft."

He rides up, angrier than hell. "I'm trying to get our son away from the likes of him and you're tying the whole city into dealing with that bastard. He's employing kids, so-called collecting and delivering. I'm scared to death it's drugs. And they do site clearance, that's what Adam said. Haven't you thought about that? He wasn't just burning down a school, he was clearing a site!"

There's white noise between her ears, her eyes glaze. Site clearance. The Meadows. The explosion. How could she have dismissed that so quickly? She rages at her own stupidity. She has to get out of here.

"Don't run out now, Anne-Marie. Where are your priorities? Think about Adam. You're his mother."

"I'm thinking about all our futures. Adam, Ben, our friends, our estate, the city and the Council, which includes mine and yours, I make no apology for that."

Frank has done his worst. "Piss off, Anne-Marie. Who do you think you are?"

"I'm doing what I can."

"You're in complete denial. We have to get Adam away from Croft. You're making good people redundant, delivering a poison palace that no-one wants or needs. You've ended a relationship, god knows what for. A few weeks ago I thought we needed good people like you to do the difficult jobs, but now I'm not sure whose side you are on."

"It was never about sides Frank and I'm not listening to any more of this."

She keeps her head down and makes it to the door. An empty can on the pavement invites her to kick the shit out of it. She screams as loud as she can and doesn't care who hears. She shouts at the building. "You're a bastard, Frank. You're just like my dad and twice as bloody preachy, but all your talk amounts to nothing. Sweet FA. Don't blame me. Just leave me alone."

She leans against a pound shop window, trying to catch her breath. The street is empty. The town is empty. That's the problem, isn't it? She's badly wounded. She crawls into the back of a black cab, bashing the back of her head against the rest.

Slamming the door of the cab shut and staggering along the path, she remembers she's not drunk. There hadn't been time. There is now. The lights at home blaze. Someone else can fight for the environment. Looking for her keys she notices the decorative plum slates shimmer with icy drizzle. The TV is on. It must mean Adam is home. That's good. She takes her coat off and composes herself. Come on. Think straight. Take it easy. You're home. You're OK.

"Adam?" There's no answer. She drops her bag on the floor and opens the door to the lounge. Her first thought, in that first shaving of a second, is that he's dead. He's lying on his back on the floor. His eyes are closed. There is vomit around his mouth and on his hoodie. His mouth is closed. Anne-Marie falls onto both knees by his side, putting her ear to his mouth. There is the hint of a breath. He's alive. Thank god. She dials 999, trying not to scream at the woman on the phone. Frank doesn't answer his phone. She keeps the message short and tells him to meet her at the hospital.

Trying to roll Adam onto his side into the recovery position is harder than expected. He's heavier than she realised. His body twitches. In his throat is the quietest sound she's ever heard. Her beautiful boy is trying to breathe, but without any reflexes. He's choking on his sick. Quickly she thrusts her fingers into his mouth, trying to keep it open. The smell of the mustard green liquid on his clothes rushes up her nose. She tries to hold up his head, which is in a puddle of sick. She frantically rubs his back as hard as she can, not knowing if anything she's doing is right. There's the slightest twitch in his back muscles. He's trying to vomit again. She fights to get his tongue out of the way of the next heave, but nothing comes out.

"Come on, ambulance. Where are you? Adam, Adam, can you hear me? You're going to be OK, love. They bloody better be here in a minute or I'm driving you to the hospital myself."

She's rambling, pleading with him to live. Her fingers are covered in streaky mucus and bile. She looks at his grey face, seeing the reality of death's door for the first time.

Finally she hears the ambulance, waits until they bang on the door and then speeds to open it. Then she sees the empty vodka bottle by the side of the sofa with a few crushed cans of Coke; a whole litre of vodka. He'd always been allowed to have a beer if there was one. He didn't bother with wine, but this? Why, Adam, why? What's happened? And why did she buy it and leave it here in harm's way?

The 'what if's' hit her thick and fast. What if Frank hadn't laid into her like that? What if she'd been feeling stronger and argued the toss? She can argue all night if she's in the mood. What if she hadn't got a cab? Christ, the de-regulation of taxis has been on her to-do list for a while. She uses them all the time and they are fine early on, but what if there had been a cricket match on in

Pakistan? You can never get a cab then. What if she hadn't got home when she did? Her son would be dead.

The paramedics are so fast she blinks and there are tubes in his mouth. "He'll be alright love," one of them says to her. "That's a new shade on our vomit colour card. What was he drinking?"

"Vodka."

"And weedkiller? Or Kryptonite?"

She assumes they are trying to make her feel better, but of course she doesn't until they are through the hell of reception and into a cubicle with a doctor in front of her.

The doctor's voice is tired and neutral. "Probably fake vodka or anti-freeze. He'll live, but he might not have and he might still have sight problems."

"Hang on, I got that vodka in an off-licence on Denman Street."

"You bought vodka for a 17-year-old boy?" The doctor seems too young to have seen it all. "I could report you to Social Services."

Anne-Marie is thinking about reporting the incident to the Police and Trading Standards, not being reported herself.

"He took that bottle without permission while I was out. What do you mean sight problems?"

"Massive doses of methanol in fake booze can cause blindness or even death."

They aren't going to pump his stomach. Apparently they don't do that automatically these days. They would like to admit him, but there are no beds, so he sleeps on in the cubicle for now.

Anne-Marie's nerves are raw. She asks a nurse if she can go out for a fag break. The nurse looks at her with a 'whatever' face. He might be blind, he could have died while she was busy arguing about more pubs and a bloody casino in the city. Frank's right, Adam doesn't need that.

She's alone in the smoking area, under the searching strip light. The cold bites her ankles. Should she get down on her knees on the pavement, on a bed of cigarette butts, and pray to god to make sure that Adam will be alright? She looks at the floor and decides against kneeling, but says a silent prayer and then slaps herself for being pathetic. Religion is not her road. She has faith in herself, in humankind, in people's power to think, to make the right choices, to look after each other, to act in the interest of the greater good.

Flicking at her plastic lighter, she manages to get a weak bluish flame. There's no heat, no fuel. The flame dies. She's been focusing on the wrong problems, not thinking through the consequences. If Davina's deal goes ahead it opens the door to the Crofts and worse. Those that will squeeze the breath out of the dying and sell it back to them for profit. Buy more drink, gamble more and degrade yourself lap-dancing as you go. It's not like it's not all here in the city already, but what are we doing building it an official residence? Announcing to the world that this is what we think of ourselves, this is what we're here for, this is what we're worth?

She sits through the night by Adam's trolley, listening to stories between plastic walls, about the fights, pain, accidents and other self-imposed injuries. Since when was Sunday an extension of Saturday? Around 6.30am Frank arrives. Adam has opened his eyes. They sit together awkwardly, not mentioning last night, quietly waiting while Adam is wheeled off for a further assessment. Around 9am a new doctor announces that admission won't be necessary. On the basis that his eyes seem OK, and if they are at all worried they can bring him straight back, they wheel him in a chair to the car. He's better at home.

At lunchtime he wakes briefly, groaning, and says, "Mum, I've got to call Ben."

"Take your time, love. I'll get you some water."

Before she reaches the door he's passed out again.

CHAPTER 39

JESSICA

Monday 6ᵗʰ December, 1pm

Anne-Marie is lying, but Jess doesn't care. The fact that she's 'off sick' saves Jess from having to have to walk into the Council House as if everything is alright. It's strange, though, that she's ended up here, at Anne-Marie's heavy, matt-finished, black front door. Despite their recent antagonism, there is recognition of their differences, there is history to draw on and there had been a warmth between them at Frank's party. Jess is sure Anne-Marie can help her and finally, reluctantly, admits, there's no-one else. Anne-Marie doesn't smile, but ushers her in as if she's expected.

"I thought Frank might call you," she says. "God, you look worse than I do. Come in. We'll go into the kitchen. Adam's on the sofa. We've only been home a few hours."

"Something's happened to Adam? Is he OK? Sorry, Frank didn't call me. I don't know what you mean."

"We spent the night in A&E. Adam's been poisoned by fake vodka – that I bloody bought from a local offy."

Jess hears the washing machine going and smells the disinfectant.

"Hold on," Anne-Marie gently touches Jess' elbow, "you've got your glasses on. Have you been crying? You can't get your contact lenses in? God, what a pair. Don't tell me it's bloody Stewart?"

There's an awkward moment where she feels Anne-Marie's arms around her and fails to contain her rage and remorse. It would be maybe thirty years since Jess has cried in front of Anne-Marie. She shakes her head, rubs her eyes hard to avoid tears.

"Sorry, I'm a mess," she says quietly.

"What is it?"

Jess sucks in air, three short breaths, her neck stiffening and rising. The room's moving, the time on the digital display on the oven jumps out at her.

"It's Shaz. She's dead."

Anne-Marie shakes her head. "Shaz?"

"Sharon. My friend Sharon. Our friend Sharon. Sharon Wright. Shaz from school, who lives at the top of Highlands Lane."

"No, she can't be. She's our age, Jess. What happened?"

"She committed suicide." Jess feels almost breathless. Her mouth is dry. She swallows hard, hoping that the focus on the action will help her regain her composure.

"Do you want some water?" Anne-Marie asks, getting a glass and blasting the tap so that it runs cold. Jess sees she's giving her a minute and musters her reserves to speak, perching on the pine table, staring out at the unkempt garden. The kitchen is silent.

"She overdosed on pills and alcohol. It must've taken her hours to die."

"Are you sure it wasn't an accident? The doctor said that vodka could've killed Adam."

"I'm sure. She left a suicide note, a video message for Ben on her phone. She wouldn't return my calls or answer the door. I told her about Croft and Ben working for him. She already knew, said it was her fault, and she told me she'd been attacked by one of their men."

"Christ, no. Where's Ben? Adam must've found out. That could be why he went for the vodka. If Ben was here drinking he might be sick, too."

"No, no, he's alright physically. He's at his nan's. Shaz didn't speak to her mum, not for years, but Ben's OK to stay there for now. He knew there was something wrong, but thought she was sleeping. Eventually he called an ambulance."

Jess sees a crimson fury flash in her friend's aura. Anne-Marie head-butts thin air and stumbles against the worktop. "I'm going totally insane with this. I nearly lose Adam. Ben's lost his mum. He'll be torturing himself that he didn't call the ambulance earlier. It's a mess."

Jess is torturing herself, too. She can't shake off the fact that Shaz killed herself 24 hours after she'd told her about Ben's involvement with Croft. Telling Shaz had made it real and unavoidable, but had she needed to do it then, when she knew Shaz was so vulnerable? A black, bluish soaking of grief covers them both.

Anne-Marie asks her quietly, "When did it happen? How did you find out?"

"Stew's supporting the murder enquiry. He saw the report sheet this morning and rang me. I'd told him last week Shaz was in trouble." Hearing Stew telling her that Shaz was dead had been a horror. His work voice hadn't hidden his indifference.

Jess reflects on her actions over the weekend, the driving past Shaz's house, the phone calls and texts. It had been an unconscious suicide watch – one that had failed. She grabs the kitchen roll and blows her nose. Anne-Marie blows her nose too.

"What a bloody mess. Has Ben seen the note thing? The video?"

Jess had watched the video clip alone and in agony. A kid shouldn't see that. "We can't show Ben yet. It's evidence."

Anne-Marie's response is clear. "Jess, it might help him. Surely you can put it on a secure file or something. Does Shaz say she loves Ben?"

Jess nods.

"He needs to hear that. Forward it to me. I'll take responsibility. I'll show him."

"I can't tamper with evidence." The words sound limp in her mouth.

"Sod that. What is it with you and your rules. You've got to think about Ben."

Jess takes a long drink. It's not about following rules for the sake of it, it's the law. Anne-Marie may be right, but if she's going to do this, she'll have to justify her behaviour, and at the moment she's too emotional, too uncertain.

"I need to think about it. I'll talk to Jonesy. I've spoken to Ben's nan. He's safe for now. How's Adam. Can I ask him a few questions? He might know something."

In the lounge Jess watches Anne-Marie kneel down next to the sofa, touching her son as if he's a newborn in an incubator.

"It's OK, I know about Ben. Why didn't you call me last night? I was only in the Mechanics with your dad. Poor Ben. Poor you." Adam buries his head in his mum's chest.

Seeing what is clearly love, Jess retreats to the kitchen to put the kettle on. She stares out at the garden again, wondering about the video message. It's questionable how useful it will be as evidence anyway and it could help Ben, although it might enrage him and he'd been violent at college. He'll probably want to kill Croft, and the attacker, or both. Underneath her misery and her uniform, she feels pretty much like that herself.

Anne-Marie comes back into the kitchen. She's coaxed Adam into the shower. "His throat is sore from all that puking, but he'll survive. He wants to see Ben. What do you think? Maybe tomorrow?"

Anxiety is etched into Anne-Marie's forehead like a wood-carving. Her brain is still working on processing the information. "Shaz was raped?"

"She says she was too drunk to fight him off, but she blames – blamed – herself."

"For Christ's sake. Do we know if it's the same bastard that murdered the girl and attacked Kerry?"

"Not yet. We're narrowing it down to a handful of possibilities."

Anne-Marie's anxiety is expressing itself in a hesitancy Jess hasn't seen before.

"I said on Friday night we needed to talk. I'm sorry, I didn't think. I mean, I've been working on a development. There's a development, a deal between Croft and the Council. It's on the old Meadows site, but it's only outline at the moment. It's not public yet."

The words smack Jess out of her despair. "What kind of development?"

Anne-Marie steps back, weighing up the impact of her next words. "It's an entertainment centre, regional casino, night club, restaurants. I haven't worked out the connections yet, but Davina is making sure Croft's the only player."

"You're kidding?" Jess snaps. "You've known about this all along. You've been protecting Croft haven't you? Keeping the Girl in the Bin story quiet, undermining the alcohol work, refusing to acknowledge there's a problem. Why didn't you tell me what was going on?"

"I couldn't..." It's unlike Anne-Marie to falter, not to argue a case.

"Of course, you could. You chose not to. You say you want to work together, but it's always on your terms, always your way. You don't care about the rest of us trying to do things properly, the right way." Jess senses her friend's defeat.

"Believe me, I see things very differently today, but things aren't that clear-cut. I honestly don't know how the money stacks up or what Davina's interests are, but as far as they're concerned I'm still with it, I'm still on the inside working for them, and that could be useful. This deal can't go ahead. It'll be a disaster. I can't leave Adam now, but I'll do some digging from here, make a few calls."

Jess is already putting her coat on. "I'm going back to the station. I have to talk to Jonesy. I'll see about the phone. Get Adam to text Ben. Depending on how both of them are, I'll bring Ben round here tomorrow."

Anne-Marie puts a hand on Jess' arm. "I'm not letting you go unless you promise to come back later, as soon as you know more. Are you going to be on your own tonight? Come on, it's as much for me as it is for you. I need someone around. We can talk about what to do next."

There might be some solace in shared suffering. "Thanks, I'll think about it."

Although the station is always quiet on a Monday afternoon, it's unusual for the incident room to be empty. She focuses her attention on the display boards, the map of the city with Croft's pubs circled in red, the location of the girl's body, where Shaz had been that day and the Meadows site. The city now seems small and claustrophobic, as if there isn't a street or alley that couldn't be linked to this case. Her eyes are drawn to a series of photos on the edge of the board. One catches her attention. It's Stewart's mate from tae-kwon do. His name is scrawled next to it. She calls Jonesy.

"I'm back at base. The guy on the board, Ray Turval, he's Stewart's mate. Did he tell you? How did he react?"

"He said he'd seen him around, that was all."

"What've we got on him?"

"He's clean, ex-army, but he hasn't got an alibi and there's witness ID in Silver Street at the right time, though."

"Have we got the warrant for Croft's pubs? Found any offices they might have?"

"Boss, I'm on it. I'm down at the Magistrates now."

"Good. Who's on duty this afternoon?"

"Mrs P."

"Could you warn her that we might need to extend the search area. See what turns up at the pubs. There are some derelict buildings down on the Meadows site that might be worth a look and, keep this to yourself, the Council House."

"The site isn't a problem, but is there a link to the Council House? What's your thinking here? That's way beyond me. The Chief will need to sort that."

In his shoes, she might also be doubtful about a warrant to search the Council offices. It would be a first and would ignite a political storm. "You're right. I'm getting ahead of myself. We don't know what we might find yet and I might need a quiet chat with the Leader of the Council first. I don't want them getting notice of any suspicion, though. Likewise Croft." She hears a pause at the other end of the phone and prepares herself.

"I'm sorry to hear about your friend," he says.

She takes a deep breath. Concerned colleagues are hard to handle. "Thanks. We'll speak later."

While her focus has been on the display in front of her and the call, Jess realises someone has come in. She composes herself before turning around.

"Surprised to see you here," Stewart says. "I thought you'd be at home. You know, the shock of it."

Jess can't tell whether or not he's heard the conversation about the warrants. She can't help thinking he will be desperate to phone Turval, but checks herself. They are friends, but would Stew go that far? Would he deliberately obstruct the investigation? She stays calm.

"I'm better here to be honest. I've got a colleague staying at the house at the moment."

How long has it been like this? Normal-sounding sentences which are empty of both meaning and enquiry. It's all for public consumption and under these circumstances couldn't they cut the crap?

"I'll be at Anne-Marie's tonight."

She watches as he leaves the room, forcing himself not to rush perhaps? Jess is aware she's making a leap. She thinks of Shaz and

Ben, collects her coat and makes her way to the evidence store. "Is the stuff bagged up for Sharon Wright yet? It's the phone I need for a bit."

The old sergeant knows her well and her father before her. "Yes ma'am," he says, giving her the eye to let her know it's not evidence preservation procedure, but he hands over the plastic bag with the phone in it.

She carries it towards the car park, slowly slipping it into her bag as Stewart comes into view. They are alone, hovering on the edge of the cold afternoon and the empty corridor.

"Where are you off to with that?" he demands.

"None of your business," she flashes back.

"It's an offence to tamper with evidence." His official tone is empty and pompous. Jess pushes past him.

"There's nothing on there that will stack up, just the ramblings of an unstable drunk."

She could hit him hard. She imagines his oily blood on her hands and how good it would feel. Turning back towards him, she thinks, stay calm, don't lose it. He must be winding her up deliberately.

"Have you seen it?"

"I'm on the team. I can look at it whenever I like, but I'm interested in what you're doing with it... ma'am."

She ignores him and walks to her car without speeding up.

"I'm coming with you. You're emotional and you're way out of line here. I told you before, Croft is nothing to do with this. It sounds to me like you're deliberately on the warpath against a major financial player in the city. You don't know who you're dealing with here."

And you do, she thinks, so why aren't you helping us with that then? She slams the car door shut, pulling out, hoping he won't follow her. She turns left and heads back to Anne-Marie's.

CHAPTER 40

ANNE-MARIE

Monday 6th December, 4pm

Adam makes it upstairs, propped under Anne-Marie's arm. They are getting better at this double act, but the stairs are too narrow. Still, she enjoys the physical contact, mingled as it is with the euphoria that he's alive. "My god, you need to change your clothes. Jess'll be back soon. Fancy some flat Coke? You don't look ready for solids."

She's not sure she is either. Jess' questions and how to answer them feel like a new mountain to climb and this time she'll need fixed pegs hammered deep into the rocks to support her. She'll need a map that can tell her which way to go in the dark and a compass that can provide direction into the future. Except all she's got are her own resources, doubtful and depleted.

She sits outside the bathroom, leaning her back against the door, picking tiny loops of fluff from the carpet. She's there in case Adam needs her.

She realises now that when her mum left she'd desperately needed someone other than her dad to help her. Mums don't leave – or they didn't then. Dad needed someone to help him, too, but that wasn't an option back then and still isn't for most men. It's almost a cliché now, but it was a bereavement of sorts. Her mum had gone off with another selfish sod who'd left his family and the two of them had moved into a massive four-bed detached place on the outskirts of the city. Anne-Marie was no longer wanted. She'd held it together for about six months, then had impulsively chucked a brick through the window of the Con Club. Seeing her mum, sitting there with her bloody gin and tonic, smoking her Du Maurier menthol cigarettes, had lit the torch paper. The intention was to give her mum a fright, not to hurt her, but it clearly wasn't one of her brighter ideas. The new actuarial husband didn't want the fuss, so nothing came of it. The violence of the action hadn't scared Anne-Marie. She'd loved the glass shattering, the look on their faces, the statement she'd made.

She'd adored her dad until then, seeing him as a rebel, someone who would stand up for the underdogs, but he couldn't stand up for himself and he couldn't fight a grief-stricken teenager. When Jess had been on a psychological profiling course in their late twenties, she'd said Anne-Marie was a text book case, coping with the trauma of abandonment by self-medicating with alcohol and sex. Maybe it's because she's sober today, but even she can see that hasn't changed much in the last twenty years.

There is no way she's letting Adam get into that kind of behaviour. It hits her like a baseball bat to the back of the head that Adam had his own childhood trauma. Neither his mum nor dad had run off, but she and Frank had split up when he was three. They'd done their best to keep up the appearance of a warm loving home, but young Adam was acutely aware of having two homes and a mummy and daddy who weren't together. At the age of about seven Adam had started asking, "If I'm good will you and dad get back together?" She's getting carried away, though. It must be the after-effects of last night. She reminds herself that Frank has never been weak like her dad. He'll be there for Adam and so will she.

An hour passes in a blur of early evening TV news and inane chat. Her laptop glows on the sofa next to her. What she's got is time and in that time she can plan. "Plans are useless, but planning is priceless," she groans at herself, but it's true. The sound of a car draws her to the window. It's Jess. As she comes up the path, another car, driven by Stewart, pulls into view.

"Quick, let me in." She pulls the door to after her, whispering, "Can we pretend to be polite until I can get rid of him?"

Stewart stands waiting for the door to re-open, slowly taking off his tan driving gloves.

"Come through," Anne-Marie says. She realises she hasn't seen Stewart for a couple of years or more. The bitterness is evident in his thin, tight-lipped mouth. His career has gone nowhere, while Jess' has blossomed. Anne-Marie is only surprised that they stayed together this long.

Jess uses her work voice. "We need to look at Sharon's recording. Stewart, you can look at it anytime. Could you give us some private space? Then I'll take it back to the station."

Anne-Marie wouldn't normally play along with this kind of strained civility, but says to Stewart, "You can find your way around a kitchen can't you? Why don't you make tea?"

He's reluctant to leave the lounge and far too keen to see this. What's his rush? Jess pulls on a pair of clear plastic gloves and brings out the evidence bag. The phone has been upgraded recently. It's slick, black and the screensaver is a picture of Shaz and Ben, passport photo-style. The reality of what it is they are about to see hits and Anne-Marie isn't sure she can do it.

Jess warns, "You don't have to watch it if it's too much. You can just listen to it. She's sort of filming herself at the beginning, but then she drops the phone and it's pointing at the ceiling so you can't see her anyway. I shouldn't have bought it here, but it's saved to a secure file and I was thinking about what you said. Watch it and if you still think it's a good idea we'll show Ben."

Jess presses play and lays the phone flat on the coffee table. Shaz is propped up by maybe three or four pillows. They look clean. There's an embroidered silver stripe down the side of the matching duvet. She's wearing a plain pink hoodie. It doesn't look like it's pyjamas. It's fairly dark and the curtains are partially drawn. It's some relief that no pills or whiskey are on show. Anne-Marie gulps, imagining Shaz planning her note to Ben, thinking about what to wear. Shaz wipes her fringe out of her eyes, her quiet voice begins hesitantly.

11.01am: Ben, I love you. I hope you know that. I do love you and you mustn't doubt that ever - never. When you were small I would tell you every day, every night when you went to bed, and I'd do it now if it didn't sound so stupid. I couldn't, you know, write anything. It would come out wrong. I mean it's all coming out wrong anyway. I'm so sorry my love, I'm so sorry.

11.15am: What I want to say is that I can't live with it anymore. I can't. You've only tried to help, all along you've helped. Ben. I know you're going to be so angry with me and you're right. I've let you down so much I don't know where to begin apologising. Don't hate me, though, Ben. I know what you've been doing and it can't go on. This is the only way for you to get away from those bastards. If I'm gone they've got nothing on you. And I want, I want to do this. You'll think I'm mad, but I'm not doing it because I've lost it. I know it'll be hard to understand, but it's my choice. It's the only thing I can think of that will help.

11.45am: I just feel tired. So tired. I mean, I know I've failed you. It might've been different if I was still at the Peartree. They were my lifeline for a while. I was better then, wasn't I? How're people like me supposed to sort ourselves out with no-one to help? I mean you helped, helped so much, but that's not a job for a young boy. No son ought to see their mother like that. I see myself much clearer now. It's honestly the calmest I've felt in ages. Listen to me. I needed proper psychological help and it wasn't there. If you want to blame anyone, blame the bloody Government, the Prime Minister, the Council, the lot of them. It always felt like you and me on our own. And the thing is, what I know now, is that you're better off without me.

12.30pm: Ben, you're going to be alright, but don't stay here. Get away from this business. Get as far away as you can. Don't stay at your nan's or they might be in danger. Go to Dundee. Jess will help you. Someone must help you, because you're not 18 yet. I know what it's like. They only help children. You can stay with my cousin Alison. Her number's on this phone. Don't go to your nan's. It's too close and...

1pm: Ben I love you. It could've been different. If...

1.45pm: Get away Ben. Don't go anywhere near the pub. Keep away from the Meadows. Stop delivering. If you see any of Croft's men, run and never stop, my love. Do anything to get away. You know what they can do. Tell Jess about everything. She knows how to stop them and keep you safe. The whole thing has to stop. You'll be fine. You can make something of yourself. Whatever you choose, do you best. I trust you Ben, you hear me...

2pm: Love...

Tears stream down Anne-Marie's face. No mother should ever get to the point where she thinks killing herself is the best thing to do, yet if she genuinely thought she could save Adam's life in return for her own she would do it. Every time, she would. Not that she underestimates the courage needed. Shaz knew what she wanted to do and had the courage to see it through, but that didn't mean she wasn't scared. Her hesitancy, her determination to say the right things for her son couldn't hide that. What will stay with Anne-Marie is the audible fear in Shaz's voice.

The end of a life, a fragile record of love and the components of despair, squashed into a tiny screen. It threatens to overwhelm her. She's imagined saying goodbye to Adam. She's imagined the natural separation that will come when he's old enough to leave home, get his own place or goes off to uni, but to say goodbye like that? Shaz saw herself as a failure, but it's not her failure, it's all of ours.

Anne-Marie realises Stewart's been watching. He takes a deep breath, appears to be relieved it's over. Adam has come down and is standing behind him. Jess quickly picks up the phone and presses the stop button.

"It was Ben's mum, wasn't it?" Adam's watery eyes don't move from the phone. "I want to hear it. Where's Ben? Has he heard it?"

"No son, it's evidence." Stewart sounds calm, putting on his court voice to match the uniform.

"Ben needs to hear it," Anne-Marie snaps. "He has a right to hear it."

"He's in no state to see this. Think about it from his point of view," Stewart says, as if Ben's point of view is one he would ever be interested in.

"You've got to show Ben." Adam looks like he will burst.

Stewart attempts to sound like he's in charge. He picks up the empty evidence bag and holds it up for Jess. "Ben is at his nan's house. He's safe. We have a car outside and he's told us he doesn't want to see anyone. He's just trying to get his head around what's happened." Stewart's waiting for the phone, his arm out-stretched.

"That's exactly why he needs to see it," Anne-Marie insists. "He needs to know his mum loved him. You can't keep that from him. Jess, please, why don't we all go? Let's take it to Ben now."

"You can't do that. I told you, it's evidence. He'll get to see it eventually."

Anne-Marie wants to smack Stewart's patronising face. "That's not good enough. Ben'll be blaming himself and that's not fair."

Jess cuts in, "There will be an enquiry and it'll be months before he sees it."

Stewart raises his voice. He's looking straight at Jess. "I have to talk to you outside. I mean right now. I told you we should've done this at the station." He steps towards her. The room suddenly seems too small. He's invading their space. "This phone should never have left the station."

Anne-Marie sees Jess shake. "Don't tell me what to do."

Stewart lunges forward, trying to grab the phone. He's unbalanced and can't quite reach, because of the coffee table. Adam tries to grab his arm from behind to hold him back. Stewart jabs an elbow, catching the corner of Adam's jaw. Still groggy, Adam falls backwards onto the floor.

"Don't you touch my son," Anne-Marie yells at him. "Get out of my house."

Jess puts the phone in her pocket quickly. "For god's sake, Stew, back off right now. I'm in control, I'm in charge and I'll decide what happens."

Anne-Marie tries to get to Adam, but Stew isn't interested in her son.

He points a finger at Jess. "I told you it's a mistake. The wrong people could get hold of this. We can't let this get out in public."

"Who are the wrong people, Stew?" Jess flares.

Adam staggers to his feet and moves towards Stewart, who swings round, arm raised, in a martial arts stance. There's no contact this time, although the threat is clear. Anne-Marie jumps the coffee table and puts her body between Adam and Stewart. "Adam, get to the kitchen and ring Frank. Stew, get out of my house. Didn't you hear me?"

But Stewart's focus is on Jess.

"Who are the wrong people?" she asks again. Anne-Marie sees contempt and a new resolve in her friend. Jess squares up to him unflinching, face fierce. "I'm not afraid of the truth now."

As Stewart slams the front door, Anne-Marie hugs Adam, careful not to touch his chin. "Where did he catch you? It looks alright, a bit red maybe." She cajoles him to the sofa and joins Jess in the kitchen. Stewart is right, the message could be political dynamite, but both his and Jess' reactions were wrong, too extreme. Jess' tone had an edge of ultimatum. It wasn't clear how much Adam heard, but Shaz clearly said that going to Ben's nan's might put them in danger. She can't let Adam near any kind of danger either.

"Jess, what's going on?"

"I'm so sorry. I couldn't keep it under control. I shouldn't have let him in the house, but I can't leave this now. I need your help."

"Of course. Don't go home tonight. Come and stay here. He's a bastard."

"He's already moved his stuff out, but I've got someone else at the house. Barrington. Barrington Edwards."

"Don't tell me...?"

"100 per cent no way, Anne-Marie. It's more complicated than I can tell you at this stage."

Jess rubs her hand over her face. The daylight has gone outside the house and the kitchen is dark.

"Look, we'll have a takeaway." Anne-Marie turns on the warming spotlights. "If there's anything else we need we can get it, but now you really have to tell me what's going on."

"Yep," she says, but doesn't. "I need to let Ben know that we'll come over tomorrow."

Anne-Marie has had years of practice holding things back, but Jess is almost ready to burst. Before they get into detail, she wants to know what going to happen with the phone.

"Had you decided to show Ben the phone before you came here?"

"I had and I hadn't. I agree with you mainly, but if we show Ben, yes, he'll know his mum loved him, but he might also want to go and do something stupid, maybe even go for Croft. I can't risk that."

"Adam would go with him and actually I might as well."

They are satisfied that Adam didn't really hear any of the detail of what Shaz was saying and by that point it was pretty slurred and incoherent, but could that really be evidence?

"Let's come back to that later."

"You're right," Anne-Marie says. "Let's go through what we know."

"Are you going to work tomorrow?" Jess asks.

Work. "I'm due to see Davina first thing tomorrow morning, but I'm not ready for it. I…" Work. She takes a dip herself now. Work has become her identity, it's emblazoned across her shield, but it's a shield that no longer provides cover for her core, that her arms are now too weak to lift. "I need some air. I'll check on Adam and then we can drag ourselves down the shops."

Anne-Marie decides to call in sick for the morning, stay with Adam, cancel Davina. Frank might be able to come over later. Then she can decide whether or not to go into work in the afternoon. Her bones don't want to go in that direction, but she needs to re-group. Remind herself of some basics. Patch something together that she can defend herself with, something that could become a weapon.

CHAPTER 41

JESSICA

Tuesday 7th December, 5.30am

Avoiding the springs on Anne-Marie's sofa bed has been like that kid's game where you navigate a rod with a ring on the end around a squiggly wire. If you touch the sides a buzzer goes. She'd eventually dreamt she was naked in the middle of a football stadium, the floodlights highlighting every mole, spot, freckle on her skin. She'd jolted awake, telling herself it was a classic anxiety dream, but sleep was impossible. There had been men in that dream, men watching her from the stands, from around the edge of the football pitch, a groundsman, his eyes boring into her. She's been staring at the bedside clock for over an hour now.

They hadn't sat up all night talking. By 11pm they were drained. Anne-Marie had said it was the first time in years she'd opened a bottle of wine and not finished it. Jess had been relieved about that. How much was Anne-Marie drinking, she wondered? Maybe more than Shaz had been. On her salary she could certainly afford it. Should she risk mentioning it or make the same mistake again? Was that when she'd started to let Shaz down? Not talking to her about her drinking? Or not talking to her about her life? Either way, Jess' vocal chords have had a habit of failing at the critical moment.

There are hours of darkness to go. She can't wait for the night to become morning. A hostile anticipation drives her to get up. She decides to go home before Barrington wakes, get her stuff and come back here for a shower. She'd been relieved that, despite

Anne-Marie's initial curiosity about Barrington, she'd managed to explain the events without any real scrutiny. It had meant at least one more night to draw her thoughts together, to think it through. And why would Anne-Marie think there was more to know? What might Jess have said if she'd probed deeper? Probably the same lies she'd constructed all those years ago, so practised and internalised they had meshed into a truth-like web. Or maybe not this time. What would it feel like to tell the truth?

She'd convinced herself that if she was a good girl and did what she was told she would be alright. Miraculously that had worked and, in some ways, it continued to work. That was the thing about the Force. It rewarded silence and if she had to accept that her promotions might not have been on her own merit, well, that wasn't so bad either. She still got promoted. Stewart and their deathly relationship was part of her penance, but, actually, until the last few years he hadn't been so bad to live with, and keeping up lies has kept her alert, forced her to think creatively, helped her develop.

What about being under oath? How would she hold up? Actually, a reassuring wooden witness box in a quiet orderly courtroom would be a relief. The whole truth would be a relief, but how would she get into a witness box when no-one knew what questions to ask? For years Jess has thought that the truth will be her medicine, that it will, in the end, clear her head and her heart, heal her guilt, but now she is so close to it she remembers that there are side effects to all medicines. She will feel worse before she can ever feel better.

Which brings her back to Shaz. She's lost a friend; a lovely, caring woman who was alone and in no-one's sights. No-one, including Jess herself, had seen that Shaz had lost her way. The people at the Peartree Drug and Alcohol Service probably knew best what was going on, but their funding had been cut and their service shut down. No-one had picked Shaz up and thought to ask what she needed. There were other professionals who could've made sure she got it, but Shaz didn't make it onto anyone's priority list. They'd all decided that basically she was OK and moved on to the next. We all had other priorities, she thinks.

In the course of Jess' career she's consistently told herself that the truth isn't always possible. As police officers all they can often do is shine a light on what's known. Get a torch out, a cool beam to flood the facts with transparency. Jess decides she'll shine whatever light she can on Croft. It occurs to her that Ben and Adam might be able to help with that. It might offer Ben something – the chance to contribute to Croft's downfall. To see Croft and whoever attacked his mum in court would be a painfully small and highly uncertain piece of justice compared to losing your mum, but it might be a comfort. It's her job to make that happen, but she needs to do more. She'll shine a light on the hidden corners of her own life, too; on all their lives. She'll see what that reality looks like and live with the consequences.

Jess pulls up a few metres back from her house. It's 6am and it's in darkness. A lone porch light opposite provides the only sign of life in the cul-de-sac. She's not keen to disturb Barrington and plans to be in and out in ten minutes. The alarm isn't on and the kitchen smells of bleach. She can negotiate her own home in the dark. Creeping around forms part of police training and the deep pile carpets muffle most of the sound. Feeling cold, she spots that the bathroom window is open and so is the small window in her bedroom. Relieved that the door to the spare room is closed, her sympathies go out to Corinne.

In the gloom of the bedroom wardrobe the stripes on her jacket guide her. She fumbles the uniform and a white shirt into a suit bag. In the drawer she finds her soft jersey yoga trousers and puts them into a regulation holdall. As she collects her soap bag from the bathroom she thinks she hears another car pull up.

From the bedroom window she sees Stewart's car. He's already walking to the front door. Damn, she hasn't got his keys back or changed the locks. Anything they need to say to each other has to be outside. She has to head him off, but as she gets to the bottom of the stairs he's in and has switched the hall light on. Her eyes are grateful for the low energy bulb as it slowly warms up.

"What do you want?"

As the light brightens she sees his scowl. His eyes are red-rimmed and angry.

"I followed you from Anne-Marie's."

Jess shudders. "Why? This early? What's going on? If you want to talk let's go outside. My colleague is staying over, remember."

Stewart is blocking the way out. "What the hell did you think you were talking about yesterday."

"You must see that Shaz's death has changed things for me…"

"I see you're losing it. Your judgement is clouded."

"No, I'm seeing things more clearly than I have in years."

"I've told the Chief that you're grieving, need to get away for a break somewhere. You can't be involved with this anymore."

"How dare you. That's not happening, but I do need to talk to you." Jess is trying to keep her voice down.

He takes two steps forward into her face. His breath is stale. "You're tampering with evidence in a murder enquiry."

"Are you still talking about the phone? It's more than that. I've decided to go and see Darren's family, but we can't talk here. Not now."

This isn't right. She's not ready. He grabs her forearm.

"Back off, you're threatening me again and I won't have it."

It had been clear yesterday that she still held the upper hand. Her implicit threat trumped anything he could come up with. They'd both known this from the start of their marriage, but he'd always said it was her career as well as his that would be destroyed. To her shame, she'd accepted that as true. Last night had changed things. She no longer cared and in that moment he saw it.

"You bitch, you'd do it wouldn't you?"

His voice is raised. Barrington is upstairs. He's bound to wake up and hear. Jess glares at him. "Stop it, now." Her priority is Barrington. He can't hear this. He can't hear this now.

"This is nothing. I know how to keep you quiet. And it won't just be me. You go to the Chief and you think he's going to listen? He never did all those years ago. Don't kid yourself. This is the Force you're talking about. No-one will believe you. You're distraught, unbalanced. It was an accident. We've been through it all before."

Jess hears the bedroom door above them open.

"And you think you're going to send me to jail? For what? For fuck all. The poxy life of a thieving black kid." The shock of seeing Barrington at the top of the stairs makes Stewart falter. He backs out into the street, slamming the front door as hard as he can behind him.

Jess is sure he doesn't know who Barrington is, but it doesn't matter. Barrington's heard enough to ask. She'd wanted time to prepare for this conversation, time to plan it safely, for her and Barrington. He shouldn't be the person either. That person is Darren's mother, Hermin. She's imagined the conversation a hundred times, but her courage has always failed her. This time her anger will carry her through.

"Who's that? What's going on?" Barrington rubs his eyes. He's wearing an old cycling T-shirt and shorts.

"Come into the kitchen a minute will you?" She steadies herself on the breakfast bar, her arms taking her weight, elbows locked. Panic shoots through her. She could make something up. She could tell a partial truth. Stewart is her ex-husband. It's domestic. Lies are forming on her lips, but no, this is the chance she's been thinking about. This is the chance to make things change. She's got to say it now.

"My ex-husband, Stewart," Jess begins quietly, "killed your cousin, Darren."

Five seconds is all it takes. That's it – it's done. Those few unspoken words have shaped her life for the last twenty years. Suddenly they are said. She feels like the ground should start shaking, a huge crack should appear, a crack that travels from this spot at her kitchen table, through the house, the city and across the region. It should stretch and deepen all the way to London. It should swallow up her, Stewart, the station, HQ, the Home Office.

"How do you know it was him?" From Barrington's face it's clear these words have no such import. He looks confused, like his brain is working through a logic puzzle.

"Because I was the first to arrive on the scene. I was only minutes away, but in those few minutes, he died. I saw Stewart's reaction. We weren't married at the time, but we'd started going out. That night he admitted that in the heat of the moment he'd used one of his martial arts moves, a neck hold, and…" Jess braces herself for a cleansing blast of Barrington's anger.

"My cousin died of positional asphyxia. The flow of blood to his brain was obstructed. The Police said he'd been drinking, but he died at 11am in the morning and no evidence of alcohol levels was presented at the enquiry." There is no emotion on his face.

"I know Stewart used excessive force." Jess is trying to keep it as factual and as calm as she can. Her instinct is to comfort him, to touch him. She looks at the cut above Barrington's eye. This man has been through some sort of trauma and his relationship is breaking down, and she's telling him this.

"Of course he did or my cousin would not be dead. That was clear to everyone. The inquest wasn't based on fact. That you happen to be married to him is new, but what does that change?"

She's stunned. How can it change everything for her but nothing for him? "What about your family? Your Aunt Hermin?" Jess recognises that she has needed to say this, but he does not have a similar need to hear it.

"Hermin will speak for herself."

"But there could be another enquiry." Jess sees he's unimpressed. All the time she's been painfully burying this away, it's been about her own need to be punished.

"In the last 11years there have been 333 deaths in custody. Do you know how many police officers have been convicted?" he asks.

She shakes her head.

"None. Zero."

If she'd thought about it, it was predictable that he'd respond with a statistic.

"They've changed the system. It will be better now." The system has done a good job of ensuring she's kept her mouth shut so far, though. The pressure from Stewart had been overt; emotional blackmail backed by a silent physical threat. From the men at the station it had been the 'take a hit for the team' message and from the Chief it was cerebral and insistent persuasion. And she'd done what they wanted, because her whole life her dad, a man who had worked for a system and an institution he believed was inherently good, had taught her to be a good girl.

"Where is your evidence for that assumption?"

"I'm sorry" is all she can say.

Her phone bleeps, breaking the tension. It's a text from Stewart. *Come outside we need to talk*

Now a wave of fear hits her. Stewart is still outside. He's angry and has said he'll do anything he can to stop her doing this.

"I can't stay here." Barrington says with urgency.

"I know, I understand. Are there any other options? Are you sure you can't go to your Aunt's?"

"No. I can't explain. I… "

"What is it Barrington? What happened?"

"Can I have some water?" he asks quietly, then, while she lets the water from the tap run cold, he says, "I can't go there. I am disgraced."

How can he be disgraced when she has just told him about the cover-up of Darren's death and her central role in it? What a bloody mess. Barrington, Corinne, Anne-Marie, Adam, Ben, the Chief, the list could go on. We are choosing not to see the mess we're in, choosing not to deal with it. She has one of those 'Keep calm and carry on' mugs on the draining board. It's an insidious phrase. No, don't keep calm, don't carry on. Stop, think, shout it out loud, this mess has to be cleaned up. "I have to leave."

Yes, that's right, Jess thinks, be practical.

"Can I take you to a hotel? There's that new chain hotel that's opened by the motorway. It'll be clean, standardised, quiet."

He nods. "But I need to do something. I can't sit in a hotel room doing nothing. I can't."

"You can work. I mean, have you said anything to work? Do they know where you were yesterday?"

"No, I've lost my Blackberry."

"Use my phone and leave them a message. You can't go in today. Do you want to see a doctor?"

"I am a doctor and I don't need to see one."

He looks only slightly better than when she'd found him wandering the ring road.

"Can you drive me past my work? I'll pick up my laptop."

The practicalities are a relief to them both. He looks alert.

"We still need your help with the alcohol work, the evidence – all that. The murder enquiry into the death of the Girl in the Bin has been expanded. There are more victims."

"I know."

Jess is shocked. "You know about Shaz?"

"No, I don't know about anyone called Shaz." He says this as if he has checked a database of names. There is no inference or implied snobbery.

"Shaz is my friend and she's dead. She was another victim, dumped in a skip. It's related."

"Right. I see. I've got the information from the hospital tracking the admissions to A&E and a series of qualitative interviews from Anil."

Jess texts back to Stewart.

Will both be leaving house in 10 mins. Will call later

She's in no hurry to speak to him. Why did she stay with him all that time? It's such an obvious question, but she knew what he was, and still is, capable of. Jess understands that she tied a blindfold across that part of her vision, a blindfold that had become so comfortable she'd forgotten until recently that it was still there. The new light of truth is going to hurt, but for now there's the relief of telling Barrington the truth, although this is balanced by the threat that Stewart, the Chief, the Force might still represent. She knows she's changed, but she isn't confident that they have.

CHAPTER 42

ANNE-MARIE

Tuesday 7th December, 6.15am

Smoking in bed feels like having her lungs wrapped in an extra duvet. The light, hazy effect it has on her head cushions the early start. She hears Jess closing the front door and decides to give it another 15 minutes for the house to warm up. She's missing Bob in her bed. Not that she'd have had the mental space for sex, but his physical presence would've been good. Even if she can block out the feeling that he hates her, though, she's still left without his company and support.

There wasn't a peep from Adam the whole evening, but she imagines he'll soon be in a state where he could eat a pit pony. Her craving is for white toast with a puddle of salty melted butter and a smidge of strawberry jam. There's a corner shop near the station that she's confident will be open, so she pulls on jeans, trainers and her thickest work coat against the despondent December morning. Driving into town will be easy, she'll get what she needs, embellished with Jaffa Cakes for Adam, and be back in ten minutes.

What catches her eye as she pulls off is an old sign for Bentley's site traffic. The development location is only a few minutes away and she decides to take a quick look. Strange that with everything that's happened she hasn't actually been down here for months. The dense fog is filled with grime. She puts on her beam, then draws up beside a boarded up pub. A dusting of powdered frost turns out to be shattered glass. Knowing that

Croft owns the building, she gives the sheet metal that's nailed across the front of the door a good kick. A buddleia grows out of the roof and there's a mess of graffiti layers almost blacking out the entire side wall.

A chicken wire fence covers a vague entrance to a concreted section of derelict land that stretches into the distance. The streetlights peter out and it's darker here. It was a bad idea to stop, but her brain has started piecing together what lies in front of her with a plan of the land ownership. There is half a fence with what she thinks might be a Council warning sign of some sort. She turns to her right and can see the station. Never mind Davina, it's so close to the City Centre that they have to do something with this place. "Over my dead body," she shouts to the dim street. There are footsteps behind her. Christ. She's jolted out of her skin, fists clenched tight. She prepares to run, but which way? Her route back to the car is blocked.

"Watch my ears, will you. Very tender they are this time of the morning."

It's a large man walking a small dog, who seems desperate to water the rusted gate post. Anne-Marie takes a deep breath and looks at his face.

"Sorry love, did I give you a fright? We don't usually see anyone down here this time of the morning."

It's Mr Sizzle. There's no need to run, although she's not keen on the interest the dog is showing in her trainers. Sizzle is wearing what look like steel re-enforced boots, an old donkey jacket and a thick woollen Benny hat.

"Stop that, Cromwell. Can't take him anywhere." The dog is a King Charles Spaniel with a white stripe, soppy face and gift card eyes.

"Come to enjoy the sunrise over the Meadows, have we?" Local sarcasm. Normally it can't be beaten, but today it's too early and her nerves are rattled.

"Does the sun ever rise here, then?"

"No, bab. Always was a dump, always will be."

"And you're going to say, but it's our dump and that's how we like it?"

"Correct!" He sounds delighted. "Not sure I could live with it any other way."

That kind of attitude has always irritated Anne-Marie. She sees it as a mixture of reverse snobbishness and negativity that sucks the ambition out of working class communities. "But it doesn't have to be a dump," she says, her voice disappearing across the concrete expanse.

"I wasn't joking. Always was a dump, since my dad was a nipper and his dad was a nipper's nipper."

She smiles, remembering the muscle movement in her cheeks, then looks him in the eye and sees he's serious. What if he's right? She turns her back to look at the road. It's the New Road. If there's a new road there must've been an old road, but where? In the far corner of her field of vision is the shape of the burnt-out warehouse, the site of the explosion she and Bob had been caught in; the explosion supposedly caused by joyriders. If this was all one big dump the land could've been toxic. It could still be toxic. The clean-up costs would be enormous. It could kill the Pleisureland finance package. She imagines flammable gas billowing from underneath the foundations of the shell of the new building. It could all go up. Don't get ahead of yourself she thinks, but it's something to work on.

"There you go." Sizzle is almost smiling. The morning sun is starting to rise. It has no warmth, but the light picks out the beautiful brick work of an old bridge leading to one of the canals. She bends down to tickle the dog under his chin. "You're lovely, you are."

"Not as lovely as his owner, don't you think?"

Anne-Marie turns. She needs to get back to her son.

When Adam wakes up later he seems brighter. He's going to see Ben tomorrow and says he's never drinking again. Or at least he isn't drinking that poison again. Once he's back on the sofa she can't avoid checking her emails. There are 492. Four from Davina, marked urgent, remind her that she needs to be increasingly vigilant from here on in. Davina is pushing for an early outline planning application. At this stage it will only be a red line around the site, but they must be getting ready to move.

The news about the economy is deathly, never mind the potential toxicity of the site. The deal won't withstand another financial dip and it makes sense that Davina wants to make fast progress in case there's another collapse. Unless some of the money is coming from overseas. One neighbouring council has been creative about attracting decent foreign investors and has a Canadian pension company, no less, on board. She wonders whether they could pull something like that off. After the Iceland debacle their councillors are unlikely to go for it, but it could be her own lack of courage, her learned limitations, that means she dismisses alternatives before they've been aired.

Frank arrives mid-afternoon to sit with Adam, so Anne-Marie and Jess can get out for an hour or so.

"What took you so long?" Frank says, and he doesn't mean to open the front door.

"Davina's scheme has some merits."

"No." He gives her a long look. "Don't tell me you're starting that again."

Her texts to him during the morning have already told him that she's seeking an alternative, but she holds off with the smile until he knows he's been had.

"So what are we going to do about it?"

"I don't know exactly yet. We ought to be able to pull something together on that site."

"Who's we?"

"I don't know."

"What about the alcohol issue? What about Croft?"

"I'm working on it."

Anne-Marie means she's thinking about it. She still needs time to reflect on her own response to alcohol. It's on her list, in a deeper way than before and with plenty more reason, but that won't stop her opening a bottle of red wine tonight. What happens when she drinks is that it helps her think. It enables her to cut through the crowded, impenetrable complexity that surrounds her life, to get to the heart of the matter, to access a deeper level. Frank's never understood that.

"You just jumped seamlessly from 'we' to 'I' again," Frank says.

"You know what I mean. I need to think it through first, but we need to do something."

He starts to form his lecturing pose, fist tight, tucked under his chin. "This is the best opportunity we've ever had to do something about harmful drinking, give it an almighty shove, do something meaningful. Jess is right. If it was a gang shooting we'd be under the spotlight, firing off initiatives. We'd all be involved. This isn't just Adam. We aren't the only parents worried about this. I've got plenty of alcoholic and drugged up students to worry about and…"

"Frank, you're doing it again." Her hackles are itching to rise, but she does what she can to keep a lid on it. Don't diss the pep talk, as Adam might say.

"I'm serious, girl," he continues.

Frank hasn't called her that for a while. Things must be improving.

"Don't just present us with one you prepared earlier. Talk to us. Talk to Barrington."

Thankfully Jess rings the doorbell, tired but clearly on a mission.

Frank puts a sincere arm on Jess' shoulder. "I'm so sorry to hear about Sharon."

"Thanks." She looks across to Anne-Marie. "We'll be out for an hour or so." They grab their coats.

"Where are we going?"

"The Rendevue Hotel."

"Because?"

"Barrington is staying there. Don't roll your eyes. We need him to nail Croft. We've got to work together. I mean properly, not lip service, not playing at it."

What surprises Anne-Marie is that they still think she won't pitch in. She doesn't need telling. She nearly lost her son. It's clear her motivation has changed, but that doesn't automatically mean she has to work differently, does it? Good question. She needs to think about that. For now she says, "Yeah, yeah I know, but I want to hear the full story first. What was he doing at your place?"

Jess' eyes are fixed on the road as she begins the story. Anne-Marie's are wider than a mile. Good job she's not driving. That Stewart was a bastard is nothing new, but she's amazed at Jess' confession, her involvement. She can't believe her exceptionally competent, thoughtful, often pain in the arse, preachy friend could be part of it... except that she knows the compliant, easily manipulated side of Jess, too. Anne-Marie now feels slightly guilty about having leant on Jess herself. She thinks back to what Jess was like at 19. She'd started her police training and they'd hardly seen each other, but her own first year at college had been pretty ugly and she doesn't feel capable of throwing stones at the moment.

Anne-Marie has a hundred questions, but the thought in her head now is that Stewart was right to say Shaz's video can't get into the wrong hands. Strange that he'd understood mass exposure of that video would unleash a further tide of torment, but his reaction may not have been over the top if there does turn out to be a connection to Croft.

They arrive at the hotel in silence. Barrington isn't in his hotel room.

"I've got an idea where he might be." Jess drives off again.

In ten minutes they get to the park. It's cold and getting dark, but now they're here Anne-Marie can guess why Barrington might have a thing about this place. She remembers responding instinctively to a small poster on a lamppost near her house, a rallying call to protest against Darren's death in custody. She'd been there in the snow all those years ago, waiting for the demo to start. The anger she'd felt as a student hadn't been enough to insulate them from the cold.

"They'll be locking the gates soon. Let's make it quick."

Linking arms they begin a circuit of the park. Anne-Marie tells her about her early morning conversation and her suspicions. She'd found another potential piece of the jigsaw about 11am and celebrated with more toast. Even at the first meeting with Croft and Davina they'd talked about potential access issues. For any development of this size access is the showstopper. If they can't get direct access onto the ring road and out to the motorway, it's dead in the canal. What Anne-Marie has discovered is that old man Bentley owns part of the access for the site. Bentley is a medium-sized employer, used to be a councillor years back, but he's now Davina's party chairman. He effectively has a ransom strip, a crappy bit of derelict land that he can name his price for and is Davina going to say no? To her own party chairman? Is she buggery. Anne-Marie senses there's more and this isn't just about feathering the nests of a few of Davina's cronies.

"Are you sure Barrington will be OK with you? I mean, if it was me…"

She nods. "I hope so. He's, you know, unemotional."

Anne-Marie is unconvinced. Barrington is definitely on the autistic spectrum, but then what bloke in management isn't these days? Being arrogant, lacking social skills, thinking you can do everything on your own, it's not in the person spec, but it's the sort of behaviour that gets men the jobs. Then again, this isn't work.

They stop at a low-gated play area. This is one of the remaining good play areas in the city. She loves the swings. At some level everyone loves swings, don't they? That first experience of motion, the fear and exhilaration of being pushed higher and higher. At the top of the swing's arc you see sky, looking down you see the ground rushing towards you. The feel of her dad's hands on her back, pushing her for as long as she'd wanted.

Still, she's a Council officer and the cost of the insurance for play areas and the hours her officers have spent discussing which flooring meets the safety regulations threatens to kill the moment. The kids that need these play areas most don't get them because grown-ups looking for a quick buck make spurious claims against the Council. Then the Council runs out of money to maintain them and they get shut down.

"Come on then," she says, unable to resist. She works hard, pulling at the chains and thrusting her legs forward and back to get going. The wind scalds her cheeks, but she doesn't care. It's great to know her backside still fits on the rough, red plastic seat. Jess is scraping her feet along the ground. "It's only a swing, Jess. Come on." As Jess gradually gets going, Anne-Marie spots Barrington and shouts across, inviting him to join them. Barrington responds hesitantly, settling himself on the bottom of a see-saw, not moving but clearly listening.

"What did you get from the hospital data?" Jess asks him.

"I've identified – sorry, Anil identified – a definite pattern of incidents. In addition to the three cases we know about, there are possibly a further eight involving Rohypnol over the last year. Significantly more incidents without drugs, but with similar levels of alcohol consumption to the Girl in the Bin."

"Shall we all call her by her name now?" Anne-Marie says. "It was Laura, wasn't it?"

Barrington continues. "And there's a similar range of injuries, including GBH, ABH, broken bones, broken teeth, extensive bruising, cuts requiring stitches and some visible disfigurement. Not all assaults end in rape, but the interview-based data suggests a similar mode of operation. The women are often drinking in fairly large groups, five or more, similar ends to the evening, isolated, dragged into alleyways and the like, dumped close to waste units. There are multiple starting locations for these evenings out. The only definite commonality is the Anvil and the Three Lions."

Jess thanks him. "We have to get this to my DI. He's been closing in on the Anvil and one or two suspects."

Anne-Marie thinks about the time she was there with Bob, the Argentinian, as she'd called him, the behaviour of the bouncer and Croft. Where's Croft in all this? Nowhere. Where's Davina?

"The issue isn't whether you'll get the bastard or not. I know you'll get him – or them." She shudders at the thought that these attacks are organised. "Our bit of it, why we need each other, is that it's about the place. It's where it's happening and who is responsible. We're all responsible. It's up to all of us what happens next. We all need to do this, together."

Anne-Marie finds staring up at the black clouds a release. Can she swing higher? Think bigger? All three of them are in the midst of a hurricane, who cares if it rains? They are already soaked, through their skins and into their bones.

"Is that the best you can do?" she goads Jess.

As Jess gradually begins moving, Anne-Marie's head starts to flood with ideas. Jess throws her head back and blows off steam into the cold air. As they work themselves higher and higher an irritating dry squeak from the swing threatens to spoil the moment. A childhood memory pushes its way through Anne-Marie's buzzing brain. She'd been here with her dad when she was maybe eight or nine. There'd been something on in the park, one of dad's things, lots of stalls, banners, music, old people, but she had refused to move from the swing.

"What're we doing here anyway, Dad?" she'd asked.

"Come on, love," he'd replied. "We're changing the world."

CHAPTER 43

BARRINGTON

Tuesday 7th December, 4pm

Barrington refuses a lift back to his hotel. He needs to regain control and begins walking as fast as he can to the park entrance. The probability of each of the random occurrences that he has experienced in the last week is, without question, zero. From his point of view that is. The barmaid in the nightclub – he shudders at the thought of her luminous bra strap – seemed unsurprised that he would be drugged and beaten up, given that he, being him, had been in that pub at all. The probability of such a series of events, the behaviour of the chain, the system, is too random to be quantifiable.

How could he end up sleeping in the home of a female colleague he barely knows, who, it turns out, was involved in the death of his cousin? It's helped him in the past to see the connections between the events and the people in his life as practical, biological and economic transactions that expand and contract in number depending on actual lived events. It doesn't help now. If he was treating himself, as a patient, he'd expect there would be feelings of shame, anger and resentment. He recognises they are there, somewhere, but he needs Corinne to help him make sense of it all. He files those thoughts away, labels the route to find them carefully, and holds on until he can be sure he knows how to behave.

He's never liked or accepted the lazy way systems are thought about or talked about, although, as he'd sat in the park watching and listening to the two women on the swings, there were other factors in play. There was undeniably more. There was commitment and belief in each other, a different kind of drive and desire from his. Thinking it through is hard. He recognises that underneath it all there are some of the same elements, the desire to protect his family, anger at his father for his drinking and the death of his mother. At work, though, those emotions are hidden under a mass of evidence. Anne-Marie had once said that his statistics weren't neutral. She'd accused him of hiding his own moral prejudices beneath the numbers. He thought he'd been careful to screen for that, but recognises she's partially right. There's always interpretation, nuance, untested hypotheses. Chicken or egg? Belief or justification? Was his belief in the severity of the alcohol issue there first, before he'd charged in with the numbers he decided needed showing. It might have been, but in this case the numbers don't lie.

The women were in the park, in his territory. It was wrong to see them here, especially Anne-Marie, behaving like a child. Witnessing their abandon had heightened his need for control. He's starting from zero. No home, no bike, no phone and he'll need help. But help, even in getting the basics done, is something he hasn't previously considered sufficiently important, because he's always had it – from Corinne, from Aunt Hermin, from his colleagues, mainly female now he thinks of it. His needs have been intuited, understood and shared. Some are glaringly obvious and, over time, he's learned to articulate others. Barrington knows that, essentially, he's been able to perform, supported to do what he does best because of others, others who see his weaknesses and have either made allowances or excuses for him, or have chosen to help him anyway.

As he reaches the park gates a warden is about to lock up. He stops to tell the young man in green overalls that there are two more to come. It is simple. It is the right thing to do. All is not lost. He has resources, he has knowledge, he has a family. Right here in this park, right now, he is no longer that terrified teenager, alert for any opportunity to escape the demo crowd, witnessing the anger of his family and community, and crippled by the fear that any reaction will be wrong.

Before he'd left them, Jess had given him a piece of paper with Anne-Marie's address on it. "We're getting some people together later to start work. We need you there." He hadn't panicked, but remained unsure about going to another colleague's house so soon. Then, catching himself doubting what he can contribute, he thumps his fist hard on his thighs. Come on. Think man. Retrieve your bike. The hotel is acceptable for one week and after he's been to Anne-Marie's he will try to find his Blackberry at the club.

Anne-Marie's house is reassuringly similar to his, in layout that is. The faint disinfectant smell is also a bonus. What is disconcerting is the noise. A bright red sofa and two chairs are full, the room is full. The people he knows are Frank, Sandra, Zoe, the Partnership Manager, who has a rolled up flipchart under her arm, and Anil, who stands and offers his hand. How is it that Anil's here? They've only communicated electronically in the last few weeks. In a faded out T-shirt and jeans Anil looks younger than he remembers.

"I wanted to come along. I hope you don't mind?"

Barrington shakes his hand. He adds another emotion to his 'buried until later' list. "The information you collected has been useful. I apologise," he says "for my... behaviour." As Corinne might say, a different perspective can be helpful. Although Jess pulls Anil to one side, Barrington can hear the conversation.

"Sorry, I didn't get a chance to return your message. Was there something about your family, the Booze2U service?"

Barrington's ears tune in.

"There was. My family are no longer involved, which is good for me and hopefully good for them. It wasn't their choice, though. There's been more trouble."

"What kind? Are they OK?"

"My cousins got warned off by the new distributors. There was a fight with some of the new lot at the College I think."

This isn't the different perspective Barrington expected.

"And they didn't report anything? Your cousins, I mean." Jess doesn't seem to expect an answer to that and continues, "Do you know who's behind it? Any names? Is it Croft?"

"I don't recognise that name, no. Sorry."

"Let's talk to Frank later. He told me that they were investigating a fight at the College. Adam might also have been there." She points to the boy on the floor.

It's the kind of information Barrington would never normally get to hear, but which suddenly sounds so relevant. Supply chains and distribution. That might provide him with another avenue of approach.

Then he's introduced to Pete, a drugs and alcohol community worker, and Andrea, who gives herself no title. He has to step over Anne-Marie's teenage son, who is lying on the floor propped up by moss-green cushions. The boy is wearing headphones and doesn't acknowledge him. Barrington takes a seat at the far end of the dining table, where it's easy to hear, but he has space to breathe. He imagines it's like a party, people talking in twos and threes at the same time, over and with each other. He can't tune in to any one thread. Until Anne-Marie shocks him. "My suggestion is that we start with the family. Sharon, Ben, Barbara and Stan. They are a normal family, typical in many ways, a nan who's had a stroke. That's common enough, should be manageable…"

Barrington can't help himself staring at her. Barbara and Stan. He's been to their house. The picture of the mixed race boy he'd seen in the hall is Ben, their grandson. Sharon, the dead woman, is the estranged daughter Corinne mentioned.

"Shaz, who some of us knew, was lovely, bright, hadn't got any qualifications, started drinking not that long ago by all account, nothing that serious so she couldn't function, liked a drink but was never a drunk, but then you add into the mix debt and loan sharks and we're onto a different level entirely. Then there's Ben..."

Anne-Marie's son turns round to face his mother. He has been listening.

"...just trying to help his mum, gets into trouble. We're all connected to this family. They're part of this city, they're part of the Highlands Estate. Just like we're all connected to Laura Awsworth, the Girl in the Bin, and to Croft. As I said, this family is normal in many ways, not in enough trouble to come up on our radars, but as our thresholds get higher they become an ever more distant blip at the corner of a screen. They don't make it onto a spreadsheet, let alone a multi-agency team list. They don't qualify for support and we never see them until it's too late, when, because they haven't got the reserves to help themselves, it all breaks down big-style. We scratch our heads and everyone tells us we should've done something. So we need to work out the fault lines. Where did the system break down? Don't worry yet about what we can and can't do, my job is to untie your hands. I'll deal with the blockages, the well-poisoners and naysayers. This is the good bit. We need to thrash out what needs to be done."

There is a burst of energy. The noise level rises. Barrington can't focus effectively. Words, sentences, over-lapping, a jumble of issues, cutting across people, time, space.

"What are our treatment numbers like?" "We have to increase the capacity of our enforcement teams to deal with licensing and

trading standards." "Will Kerry come forward?" "We could train a thousand people in the community, including those who've been there, users, family members. They should do the alcohol advice." "What are the councillors saying?" "What about CCTV from the pub?" "Where's Bob Jackson? We need Licensing here." "Jonesy, can you get over to 43 Highlands Road." "What was she wearing? Can we get the clothes? Anyone got a photo?" "There's the last bit of the Performance Reward Grant. We could put that money into a package." "Let's make sure we're redesigning services, not just propping up the same old crap." "Minimum alcohol pricing per unit in the supermarkets – what should it be?" "Council houses on the Meadows?" "His only answer is to have a bloody restructure." "Are rape crisis still going?" "Let's set up a big debate on alcohol with young people in schools and colleges across the city." "We need a lobbying strategy." "We can't do anything about that, it's central government's role." "She won't co-operate." "The attendance data at A&E cross-referenced with the pub showed..." "We need someone to talk to the Coalition council-lors." "We've got to get rid of the industry reps on the board." "We can do more, push the boundaries." "I'll see where Bob is on the cumulative impact. It might give us some leverage." "Don't tell us the police are interested in date rape. Her friend's mum had to ring the Police 17 times before they even questioned the bloke." "The opposition is dreaming of a council house building programme." "We're struggling without the DNA." "Let's make sure this is tight before we take it anywhere." "We should launch community-based commissioning for alcohol services, starting with a pilot on the Highlands Estate." "We need a windfall tax." "Where are Adult Services?" "I'll work on an agreement that says that despite budget constraints the Council and PCT will not cut alcohol services on the basis that savings will follow and we'll work out how much we can save."

There is a pause and Frank says, "We need to think bigger, widen our horizons. It's not just us who has these problems. Sorry to use the 'B word', but we need to talk about Birmingham."

He's not joking, but people laugh at a reference that Barrington doesn't get. "The region, Leicester, Derby, we need to protect our economies, together."

There is a fluorescent rainbow of Post-its, imprecise diagrams, pieces of paper stuck over a large mirror in Anne-Marie's front room. Is anything being communicated? Is it different from other times they've said the same or similar things? Is there sense or meaning? Or just more words? Barrington hates Post-its. They come unstuck, fall behind desks never to be seen again or are typed up by someone who doesn't recognise that those words once had meaning or value.

What he decides is that there is deliberate intent here. Intent linked to values, to the sort of things the people in this room believe. Before he would have said that values weren't important, that they were only important if they meant people did things differently as a result of holding those beliefs – and usually they didn't. Organisationally speaking they never did. He can hypothesise that it might be different because the relationships are stronger here than he's witnessed before. He would still want to see the evidence, but this feels different and it is different because he actively wants to join in. Despite his disgrace, he's motivated. He wants to be part of the team.

In a break in the hubbub, Anne-Marie shouts, "What are you going to do Barrington?"

He's unsure what to say, he wants time, time to reassess the whole thing. "What do you think I should do?"

"Steps back in amazement!" she replies.

"That isn't an answer." He smiles, glad to have interpreted the intention correctly.

"Do what you do best." Anne-Marie turns away to talk to Frank.

Would his answer be the same as theirs? He's never been remotely interested in how these people might assess his strengths. In reality, the discussion isn't that far away from what he'd wanted to happen all along. What he can't deny is that he wasn't able to generate this kind of intent or commitment on his own. People are self-organising, visibly collaborating. It's not the sort of control he's after, but the energy in the room refuels him. He sticks to what he knows. "I'll get the evidence."

Jess immediately comes over to his end of the table and sits down. Her voice is quiet and strained. "Thanks, but work with us, you aren't trained. What we need is your analytical policy brain in gear."

"I'll get the DNA."

"How?"

He stops himself from reminding her that he's a doctor and follows her lead in keeping his voice down. "It's clear you think the man who murdered Laura Awsworth works for Croft. That's what you're saying, isn't it, but you don't know who?"

"Yes, we have photos of the main suspects, but two of our victims are dead and we don't know if Kerry will come forward."

He is swinging on the back legs of Anne-Marie's chair, his hands holding the edge of the table, momentarily swayed by… what? "I was attacked by Croft's men. It could have been the same men. It's not only women they drug. I'll be a witness."

Jess presses her hands together. "Thank you."

The implications of his words now seem daunting. He's offering to engage with a system that hasn't brought justice to his family – but might it to another family? Wouldn't that be what Corinne would want? If she thinks it will bring justice for the old couple's family, he'll go through with it. The feeling he has now is not agitation, but it's not quite optimism either. Maybe he just feels better?

Jess continues, "We can't ask all Croft's staff for DNA samples.

There's not much from forensics. All we've got is a wavy silver hair on Laura Awsworth's jacket. Barrington…" he doesn't want to meet her eye, "will you make a statement?"

"I can't, not now." Staying there, in that living room, is too hard, too loud. He needs fresh air.

Jess nods. "No, that's fine. I didn't mean now. I'll ask DI Alan Jones to come to your hotel in the morning."

He realises he can't do this on his own. The thing about getting help, especially from men who don't know you that well, is that you have to ask for it. Barrington begins planning. "I know someone else who could assist."

CHAPTER 44

ANNE-MARIE

Wednesday 8th December, 2am

The house is quiet now. The only evidence of the evening's activity is a faint, lingering smell of bodies, a warmth of sorts, and she wants to sit with the mess of words and papers surrounding her, absorbing, ingesting, letting it settle before sifting. Jess had tidied up and gone to bed after a terse exchange. Anne-Marie had been trying to point out the potential scenarios Jess could face at work if the case of Darren's death in custody were to be re-opened and none of them were positive. "Don't think I don't know all this," was what Jess had said, but it hadn't sounded convincing.

The spectre of work scenarios forces Anne-Marie to consider her own new realities. Buoyed up as they had all been by their ideas, the spirit and potential of their evening, Anne-Marie needs the heating on and reaches for a final glass of wine. What they've come up with is energising, completely in the right direction and ought to be do-able, but it could easily be dismissed by the Leader of the Council. Nothing is deliverable without political support. For that they'll need leverage and any leverage that might persuade Davina to change course will be buried deep and costly in ways she's only just thinking about. She doesn't expect Davina to suddenly change her views, of course. Ordinary people and their problems will never be the real priority, but if they can strengthen their collective hand, maybe trade what they've got for an ace or two? The thought that they are up against legitimate power drags her back down to the bit of the earth where the Council House sits, solid and unmoveable.

Her eyes are closing fast, her body temperature dropping, but she forces herself to re-read the files. There's something she's missing – hopefully a direct connection that will prove Davina is going to benefit financially from the deal with Croft. She needs something more than an indirect benefit for the party chairman from a ransom strip piece of land. That might get a raised eyebrow or two, but it isn't a story she can get anyone interested in. She needs some evidence of corruption, a rumpled piece of paper, preferably with Davina's signature on it. That could force her hand.

It's been almost a week now since she's seen Davina. The emails have stopped and it's now up to Anne-Marie to contact her. In normal circumstances you would ring the Leader straight back. Davina isn't stupid. The disappearance of a Director, albeit for personal reasons, at this crucial stage will be interpreted as deliberate avoidance and a lack of commitment.

Anne-Marie remembers that she'd gone along with Davina, because it suited her career. It had been exciting to play with developers, with people with real money. It flattered her ego as much as it did Davina's. It's cold comfort to Anne-Marie that she wasn't alone in buying Davina's line. Owen had been frothing and fawning. There had also been the constant background noise from the Government and media saying it's the public sector's role to ease the way for businesses to create jobs and wealth and if it wasn't for the state strangling business in red tape the city would have all the jobs it needs.

Anne-Marie has even better excuses than that. She's not there to be political. It's not her job. Like the Civil Service, she's there to do the bidding of the elected representatives, only following orders etc. Except that doesn't wash these days either. Anne-Marie could name four or five chief execs who are card-carrying members of the main political parties.

The problem is that she's forgotten what she always knew. Through her dad's careful explanation of who pays for parks, leisure centres, hospitals and schools, she could've put together an argument for the value of public services at the age of 13. It sounds so obvious that the aim of public services is to serve the public that she hasn't bothered to refresh it. Public services have become about how you are treated by the staff member on reception, the number of rings before someone picks up the phone, the quality of the frozen ready meals on wheels. That the public sector has been trashed, knee-capped, ridiculed for health and safety, not celebrated for protecting the public, is also obvious. They are on the wrong battlefield. The public sector isn't just there for those who can't afford to buy their own, non-subsidised ready meals in a 'nice' supermarket, it's about what's on the menu. That's the fight they need to have. What's driving her now is that Davina will control the city in her way and that the likes of Adam and Ben won't have a future here. That she'll fail her son again.

In amongst her papers are a couple of groundwork site investigation reports on the Meadows. It's hardly a surprise, but there are conflicting views about site contamination. Normally she'd be asleep in minutes, the words themselves do draw her head towards the cushion, but she senses that there could be something in this. Old George, a planner who they allowed to take early retirement, but who still comes in to help out with the workload, has found the reports in the archives. Indeed, he alone knows where the archives are. It's all before her time, but she notices Owen Cork's name on the Planning Committee papers. That's interesting. Maybe they've been at this before? Twenty years before, the last time Davina was in power?

Anne-Marie walks to the art gallery café for a lunchtime meeting with Frank, Jess and Barrington, glad to have something to boost the new team's morale, pad out their hand. She's also had a productive morning talking to her contacts in the Department in London, sent messages to the office and booked in a meeting with Owen and the management team. Normal service is being feigned. There are still cuts to focus on, but the priority is to shape an alternative that she'll be proud to front up.

While she has been wondering about Davina, and not phoning her, the Leader has been skulking in Whitehall corridors, scaring the juniors. "Davina's apparently been busy demolishing the planning system. It has to be linked."

Barrington is studying the menu. Jess' eyebrows knit. It looks like she has news of her own.

"Davina's offering us up for a nuclear waste site is she?" Frank is pleased with his quip, but Anne-Marie wonders if it's possible that they've underestimated Davina.

He coughs and laughs. "No, they wouldn't put it in the Midlands where they have a chance of building on their vote."

"It sounds like she's lined up a licence for the super-casino," continues Anne-Marie. "That isn't even controversial. The centre wants to reward her for winning the Council with funding for an enterprise zone and money for capital remediation."

Jess is intently engaged and still looks tense. She asks, "So even if it's a casino, can Davina argue it's in the public interest?"

Frank clarifies. "Yes. They don't talk about public interest anymore, it's economic interest. The idea of public good, public space, public anything is part of the past. What's left is the jobs. That's the answer to every question."

There's no malice in his voice, but Anne-Marie cringes hearing it, understanding how specious she must've sounded to Frank back in the Mechanics.

"Has Davina been lobbying on state aid regulations or European grants to private companies?" Frank asks.

"I'm ordering potato and leek soup." Barrington stands to go to the counter.

"Good idea." Jess goes with him.

There's a lull in the kitchen clatter and Anne-Marie drops her voice. "That was my thought, too."

"Who did you speak to? We don't want to alert her." He sounds protective.

"It's safe enough. Apparently there wouldn't be a problem if there was contaminated land involved, even if the costs rocketed and we had to bail out Croft or any other dubious property company."

Frank nods. Anne-Marie is thinking about the timing of this again. Davina needs it to happen before the market dips again. They regularly clean up all sorts of mucky sites in this region, but if Davina is a shareholder in a company directly profiting from it and has deliberately sat on a site contamination report that could be useful. Davina's husband has a construction company, but she'd need evidence of a kickback and there's no way that trail wouldn't be covered. Even if Davina's husband is a sub-contractor down the line, she could step lightly aside from the decision-making, pass him information and no-one would ever know.

Frank sits back in his chair, following a different train. "OK, it's a casino. It's not right. They'll be plenty of objections and Scrutiny around it. Who knows about it now? Let's consult and let's get the councillors to call it in. Get the system to do its job."

"Since when did the system ever find anything we didn't want them to?" Anne-Marie knows it's a wobbly stick, but Frank could be right about using the system. Her mind jumps back to the previous point. The heartsink of Scrutiny. She's treated it as a disdainful waste of time for years. Backbench councillors scrutinising the leaderships decisions has never changed anything, but seen from another angle there is potential.

"If this is what you mean," she smiles at Frank, "it's genius. The system won't discover anything, but Scrutiny could delay the development for months. If one of the Coalition councillors calls it in, that's even better. Cause trouble in the ranks." She dips into the official toolbox for any other tools of the trade she's forgotten about. The 151 Monitoring Officer will be important, but she keeps that to herself. Anne-Marie will stay on the straight and narrow, and do some more digging. It's a start.

Jess and Barrington return with trays and hearty steaming bowls. Jess plays with the lumps in the soup, trying to cool it, unable to keep in her news.

"I got an unlikely phone call from a Home Office PR advisor, asking me if I knew anything about some possible negative video going on YouTube. He meant Sharon's phone message. The Government let me down bit."

Jesus H Christ, Anne-Marie is now worried for them all. The kind of visitation from Whitehall that could follow would mean that there would be no possibility of a local solution.

"How could they know that?" Barrington asks.

"Stewart could've alerted the Chief."

Anne-Marie sees immediately that the Chief might want to cover his own back. They probably think that Jess or Ben might leak it. This could be a useful bargaining tool for Jess if she needs it.

Barrington finishes his soup noisily and get's up to leave. "I have to go. I don't have anything to add today, but my investigations may bear some fruit tomorrow. Are we meeting again?"

Anne-Marie is happy for him to go. Home Office involvement could mean trouble and she needs to think through the news. Their hand, their project, their team could be dead in the water if that video gets out. She volunteers to take the trays back to the counter. Watching as a woman cleans the coffee machines and the industrial toaster behind the till, she notices a framed certificate from the Rotary Club. It commemorates the cafe's donation to Make A Dream Come True, a fundraiser for mini-buses for disabled children.

This jars, because Anne-Marie has never liked the Rotary Club, seeing it as a charitable front for a small group of mainly men to do business behind. She'd bet on Davina's husband being a Rotarian. Then she remembers someone else who is a good businessman and knows everyone. Steve Bolter gives the private sector a good name. He'll turn up to a meeting and critically engage with the city. He chaired a local group for them about five years ago and cares about the people who work for him. It might be a distraction, but he'll talk to her over a glass of wine. It's an over-stretched clutch at a short straw.

CHAPTER 45

MR SIZZLE

Wednesday 8th December, 9.30pm

Before there were burgers, there were chips. He'd slathered at the thought of taking over the chippy at the Poet's Corner shops. The previous Captain Cod was leaving town. The bastard, well, the poor bastard, had borrowed money for the fryers from Croft, couldn't pay and had to leg it. As the new owner, Croft had expected him to pay. He was using the kit, it became his debt, but not just everyday debt. He'd paid up the first time, but one of Croft's men had come round demanding double what he'd been told the week before. Compound interest, he'd said, banging his fist on the counter, sending the salt and vinegar flying.

The punters seemed to like him. Bags of chips in grubby hands went moseying out the door. He managed to pay for the first month, but the debt grew. There was no doubting they were good chips, but they weren't frigging made of gold. No-one could have afforded that.

It was early on a Wednesday afternoon. There'd been a few school kids bunking off at lunchtime, but the place was empty when Croft's collector arrived; a rough-arse, Hell's Angel type, leather studs and greasy hair, mean. There was no money. If he'd had the money he would've paid, but a few 50 pences for chips wasn't going to save him.

The man took him by surprise, opening the hatch, walking straight round. He'd found himself kneed in the bollocks, fit to crumple with pain. The sadist had grabbed his forearm and thrust his hand into the deep, boiling fat. The top layers of the skin on his hand crisped up hard, flakes hung off, leaving burning flesh dripping with oil.

While he writhed on the floor, wishing his hand was no longer part of his body, the man dragged his wife into the shop to watch. He tried to stand, to protect his wife, and found his face smashed into the tiles. Try that again, he was told, and the missus is next.

It was the worst eight weeks of his life. People on the estate looked on and did nothing. They were shocked, scared that similar treatment would be meted out on their doorsteps, but it didn't stop them taking out loans. The Government thinks if you're stupid enough to borrow it, it's your lookout, but he hadn't borrowed money knowingly. There was no justice in that.

He'd left his keys and car, and gone, although only ten miles down the road. The scars and the humiliation remained, the fear in his wife's eyes. Until she left him, that was.

The collector still sneers when he sees him around town. He owes no-one anything now. Not even a week's pink ticket for the *Post* at his local newsagent. He's lost count of the times he's gone into a Croft pub with a baseball bat and done his worst. Just in his head, though. Just in his head.

CHAPTER 46

BARRINGTON

Wednesday 8th December, 9.45pm

Getting back on his bike, focusing on his cadence, restores Barrington's sense of well-being. His muscles can still produce the sort of speeds he expects and his lung capacity seems normal. He cycles to his house and pushes a note through the door asking Corinne if they can talk. The flap scrapes his thumb, drawing blood. She will be getting ready for the morning, almost ready for bed, and now isn't a good time to ask her advice about Darren or Croft, but he wants to say goodnight to her and to line up his son's Action Men, right to left, as he used to do. He knows it makes his son smile. His list of wants at this stage is unrealistically long. The first thing is to be allowed to move home.

It feels to Barrington as if snow is on the way. As he cycles up to Mr Sizzle's van, the pungent smell is familiar, but the man is not.

"Where's Mr Sizzle?"

"I am he," says a wiry man with glasses.

"No, the normal Mr Sizzle."

"I can assure you I'm as normal as anyone in this town."

"The other Mr Sizzle?" Barrington steps back, noticing the van does look slightly different.

"I am 00Sizzle – licensed to fry. Would you be after the Sizzle Supremacy? RoboSizzle, Samurai Sizzle or Die Hard with a Burger?"

These are clearly jokes, but Barrington has no time for them. "Where's the one who's normally here?"

"Over at the Blackwood Christmas Fair and look out for the latest addition to our empire, the Sixth Sizzle."

A Christmas fair? Christmas? Already? He makes his way across to Blackwood. Calling it a fair is an overstatement. There are two rides and three stalls, the traders blowing steam into the cold air outnumber the frozen punters.

"Alright, matey? What, no Lycra?" Sizzle seems pleased to see him. "Hold on there, I'll come out." He wipes his hands on a stripy tea towel, disappears, then emerges beside Barrington and crosses to an adjacent stand, insisting on paying for a bag of five hot doughnuts, despite his fellow trader's protests. They lean against an upside-down beer barrel. Barrington holds a doughnut in a paper serviette, licking the grains of sugar cautiously. The first one goes into Sizzle's wide mouth without touching his lips.

"I was wondering how you got on."

"I was drugged and beaten up. I achieved nothing. I was..." He stops.

"I know the feeling, mate."

"Do you know anything about the men that work for Croft? The bouncers?"

"Everyone round here knows about them."

"I'm trying to help the Police with evidence." Barrington says. "DNA samples maybe? We need a match with the curly silver hair found on the Girl in the Bin's jacket."

"The Girl in the Bin?" Sizzle shakes his head. "Was she killed by one of them?"

"Jessica Reid, Deputy Commander, thinks it's the main line of enquiry."

"And I'm thinking you've got a serious death wish. Listen mate, I told you. I know how you feel, but you can't go near a Croft pub again. They don't forget a face and they don't have many black punters in their pubs. They'll know exactly who you are."

"Could you help?" Barrington has to ask. Where else can he go?

"No mate. Do like the rest of us do, chalk it up to experience, become bitter," Sizzle says flatly.

There is still no-one around. Barrington hesitates. "What about witnesses?"

"No, son. Not you. Not me. You think of yourself. Think of your family."

Sizzle screws up the paper bag and brushes the sugar from his white overcoat.

It's nearly 10.30pm. Barrington is frustrated again, but what had he expected? Before he heads back to the hotel, he has it in his mind to see if he can retrieve his phone and maybe gather more information. He has nothing better to do and feels like he ought to go back to the club and apologise to the barmaid. It's his duty. As he passes the Anvil he sees the bouncers, speeds up and keeps his head down.

When he arrives, there is no-one on the door. He makes his way inside, not remembering anything of the layout. The navy sofa jogs his memory.

"You took your time," she says, all smiles.

"I apologise. My behaviour was unacceptable and my physical condition was no excuse. Have you got my Blackberry?"

"What if I have?"

The indiscretion in the storeroom was a mistake and had degraded them both, but beyond that what does he remember about her? In a sober light he now sees he guessed rightly that she is about 17, maybe 18. She is assertive, smart if not intelligent, and sexually predatory, but not a prostitute. Barrington is confused. She doesn't fit any of his categories.

"Give it back if you have it." He doesn't mean to sound so blunt.

"What's it worth?"

"Are you asking me how much it cost?"

"No, like, how much do you want it back?"

He fishes in his pocket for his wallet.

"How about you give me a 'thank you' for finding it? The tight wads here don't even pay minimum wage."

Barrington calculates minimum wage times five hours times three nights, then decides to give her £50. She hands over his Blackberry and then his keys.

"OK, you're alright. Stay for a drink if you want."

"No thanks, but I do want to ask you something about that night?"

Her face flicks from smile to frown.

"You said Croft drugged people for fun. How do you know?"

"Keep the noise down. This is one of his bars."

"Did you ever see Croft or his men beating anyone up or putting drugs in a drink?"

"You're not Police. Why are you bothered?"

"We're all bothered. It's our job."

"Nah, I don't know nothing and I wouldn't go around asking questions like that if I were you. They'll get to hear."

"But you told me…"

"…nothing. You better go."

It's another dead end and her reaction has been stronger than he'd expected. He realises he should have predicted this and tried to gain an insight into who she is, so that he could have approached her with more sensitivity. In the past Corinne has made him practice behaving in a more socially acceptable manner and it hasn't been that difficult to learn the right skills for work situations, because they are so much more predictable and present repeated opportunities for self-improvement.

"Listen," he says.

"Why should I? You aren't listening to me."

It's true, he isn't, mainly because he can't be bothered. Other people's contributions aren't as valuable as his – or he quickly gets bored by other people's views, which he appreciates is a version of the same thing. This young woman clearly sees any connection to Croft as a threat and he's a threat related to that. She's scared. Despite his self-assurance, Barrington is embarrassed.

"I'm sorry. I've forgotten your name."

"Holly."

"I'm just trying to…"

To get revenge on Croft? Stop another girl dying in a bin? Or is it about his parents? Professionally speaking, it's still about preventing the harm that alcohol does, but that will sound incomprehensible to a young woman in a nightclub. It's probably all of the above, but in the end does it matter what his drive for change is, as long as there is one? He's spent time looking at the research on how to change other people's behaviours and is realistic about how hard it is. When doctors tell heart patients they will die if they don't change their habits, only one in seven are actually able to do it. The question is, would he be the one who can follow through or one of the six who would rather risk their lives than change?

"I'm trying to make this town safer and get rid of the likes of Croft."

"Help yourself, then," she says, "by keeping well out of it."

"I can't. I don't want to."

She looks at him directly. He turns his gaze back to the bar. "I'm not blind," she says. "I can see that."

"So," he says, aware that a normal conversation with this young woman is improbable, but that it shouldn't be beyond him to try, "can I have a bottle of water please?" He settles himself onto a stool.

CHAPTER 47

JESSICA

Thursday 9th December, 7.45am

Barrington has left an obtuse message asking Jess to drive to the station, pull into the drop off-only area, park immediately to the left of the barrier and wait there until 8am. If it had been anyone else she'd have thought the message deliberately mysterious, but with Barrington, who knows? It took her until late last night to get official clearance to show Shaz's phone to Ben and she's been trying to focus on how best to handle it. She's seeing him later and taking Adam with her to Ben's grandparents will help. She recognises that the boys need each other more than a few carefully chosen words from her, but Anne-Marie still doesn't trust the lads not to try and take things into their own hands. Like mother, like son.

Jess is relieved that Anne-Marie didn't criticise her directly about her role in the cover-up of Darren's death, but she hadn't said she'd understood, or even that she might've done the same thing if she'd been in Jess' shoes, because she wouldn't have. In the last few days Anne-Marie has had the same indignant, self-righteous, steely focus about her that Jess recognises from when she was a teenager.

Normally she's too early to hit the morning rush hour and it's a new and vaguely irritating experience. She parks next to a red hatchback, with a small dog barking loudly in the back. A hefty man in a donkey jacket struggles to get out from behind the wheel. He walks round to Jess' window and motions for her to wind the window down. She doesn't recognise him, nor can she see any obvious connection with Barrington.

"Morning. Are you Barrington's friend?"

"There's many an answer I could give to that question. Shall we say 'acquaintance' will do for now."

"How can I help?"

"I've got something for your investigation." His ample hands are clutching a clear plastic bag, with what looks like a half-eaten burger in it.

She holds the bag up to the light. "And this is?"

"DNA in a bun." His downbeat delivery can't hide how pleased he is with himself.

"And who's been eating it?" Jess asks.

He fishes inside his jacket pocket and pulls out his phone. The blurred picture mainly catches the back of an ageing, curly head of hair. She realises it's Turval, but it could be clearer.

If there's a match between that and the girl's dress, they can bring him in. "Could you…"

"No, love, don't be asking anymore. I must be off now."

"Could you text that photo to Barrington?" Excited, she calls Jonesy, tells him to get there fast. Special delivery.

Ben's nan, Barbara, is sat with Stan in their chairs in the front room. Barbara has a pile of small china plates on her lap. A bandaged hand steadies the tower. With the other she wipes each plate tentatively, firstly with a damp cloth, then a tea towel. Stan is listening to the local radio travel updates.

"Must be a bit clearer by now?"

Jess nods, forgetting he can't see her.

"I say, the traffic sounds dreadful." Stan wants a response from their visitor, whom he knows to be in uniform.

"Sorry," she says. "I'm glad I don't have to drive in the rush hour every morning."

It's strange to think Shaz grew up in this house. It smells of dust and unwashed hair and reminds her of vivid and vitriolic rows between Shaz and Barbara about hairdying. The ferocity had been shocking to Jess, in whose house voices were never raised. Best not to remind Barbara that they've met before. Things are complicated enough for an old lady in ill health who's lost a daughter and gained a teenage lodger.

"Ben, love, you and your friend sort us out some fresh tea and bring the police lady the biscuit tin." Adam and Ben shuffle into the kitchen, glad of the escape from the smothering electric bars.

"How are you coping with a teenager in the house?" she asks.

"We barely know he's here. Has his headphones in most of the time. And he's got that computer."

"He's a good kid." His attitude seems to have dissolved with his mum's death."I'll check on that tea," she says, thinking that she'll talk to the lads alone, in the kitchen. Ben is glad Stan can't see his mum's suicide note and that Barbara prefers not to. They settle around the kitchen table.

"Are you sure you're ready for this?" she asks. "I know the thought of it is upsetting, but she's amazing your mum and you can switch it off at any time or just listen if you prefer. The only thing is, and I mentioned this before, didn't I, you can't keep the phone now. I have to take it back to the station."

"She looks beautiful, doesn't she?" he says. Then puts the phone to his ear and walks upstairs to his bedroom, concentrating on his mum's voice. Adam will stay here with Ben today, to make sure he's not alone, and while they wait Adam talks nervously about Frank, college and studying. He's on his best behaviour, trying to convince Jess that he's not the gang type, but there are crucial bits of that delivery story missing.

Ben's eyes are watery when he re-emerges in the kitchen. Adam gives him an awkward hug.

Jess says, "I looked up to your mum so much as a kid. She was braver than I ever was. Ben, you were always her greatest joy in life and you're a credit to her."

Shaz never complained about anything. It was true and also part of the problem. Shaz was strong, but tried to carry it all herself and she had caved with the weight. Although Barbara loved her grandson, the support hadn't been there. Difficult mothers were something Jess, Anne-Marie and Shaz had in common and had talked about a lot in their teens. In their thirties they'd thought they'd got over it, but maybe not?

"Your mum was devoted to you, and the last thing she wanted was to be separated from you." Jess is beyond tears now and focuses on what Ben needs. Her voice doesn't falter. "She just saw no other way. Her life had become so painful and she succumbed to the pain. Don't be angry with your mum, none of us should be, but..." she puts a hand on Ben's shoulder, "I'm angry that we've lost her. We'll always love and remember her."

Still Ben says nothing. Jess holds back. What can she say about Shaz's choice to die? What were her choices? In the midst of depression, she desperately tried to sort herself out and used alcohol to numb the pain. That led to addiction, debt, a loan shark and an attack she wasn't able to come back from. Ben doesn't need to hear that.

Her lips are moving, but words aren't coming out. What she wants to say is that she's not going to let it lie. Anne-Marie had been right that, as a family, Shaz and Ben, Stan and Barbara, had so few resources to draw on. Sod the no-blame culture they so banally talk about at work. Sod the learning lessons. Justice is what she wants for Shaz and Ben and everyone else who ends up clinging to that kind of raft. From now on she'll be Ben's back-up, his resource.

"Are you going to make an arrest?" Ben blurts out.

It shakes her out of the silent maze in her head. "We hope to – soon. We've got evidence that looks like it means we'll be able to make a conviction stick on the man who murdered the Girl in the Bin." She shouldn't have said that much really, but what else could she give him. Even if they get a DNA match, it won't prove that Shaz was attacked by the same man.

Ben stares intently back at her. His body steady, his challenge solid, knowing, critical. He says, "You've got him, but you haven't got them."

Jess looks down at the lino. There are crumbs in the grooves of the squared pattern. There's a tea bag on the floor next to the bin. The kitchen isn't clean. The windows are dirty. Stan and Barbara can barely look after themselves let alone Ben in his traumatic state.

"I'm sorry, we can't say just yet."

Ben turns away from her, thumping his fist down on the kitchen table. A mug falls onto the floor.

"Trust us Ben." She's embarrassed at how feeble her own voice sounds, like a mouse when he needs and deserves a lion.

"Smashing up the place are we?" Stan shuffles to the kitchen doorway.

"I am, yes, but nothing broken. I'll mop it up for you." She decides she ought to mop the floor while she's at it. "I'll leave you lads here for a bit. I'll see what else I can find out and maybe I'll see you at Adam's house later?"

As she drives off she's distracted by seeing Corinne pull up at Stan and Barbara's house. It's a relief to have missed her. They haven't spoken since that disastrous morning. Still, time to think about that later. She's due at HQ for a preliminary meeting with the Chief.

Ben's right, but she didn't find the courage in that moment to say to his young, angry, heartbroken face that they haven't got a hope of a conviction against 'them', against Croft. They are miles away from making anything like an accessory to murder charge stand up. They'll never pin corporate manslaughter on him. They've got no-one who says he's carried out any violence himself. They will certainly get HM Revenue and Customs onto him and hurt him in the pocket, which will curtail the loan sharking, albeit temporarily. He could also lose his licenses at the Anvil and the Three Lions. They'll get Trading Standards after him for illegal trading, too, and pull out the stops to see if they can make a prosecution. It's pretty poor though, isn't it, for Ben, and, increasingly, for Jess herself. It'll mean nothing if Croft doesn't end up in prison. How else do we judge justice?

Jess has stepped up and eventually done the right thing by Darren, but she knows all that's really happened is she's activated another process, another part of the system which, like last time, is unlikely to deliver justice for the family. The system can work in its own interests when it needs to, but it didn't work for Shaz and it can never be immediate enough for a young person like Ben in such crippling pain.

CHAPTER 48

ANNE-MARIE

Thursday 9th December, 8am

The silent bad mood that normally greets Anne-Marie when she's forced to be up before 7am has been replaced by a state of alert. Today requires a Saturday-sized breakfast: extra toast, three coffees and a Kit Kat. She's drying her hair naturally today and applying lipstick in slow motion to avoid a circus clown look. She resists poking her head inside Adam's door and instead blows him a kiss through the woodwork, wondering if he'll make it out of bed by lunchtime. Outside the roads are icy and the frost is thicker than a rink. She switches on the engine and lets the car warm up while smoking a quick fag on the doorstep.

Jess, Frank and Barrington have helped shore up her force field and she feels as prepared for today as she could be. They've crafted an alternative case and at least there's a choice on offer now. Andrea has translated it into plain English. Frank's speedily done the grassroots work and briefed the opposition and local councillors. They seem willing to ditch Pleisureland in favour of New Horizons – for god's sake, it needs a better name – an integrated community housing, alcohol and family support strategy.

What Anne-Marie loves about the scheme is that it's integrated with the Highlands. The Highlands will be linked physically, through the site, and through a new service configuration, to the City Centre. Davina's strategy to keep the Pleisureland scheme quiet has worked and no-one knows much about it anyway. The question is what the Coalition councillors will do. The corridors have been buzzing with a press statement made by one of the backbenchers condemning the job losses and cuts. Bob's been busy and that could be useful, too.

It's 7.30am when she arrives in the Council House car park. Davina's clean black Beamer and Owen's Range Rover are nuzzling together. They aren't due to meet Davina until 9am to pitch the alternative scheme, but Anne-Marie needs to talk to Owen first. She quickly makes tracks around the rear of the building and walks up the back stairs. One flight up and she becomes aware of a woman below tracking her steps. A click of court heels echoes on the concrete stairs. Glancing down, she catches a glimpse of Davina's camel coat. It's a good idea to stop and wait for her, Anne-Marie thinks, at least start off on a civil footing. Then Davina stops, too. Anne-Marie walks on a few paces. She does, too. It's creepy and unnecessary. It irritates Anne-Marie, but somehow she doesn't want to go down and confront her. Anne-Marie presses quickly on up to Owen's office, where none of the PAs are around. It's as if someone has pressed a mute button for the whole floor and it's lit only by a single light coming from Owen's office.

Anne-Marie has alerted Owen to the potential 151 Monitoring Officer issues – local government code for corruption – and that is what has prompted this morning's war paint. It's unimaginable to Anne-Marie that after the deaths and the growing links to Croft the deal will survive. Still, there's nothing proven against Croft and she doesn't put it past Davina to find a friend at the Golf Club with deep pockets to give her scheme another lease of life in the new year. The irony is that having spent so much of her career avoiding red tape, she's now glueing herself to it until there's a result. She's hoping it'll hold firm, a patchwork of precedent, an often mocked shield of procedure, a Sellotaped together mesh of good practice.

"Morning, Owen." She knocks, recovering her composure and pulling the door closed. He motions her to sit down on a boxy, lounge-style chair, as the door bangs open.

Davina snorts a short, hot breath from her nose. "You want to accuse me of corruption? You have disappointed me, Anne-Marie. I thought you were interested in seeing things happen in this city."

Davina leans against Owen's desk, partially obscuring him from view. The careful sycophant has told Davina about the meeting and hasn't even had the decency to hear her out first. That's not 151 protocol. Anne-Marie pulls out a note book from her bag, aware she's in danger of looking like a secretary about to take dictation. It's Owen's duty to investigate 'any proposal or decision that might be illegal, classed as maladministration or a breach of statutory code under Sections 5 and 5A of the Local Government and Housing Act 1989'. That won't bother Davina, but she makes a note of Owen's procedural mistake and takes her time answering.

"I'm committed to making this city a better place, Councillor. We're supposed to be meeting at 9am to discuss that and we'll be talking about our response to the recent alcohol-related deaths, the City Centre and how we work with other agencies to tackle it. It has implications for the Meadows/New Horizons scheme."

Anne-Marie can smell Davina's disdain. "You can forget that. It's a press conference, recognition of an unfortunate event, a drunken teenager, that's all."

Christ she's worse than Croft. He ignores anything that doesn't affect his interests, but Davina, that's the job she's elected to do. It's possible that Davina doesn't know about Sharon, Kerry, the latest from the Police. Anne-Marie holds herself in while Davina huffs again.

"And the issue of funding for the Meadows is nothing to do with anyone but councillors."

She's ready for this. "We are required to consult with our partners and taxpayers on local spending decisions. The Government…"

Davina scoffs. "Since when have you been interested in complying with requirements? The Government won't require us to do anything. I'm part of this Government."

Anne-Marie is sweating. She feels like she's got a bout of flu coming on. Her sinuses are blocked and her head could burst with the tension. Sticking to her plan she says, "There has been an official request from Council members on the Scrutiny committee to call in the Pleisureland proposals."

Davina grunts, "We need this development to happen now and no backbench committee is going to stop it. You're in a politically restricted post and you're bringing this down to party politics."

Anne-Marie manages half a smile. "It's one of your Coalition councillors on the Scrutiny committee who is asking the questions and I ceased to have any involvement in party political activities when I became a manager in 1994. I've acted in accordance with the Nolan Standards in Public Life." The words sound almost ridiculous, but right now they mean everything. She leans around Davina to look deliberately at Owen, "However, I'm aware that, Owen, you attended Davina's party conference this year and you've been involved in fundraising for them."

Owen looks shaken, but manages to stutter back, "Many chief executives accompany their leaders to the party conferences." She can tell she's got him. It's a useful blow. Even if he doesn't want to retire, he won't want to damage his interests.

Davina juts her chin out dismissively. "That's immaterial. Tell me what you think you've discovered."

There's something about her movements, the slowly folding arms, the natural but manicured finger nails contrasting with the camel coat she has kept on. It's the way Davina cares so totally about herself and no-one else that reminds Anne-Marie of her mother. Careful she tells herself, don't blab this out like a 12-year-old.

Davina spits, "I've made the appropriate declarations of interest, so let's not waste time. You won't find anything. No corruption, no financial wrongdoing, nothing. Your working life here is over."

Anne Marie prods her again. "Are your declarations up to date?"

Davina interrupts. "Didn't you hear me? You'll never work in public service again."

Anne-Marie puts her notepad down and stands up to face Davina eye to eye.

"You've been offered a directorship of Willow Homes. They think you're a smooth political operator, who'll be useful for them as they move into the provision of a wide range of care services, right next door, in our neighbouring authority."

Davina sweeps her coat off, spraying papers from Owen's desk across the floor. "I don't know how you know that, but it's of no consequence. There's absolutely nothing wrong with it."

Anne-Marie's face burns. "That's exactly it, Davina. That's the problem. You don't see anything wrong with it. That company are owned by a syndicate of American investors who provided sub-prime mortgages. DNB Holdings, who have land on the Meadows site, aren't registered to pay UK tax. And don't get me started on Daniel Croft. Do you really believe he's going to create wealth for our city?"

Davina starts to speak, but Anne-Marie is aflame. "No, of course you don't. You know they don't care, because you don't care either. You've never believed in trickledown have you? Just by being wealthy it doesn't magically rub off on other people. No, you're smarter than that. You're putting money in the pockets of people who have no interest in us, people who suck the life and the money out of our economy, and it's not a problem, that's just the way business is done. It's double standards and it makes me sick. You keep the money for yourselves."

"That's enough, Anne-Marie." Owen tries to intervene.

"It's not enough, Owen. We're supposed to cheer that we get a few contracted-out, part-time, minimum-wage jobs, while Croft gets public grants – that's taxpayers' money and our land assets – and a clean site he can hold onto and sell when it suits. And what that means is he'll leave it derelict for another twenty years. It might suit you to have a local landowner's face on it, but Croft's money is dirty. I've got proof."

Before they can ask for that proof, Anne-Marie shakes her head and picks up her bag. "That's what got me in the end," she says. "I can't believe I was ready to settle for so little, as though we should be grateful, as though that's all our communities are worth. I know we can do better in providing a good future for our young people and there are plenty of others who believe that, too."

"I repeat," Davina says, "you have nothing on me and I have the right to suspend you for your behaviour."

Anne-Marie rocks back on her heels. She's half-expected this and holds firm. "That's fine by me. I don't mind an investigation into the reasons for my suspension. Do you?"

"Get out," shrieks Davina.

Anne-Marie toughs it out. "Then I look forward to an official email from HR setting out the basis for my suspension, but in the meantime I've got work to do."

CHAPTER 49

BARRINGTON

Thursday 9th December, 11am

Barrington is grateful that the meeting with his family had been strangely quiet and quick. Being back in his aunt's house was comforting, but still not comfortable. That Corinne was sitting at the breakfast bar on a high stool was good. He'd wanted her to be there, but she'd said nothing. He'd asked to be allowed to move home, but that proposal had met with a flat no.

Jess had been invited to take a seat and had sunk low into the old sofa, the back of which was covered by a red and black blanket with a map of the Caribbean on it. Barrington had noticed her head was almost the same size as Trinidad and a similar shape. She'd sounded as though she was reading an invisible statement.

"On 10th November 1985 I was witness to a series of events surrounding the death of your son."

"We appreciate you coming, Commander Reid," Hermin had said calmly. "My son's name was Darren."

"I'm not here in an official capacity today. I'm..." Jess had started a sentence, but hadn't finished it, and Barrington had registered that was unusual. She was normally clearer than most.

"I don't intend to shoot the messenger, even if she is more than two decades late," Hermin had said, shaking her head.

Jess had stuttered, but related a fuller version of the story than the one she'd told Barrington that first day. Hermin had offered them all a cup of tea and a dense slab of coconut cake. There were few questions.

"We knew that all along." The words had seemed to stick to the back of Hermin's tongue.

Barrington had watched Corinne's face. She'd briefly got up to place a hand on his shoulder as Jess had replayed her arrival at the scene and Stewart's confession later that night, and he had felt pleased by the physical contact. Hopeful even.

Jess had said that her ex-husband, Stewart, had described the particular tae-kwon do move he'd used as "necessary to survive a violent opponent intent on causing injury". That was untrue, of course. None of the family had ever believed anything Darren's killer had said.

"We don't need details of the incident. We need to know how and why your evidence never became part of the inquest. Are you going to make a new statement that could be of some use to us?" Hermin had looked directly into Jess' face. Barrington was unsure, but it looked like Jess had shivered.

"I can't tell you how sorry I am," Jess had said and had explained quietly how she'd argued with Stewart about his confession that night. She'd gone to the Chief, who was a DCI at the time, but she had been 19 years old and scared. The Chief had covered up the information and she had let it happen. The process the family had been through had come to the only conclusion it could have done with the information available.

"Now, if you don't mind, I need to think this through." Hermin had stood up and held out a hand in the direction of the door. There had been no knee-jerk reaction, no slamming the table and calling for a new enquiry, but that was just like his Aunt. She would keep her counsel until she was ready.

Hermin and Corinne have provided no guidance. Should he even be speaking to Jess? There is anger in him, but he's conflicted, unsure how to express it. Once outside the house, he asks Jess for a lift back to the office. It's pragmatic but awkward.

"How long will you be staying at the hotel," she asks?

"Three more nights. The hotel food is acceptable, but not nutritionally balanced. Then I'll stay with Hermin. I agreed with Corinne that I'm going to see Nelson tomorrow. Give him his bath."

"That sounds better?"

"Better than what? If you mean better than divorce, I agree. I completely refuse to add to the estimated one in three boys in the UK who grow up without a reliable and present father. Thanks for the lift. I'll see you at the meeting." The wind catches the car door and it slams shut.

The sanctity of his office is healing. The others, his colleagues, have been told he's recovering from a contagious virus. They'll be irritated that he's causing a health risk, exposing them to germs, but it means he has a quiet space to work and reassess. Flicking on his computer to check his emails, he notices Anil has forwarded him an update from Bob Jackson, the Council's Licensing Manager, on the fake vodka operation.

The spreadsheet attached confirms the anonymised results of random visits to more than 70 licensed premises in the city. Fake vodka with high levels of methanol is being sold in 25% of them. This constitutes a clear public heath danger and a threat to anyone working in the production processes.

The fake vodka is being delivered to shops by van in a fairly ad hoc manner. We haven't found the source yet, but the scale is such that we can't rule out the possibility that there is more than one factory. Identifying the source or sources must be a priority.

CHAPTER 50

JESSICA

Thursday 9th December, 6pm

Dragging her aching body up to the Chief's office on the top floor is an achievement. Time is what she really needs, time to think. Her dad used to say "Time is the enemy" and he was right. Without it she's in danger of getting lost, when she most needs to stay on track. The DNA evidence is a breakthrough and they are closing in on Turval. She's waiting for Jonesy to pull him in for interview, but that's not her call. There's the forthcoming Council meeting, there's Shaz's funeral and then there's Ben. She's exhausted from talking to Hermin and she needs to get herself a lawyer.

As she knocks on the Chief's door and waits to be invited in she realises she's too tired to be nervous. There he is, in his courtly chair, his back to the expansive window, his egg-shaped silhouette now almost invisible against the black sky. The Anglepoise lamp points at a white file with her name printed on a sticky label. The file is open.

"Interesting," the Chief says slowly. "I had a premonition about this. You've been building up to it, haven't you."

"Have I?"

"Indeed you have. It's a measure of your development as a human being."

Jess really hasn't got time for his philosophical meandering now. Stewart has told the Chief that the family know about the cover-up.

"And if I tell you I find that comment patronising, will I be giving you another measure?"

He nods sagely.

"It's a measure of mine that I have lived with the decisions we made surrounding Darren Wilson's death all those years ago and that I remain unwilling to change."

Jess slips down in her chair, while he stands up, close to the window. It's not a surprise. Why would he support her now? Discipline is liberation for him.

"I no longer feel I have a choice."

She imagines her dad sitting in the Chief's chair, not that he'd ever wanted to be management. If it was her dad would she say what she never could while he was alive? That she's always tried to be the good daughter, the good wife, the loyal colleague. That she'd thought that if she could pull those off she'd be accepted, loved even?

The Chief's voice interrupts her hypothetical conversation. "You have thrown away a good career."

She rests her chin in one hand, rubbing her cheek bone. No, she thinks. I'm forty. If I'm going to be accepted, respected even, I want it to be for who I actually am. "I needed them to hear the truth," she states.

"Well, you know the drill. We are now in a formal process. Don't underestimate the Force. You've chosen a hard road. Going straight to the family and not coming to me first was a mistake. We could've worked something out. Now you must be prepared for the bitumen to burn your soles."

She's avoided conflict all her life, tried to mediate, conciliate, smooth the edges. She half-laughs to herself, knowing she's picked the biggest fight she could, as if to lay down a new path, one there's no turning back from.

"Don't expect this to get to court, whatever you or the family might say." He sighs, "What about the other work you were so passionate about? All that will go to waste, disappear into naught."

What might it be like on her new path if she now puts her foot down on the conflict, accelerates it.

"No, I'll leave that to you. It should always have been you leading it, but I see how awkward that would've been for you, the Leader of the Council and your golfing pal. You know Croft is linked to the investigation about Laura Awsworth and the others girls dumped in bins, don't you?"

She wants to let the Chief know, if he tries to protect Croft, she'll be watching, and so will others.

He scribbles a note on his pad. "Stewart has informed me that you're involved with Dr Edwards. He's been sleeping at your house."

Anne-Marie had said to watch out for the smears and dirty tricks to start.

"He stayed one night. Neither myself nor Stewart were there. I stayed with a friend who will confirm this."

"And you tampered with the phone evidence."

"You know that I took the phone for a few hours, once the evidence was securely recorded, and I subsequently received permission to show it to the victim's son."

The reality of an enquiry into her every move, designed to discredit her, is wearying.

"The state of your relationship with Stewart won't help you or the family.

She can't see his face, but hears the finality in his voice.

"You're wrong, though," he continues, "if you think the Force is the same as it was in the eighties. We've moved on. We're better." The Chief has delivered this with more conviction than she had.

"You're right in some ways, but we still get stuck on the same old things, don't we?"

"The inconvenient course of action you've chosen will be resisted at every level. I've spoken to HQ. From tomorrow you are suspended on full pay while we carry out an investigation. I haven't decided how we'll manage the message yet. For the next day or so, we'll say you're on sick leave, then HR will confirm the details."

"I understand," she says, walking out into the bright light of the corridor.

Momentum carries her down the stairs. Now she has time, but it'll be eaten up by HQ, HR, legal advisers, a formal statement, the implications and the involvement of a range of parties. The likelihood of a referral to the Independent Police Complaints Commission will keep the Chief occupied, not her.

Her belated honesty is an immediate declaration of herself as other, black to the white, an outsider. Her career is now over. It was what she'd expected and it ought to be liberating. The reality is that she'll be thrust into an acrid, procedural fog, tossed out into the freezing cold of December gardening leave. People in public service dream about gardening leave, paid time out, normally while a deal is brokered. They imagine mowing the lawn and watching tennis while the pay cheques continue to arrive. Jess sees the reality as wandering around outside a walled garden, unable to move on, insecure, scrutinised and judged.

She can't stand the defeated box of personal items routine, so stuffs the laptop in her bag and strides down to the car park. Sitting in the car she wonders what she can do in her last couple of days, while she's officially on sick leave, to help Jonesy and unpick the connection between Stewart and Croft.

The three-mile drive home becomes a test of physical endurance. She's missed most of the traffic, but it's as if she's in a right-hand drive car and her arm struggles to shift the gear stick properly. The car jolts into second when she wants fourth. She slams on the brakes and stalls the engine. Stopped in the middle of the road, a double-decker bus, windows misted, hiding irritated passengers, blasts its horn and goes round her, blocking the oncoming traffic. She puts the hazard lights on and kangaroo hops the car into the curb.

That's all she needs now. Leaving the engine a minute or two, she switches the radio on and checks her phone. There's nothing. No missed calls. No messages. The car starts as normal. She pushes the button to open the window and gets a blast of bitingly cold air, then links her fingers behind her head, pulling down hard to stretch out her neck muscles. It slowly becomes apparent that the problem might not be with the car. Her brain is dead and it's not communicating with her body. There's a deep fatigue paralysing her limbs.

Get home, just get there, she tells herself. Keep the window open, break the journey down, drive one road junction to the next, slow up well before the roundabout. It's only ten minutes away. She crunches the gears. The car drifts. Don't cut the corners, turn left, turn right. The lights of the corner shops and her local garage blur. The window is still fully down as she pulls into the drive. Like a dying battery, she uses the final flickers of energy to grab her bag, put one foot in front of the other and get to the front door. She rattles the key in the lock and stumbles into the house. All she can think about now is being warm. She climbs the stairs like the end of a marathon. The heating is on, but doesn't make an impact on her shivers. She sits on the side of the bed to take her boots off and falls rather than lies down, pulling the duvet over her as sleep engulfs her.

Jess is woken by the phone ringing on her bedside table. Picking it up in the dark she feels for the accept button. It's 1am.

"Hello, it's Barbara here. I'm Ben's nan. I'm sorry to be ringing in the middle of the night, but you gave me your number and I thought you seemed like one of them who cares."

"Yes, yes, don't worry about that. Are you alright? What's happened?" Immediately alert, Jess throws back the cover and begins to stand.

"He's gone, ducky, and I'm worried. He's been fuming all evening. Livid he was. Wouldn't calm down, wouldn't say much. I was so worried I decided to stay in my chair, couldn't face the stairs anyway, so I heard him. I told him it's too late to be going out, but he wouldn't listen."

Unsteady on her feet, Jess is pleased to find she's fully dressed. "I'll find him, Barbara. What did he say exactly?"

"Out. He said he was going out, but I heard him in the kitchen talking to his friend, the young one you brought round here. He said he was going to the warehouse."

"Do you know what he meant?"

"That's where he works, but he wouldn't be working this time of night, would he?"

Jess keeps her voice calm. She doesn't want to upset the old lady even more. "Do you know where it is? Think, Barbara. Did he say anything else?"

"I think he said something about meeting at the train station. They could go the back way round Bentley's."

"That's great. Thanks for ringing me. You did exactly the right thing. I know you'll be worrying, but he'll be fine. Leave it with me. I'll go out now and look for him, and phone you as soon as I know anything."

Jess grabs her keys and a bottle of water. Sliding into the driver's seat, she's vigilant and focused. Her body now remembers exactly how to operate the car and the engine ignites first time. It hardly needs great skills of deduction. Ben thinks we won't get Croft. He's angry. He wants to do some damage and he's stupid enough to put himself in danger. Anne-Marie had described the Meadows site at her house that night. It's got to be the first place to try. Should she ring Jonesy? It's not Police business, but if Ben's gone out with revenge in mind it might be a good precaution. If Adam's with Ben, should she call Frank for back-up? Anne-Marie's too unpredictable, so that seems a better option. OK, she thinks, get down there first, see if there's anything obvious, then decide who, if anyone, needs calling.

As she leaves the main road, the street lamps peter out. Jess puts her lights on full beam and slows down into second gear. She'll drive to the far end of the site and work her way back, then check the side roads. The front left wheel crunches into a small pothole. She straightens up. She can't afford to keep her eyes on the road. There's the derelict pub Anne-Marie had mentioned. It's not what anyone would call a warehouse, but she knows she has to check. There's a small torch in the glove compartment. Quickly she gets out, locks the car and jogs round. It looks truly abandoned, but there's a sound, a shuffling noise. It's pitch black. The torch picks out a boarded up door. There's a scream, like a baby. God in heaven. Her body tenses up. There's the clink of a glass bottle being kicked across the road. Quickly she flashes the torch and sees a fox with a cub diving into a hole behind the metal casing over the door.

The release of tension steadies her as she gets back in the car. She rings Frank, but he doesn't pick up. She drives on. Metal fencing that had once been attached to a gate post is being blown like a flag in a bitter wind that seems to have followed her onto the Meadows. Ahead in the darkness her beams begin to pick up the rectangular shape of a building. She'd rather not drive straight up to it, but it seems there's no other way. She slows to a crawl. It looks like the kind of garage that replaces tyres and batteries. There's an industrial roller shutter covered in graffiti. There's nothing else here. If her hunch is right and Ben was heading this way, this has to be it. She stops the car, deciding to walk the last thirty metres, satisfy herself that the building is abandoned and get out of there as quickly as possible. There's no earthly sign of life from the front, but to be sure she makes her way round to the left to check the back.

Her heart lurches. No. No way. There's a dim security light above a steel reinforced door and there are two cars – a black BMW with its driver-door open and a silver Lexus. It's Stewart's car. Shocked, she retreats a few metres, crouches down and fumbles for her phone. Then she hears raised voices echoing in the empty garage space. Tracking round, it's clear they've just arrived and have left the security door open. There are two vans in the main working area, boxes everywhere. A partition with another door is to the right and to the left there's an office with a light on. It's Ben. They've got him. Sprinting across, she yanks the door open. "Stop there. Police. Stop now, Stew, touch that boy again and you'll never..."

Ben is on the floor. She sees Stewart's foot strike him in the stomach, as if he's taking a penalty. He lines up to take another shot, this time at his head. Ben is crumpled in a ball. His hand moves to cover his face. Jess launches herself at Stewart, temporarily knocking him off balance. They are all frozen, momentarily paralysed by her unexpected intrusion in the middle of a beating. Croft is leaning against a desk, watching with a sick grin on his face. Another man, it could be Turval, the face seems the same, but his head is clean shaven, has got Adam. His nose is bleeding. His arms are pinned behind his back.

"On your own are you, officer?"

Jess is half-dressed in uniform. She has her badge and tonight she's still a police officer. Stew stands away from Ben. Croft coolly shakes his head.

"What the hell do you think you're doing?" she rages at Stewart.

"The kid was resisting arrest," he spits back.

"For god's sake, I just witnessed you assaulting that boy."

"That's the trouble with the Police these days," Croft interjects. "Never here when they're needed and when they do turn up it's a woman on her own. Not got the resources, have you? Not got backup, have you?"

"It's on its way," Jess barks convincingly at the men.

"My security team have just found two intruders on my premises. We caught them trying to set fire to the place." Croft kicks at a litre bottle of clear liquid on the floor. It could well be what they had in mind, the stupid idiots. Ben knows what these people are capable of, though. He should know better.

"Your security team? You're working for him?" Jess jeers. There are three men and she's on her own, unsure if Jonesy will have picked up her call.

"I told you, it's the future" Stew says.

"Then you aren't arresting these lads, are you? You're not in uniform, are you, Stew? You're just like any other thug who thinks they can take the law into in their own hands." Jess draws on all her experience. She stands tall, tries to take control. "I'm taking these lads with me. If they need arresting we'll do it at the station and you'll all need to give statements." Croft won't want to be around if he thinks a squad car is arriving. Too many questions to answer.

"Ben's coming with us," Croft commands. "He works for me, he owes me and he does what I say. This is an internal dispute. Nothing we can't handle ourselves. You can take his little girlfriend here and leave us to get on." The man holding Adam pushes him to the floor, laughing. Adam crawls behind Jess.

Croft's eyes drill into her. Unafraid of the glare, she stares back, stares through the shallow façade of a business man, through the layers of local man done good, the celebrated geezer, the rough diamond. At heart there's a selfish man who's used violence to get power and fear to get compliance – a grown man who has no problem preying on young boys and girls. Stripped back, a hyena is refusing to give up his roadkill.

"Get up, lads," she says. Adam and Ben scramble to their feet.

"They're both leaving with me now." Stew blocks the office door. There's no way she can get out unless they let her go, but she's unafraid now. He's a bully, dazzled by whoever gives him the slightest encouragement to show off, flexing his muscles like the Force of old, like he always used to.

"Twenty years go by and you've learned nothing. You're the same…"

Stew interrupts her, not wanting Croft to hear more. "She's brass, police management."

Jess keeps her focus on Croft. He clocks the word management. "Then what's she doing here?"

"She knows the boys. It's nothing we need to worry about. The Chief's got her in his sights. She won't trouble us," says Stew.

Croft turns away from her gaze. "Good. I'll have a word with the Chief and you piss off out of here."

Jess protects the boys as they anxiously edge towards the door.

"Ben, we'll see you later," says Croft. His casual, almost friendly, tone, is all the more chilling with his malicious sneer.

They pick up speed, bundling their way through the darkness of the main garage, out of the security door, then all three of them break into a run for the safety of Jess' car.

Jess' first concern is for Ben. He's breathing heavily, holding his ribs. I'll call base and we'll get you straight to the hospital."

"Nah, get out of here. I'm alright. We need to be safe. Not the hospital, anyone can walk in there."

"You're injured, Ben."

"I got a bit of protection," he says, pulling an A5-sized Moleskine book from inside his jacket. "No way were we going to set fire to the warehouse. Those are serious chemicals."

Jess begins dialling the station. She doesn't want Croft clearing out that place before Jonesy's had a good look around.

Adam wipes the remaining blood from his nose and Ben smiles. "It's the delivery book. Croft won't use a computer."

CHAPTER 51

ANNE-MARIE

Friday 10th December, 6.45pm

From her office window Anne-Marie sees the councillors' car park is full. Dressed up for the occasion, as if it were being televised, they straighten ties, lick their fingers and comb down stray hairs. The normal buzz of the Full Council is laced with neat anticipation. On the agenda is the exotic rarity of a real choice, not just a set piece of reports that have been to so many pre-meetings they've all heard them five times already; not just grand-standing for the benefit of a few junior hacks with headphones in and the usual suspects, older members of the public who prefer a tame live soap opera to a shouty small-screen one.

Anne-Marie isn't sure her frayed nerves will last the evening. She'd managed two hours of sleep, between midnight and 2am, when Jess, Frank, Adam and Ben had burst noisily into the house. The boys were both OK and needed to be taken somewhere safe. They'd compromised on Frank taking them to his sister's in Blackpool for a week.

Jonesy had got to the warehouse as some of the Chickenshack gang were attempting to pull out the gear. There was enough fake vodka to blind the whole city. Neither Croft nor Stewart had been there. Ben had patiently explained the features of the system set out in the notebook; the deliveries, the collections, the debts and the name of the bent accountant who came in every Friday. She'd watched Adam, as he'd kept his focus on Ben, in equal measures of awe and terror. In one way Anne-Marie is glad that, although they had suspected drugs, no drugs had been found. Or was it worse because alcohol is just as addictive and legal? It was bootlegging, something that people do all over the world, something that most people wouldn't consider a crime. The important thing is to start the story, spread it as accurately and as fast as she can, that Croft and his money are toxic.

She's been up and down the stairs all day. The presentation boards setting out the choice are up at the back of the Council Chamber. Option A: Pleisureland. They have thrown money at it; computer-enhanced images of boxy, brightly clad, modernist buildings with diagonally shaded uniform trees and square planting. There are no people on display and it can't buy them content.

Her heart still sinks. Option B: New Horizons. The housing and community health scheme still needs a new name, has too many words, plenty of statistics and no pictures. What were they going to do? A before and after version, one with pictures of drunken affray in the City Centre and the other a sanitised, squeaky-clean version? Every time she's got excited by the potential of the scheme, the way the team has worked creatively together, managed to laugh even, the same shadow begins to fall.

It's not that their vision isn't exciting or plausible. She'd rather build on reality. Except that's the problem. The reality is that they'll end up with all the support in the world and Davina and Croft will still win, because they have the trump card – money. However dirty it is, they have pound notes, figures and cash flows, not statistics. Anne-Marie is scraping the bottom of an empty wooden barrel. Her best hope is that they pick Option B and the public sector wins a chance, a chance to make a different story happen.

What she's hoping for is the possibility of persuasion. She's aiming for a story that will resonate, not just because the councillors might have witnessed the chaos of the city on a Saturday night or watched a gore fest A&E reality show. She's aiming for a story that illustrates a deeper truth, for them, their families and the city – that they can and should influence the ending. They can trigger a stop signal, stand up and say, "I'm persuaded of the case for change." It has to be good, because her fear is that what politics is reduced to is an instruction to vote without thinking, along the lines of outdated tribes. If that's all politics and their politicians can do, they are doomed.

She makes her way downstairs to the toilets in the Committee Suite. They are the best in the building. They have a series of small dressing tables with stools and a freestanding, full-length mirror. She's managed to avoid Davina until now and she'd guessed right that Davina wouldn't suspend her. That's not the Leader's style. Davina was right in the sense that Anne-Marie didn't have anything directly on her. It was an anti-climax, but in a way she was perversely pleased. Those sort of lazy corruption stories do no-one any good and smear the whole public sector. Still, to Anne-Marie it's corruption nonetheless and applicable to thousands of people at the top of organisations who act in the economic interest of themselves and their tribes.

As she tries to brush away a lump of mascara, she reminds herself that it's not just her story. She's told Frank and the opposition councillors about Davina's directorships, the land ownership, the ransom strip and her husband's building company. It's not a great news story though – 'Leader Fails To Demonstrate Standards Required In Public Life'. Davina's morally compromised, she lacks integrity, objectivity, openness and her leadership is questionable, but so what? Davina isn't going to slip up tonight.

Anne-Marie might've been manipulative, arrogant and vainly naïve – or as she applies her lip gloss, naively vain – and she definitely lost her own plot for a while, but she certainly didn't gain from any of it. In fact, she almost lost her son. As she straightens her suit and prepares to go into the Council Chamber, she's just about calm enough to do a good job, to get this right.

At 7pm on the dot the Committee Clerk calls the Full Council Meeting to order. The grand room, so often let down by underwhelming attendance, is pumped up, full of expectant air. There's a slight reverb on the microphone system. Anne-Marie stumbles to her seat. The colours look bolder, the expensive gold leaf of the City crest is shining bright, the brilliant blues and reds behind the platform and the tiered green leather seating give it a theatrical quality. Time to perform.

"Thank you ladies and gentlemen. We'd like to make a start."

The chamber rattles with expectation. Word has run around the building. Every seat is taken, every single councillor, every officer with the scantest of reasons, is here for the show. There's standing room only in the press and public gallery. The officers, the partners are, in effect, challenging Davina. If it wasn't for the back story, the special circumstances of the last few months, this would have been sorted in private. Anne-Marie tries to slow her brain down, slowly picking up the jug of water in front of her. She looks up and sees Bob, hovering by the fire door.

The clerk asks for apologies or declarations of interest. They could be here all night if Davina has taken a truth serum. Through custom, the Mayor, wearing his ceremonial chain, takes the Chair. He sits uncomfortably in the carved wooden throne. A genial backbencher, he's better suited to eating cheese sandwiches and smiling in the local paper than directing the action. Tonight, though, he looks like bad news is about to arrive. Anne-Marie chooses to take this as a good sign. Owen is beside the Chair, flicking over the pages of the legal statute books generously spread out in front of him. Davina is in the most prominent seat to his right. She's wearing a pink cashmere sweater and pearls. It's misjudged under the hot lights, unusual by her publicly serene standards. The Chief is next to her, looking far more attentive than usual. That's a bad sign.

"Welcome to you all. We'll take the minutes first," the Mayor says, pressing the pause button on the meeting. Papers are thumbed, people fidget while one of the councillors asks for the spelling of his name to be corrected. Anne-Marie massages her palm. She's flanked by Barrington and Jess, who's in uniform. She'd wanted Jess next to her, in defiance of the Force and to give her friend a last chance to speak, an opportunity to thank and be thanked by the community she's served for the last twenty years. Frank is sitting behind the opposition councillors. That's interesting. Sandra, Andrea and Anil are above them in the gallery. There's no sign of Croft, which is a relief.

"The first item is the way forward for the City Centre. We have two options to consider and I'm asked to remind members that we are deciding only on the concept." He reads this anxiously from his notes. "I understand the Chief Executive will give us a brief introduction to the Pleisureland proposal and the Director of Regeneration will speak about the New Horizons proposal. The papers have been circulated and we will take questions after."

Owen is on his feet. Anne-Marie lets the words flow over her, hearing only the grating tone, a vacuum cleaner grinding over a thin carpet. "Wealth creation... entrepreneurial culture... sustainable economy." He has two aces in his hand. "Local jobs..." that's one. He finishes with the other. "Fully costed and funded."

Anne-Marie rises firmly to her feet.

"Thank-you Chair, Council. It's been a tough few months for our city. We've been horrified by the loss of 16-year-old Laura Awsworth, a young woman who tragically became known for the location of her death and the violent circumstances that led up to it. Alcohol was at the heart of Laura's death, not just her own consumption, but the whole economy surrounding it. We've been forced to confront what it says about our city and the way we live our lives. Although this is a criminal case, it raises bigger questions. Could we have prevented it from happening and how do we avoid it happening again?

"The New Horizons scheme is completely different. It's not about a flagship building, it's about taking control of our city. We are saying, our city can't be successful unless we tackle alcohol. The report illustrates devastating patterns of behaviour that we've come to accept as normal and not our problem, but alcohol impacts on all of us one way or another, young and old, whether that's through illness, debt, violence and particularly domestic violence, unemployment, even underachieving at school or in college. Maybe we avoid coming into the City Centre for a night out, because of the weekend mayhem, or we buy one too many supermarket bottles of wine and sit on our sofas drinking at home. We all do it." She stops, smiles and points a finger at her own chest. There's acknowledgement, but they don't want a sermon.

"Drinking at home makes us isolated. It limits us in so many ways. The more we drink, the more our economy suffers and the costs to the public sector rise as we fail to deal with the aftermath. It's not that we don't want people to enjoy themselves, especially young people, but we've got to get the balance right between a lively attractive nightlife, safety and the real costs to all of us, to us as individuals, as taxpayers, families and communities."

That much the audience will accept. The leap is this. "New Horizons is about what we want to make happen, what we choose to do and how we work together. As public agencies we say this a lot and it's not through want of trying that we haven't done a lot, but it's complicated and we're up against the interests of big and small businesses, which simply don't accept that we, that you, Councillors, should intervene. At the moment, we, as a city, bear the costs, but if we intervene there will be a cost to businesses. Good and bad employers the same, everyone needs to play by the rules and the rules need to be tougher. We all need to respond together. We've got to act in everyone's interest." Anne-Marie sees Frank nod.

"And the good part will be that we'll all be working towards a City Centre we can be proud of, a safe City Centre that we'll want to use. It will mean shifting resources to families who are struggling with alcohol and poverty, and we are proposing to build, but we'll use the land for eco family homes in the City Centre, affordable housing, that communities can get involved in building and designing, homes that don't rack up fuel bills and perpetuate fuel poverty. In hard times this might sound like a stretch – it is! – but cuts aren't the only story. We need to use all our resources wisely. Of course, it's not profitable in the market sense, but this way our public investment gets a social return. It has social value. It's human capital. It's what makes our city part of us." She pauses for breath, hoping not to have over-cooked it. "We're asking for time. Time to put the funding together, because we want to do it the right way, so that what we get is a new direction."

There are nods, a faint but stilted murmur of approval.

"As this is a team approach, I've asked two of our partners, Dr Barrington Edwards and Deputy Commander Jessica Reid, to say a few words."

Barrington stands and says, "The statistics speak for themselves. I've done an analysis of projects broadly comparable to Pleisureland. I've made allowances for particular variables to account for the fact that many of these schemes are in the United States. The impact we might expect to see is this: a 22 per cent increase in problem gambling and a related increase in alcohol and tobacco consumption. I estimate we could have over 8,000 dependent drinkers in the city in three years' time. Total crime has increased by an average of 6 per cent in every case study I have reviewed and, particularly relevant, there has been a 24 per cent average increase in prostitution. There will be an increase in suicide rates for unemployed males under thirty, a key risk group. Life expectancy will decrease. Lives will be lost."

Anne-Marie can see he's scaring the horses. Good.

"I have also examined the business case for Pleisureland. There is a predicted profit return to the pockets of the private sector investors of 8 per cent, with 75 per cent of this coming from the alcohol- and gambling-related components. This is predicated on public sector investment, using taxpayers' resources worth over £60 million. It seems we can afford whatever we want as long as we accept the consequences. Councillors, I present the evidence. It's your job to weight it up, but I ask you, can we afford the costs?"

She's glad he said that not her. Well done, mate. Barrington looks like he's about to sit down and then says, "I have a final observation. I was glad to see the report in the *Post* about the community pub protest at the Three Lions. The community want something done and is prepared to take action themselves on this. I interpret that as political support for this option."

Anne-Marie wouldn't have gone that far, but that's good. Really good.

CHAPTER 52

JESSICA

Friday 10th December, 7.50pm

"You're whatever you want to be now, aren't you?" Anne-Marie had put her finger right on the spot, the spot where there's no uniform, no system to hide behind, no structure or institution to mould yourself into. No back, only front. The 'now what?' spot, where it's all up to you. Put your energy where you choose and live openly with your choices.

As she'd walked to the meeting Jess had taken a diversion, a loop past the Library and the Chickenshack takeaway. There was no sign of the gang. Jonesy had picked up the leader, Leeroy, at the Meadows warehouse. Down towards the University and the station, the Christmas lights were doing a good impression of seasonal cheer. She passed young people with excess baggage, suitcases no doubt full of washing, hauling themselves home. Tomorrow she'd been leaving. First down to her sister's in North London and then, who knows? She stops herself from calling it another challenge and underlines the word 'transition' in her head. And in this transition, she'll try her hardest not to grab onto the first structure that comes along. She'll try and camp out a bit, live lightly, see what emerges. Anne-Marie has instructed her to have some fun.

Jess stands to say her piece or is it 'peace'? She wants to get this right. She can't let the team down now. It's not exactly her day in court, the day she'd imagined when she could tell the truth to the world. That isn't in her hands. Whether there is a new inquest into Darren's death or not, Hermin and Barrington will determine the next steps. Jess still hopes Stewart will be prosecuted and her statement is damning, but either way he is out of the Force now. He's chosen the private sector and there will always be men like Croft, willing to pay good money for police-trained bad apples. Staring out at the faces in the Council Chamber, Jess refuses to wobble.

"As a rule, while in uniform, we remain impartial, but I'm speaking personally now, because I'm in no doubt that New Horizons is the way forward. I feel we don't really have a choice. Preventing crimes like the attack on Laura Awsworth is complex. We have to balance competing agendas, feel our way through a maze of issues, and the temptation is to simply do what's required of us and nothing more. In the case of the Police Force, that's catch the criminals. Yes, we do that, but it's not enough. We have to use all the levers we've got to make a more significant impact. We need to act smarter.

"You've seen the detail, but let me give you an example. We have to use the licensing regulations to shut down pubs and clubs that generate incidents of rape and sexual assault. We've successfully used regulations to stop people ending up with a glass or bottle in their necks, so why not do more of what works? Here's another good example. We need a hard-hitting campaign to target men's behaviour. We need to talk to men and support women to help them reduce their own vulnerabilities. We can change the environment in the City Centre. It's not a big-money change, but it's about us changing the way we work and targeting our efforts where it matters.

"Other forces have taken a more proactive view of their role and we can too. The Police are accountable to the community and the Police Authority. If this is what we all want – what they, you and the community demand – we can make it happen. As I said, I'm in no doubt that it will make a difference, but it'll take hard change, individual and collective change. If it was simple, we'd have done it by now. Without hard change there's no hope and hope comes from working together. So, I'm asking you to get actively involved in the coming weeks, months and years to make a long-term improvement in our city. Finally, I just wanted to say that, sadly, I will shortly be leaving my role as Deputy Commander, but I am extremely proud to have served this city."

There is a generous round of applause, started by Frank. That's it. Jess sits down, relief showering her body. It's all coming together. The connections have paid off, what they've created is integrated, but it's not a web, it's a net, and the more they work on it, the safer it becomes. They'd been expecting a queue of hands up, questions for them to field on the detail, but no. There are no councillors wanting to show off and score points in front of such an audience. No lights flicker in the consoles in front of them. No-one presses their button to speak. It's unbelievable. Jess shrugs at Anne-Marie. She clearly doesn't know what's going on. In the unnatural silence, Jess senses a shift. They all look at the Chair, who leans across to Owen.

"In that case, members, can I ask you to indicate your 'in principle' support for the options in turn. Firstly, option A, Pleisureland." Davina raises her hand, but the rest of her party are slow to show theirs. As Owen begins to count, Jess realises it must have been co-ordinated, planned ahead. The minority group in the Coalition aren't voting with her. The Mayor tries not look flustered. "Thank you," he says, "and Option B, New Horizons." Hands fly up. There's overwhelming support. A landslide even. She can't help but smile. That's it. People start to move their shoulders, relax and turn to speak to their neighbours. The noise level rises. Owen stands and lifts his hand to seek silence. "Thank you, colleagues, partners, ladies and gentlemen. We will now continue with Council business. This is a public meeting and you are welcome to stay." No-one moves from their seat apart from Anne-Marie. Jess sees her trying, unsuccessfully, to hide her delight. Jess turns to Barrington. They are both unsure whether to follow her or not. It takes some minutes for the room to settle. The ground has shifted.

CHAPTER 53

FRANK

He'd been right. He'd said to Adam on the phone he thought the Coalition would split and, when it did, Les and the opposition would call for a vote of no confidence in Davina. "You sound like Mum," their son had said. "I thought you didn't do politics anymore." That had brought Frank up short, because in his mind everything is political – his cup of tea, his choice of newspaper, the establishments he frequents, the company he keeps. Socially speaking he couldn't be more interested, but politically speaking what is his position?

He's glad he hasn't had to speak tonight. He'd considered it – speaking out in public, telling people about Croft, even holding a press conference with Adam and Ben – but not for long. That would have been a lot to ask of two young lads. The stakes were too high, although that was the point – the stakes are high. Anne-Marie had been right about not waiting, Barrington was correct about focusing on action and Jess' insistence on pushing the boundaries of what they were here to do had taught him something.

He'd left the Party years ago, because the membership, solid supporters like him, were treated like embarrassing uncles who should just shut up. The tired formula, the rhetoric, the posturing drove him mad, and the way the anti-war demo had been ignored was the straw that had broken his activist back. Now, though, talking to councillors about their option for change, he felt fired up. They wanted something different and he saw he could be different. They'd talked openly about what the city needed. He'd been curious about their views, not stifled by conforming to a party line, but honest about the possibility of failure. Let's have a go, he'd said. Make some mistakes and make them big! And this had been the shift for Frank: don't just sit in the Mechanics and talk about it, get out there. They need good young people, like Ben and Adam, to get stuck in, too, and they need to be working with people in the community, like Andrea, but he can't expect others to step up without being prepared to do something himself.

"Well, lad, I'm thinking of putting my hat back in the ring. I said they needed a rocket up their arse. I guess I do, too." That had amused them both. "And," he'd said, "I'm wondering if we can't get you back on the streets? When you were a kid you used to love going on demos. Don't forget that son."

CHAPTER 54

ANNE-MARIE

Friday 10th December, 8.20pm

The stairs are steeper than she expected. She stumbles down, half-leaning against the wet, cold wall. It's been here for years this place. She's never been in before, but it's what she needs now. Anonymity and alcohol, space to think through what has just happened. She'd had to get out of the Council Chamber fast or she might have jumped for joy. Seeing the political power shift and Davina's face contort, watching the effort required to keep a level of composure, Anne-Marie didn't trust herself not to burst out laughing or start making unprofessional childish gestures. She flicks two fingers at the empty bar. It's a Croft place. She wishes she'd slapped Croft's face when she'd had the chance, but after tonight she'll make sure all his pubs get shut down.

The bar itself has the normal reassuring lines of spirit bottles calling out to her. Well done! You've earned it! Drink me, I'm sexy! I'll make you invincible! If only. Fumbling for her purse, she steadies herself. "Vodka and tonic, please."

Mixed emotions people say, as if that could describe the turbulence, relief and confusion she felt as the game changed. She's been on a rollercoaster, a rickety old one, with sharp turns that threaten to fling you off the rails, with a worn metal bar that's nowhere near holding you in, with a rotten wooden structure that could've collapsed at any point. They've got to the end, or the end of this ride, but what exactly have they achieved?

It's good that the Coalition has broken up. She ought to be

celebrating the fact that Davina no longer has a majority and won't be able to control the Council or the city, but the reason it feels like an empty victory for Anne-Marie is that, in the end, it was a political numbers game. Frank and Andrea had done the ground work, talking to the other councillors. It was their legwork that made the difference. Were the councillors really voting for their option or had they just had enough of Davina? Had Anne-Marie's speech meant anything?

The barmaid is young, attractive and bored. The only other punter is a middle-aged man propping up the other end of the bar. He looks like a regular she wants to avoid.

"Do you want a double? It works out cheaper?"

"Go on, then." Anne-Marie smiles, intending to just have one.

"I know you're supposed to put lime in it, but the boss is a tight-arse and we don't have any."

Classy place. Even the glass feels thin.

Anne-Marie drinks the vodka quickly, noticing there's only a hint of bitter quinine in the tonic. It's basically fizzy pop with added sugar, but that's alright for now. It'll quench her thirst.

"Another?" the barmaid asks, as Anne-Marie leaves her bar stool for the leather sofa. Good girl. She nods. That stool was too high and it made her backside feel enormous.

"Alright there, love, I'll bring it over." The bloke at the bar turns to look at her. He's probably on the staff, she thinks. It's dank and there's no heating, so she keeps her coat on.

This city is small, small-time, no more than an overgrown town. All that's happened is they've been playing around in their own backyard while the world motors right on. Other places reach out, punch above their weight, grab onto the coat-tails of their bigger neighbours. The Girl in the Bin asked them to stand up for the city and some of them had a go, but it's never enough and it won't be enough, because a place like this can't do anything on its own.

Her mood takes a deeper dip. This must be the first time she's walked out, left before a win in the red corner was declared. Was that wise? Problems start to pace around inside her tired brain. Has the Coalition really collapsed or was that a one-off? What will Les, the opposition leader, do? Nothing probably, until it's politically expedient, but will he trust her? She thought Frank trusted her. How come he knew what was going to happen and she didn't? Calm down, she tells herself. It's alright. It's a result. It's good that she's given herself this breathing space alone to work out how to respond, because Les will probably be in the Mechanics with Frank later and it'll be important to play it right.

Her sense of her inner self, in constant flow, the ups and downs, the competing needs and desires, still sounds tru-ish, but not exactly appealing. She wants the ride to be over for the moment. She's just glad to have a son, a job for now and a few colleagues to have a drink with. Maybe she should just get down to the Mechanics. As the second drink relaxes her, she feels a looseness in her fingertips.

"Gin and tonic for the lady?"

The bloke who's been at the bar brings her a full glass. He stands by the opposite end of the couch, but he doesn't try to sit down. She can deal with him. He's local alright, Not that bad looking she supposes, trying to forget she's single now.

"Thanks." She gulps at the liquid.

"Celebrating is it?"

"Yeah, you know what? It sort of is."

That's better. Her mood begins to pick up. It's been good to feel part of a team, a team doing something good. Davina will be gone. They've bought some time to develop a new direction, a new proposal. She knows how to scratch together some resources. Hopefully with Les and Frank in charge the story of the cuts will shift. They'll do it their way. And it won't be a story, it'll be a campaign, a proper campaign against the policy of cuts. She feels giddy with the prospect of temporary respite, the possibility of different conversations.

"Sorry, I didn't catch your name," she say to the man.

"Didn't I tell you?"

Jesus, he's not expecting her to guess is he? Strangely she finds this funny.

"You're not a Paul or an Alistair are you?" He plays along, shaking his head. "Not a Nigel? Not a Kevin? Maybe something more mannish? Mark? That's it, I'll call you Mark." She's starting to feel better. This guy is alright. He looks familiar. The only problem is that he's not Bob.

This morning seems a long time ago, but it was this morning that Adam had asked her who would be making the gravy this Christmas? She'd paused, then thrown it back at him. "Isn't it time you took over that job?" They'd borrowed their Christmas tradition from an Australian folk singer who looked like her dad. The men in the family get the job of making the gravy for the Christmas dinner. She's still the sharpest knife in the draw, so there's no contest over the carving, but Adam had been clear. "Nah, not me. I mean, Bob's gravy's the best, isn't it?" She decides to send Bob a text, but struggles to find her phone and to press the keys.

Gravy maker requested for xmas day? x

Her attention turns back to the man now perching on the corner of the sofa.

"Sorry, that was rude. Are you sure we haven't we met before?"

"Not in this life," he says.

Anne-Marie can't place the voice.

"There's not just one life though, is there?" She doesn't mean reincarnation, she means the many lives lived in parallel, the many paths, the many unpredictable outcomes.

"I'm not the deep and meaningful type," he says bluntly.

Anne-Marie laughs. "Yeah, sorry, it's just that I've had an

eventful night." Unfortunately, right this moment, she can't actually remember what's just happened. "I'll buy the next round." She laughs again. It's impossible to look ladylike getting out of these low sofas, so she gives up. There's a tea light on the table, shoved in the middle of an old ash tray. She stares into its washed out flame. It gives off no heat and barely any light. This place is too dark and lifeless. She wants to be with people who understand her, who speak her language. She struggles to stand.

"You look like you need a breather. Fancy a walk then?"

She looks at him again, closely this time, and recognises something. It might be the gypsy earring. The strength of his arm lifts her easily. She likes strong men.

"Not going already are you?" the barmaid shouts across. She looks odd. "Don't go yet," she says, insistent. "Come and chat to me."

"She's had enough," the man says. "I'll get her home."

They negotiate the steps in an ungainly fashion. Anne-Marie leans heavily on him. She's glad to be outside, not feeling the cold now, but wishing there was more light. Her sense of direction has abandoned her. Which way is the Mechanics? Which way is he taking her? Vaguely she thinks about getting a cab.

"Feeling sleepy are you?"

Anne-Marie nods. She is. She just wants to be at home with Adam. She wants her own sofa, she wants... Her legs crumble as she drifts off. Her brain has stopped talking to her body. It's shutting down for the night.

CHAPTER 55

BARRINGTON

Friday 10th December, 8.25pm

Running isn't Barrington's preferred sport, but given a challenge he knows he can cover some ground. He realises he's left his bag. He's sprinting, arms pumping, phone tightly gripped in his hand. When he got the text, Barrington had crashed his way to the fire exit. A Council officer, a tall, thickset man standing by the door, had put out a hand.

"Whoa, what's wrong mate? Can I help?"

He's read the text aloud to make sure he's understood it.

Get here fast doc. Bin guy has got a woman. Holly

Should he stop to call 999? There are police in the meeting. Jess is there, but getting her out would take time. He can be quicker than anyone else. Up the High Street, to the back of the Anvil, down the alley.

"Where? Where is it? Do we need a car?" asks the Council officer urgently.

"The Cave."

"Right, come on." The other man leads him quickly out of the back of the building, via a narrow corridor, but as they hit the street Barrington overtakes him.

"This way."

For the first few minutes Barrington can hear the man's slow tread and panting breath behind him, but he can't keep up. As they pass the Anvil, Barrington turns to shout directions, but the man is nearly a hundred metres back. The only light is by the moon. It's silent, empty. Barrington makes his way to the back of the pub and round into an alley, but he's got it wrong. He backtracks slightly and sees the opening to a further alley. There's another man, arms outstretched, dragging a woman face down by her wrists. Her coat trails along the floor. He bends in to pick up the limp, heavy body.

"Stop!" yells Barrington.

Immediately the man stands, dropping the woman. Her head cracks back on the pavement. Barrington takes a run at him, shoulder down, hoping to barge him over. The man dodges, stepping back at the last moment, standing firm, looking as if he's ready to run.

"You," he sneers. "You want some more?"

Barrington recognises Croft's man from the Anvil. It's Turval. His head is shaven but it's him, the one who beat him up, murdered Laura, attacked Sizzle. The physical threat paralyses him. He doesn't want more, but he won't leave this woman. He jumps up, deciding to block the escape route to the alley as best he can.

"I'm calling the Police," Barrington shouts, holding up his phone. "We're here. Down here."

Turval taunts him, pulling his jacket sleeve back, forming a fist. Barrington hears footsteps. The Council officer is behind him. He roars, picks up speed, throws a heavy right hook to Turval's jaw, then the left jabs sharply into Turval's face. Staggering backwards, Turval almost trips over the unconscious woman, turning her body over. Her face in the moonlight is clearly Anne-Marie's.

Turval doesn't see the final blow as it rains down two-handed on the side of his head. While he's flat out on the floor, Barrington sits awkwardly on top of him, dialing 999.

"Come on, Anne-Marie. Come on, love. Wake up. You're OK. I'm here. It's Bob, love. Please, please be alive."

CHAPTER 56

ANNE-MARIE

Friday 24th December, 7pm

It's good to be out. Anne-Marie's walking back through the City Centre with four bags of Christmas shopping. There are people here looking at stalls full of wooden toys, hippy crystals and woollen hats with furry animal ears. There are families even. It's Eurotat, but she likes the German Market and while they might be late adopters, it makes her feel as if they are at least holding their own with other towns and cities.

There's time to call into the Mechanics, to wish Sandra and Andrea a festive break, before making tracks to see Adam. The place is packed, full of shiny tops and open collars, heady with the cinnamon smell of mulled wine. Groups of workmates cheer the Advent. This most public of houses feels important, somewhere where just battles are remembered and future plots hatched. "I'll have a small glass of red," she says and gives a fifty pound note to the barmaid. "Put this behind the bar for the table on the left."

She wants to change the story of her relationship with alcohol. It's one of those things that she thought she had control of, but, of course, it was the other way round. It's only 125mls, she thinks, and acknowledging there's an issue is enough for now. It's Christmas, after all. She gives Sandra a hug and grabs a seat next to Andrea.

"Thanks, you know… for everything." Anne-Marie toasts the two women. "The Highlands wouldn't be the same without you."

"And it won't be the same without neighbourhood management," Sandra says pointedly.

Anne-Marie doesn't blame her. She'd feel the same if she had an 'at risk of redundancy' letter sitting on her table top at home. "I'm doing everything I can to keep the budget in place and at least we've got a chance now."

Andrea says, "Can we trust the new lot though? Les isn't exactly a breath of fresh air."

"If you can't beat them, organise them?"

"Ha!" says Andrea "Exactly."

Her laugh has an edge of determination – self-determination. Maybe she now feels better equipped to battle the system, whether that's as community rep, a Councillor or both. There might be fewer of them in the Town Hall in future, but they're building a different team, new alliances.

At 7.45pm Anne-Marie makes her excuses and wanders towards the taxi rank. She doesn't want to stray too far from the lights. Although she has no memory of the attack, the knowledge of what nearly happened is raw. Crossing the street, she sees Colin, the warden, marshalling late shoppers in a Santa hat, then Barrington in full Lycra, pushing his bike through the crowds. She makes tracks towards him.

Arriving together at the burger van, Anne-Marie is thrown by Sizzle's forehead dripping sweat onto the griddle, on account of the reindeer antlers he's wearing.

"You're here."

"Bleedin' obvious statement of the week. I'm always here. Long after the Germans with their litres of strong lager and their odiferous sausages, filled with meat no less, have gone, me and my lot, we'll still be here; the spewing, sprawling, brawling lot of us. We'll never give up our fatty burgers and our mild beer."

She expects Barrington to respond, but he lets it go. Anne-Marie can't imagine her colleague has suddenly turned over a new leaf, but maybe even he can see the difference in the city tonight. Yes, there may be alcohol on sale, but it's not the main event, the people are. He's spent his life thinking that everyone else should change, not him, and he won't change because, underneath it all, it suits Barrington to stay as he is. It's better than admitting he might be wrong. But what does she know anymore? It could be that this time next year neither of them will be in a job, but even if they're forced out from behind the desks, they'll be fighting for public services, for the city.

"Come on," she laughs. "I love the city like this. It's what it should be like all the time."

Sizzle groans. "Not another one who wishes it could be Christmas every day."

Barrington smiles without getting it. "I came to thank you."

"The only thanks I ask is that you buy a burger now and then," Sizzle replies.

"I'll buy a bar of Cadbury's Dairy Milk."

"You would. And you, madam?" He turns to Anne-Marie. "Could you put in a word with your mates in the Council and get Environmental Health to leave off with their threatening notices."

Barrington ignores that and continues. "Your evidence was critical. Turval has been committed for trial and there's enough on Croft for a prosecution by HM Revenue and Customs. Trading Standards have discovered a network of counterfeit alcohol factories. His business will be decimated."

Sizzle begins to smile, but what comes out of his mouth is caution. "It's about time you lot wised up to his type. Plenty more where he came from. He won't be the last." He rubs his stomach. "But I must say I'm glad to know Croft'll be as miserable as I am this Christmas."

Anne-Marie pats the bars of Barrington's bike. She knows it might irritate him, but it's better than a hug. She wishes them a Merry Christmas. "Looks like you've got it under control."

Sizzle shakes his head. "As much as it can be. As much as we'll ever be."

ACKNOWLEDGEMENTS

To Simon for everything. To my amazing, supportive, creative friends and readers: Sarah, Diana, Mikenda, Moira, Joanna, Angela, Sarah D, Sue, Claire, Frances and Fran. To Lisa, whose editing is a work of art, thanks for your insight and understanding. To Ben and Kate, for designing and producing the beautiful book I hoped for. To John Petherbridge, Judith Bryan, and the gang at City Lit for the learning and company of writers. And as always, to Team Reeves.

ABOUT THE AUTHOR

 **Dawn Reeves** lives in London and loves the Midlands. She makes change happen. She's motivated by social justice, is fascinated by power and all the weird and wonderful things that happen under the surface. *Hard Change* is Dawn's first novel. There will be more.

Lightning Source UK Ltd.
Milton Keynes UK
UKOW042022040113

204441UK00003B/14/P